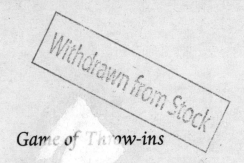

*Game of Throw-ins*

# Game of Throw-ins

## ROSS O'CARROLL-KELLY

### (as told to Paul Howard)

### Illustrated by
## ALAN CLARKE

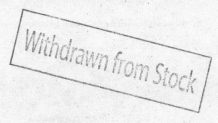

PENGUIN BOOKS

PENGUIN BOOKS

UK | USA | Canada | Ireland | Australia
India | New Zealand | South Africa

Penguin Books is part of the Penguin Random House group of companies
whose addresses can be found at global.penguinrandomhouse.com.

First published by Penguin Ireland 2016
Published in Penguin Books 2017
001

Penguin Ireland thanks O'Brien Press for its agreement to Penguin Ireland using the
same design approach and typography, and the same artist, as O'Brien Press
used in the first four Ross O'Carroll-Kelly titles

Set in 10.7/13.2 pt Dante MT Std
Typeset by Jouve (UK), Milton Keynes
Printed in Great Britain by Clays Ltd, St Ives plc

A CIP catalogue record for this book is available from the British Library

ISBN: 978-0-241-97045-4

www.greenpenguin.co.uk

For Martin Walsh

# Contents

# Prologue

The Saint Ignatius of Loyola Church is packed for the annual Castlerock College Thanksgiving Mass. There must be, like, five hundred past pupils here, filling out every pew and even spilling outside into the freezing cold night. We're all belting out the words of what used to be Father Fehily's favourite Christmas hymn, making sure we do him proud.

> *Joyful, all ye nations, rise.*
> *Join the triumph of the skies.*
> *With the angelic host proclaim:*
> *'Christ is born in Bethlehem.'*
> *Hark! The herald angels sing,*
> *'Glory to the newborn King!'*

Christian offers me his hipflask. This is in the middle of the church, bear in mind, with Father Jehoiada up on the altar still wiping the chalice clean.

'Yeah, no, I'm good,' I go. 'I'm driving.'

He offers it to JP and Oisinn, who both say the same thing.

> *Veiled in flesh, the Godhead see;*
> *Hail the incarnate Deity,*
> *Pleased as man with man to dwell,*
> *Jesus, our Emmanuel.*
> *Hark! The herald angels sing,*
> *'Glory to the newborn King!'*

When it's all over, we shuffle out of the church and into the cor pork. Then everyone stands around in the cold for half an hour, hundreds of old school friends just catching up with each other, sharing memories, swapping news and generally talking about how the whole recession thing never really affected them at all.

'I was just remembering,' JP goes, 'how much Father Fehily loved that song. I was thinking about him conducting with his hands as he belted out the lines.'

We all laugh. He used to do that.

Oisinn goes, 'You'd miss his Christmas Mass, though – and that's not being disrespectful to Father Jehoiada. His little speech at the end, then wishing everyone a *Frohe Weihnachten*. By the way, has anyone got plans for New Year's Eve?'

JP's there, 'You're joking, aren't you? We've all got kids now!'

I look at Christian and I feel instantly sad for him. He doesn't have his kids. Not anymore. Long story. It's for another time.

Luckily, he's shitfaced, and he doesn't seem to hear.

'I'm having a porty in the George,' Oisinn goes. I presume he's talking about the yacht club, not the gay bor. 'Look, it's not a major deal. It's just a few drinks to celebrate my dischorge from bankruptcy.'

Me and JP are just like, 'What?' because it's come around so quickly.

'Yeah, no,' Oisinn goes, 'as and from the first of January 2015, I'm back in the black – my debt to society paid. I thought, you know, it might be worth ringing in the New Year properly this year.'

I'm like, 'Fair focks, Dude. I wouldn't miss it for the world.'

JP goes, 'Yeah, Chloe can ask her old dear to look after Isa. By the way, did anyone hear from Fionn?'

I'm there, 'Yeah, no, we had a cord the other day.'

The dude's been living in New York for the past six months, working for the United Nations. I've no idea who they are or what they do – all I know is that it's *his* job to basically advise them on how to deal with, like, international *piracy* and shit?

'He's not coming home for Christmas,' I go. 'He's only got, like, three days off. I think his old pair are going over to him. And his brother and sister.'

God, I must put his sister back on my Drunk Dial list. It's been too long.

I suddenly spot my old man tipping over. He's got his lucky Cole

Haan camel-hair coat on – so-called – and that ridiculous focking hat he insists on wearing.

'There they are!' he goes. 'The backbone of the team that brought Leinster Schools Senior Cup glory to Castlerock College in the year of Our Lord, one thousand, nine hundred and ninety-nine!'

He's the wrong side of a bottle of brandy, judging by his volume and the focking hum off him.

The goys are all like, 'Hey, Charles!' because for some bizarre reason they all think he's great.

He goes, *'Gloria filiorum patres! Parare Domino plebem perfectam!'*

Courvoisier always brings out the Latin in him.

'Couldn't have said it better myself, Charles,' JP goes, loving my embarrassment. 'Although I'd throw in a *pendent opera interrupta* for good measure.'

'And I wouldn't stop you,' the old man goes. 'No, indeed! By the way, Kicker, there's a chap over there who's rather keen to meet you. Brother Melchior?'

I'm there, 'I don't know a Brother Melchior. Which means you're full of shit.'

'Well, you wouldn't know him, he's lived in Tanzania for the last fifty years. But he knows all about you and your extraordinary exploits on the field!'

'Continue.'

'Well, he said it to me just now. He said, "Your son was the famous rugby player – is that correct?" I said, "You're absolutely right – got it in one!" and he said, "Well, I would love to meet him – just to say I shook his hand."'

I suppose I did bring glory to the Jesuits as much as I did to the school.

'Oh,' the old man goes, 'here he comes, look!'

Brother Melchior ends up being this, like, old dude – we're talking ninety, possibly even older – and he's literally bent over double, moving really slowly, like someone who's dropped a contact lens and is terrified of stepping on it.

He just, like, extends his hand to me and goes, 'I've always wanted . . . to meet you.'

His voice is sort of, like, high-pitched and a little bit shaky.

I'm like, 'Yeah, no, cool,' giving his hand a good shake.

'I'm Brother Melchior,' he goes. 'I don't know if Denis . . . ever mentioned me . . . We were in Africa . . . together . . . oh, many, many moons ago.'

I'm there, 'He may have done. He said a lot of stuff. I mostly remember his quotes.'

'Oh, he loved his quotes . . . loved them . . . well, he told me all about you . . . in his letters, you see.'

'This is all good stuff for me to hear.'

'He was the first one to tell me . . . about this player he'd seen . . . he said watching him play rugby . . . was like looking into the face of God.'

I *was* good. I could try to be modest about it, but I'd just come across as a dick.

I'm there, 'What specific qualities of mine did he mention that set me aport from other players – the likes of Gordon D'Arcy especially?'

I'm a sucker for a compliment. I can hear Oisinn and JP both groan, but fock them.

'He said you had . . . everything,' Brother Melchior goes. 'The most complete player . . . that he'd ever . . . ever seen.'

I'm there, 'Like I said, this is a definite boost to the old ego. Of course, the man definitely knew his rugby.'

'Oh, he loved his rugby . . . He said to me, "This boy will be . . . one of the all-time greats . . . And I'm talking about on a world stage" . . .'

'If only I'd met a coach like Joe Schmidt,' I go, 'who understood what I could bring to the set-up and stopped me drinking like a rock star. Johnny Sexton has said that about me in interviews. I could have had it all. On the record.'

'Well,' the dude goes, 'it gave me great pleasure . . . later on . . . to watch your career . . . and to see that Denis . . . was absolutely right about you.'

Of course I'm enjoying the praise so much that it never occurs to me to go, What focking career? I haven't kicked a rugby ball since I was in UCD.

Instead, I go, 'Keep going.'

'To see everything you did,' he goes. 'I'm sure he was looking down on you from Heaven . . . enjoying your achievements . . . just like the rest of the country . . .'

'I'd love to think that. I genuinely would.'

'Grand Slams . . . Heineken Cups . . . captaining your country . . .'

Oisinn is the first one to cop it – he actually *laughs*? Then I hear him turn around to the old man and go, 'He thinks it's Brian O'Driscoll!'

The old man's like, 'Good Lord!'

'I used to read about you,' Brother Melchior goes, 'in the papers . . . I had *The Irish Times* sent to me in Tanzania . . . every day . . . I read about all those important tries you scored for Ireland . . .'

Fock, this is embarrassing.

The old man has to stick his hooter into the conversation then. He goes, 'The thing is, Brother Melchior, he's not actually the chap you think he is!'

I turn around to the old man and I go, 'Shut the fock up, will you?'

'You were a credit,' Brother Melchior goes, 'to yourself . . . a credit . . . to the country . . . and a credit . . . to the game of rugby.'

I'm there, 'I'll take all of that.'

'Even though he thinks he's talking to Drico,' Oisinn goes.

I'm like, 'Don't listen to them.'

The dude goes, 'I want to shake your hand again . . . and tell you thank you . . . thank you . . . thank you . . .'

So I let him shake my hand again, then off he focks, delighted with himself for having met one of the true legends of the game.

The old man goes, 'Sorry, Kicker. I should have suspected something when he mentioned the hat-trick of tries you scored in Paris. It should have rung an alarm bell.'

JP goes, 'I can't believe you stood there and let him think you were Drico.'

I'm there, 'Hey, I just didn't want to hurt the dude's feelings, that's all.'

Oisinn and JP both laugh. Even the old man looks away in

embarrassment. 'Good Lord,' he goes, 'isn't that What's-it over there? I haven't seen him since God-knows-when,' and then off *he* goes as well.

We all wish each other a Merry Christmas, then we head back to our cors. I'm the one who ends up having to drop Christian home to Carrickmines. I could weep for him. Divorceland, they call it – where Celtic Tiger marriages go to die.

He sleeps the whole way there, drunkenly muttering the names of his children and calling Lauren a bitch in his sleep.

It gives me time to think about the conversation with Brother Melchior, which has left me a little bit, I don't know, *sad*? Look, I'm not knocking Drico. He achieved all the things he achieved in the game and I'd still consider him a hero of mine, as well as a mate. But talking to Brother Melchior has made me suddenly realize more than ever that it could have been me – that it *should* have been me?

I know there were a lot of factors – we're talking bad luck, we're talking issues with my famous rotator cuff, we're talking switching from pints to shots the night I told Warren Gatland a few home truths in the Berkeley Court Hotel. All those things played a port in me not actually making it.

But suddenly tonight – at the age of, what, nearly thirty-five? – I've been reminded of the amazing career that I could potentially have had. And it's left me feeling very, very old.

# 1. *Love and Honor*

Santa Claus is coming to Finglas. That's not the title of the shittest Christmas song of all time. It's an actual fact. It's, like, seven o'clock in the evening on the last Thursday before Christmas and we're standing in a queue in the middle of some random shopping centre on the northside with six or seven hundred other people, waiting for the dude to arrive – we're talking me, we're talking Sorcha, we're talking Honor, we're talking Brian, Johnny and Leo.

Of course it's not the *real* Santa Claus? I'm explaining that to the boys. I'm there, 'It's one of his helpers,' even though it's *actually* Shadden's old man – as in K . . . K . . . K . . . K . . . Kennet Tuite – who's wearing the suit this year. It's the kind of thing that I'm sure will play well with his probation officer, what with him being out on temporary release and everything.

The boys are definitely excited about seeing him, though. The three of them are straining at their leash like feral dogs and it's taking all of my strength to hold them back. 'Focking Santa!' Leo is going at the top of his voice. 'Focking focker! Focking focker fock!'

Yeah, no, he discovered the F-word a couple of months back. But Sorcha read in a magazine that telling children that a particular word is bad actually *increases* their fascination with it? So we've gone with the strategy of doing fock-all about it, even though it's getting worse by the day. I mean, not that I care. I think it's kind of funny. Especially when strangers look at us in total disgust.

'Focking Santa!' he's going. 'Fock off, Santa! Fock off, Santa, you focking fock!'

Out of the blue, little Brian – who's given to occasional violent outbursts – smacks his brother hord across the face. Leo responds by shoving the heel of his hand into Brian's nose, which then storts pouring blood. The two of them are suddenly screaming the roof off the shopping centre, while Johnny storts crying hysterically.

Sorcha tries to calm Johnny and Leo down while I attempt to stem the flow of blood from Brian's nose.

This is actually what they do all day – Brian and Leo go at each other like Itchy and Scratchy, while Johnny bursts into tears the second it kicks off. Johnny is actually the *quiet* one? Mostly, he just sits there, saying little or nothing, possibly taking everything in. Apparently, I was the same as a baby. He's either very, very thoughtful or very, very thick.

Time will tell, I suppose.

Johnny doesn't talk, but he does eat – and by that I don't mean that he has a healthy appetite. What I mean is, everything he picks up, he puts in his mouth and swallows, we're talking fifty-cent pieces, we're talking keys, we're talking – two weeks ago? – the top from one of Sorcha's lipsticks.

So there they are, the triplets at the age of, what, two and a half? I definitely love them, there's no doubt about that, but they're a little bit like Owen Farrell – great, but focking annoying.

Sorcha is down on her hunkers, telling the boys, 'Don't be fighting! Santa will be here soon!'

'Focking Santa!' Leo goes.

Jesus Christ, it might even be Tourette's.

'That's right,' Sorcha goes, 'Santa! He's the one who comes on Christmas Eve and brings all the presents! But only to good little children who know how to behave themselves!'

I think that's when I first cop that Honor is being unusually quiet tonight. I turn around to her and I go, 'Here, Honor, I wonder does the shopping centre know that Kennet's got a criminal record longer than this focking queue?'

She doesn't answer me. She's just, like, staring at her feet – it's like she's *miles* away?

I'm there, 'Honor?'

She suddenly snaps out of it. She goes, 'What?' at the top of her voice. 'I said what – are you focking deaf?'

'Yeah, no, I'm just saying, Honor, maybe we should go and find the manager and tell him that the dude playing Santa Claus has a string of criminal convictions and he's only out of the Joy on parole.'

She goes, 'Er, why?'

'Why do you think? To get him sacked from his job! As a matter of fact, I'm pretty disappointed that you didn't come up with it first!'

She doesn't give me the excited response I'm expecting from her. She just goes, 'Whatever', then goes back to staring at her Uggs.

A few seconds later, I turn around to her again and I go, 'Hey, Honor, why don't you take your brothers over there to see the moving crib outside Argos?'

It's just so I can have a word with Sorcha.

I hand her the leash and off they go – it's like she's being dragged along by sled dogs, with Leo leading the way, effing and blinding like a focking docker.

Sorcha links my orm, puts her head on my shoulder and goes, 'Oh my God, Ross, look at our lovely children!'

I'm there, 'Okay, are we going to ignore what just happened there?'

She goes, 'We've discussed this, Ross. All of the really good parenting magazines say that children who use bad words are just testing their power over you – the worst thing you can do is let them know they *have* that power?'

'Yeah, no, I don't give a fock about the swearing. I'm talking about Honor. I just offered her the opportunity to get Kennet fired from his job and she had literally no interest.'

'It's very unlike her, I have to admit.'

'I'm wondering did she maybe bang her head getting out of the people-carrier?'

'Do you know what's weird? She's actually been really *quiet* recently?'

'I thought that, too. It's like she's, I don't know, stuck in her own head or something.'

'Maybe she's plotting something and we don't know what it is yet.'

'Yeah, no, hopefully it's just that.'

All of a sudden, the word goes around that Santa slash Kennet has arrived and the excitement goes up a few notches.

Honor arrives back with the boys. Leo is going, 'I want a present! I want a focking present!'

'Presents are for good little boys!' Sorcha goes. 'And you're going to be good, aren't you, Leo?'

He goes, 'Focking present!'

All of a sudden, I hear a familiar voice in the queue behind us. It's like, 'Theer thee are!' and when I turn around, it ends up being Ronan with Shadden and little Rihanna-Brogan, who's, like, three now? It ends up being hugs and kisses and banter all round – it's 'Sorcha, you're like a bleaten model, so you are!' and 'Jays, you're piling on the pounds there, Rosser! You'll have to keep him away from the throyfle, Sorcha, wha'?' and all the rest of it.

Sorcha turns around to little R&B and goes, 'And what's Santa Claus bringing *you* this year? Because I know *you've* been a good little girl!'

Ronan whispers to me, 'Is Honor alreet, Rosser?' because she hasn't said a single nasty thing to Shadden yet – not even about her hoopy earrings. Again, she's just, like, staring into space.

I'm like, 'We think she's either hit her head or she's planning something evil.'

Ro just nods. He has a daughter himself. It's all ahead of him.

I ask him how things are going. I can't believe he's going to be sitting his Leaving Cert next June. He's there, 'All good in the hood, Rosser. Ine godda be fiddin in me CAO application in anutter few weeks.'

I end up just shaking my head. I'm in genuine awe of my son. 'Your CAO application,' I go. 'I'm not exactly sure what that even is, but I'm so proud of you, Ro.'

While this conversation is taking place, little R&B is telling Sorcha what's on her Santa list, except it's the funniest thing – she's got, like, a half-southside, half-northside accent? She's going, 'Oh my God, I'm *so* excited, because I've asked for, like, a Flutterboy Floying Fower Feerdy. Then I'm getting, like, a Teksta Robothic Puppy and, like – oh my God – a surproyuz!'

A bunch of *wans* behind us – skanks, basically – are listening to her and they're going, 'Ah, she's a gas little one, idn't she? She should be on the tedevision, so she should!' and Shadden turns around and

12

explains to them that she spent the first half of her life in Killiney and the second half in Finglas.

I'd have told them to mind their own focking business.

I turn around to Ronan and I go, 'Are you alright for money, by the way?'

He's there, 'Ine moostard, Rosser.'

'I'm just saying, Christmas is an expensive time and blah, blah, blah. If you need moo, I can throw you a few grand.'

'You're veddy good, but we've everything bought, Rosser.'

After waiting around for, like, an hour, we finally reach the top of the queue, where we meet Shadden's old man. He's the scrawniest Santa Claus I've ever seen. He's like Hagrid out of *Harry Potter*, except on his deathbed.

'Ho, ho, ho!' is his opening line. He gives me a wink, then he looks at Honor and goes, 'You look like you're a long way f . . . f . . . f . . . from howum! Have you been g . . . g . . . g . . . good this year?'

He has some balls asking that, given that he's the one who has to sign on at the local Gorda station twice a week.

'Yeah,' Honor goes, 'I don't see how that's even relevant. I've never been good and I always end up getting whatever I want for Christmas. There's no reason to think that this year will be any different.'

That's actually true. It's nice to see Honor suddenly back to her old self, though.

Kennet goes, 'Well, doatunt be teddin me you w . . . w . . . w . . . want a b . . . b . . . b . . . bleaten pony or something. Because with the greatest widdle in the wurdled, I wouldn't be able to firrit on me sled!'

Focking widdle in the wurdled. I blame programmes like *Love/ Hate* for glamorizing the Dublin accent. I've sat through it with Ronan three or four times – I'm talking about all five seasons – and his accent is becoming so strong, I might have to hire Imelda May to interpret for him.

Sorcha turns around to Kennet and goes, 'And these are our little boys, Santa – Leo, Johnny and Brian – and they've been – oh my God – *so* good!'

He's there, 'Ine d . . . d . . . d . . . delirit to hear it, so I am.'

'Fock you!' Leo goes. 'You focking focker.'

Kennet looks at Sorcha – even *he's* in shock and he's just spent two years on D Wing.

Sorcha goes, 'We're doing the whole not responding thing?'

Kennt's like, 'Eh, feerd enuff.'

He hands the boys a present each, then he tries to give one to Honor – a massive one with a big, humungous bow on it – but she walks off without taking it, obviously figuring that it's probably shit.

Santa – sorry, Kennet – just goes, 'Okay, M . . . M . . . M . . . M . . . Meddy Carrismiss, one and all!' and then off we head.

I ask Ro if he fancies a quick pint in The Broken Orms, but he says he has a couple of hours of studying to do. Studying. Tonight. Every day I ask myself, is he really my son?

'So what are you doing for Christmas?' I go.

He's there, 'Ah, we'll be going to Kennet and Dordeen's for izzer Christmas dinner.'

'You poor fockers, eating *their* muck. No offence, Shadden,' because she's standing right there. 'By the way, me and the old man are going to pop out to see you on, like, Stephen Zuzz Day, before we hit Leopardstown. We've got a little surprise for you.'

We do – and he's going to hopefully love it.

He goes, 'What is it, Rosser?'

I'm there, 'You'll just have to wait and see. Have a great Christmas, Ro. You, too, Shadden.'

We say our goodbyes, then we head back to the cor pork, me holding the boys on their leash, walking next to Honor, Sorcha following about ten steps behind us, carrying the presents.

'Here, Honor,' I go, just as we reach the cor, 'did you get the focking whiff of drink off Kennet's breath? Hey, here's another brainwave – we could go back and report him for being drunk on the job!'

But Honor doesn't answer me, because she's suddenly staring at her reflection in the tinted rear window of the people-carrier. 'Dad,' she goes – and she says it low, so Sorcha can't hear her – 'can I ask you a question?'

I'm there, 'Of course you can! You can ask me anything you want!'

And that's when she says *the* most unbelievable thing.

She's there, 'Do you think I'm ugly?'

I'm like, 'What? Who said you were ugly? Is that why you're act-ing weird?'

'It was a question,' she goes. 'I just asked you a question.'

I'm there, 'Well, it was a ridiculous question. One thing you're definitely not, Honor, is ugly. I've seen some of the girls in your class – what I'm trying to say is, there's worse than you.'

She looks sad – it's like she doesn't *believe* me?

'Anyway,' I go, 'looks aren't important. Have you ever heard the expression that it's what's on the inside that matters?'

She's like, 'No.'

I'm there, 'Well, I see they're using it now as an advertising slo-gan for the Beacon South Quarter,' where Sorcha's old pair are back living, by the way. 'And there's definitely some truth in it, Honor. I mean, they're obviously trying to draw people in there. But I think what they're trying to say is that, yes, on the outside, it's a real fock-ing mess, but on the inside, it's actually alright. It's got Imaginosity. There's some good stuff in Bo Concept. Blah, blah, blah. The point I'm trying to make, I suppose, is that looks aren't everything.'

She nods, then gets into the back of the cor. I hate lying to the girl, but, hey, she's my daughter.


'Isn't this lovely?' my old man goes. 'I've always dreamt of being part of a big family Christmas like this.'

We've got, like, a full house – we're talking him and Helen, we're talking Sorcha's old pair, we're talking Erika, we're talking her little daughter, Amelie, we're talking me and Sorcha, we're talking Honor and the three boys.

We finished dinner about an hour ago, now we're sitting around the tree in the living room, doing the whole exchanging presents thing, with the Michael Bublé Christmas album on in the background.

We're suckers for the old traditions in this house.

I'm down on my knees, helping Brian, Johnny and Leo to open

their just, like, piles and piles of gifts. The old man has bought them each an official World Cup 2015 replica Gilbert ball. I hand Brian his one and he focks it across the room – I can't say enough good things about his throwing technique – and smashes a €400 donkey from the Lladró Nativity set.

Sorcha's old man tuts while his wife picks up the broken pieces.

'Never mind focking tutting,' I go. 'We'll all remember this moment when he wins his first cap for Ireland. Maybe even hang on to the bits of porcelain, Mrs Lalor. They might be worth something.'

Sorcha's old man hands Sorcha a present that looks about the size and shape of a book.

'Oh my God,' Sorcha goes, picking at the wrapping paper, 'what have you done?'

Of course, it turns out to *be* a book? Sorcha goes, 'Oh my God! I don't *actually* believe it!' because it turns out to be a limited edition, leatherbound copy of *The Collected Speeches of Nelson Mandela*. It's suddenly made my present of *The Notebook* on DVD seem way shitter than it needed to.

The focker loves making me look bad, of course.

He goes, 'They're all in there, Sorcha. His *Black Man in a White Man's Court* speech in Pretoria, 1962. His *Ideal I'm Prepared to Die For* speech when he was released in 1990. His *Evils of Poverty, Disease and Ignorance* speech after he became President in 1994.'

I go, 'That DVD has a special commentary by Ryan Gosling, by the way. I'm just pointing that out.'

That ends up getting totally passed over, of course.

'I'm going to read, like, one speech every night before I go to bed,' Sorcha goes. 'Oh my God, I can't believe it's a year since he passed!'

Her old man is there, 'I was recently telling one or two of my Law Library friends about those letters that Mandela sent you!'

Fock. I hate when this comes up in conversation.

I turn to Honor and I try to change the subject. 'Are you not going to open your presents?' I go, because she hasn't touched hers yet.

She's there, 'Why would I bother? I know what everything is – I gave you a detailed list.'

'Well,' I go, 'there might be one or two surprises in there as well.'

Oh, that gets her attention. She suddenly storts picking through her pile, shaking and squeezing various presents, as if suddenly remembering the joy of Christmas. 'Anything I don't like,' she goes, as she storts tearing the paper, 'you can bring it back to the shop and just give me the equivalent in cash.'

Of course, Helen has to stick her focking oar in then by bringing up the letters again. She goes, 'Are you saying that Nelson Mandela wrote to you, Sorcha?'

And Sorcha's old man sort of, like, puffs himself up and goes 'My daughter enjoyed a long correspondence with President Mandela.'

'That's right,' Sorcha goes. 'Even though I call him by his clan name – Madiba.'

He's there, 'Of course – Madiba! He wrote you, what, *six* letters, was it, Sorcha?'

She's like, 'Eight.'

I just keep my head down. I help Johnny tear open one of his presents. It's from Sorcha's old dear – a focking tennis racket. I look at her for an explanation.

'I thought it'd be good for them to try their hand at lots of different sports,' she tries to go.

I'm there, 'Yeah, no, that's great, Mrs Lalor.'

It's going in the focking bin about ten seconds after she leaves.

The Mandela thing just won't go away, though.

Helen goes, 'How did it come about that he wrote to you, Sorcha?'

Sorcha's there, 'Well, I actually wrote *him* loads of letters while he was in prison? Oh my God, I was, like, *such* a fan. Okay, this is *so* embarrassing, but the day he was released from prison, I turned to my mom – she can vouch for this – and I was like, "Oh my God, I'm going to marry him one day!"'

She didn't, of course. She married me. It's no wonder her old pair think she settled.

'Then, one day,' her old man goes, 'totally out of the blue, he rang you – didn't he, Sorcha?'

She goes, 'Yes, he did.'

He did in his focking hole, by the way. It was Oisinn. One April

Fool's Day. He used to do the voice, see, and we all thought it'd be funny – 'Your letters meant so much to me while I was in prison' and blah, blah, blah.

Sorcha fell for it, of course, and ended up talking the focking ear off him. She went on about the feelings she had for me and asked him whether or not she should switch from Orts in UCD to European Environmental Law in Trinity.

Anyway, she ended up being so bowled over by the conversation that I genuinely didn't think our relationship would have survived me telling her that it was just me and the goys ripping the serious piss out of her. So I acted surprised when she told me the dude had called her out of the blue.

But then, a while after that, she storted to get suspicious, especially when she heard Oisinn doing the impression one night in the Merrion Inn. She was like, 'Ross, tell me the truth – was that really Nelson Mandela who rang me that day, or was it Oisinn?'

And that was the moment I should have possibly told her. Instead, I went, 'Sorcha, I swear to you, it had nothing to do with me,' and then I tried to cover it up further by getting Oisinn to write her a bunch of letters, in which he talked about how things were going politically in South Africa and about me – 'He sounds like a very wonderful young man' – and about the career opportunities open to someone with a qualification in European Environmental Law as opposed to a shit-for-brains degree like Orts.

Oisinn got a mate of his who lived in Cape Town to post them to her, one every fortnight for three or four months until she stopped being suspicious.

Anyway, like I said, they come up in conversation every now and then and today it's all anyone can suddenly talk about.

I'm there, 'Sorry, why are we all banging on about this? Can we not talk about something, I don't know, more Christmassy? I hope Ian Madigan's eating light, for instance – it's a massive day for him at Thomond tomorrow.'

'Okay,' Sorcha goes, 'speaking of eating, who's for dessert? I've made my famous Nigella Lawson's Ultimate Christmas Pudding!'

Honor's there, 'Okay, I'm bored now. I'm going to my room.'

'Honor, I said we're going to have pudding.'

'Er, I don't *want* pudding?'

'I soaked the dried fruit in Pedro Ximénez.'

'Do you need your focking ears syringed? I said I didn't want pudding!'

Sorcha's old man goes, 'How dare you speak to your mother like that!'

Honor – in fairness to her – goes, 'Sorry, what focking business is it of yours?'

He's there, 'You didn't eat your dinner either – a beautiful dinner that your mother's been preparing since . . .'

'Monday,' Sorcha goes.

Honor's like, 'Yeah, for your information, I ate a sprout.'

Sorcha's there, 'A sprout is not a meal, Honor,' and I think to myself, yeah, no, you've obviously forgotten how you lost nearly all your baby weight. I don't call her out on it, though.

She goes, 'You have to eat more than the occasional vegetable, Honor.'

Again – a hypocrite.

And that's when Honor suddenly loses it with her. She goes, 'I'm not focking hungry, okay?' and she's, like, screaming the words at the top of her voice. 'Maybe I don't want to be fat anymore!'

Everyone in the room is just like, 'What?'

Sorcha goes, 'Fat? Honor, you're not exactly fat.'

Honor bursts into tears. 'I am fat,' she goes. 'And you're trying to make me even fatter – because you're a bitch!'

She runs out of the room and up the stairs.

Sorcha's old man tries to throw another ten cents into the mix then. He goes, 'That girl has no respect for anyone – and it's not difficult to see from *whom* she takes her behavioural cues.'

I'm there, 'What business is it of yours, you focking knob-end?'

Sorcha's like, 'Please don't start, you two.'

But, of course, Christmas wouldn't be Christmas without the traditional family row.

I'm there, 'Why don't you keep your focking opinions to yourself?'

He goes, 'I won't stay here to be insulted.'

'Hey, you're perfectly welcome to fock off any time you want. I don't remember even inviting you.'

'My daughter invited me.'

'Well, you've been pissing us all off since you arrived, with your book of speeches and your general bullshit. Then banging on about Nelson Mandela and refusing to let it go even when the conversation had clearly moved on to Ian Madigan.'

'You and that daughter of yours – you're exactly the same!'

'I'm happy to hear it. I'll take it as a compliment.'

Sorcha goes, 'Please, stop it! You're ruining everything!'

My old man stands up, obviously feeling awkward. 'We, em, might head off, Sorcha. We said we might pop in and have a drink with Hennessy – the day that's in it. Thank you for a lovely Christmas dinner.'

Sorcha's old man goes, 'Well, we're not staying either.'

I'm there, 'No one's asking you to. As a matter of fact, I'll get your focking coat.'

Suddenly, no one's having dessert.

'At least stay and watch me flame the pudding!' Sorcha goes. 'It's one of our traditions!'

But her old man goes, 'I think it's best we leave before I say or do something I regret.'

I'm there, 'Yeah, no, don't let the door hit you on the way out!'

He's like, 'Merry Christmas, Sorcha,' and off he focks, with Sorcha's old dear following closely behind.

That's how quickly it all happens. Literally sixty seconds later, Sorcha's old pair, my old man and Helen have all driven off and it's only me, Sorcha, Erika and the kids left in the house.

Sorcha is not a happy rabbit – of course, as usual, I end up getting the blame for what happened?

She goes, 'Could you not have bitten your tongue – oh my God, Ross – just for, like, *one* day of the year?'

And that's when Erika goes, 'Er, shouldn't you two be more worried about Honor?'

We're both like, 'Honor?' not a clue what she's even talking about.

She's there, 'Aren't you even the slightest bit concerned about what she just said? She said she thought she was fat. She said you were trying to make her fatter.'

Sorcha suddenly sits down.

'Oh my God,' she goes, 'you're right. I mean, here *I* am, practically having a nervous breakdown trying to give everyone *the* perfect Christmas – and all the time I've been ignoring the fact that my daughter is upset about something.'

Erika's there, 'Okay, I'm going to ask this straight out. Do you think it's possible that Honor is suffering from an eating disorder?'

Sorcha goes, 'An *eating* disorder?' shocked at even the idea of it. 'She's, like, nine years old!'

'You read magazines, Sorcha. There are children in America as young as five years old with full-blown anorexia. The pressure on girls to look perfect is starting earlier and earlier.'

'Fock,' I go. 'I've just remembered something.'

Sorcha's like, 'What?'

'Yeah, no, last week, when we went to see K . . . K . . . K . . . Kennet playing Santa Claus, I caught Honor staring at her reflection in the window of the cor. She asked me if I thought she was ugly.'

'Oh! My God!' Sorcha goes. 'Ross, what did you say?'

'I said I definitely wouldn't class her as ugly – especially compared to one or two others in her class. She didn't seem to accept it though.'

Sorcha suddenly whips out her phone and storts flicking the screen with her thumb. She's like, 'Oh! My God!'

I'm there, 'What?'

'I'm just checking her Instagram account. Ross, she hasn't posted a picture of something she's eaten for days!'

Erika goes, 'Do you want me to talk to her?'

Sorcha's like, 'You?' obviously a bit put out by the idea that Honor might confide in her aunt ahead of her.

Erika goes, 'I promised to bring her to Dundrum on Saturday. I said we'd have a day together before I went away.'

Erika's going to Tuscany next week for four months to study – believe it or not – ort history and appreciation. There's talk of her possibly opening a gallery when she comes home.

It's another sign that the economy is possibly back on track.

Sorcha goes, 'If it is – oh my God – what you suggested, Erika, I still think this is something she should be able to confide in me, and not – no offence – an *outsider*?'

Erika's there, 'I'm not in competition with you, Sorcha. I'm just saying she might find it easier to open up to someone outside her immediate family.'

She possibly has a point. And Honor idolizes Erika.

'Okay,' Sorcha goes, looking just about as sad as I've ever seen her look, 'please, just see what you can find out. Oh my God, I can't believe my little girl has a possible eating disorder!'

I'm there, 'We don't know that for definite yet.'

'It's all beginning to make sense, Ross. Like I said, she's been quiet and distracted for weeks now. She only picks at her dinner. And, oh my God, I made her Brussels pâté sandwiches for her lunch last week and I found them that night, still in her schoolbag.'

'Like I said,' Erika goes, 'I'll talk to her.'

Sorcha shakes her head, tears welling in her eyes. 'I honestly thought that this was going to be our best Christmas ever.'

'Fock you!' Leo suddenly shouts. 'And fock your focking Christmas.'

And somehow – despite being still a baby – he manages to totally nail the atmosphere of the day.

It's, like, eleven o'clock on Stephen Zuzz morning and I'm in bed, checking the old Twitter feed on my iPhone, when one particular Tweet catches my eye.

It's from, like, Seapoint Rugby Club and it's like: 'Players wanted. All levels. Trials on Saturday, 3 January 2015.'

Suddenly, it has me dreaming all sorts of crazy comeback dreams. I'm thinking, Hey, thirty-four going on thirty-five isn't old! I could still do a job in – where do their firsts play? – Division 2B of the All Ireland League?

It's just as I'm thinking this that my phone suddenly rings. It's, like, an overseas number, one I don't recognize, but of course I make the mistake of answering it. There's, like, a familiar voice on the other end – a woman's voice.

Shit-faced.

She's like, 'Ross!'

I'm there, 'What the fock do *you* want, you focking molehog?'

She goes, 'Hello? Hello? I think we must have a crossed line! Ross, it's your mother!'

'Yeah,' I go, 'I'm well aware of that fact. The line is as clear as a bell. What the fock do you want?'

'I'm ringing from California! I'm ringing from Malibu, California!'

'What do you want me to say? Congratulations on still being able to dial after your traditional Christmas bottle-and-a-half of gin and a fistful of diazepam?'

'Ross, I'm ringing with news!'

'You could at least say Merry Christmas – you know, like a *normal* parent?'

'Brace yourself! I'm getting married!'

Everything goes suddenly silent. I realize that this might be because I'm expected to say something, except I can't – as in, I can't form any actual *words*? I have no idea how much time goes by.

She goes, 'Ross, say something.'

What I want to say is that I can't believe she found a man either desperate or mentally unstable enough to want to spend the rest of his natural life with her. But for once in my life I'm not quick enough.

She goes, 'You're pleased for me, aren't you? Oh, I knew you would be. I said it to Ari. That's the name of my *fianthé*.'

'Yeah,' I go, 'I'm pretty sure that's not how you pronounce it.'

'He's not my usual type. He's not classically handsome like so many of my men. He's a financier and he just happens to be worth two billion dollars.'

'Two billion? Did you just say he was worth two *billion*?'

'It's something of that order. Not that I'm interested in his money. Oh, you'll really enjoy him, Ross. We're very much in love.'

'Ari what?'

'I beg your pardon?'

'I'm saying Ari what? As in, what's his second name?'

'It's Brostein. Or Berkovitz.'

23

'You don't even know his name?'

'It begins with a B. It's irrelevant. We love each other, Ross, and he's going to be my husband.'

'Spare me. Where did you even meet him?'

'If you must know, his granddaughter was in rehab with me.'

'What, was she a focking coke-head as well?'

'I'm not going to listen to you being nasty to me, Ross. We're getting married in Dublin in the spring – and I have a special favour to ask of you. I want you to give me away.'

'I'd be happy to. I'd give you to focking ISIS if I thought they'd take you. Are you not even going to say Merry Christmas to me?'

'Ari is Jewish, Ross. We don't celebrate . . . Samuels!'

'What?'

'I've just remembered. His name is Samuels!'

'I'm thinking of going back playing rugby.'

That's what I tell my old man and Ronan. We're in my cor – I'm driving a 142D, black BMW Five Serious these days – on the way to Ticknock to give Ro his Christmas present.

I'm there, 'I was thinking of going back playing the game of rugby.'

The game of rugby – I love the way that sounds.

The old man just goes, 'That's wonderful! Did your mother reach you, by the way?'

I'm there, 'Why are we suddenly talking about her?'

'It's just she has some rather exciting news!'

'Yeah, I know her news – she got me, okay?'

'She's getting married! Isn't that terrific, Ronan?'

'Ah, feer fooks!' Ronan pipes up from the back seat of the cor.

I'm there, 'I can't believe someone actually wants to marry her – and that's no offence – the focking mange-ridden bull-seal.'

The old man goes, 'Well, I think it's rather wonderful. She deserves some happiness, your mother. This chap – he's called Ari, by all accounts – popped the question on Christmas Eve, on the balcony of this mansion of his – overlooking the Pacific, if you don't mind!'

I pull up at a red light. I go, 'Sorry to cut you off – actually, I'm not sorry – how the fock is that bigger than my news?'

He's there, 'Your news?'

'Er, I just announced – *exclusively*, by the way? – that I was thinking of going back playing rugby and I might as well have said the cor needed oil.'

'The car does need oil, Ross. I noticed the little light went on just after we collected Ronan.'

'Can we stick to the subject of me for, like, ten seconds? When I said I'm thinking of going back playing rugby, I was talking about playing rugby for possibly Seapoint. They're looking for players.'

Oh, that gets his attention.

He goes, 'Seapoint?'

I'm there, 'Yes, Seapoint.'

'Seapoint, in –?'

'Ballybrack, yeah.'

That's when he says the most unbelievable thing. He goes, 'I didn't know they *had* a seniors team.'

I'm like, 'A seniors team? What the fock are you talking about? I'm thirty-four.'

'You'll be thirty-five in a week or two.'

'Yeah, and that's not even old. Do you know what? Forget about it. I'm sorry I even told you.'

We drive on in silence. After a while, Ronan goes, 'Where in the nayum of Jaysus are we?'

The old man laughs. He's like, 'We're nearly there, Ronan.'

'What's this present you're arthur getting me, but?'

'Patience, little chap. It's just up here on the left, Kicker.'

I pull up on the road next to a plot of waste ground, which is about, like, an acre in size. Back in the day, the old man owned this and another 234 acres just like it, which is now practically all houses and aportments – except that some orchitect made a balls of it when he was drawing up the plans and the old man ended up with this one acre left over.

'Merry Christmas!' me and the old man both go at the exact same time.

Ronan looks at us, his face screwed up like he thinks we're both pissed. The old man actually *is* pissed. We're heading to the races after this.

Ronan's there, 'What are yiz on about?'

'This is your Christmas present,' the old man goes.

We all get out of the cor. Ronan pushes open the heavy iron gate and the three of us step onto the site. And that's when he sees it, off to his right. It's a mobile home. It's not an ordinary mobile home either. It's the exact same one as Fran has in *Love/Hate*.

Ronan – I swear to God – can't even speak.

The old man goes, 'You happy, little chap?'

He's like, 'I . . . I just . . . I just . . .'

I'm there, 'Come on, Ro – that's not all.'

I hand him a set of keys. He opens the door and we step inside. We've had the whole interior properly furnished. There's, like, a bed, a sofa, a TV and a table and chairs – again, all the exact same as Fran's.

We've even got him his own little stash of poitín – although it's only 12% proof, what with him being still only seventeen.

Ronan is, like, totally blown away. 'I caddent believe it,' he goes, wiping away genuine tears. 'Me foorst base of operashiddens.'

The old man goes, 'The start of your empire, Ronan.'

I'm there, 'Yeah, no, I was thinking more in terms of a place where you could study for the Leaving Cert? Peace and quiet, blah, blah, blah.'

'I fooken love it, Rosser.'

'We were going to get you two or three pit bull terriers, but they do say don't buy a dog for Christmas. We'll get them for you next week.'

'Look out the window,' the old man goes.

Ronan does as he's told.

The old man's there, 'Do you see that JCB digger over there?'

Ro's like, 'Yeah, what abourrit, Grandda?'

'Well, that's yours as well.'

He throws his orms around his granddad. He's *really* crying now. Just like the old man's crying. *I'm* even crying.

Wait till he finds out about the video message from Peter Coonan – that'll finish him off altogether.

He goes, 'Thanks, Rosser! Thanks, Grandda!'

The old man goes, 'You're welcome, little chap. Now, Ross and I are going to the races with Hennessy. What do you say we leave you here for a few hours to get properly acquainted with the place, then we'll pick you up on the way home?'

'Gayum ball, Grandda – gayum ball.'

Me and the old man get into the cor and I point it in the direction of Leopardstown. I totally blank him the entire way there, still pissed off with him for what he said earlier. We're actually just pulling into the cor pork of the racecourse when I finally turn around to him and go, 'Do you seriously not think I could do a job for someone in the All Ireland League?'

He goes, 'I didn't mean any offence. Like I've always said, Ross, you've got a rugby brain.'

'That better be a compliment.'

'Oh, it's very much a compliment.'

'But you don't think I could come back and play at the age of still technically thirty-four?'

'Well, it's just that rugby is very different to the way it was when you last played.'

'That was only, like, fifteen years ago.'

'Fifteen years is a long time. The game has moved on. When you played, it was a contact sport. Now, it's a collision sport.'

'Do you want to know what I'm bench-pressing these days? It'd make you sick.'

'Then you hear about all these – let's be careful here – *alleged* concussions, not to mention broken necks. You've got children, Ross. Five of them.'

'I know how many children I have.'

That's a lie, of course – it could be any focking number.

I'm there, 'Maybe it's my children I'm thinking about. The boys are talking now. Maybe I don't want them one day asking me, "Why did you never actually make it in the game, Dad?" or "Why did you just walk away – despite your obvious talent?"'

'I'm just wondering where this is all coming from? Is it something to do with Brother What's-it mistaking you for the great Brian O'Driscoll?'

'Maybe. It's made me think about the player I could and should have been.'

'There were factors in your case, Ross.'

'I know there were factors. There were focking loads of them. But it's just, you know, in a week or two I'm going to be another Six Nations older – and what have I actually done?'

'Look, let's go inside. We'll have a few drinks with our learned friend and we'll see if we can't cheer ourselves up by picking out a winner or two.'

Sorcha has been pacing the floor for the last two hours. 'Where are they?' she keeps going. 'What time is it now, Ross?'

I'm there, 'It's five minutes after the last time you asked me.'

She goes, 'So why aren't they home yet?'

She's talking about Erika and Honor. She's been going out of her mind since they left for Dundrum.

'Look,' I go, 'you know what those two are like when they stort shopping. And that place was designed so you never know whether it's day or night.'

She's there, 'They left here at ten o'clock this morning, Ross. It's now eight o'clock at night.'

'Which goes to prove my point.'

'I've tried their phones at least ten times and neither of them is answering.'

'Look, chillax, Babes. They've probably gone for something to eat.'

'Yeah, Honor *doesn't* eat, remember?'

'Well, hopefully Erika's getting to the bottom of that – over a humungous Eddie Rockets with a bit of luck. Cheese and bacon fries, the works! Do you want to check her Instagram again?'

'I still hate the idea that there are things Honor can talk to Erika about which she can't discuss with me. I gave birth to her, Ross!'

'I was there.'

'That makes me her mother.'

'I know how it works.'

'I'm not jealous. I'm just saying this isn't how I wanted our relationship to be.'

All of a sudden there's the sound of a key in the front door, then Erika's voice goes, 'Hi! We're back!'

Sorcha runs out into the hall and throws her orms around Honor like the girl has just been pulled from in front of a runaway Luas. She's there, 'Thank God you're home!'

Honor is, like, laden down with bags from Horvey Nichs, BT2, House of Fraser, blah, blah, blah. She looks at me and goes, 'Has your wife been drinking?'

Sorcha's there, 'No, I haven't been drinking. I just missed you, that's all.'

'Well, you're being a knob,' she goes, separating herself from her. 'Auntie Erika, thank you for my lovely presents!'

Erika goes, 'You're welcome, my darling!' then off Honor goes, up the stairs.

Erika's there, 'Okay, I'd better go. Mum and Dad have been minding Amelie all day.'

Sorcha goes, 'Oh, no you don't – you need to tell me first!'

'Tell you what?'

'Erika, don't leave me in suspense. Did Honor tell you anything about what's been bothering her?'

'Yes, she did.'

'And?'

'And it's nothing for you to worry about.'

'I'm her mother, Erika. I think I'll be the judge as to whether I should worry or not.'

Erika goes, 'I'm sworn to secrecy – and, look, we've got an early flight tomorrow morning. I really do have to go.'

She turns and storts heading for the front door again. Sorcha chases after her, grabs her by the shoulders and spins her around. 'Erika,' she goes, 'don't you dare do this to me – you're a mother yourself. If Honor has an eating disorder, I'm entitled to know.'

Erika throws her eyes skyward.

'Yes,' she goes, 'Honor has an eating disorder.'

Sorcha turns to me, her mouth slung open like a yawning hippo.

'Well,' Erika goes, 'it's a kind of eating disorder. It's a boy.'

Sorcha's there, 'Excuse me?'

'I'm saying that's why she's been acting all quiet and why she's off her food. She likes a boy.'

'What boy?'

'Just a boy.'

I'm there, 'Do we know what school he goes to?' because I know it's probably what Sorcha's thinking as well.

Erika goes, 'Look, I promised Honor that I wouldn't tell you anything and I'm not going to break that promise.'

I'm there, 'Erika, as her parents, we're entitled to know what school he goes to. Like Sorcha said, you have a daughter yourself.'

'Okay,' she goes, 'he's in St Michael's – the primary school.'

I breathe a sudden sigh of relief. 'Well, that's something,' I go. 'At least it's not Willow Pork. Let's count our blessings. So what else do we know about him? Does he come from a good family?'

Yeah, like I'm in any position to judge.

'I gave Honor my word,' she goes. 'I can't tell you any more than that. But you have nothing to worry about.'

Sorcha's there, 'It's probably just a crush,' still trying to put a brave face on things. 'I'd like to think that if she really liked this boy, she would have confided in me first.'

'It's definitely not a crush,' Erika goes. 'Trust me, Sorcha. Honor is in love.'


Chloe's old pair have been robbed. They're apparently pretty shaken up about it as well.

I'm there, 'See, that's the price you pay for living in – where are they again, Shankill?'

It's, like, New Year's Eve and the yacht club is packed for Oisinn's Dischorge from Bankruptcy porty.

'It's technically more Killiney than Shankill,' Chloe goes, 'and anyway, it wasn't even that kind of robbed. They had one of those phone calls – you know, someone rings you from a call centre in, I don't know, Bangalore and they go, "We have detected a virus on your computer – can you switch it on, please?"'

'I've never heard of that.'

JP's there, 'Yeah, they tell you to log on to some website that allows them to take control of your computer remotely, then they steal all your credit cord and, like, bank account details. They robbed seven grand – wasn't it, Chloe?'

She's there, 'It's not so much the money they're worried about. They just feel so stupid.'

I'm there, 'Well, I would love to go over to – where did you say this was happening? Booba Looba?'

'Bangalore,' JP goes. 'Well, somewhere in India.'

'I would love to go over there and deck whoever did it. Look, I know my old man was as focking crooked as a Welsh put-in, but at least planning corruption and tax evasion are, like, *victimless* crimes? As in, there were no real *losers*?'

I look over at Oisinn. He's throwing the old Veuve Clicquot into him and some old dude who I'm pretty sure I recognize from the banking inquiry has his orm around his shoulder.

'A new stort!' the dude goes – and he says it as a kind of *toast*?

We all raise our glasses and say the exact same thing. 'A new stort!'

'My old man thinks the next boom is going to be even bigger than the last one,' JP goes. 'Stands to reason, I suppose. People don't ever want to feel that poor again.'

Sorcha arrives back from the jacks. She looks tremendous, by the way. Like I said, she's very nearly got her old figure back and I can see her gobstoppers down the front of her dress.

She goes, 'Hi, Chloe! Hi, JP! Happy New Year!' and it's air-kisses and all the rest of it. 'How's little Isa? Oh my God, he must be talking now!'

'One or two words,' Chloe goes. 'He's still only fourteen months old, bear in mind. He can say Dadda and sometimes he says Ma. We'd obviously prefer if it was Mom, although we took him to see a Children's Cognitive Behavioural Therapist and she said it was, like, *way* too early to stort worrying. And how are yours – how are the boys?'

'Getting big!' Sorcha goes. 'Big and bold!'

Chloe's there, 'And what about Honor?' and she sort of, like, pulls a face as she says it, like she's bracing herself for the news that she tried to kill us both in our sleep or that she burned down a care home.

'Oh, it seems Honor is in love,' Sorcha goes.

Chloe and JP are both like, 'Love?' like they can't believe she's even capable of that emotion.

In fairness, I'm struggling to get my head around it myself.

Chloe's there, 'Oh my God, so who is she in love *with*?'

Sorcha goes, 'We don't actually *know* his name yet? I'm sure she'll tell us in her own time. It's important to give her space. We don't want to be those kind of parents who have to know every little thing that's going on in their children's lives.'

I'm there, 'The important thing is that he doesn't go to Willow Pork. Everything after that is a bonus.'

I knock back a mouthful of the old Miracle of Zoeterwoude, then someone shouts, 'It's coming up on ten seconds to midnight!' and everyone storts going, 'Ten! Nine! Eight! Seven!'

I shout, 'You the man, Oisinn!'

'Five! Four! Three! Two!'

Instead of going, 'Happy New Year!' everyone just goes, 'Happy Dischorge from Bankruptcy!'

I turn around to Sorcha and I kiss her. And I very nearly do the same to Oisinn when he tips over to us.

I'm there, 'I'm so happy for you, Dude,' because I'm thinking about that day, five or six years ago, when the two of us stood and watched as a crew of repo men stripped everything out of his old gaff. His home sauna. His Honma golf clubs. His grid composition by John Kingerlee. Everything he had in the world seized then sold off to pay his creditors.

And now he's back.

'Thanks for coming,' he goes. 'Are you going to stick around? We're all going outside in a bit and I'm going to burn my Order of Adjudication and Warrant of Seizure.'

I'm like, 'I'm not missing that.'

Sorcha and Chloe stort talking about, I don't know, girlie stuff, so me, Oisinn and JP end up taking a couple of steps to the side.

'So what happens now?' JP goes. 'Any plans?'

Oisinn's there, 'One or two ideas, let's just say, percolating.'

I laugh. I've decided that Oisinn's going to be the inspiration for my own comeback.

I'm there, 'Speaking of people who everyone considered finished . . .'

They're both like, 'Yeah?'

' . . . okay, I'm going to come straight out with it. I've been thinking of going back to rugby.'

JP's like, 'Whoa! That's fantastic!'

And Oisinn goes, 'About focking time as well!'

I'm there, 'See? I knew you two would have faith in me.'

'Hey,' JP goes, 'you've still got a lot to contribute.'

I'm there, 'Keep talking to me like this, Dude.'

'Here,' JP goes, 'did you hear Accenture are looking for a coach for their women's tag rugby team?'

I'm there, 'Excuse me?'

'I don't know if there's any shekels in it. But there's a lot of good-looking birds go in and out of there.'

Oisinn goes, 'They're based in Grand Canal Square, aren't they?'

I end up suddenly losing it with them. 'I'm not talking about coaching focking women!' I go.

Oisinn's like, 'What are you talking about then?'

'I'm talking about playing the actual game. Tag rugby? I should focking deck you – the pair of you.'

JP's like, 'Playing it?'

'Yes, playing it. Why is that so unbelievable?'

'Playing it for who, though?'

'I was thinking in terms of Seapoint.'

'Seapoint?'

'Yeah.'

'In Ballybrack?'

'Let's be honest.'

'But they're in the All Ireland League,' Oisinn goes.

'I know they're in the All Ireland League.'

'I'm sorry, Ross, it's just, I don't know, the game has moved on quite a bit since we played it.'

'You don't think I can do it either. Do you know what? I'm going to do it. I'm going to come back just to prove you two and my old man wrong.'

All of a sudden, we hear raised voices. There's, like, a row going on up at the bor. It turns out that one of the staff has told Christian that he's had enough to drink, while Christian is disagreeing with that analysis at the top of his voice.

He's like, 'Do you know how many focking . . . focking years I've been coming here . . . on and off . . . I pay your focking wages!'

Sorcha goes, 'Ross, do something!'

So I go over and I grab him. I'm like, 'Come on, Christian, you're hammered. Maybe you should go home. Or on into town.'

'Your focking hands off me!' he shouts at me. 'Get your focking hands off me!'

It breaks my hort to see him like this, but Christian has been on a downward spiral for a while now. Look, everyone knows that him and Lauren had problems – we're talking financial, we're talking relationship, we're talking everything. His comic book store on Chatham Street went down the shitter along with the last of their savings and their rows were famous. For about a year, they were on and off like a fat dude's fridge light, then about four months ago, Lauren took the kids – we're talking Ross Junior and Oliver – and just focked off to France to live. Hennessy – as in, her old man – has a brother who supposedly owns a vineyord just outside Bourg-en-Gironde.

JP goes, 'We'll drop him home. We told the babysitter we'd let her go shortly after midnight. We can swing past Carrickmines, Chloe, can't we?'

I feel a bit bad. If I was being hord on myself, I'd nearly say I played a port in Christian and Lauren breaking up. I try not to think about it, though.

I'm there, 'JP, get him home safely, will you?'

Christian goes, 'Fock you – ruined my focking . . . my focking . . . whole . . . life.'

34

Then off they thankfully head.

A few minutes later, the word goes around that Oisinn is about to burn the paperwork confirming his bankruptcy outside on the terrace. Me and Sorcha shuffle outside along with everyone else.

Oisinn is holding up a red fire bucket and there's a definite sense of excitement in the air. He puts it down on a table, then he produces the documents from his inside pocket and he stuffs them into the bucket. Someone hands him a vinegar bottle filled with presumably petrol and Oisinn tips it in. He lights a match, takes a step backwards, then throws it into the bucket.

The pages go up in a blaze and there's, like, a spontaneous cheer, followed by a round of applause.

There's a definite sense that Ireland is going back to where it was in 2004 slash 2005 – and I don't think anyone would describe that as a bad thing.

'So,' Sorcha goes, as we're walking back to the cor, 'any resolutions for 2015?'

I decide not to tell her about the Seapoint trial this weekend. I don't want to give anyone else the chance to remind me how old I am.

So I just go, 'This is going to be my year, Sorcha. The year I prove the doubters wrong once and for all.'

Seapoint Rugby Club isn't actually *in* Seapoint? Like JP said, it's in, let's be honest, Ballybrack – which is why I end up locking the cor about eight times after I throw it in the cor pork.

I don't actually *have* any gear with me? That's how I've decided to play this thing. I just figure they'll know who I am and they'll know what I can do. The Rossmeister doesn't do auditions.

Bottom of Division 2B, they should be honoured that I'd even *consider* playing for them?

Like I said, I pork the cor, then I stort walking across Kilbogget Pork to get to the actual rugby pitch. It's, like, pissing with rain and there's a wind blowing across the field from the direction of Cabinteely that would exfoliate an elephant.

Even from a distance, I can see that there's, like, a trials match underway. It's blue bibs – who I'm presuming are the first team – against orange bibs – who I'm presuming are the trialists – and there's a lot of heavy hits going in. Goys are obviously going all out to prove themselves. A lot of hord tackles. Some that I can nearly feel, even from, like, fifty or sixty yords away.

Not that I'd be in any way intimidated. Back in the day, I was famous for dishing it out. There's one or two, let's just say, well-known Irish internationals who are going to have arthritis in their old age as a result of being tackled by me. They'll remember my name every time they bend down to tie their shoes.

It's the name of the game.

I actually get butterflies in my stomach as I get closer to the pitch. The grunts. The roars. The crack of, like, bone on bone. The steam rising from the scrum. The smell of wintergreen and wet jerseys. I've missed it.

They're young. That's one thing I notice as I get closer. They're a lot younger than I expected them to be – we're talking, like, early to mid-twenties, most of them.

But then, physically, I've nothing to worry about, because I've obviously stayed in shape since I finished playing. And I've also got something that probably none of them have got, and that's a Lein-ster Schools Senior Cup medal – even though it was technically taken off me for doping.

Fock, they're *very* young actually? One or two of them aren't much older than Ronan. But then I quickly remind myself that there's no substitute for experience. They'll know that that's one of the things I'll definitely bring to the set-up.

Someone suddenly puts the ball into touch on my side of the pitch. It bounces two or three times and ends up landing right in my path. The players all stort shouting at me. They're all like, 'Hey, Dude, can you kick the ball back?' and I end up having a little chuckle to myself, because they obviously haven't *recognized* me yet?

I'm thinking, Yeah, no, the joke is about to be on them.

With the toe of my right Dube, I flick the ball up into my hand, we're talking proper Cian Healy-style. Then I pick out a player, who's standing, like, eighty yords away, and I go, 'Okay, people, watch and learn! Into the hands of the full-back in blue!'

With the ball in my hands, I take a short run-up, then I pull back the trigger of my right foot. As I'm doing that, I release the ball and then –

Oh, holy fock.

My standing foot suddenly slips on the wet grass and I go flying in the air – we're talking orse over proverbial tit – then I land, with the most almighty crack, on the flat of my back.

There's, like, a moment of silence, which I take for concern, before everyone decides that it's actually too hilarious *not* to laugh? So there I am, lying on my back, staring up at the black sky, with the rain falling down on me, listening to everyone laughing, high-fiving each other and saying that they wished they'd filmed it because it would have got, like, five million hits on YouTube.

Some dude trots over. With one hand, he picks up the ball. With the other, he pulls me up into a standing position.

He goes, 'Are you okay, Mister?' not even recognizing me.

In fact, no one seems to recognize me.

I'm there, 'Yeah, no, I'm just a bit winded, that's all. I'd be used to a better surface.'

And he goes, 'You'd want to take it easy, Mister. A man of your age could do himself a serious injury.'

## 2. A Problem with the Windows

'Oh! My God!' Sorcha goes. 'What happened to your trousers?'

I'm like, 'What are you talking about?'

She's emptying the laundry basket while I'm, like, bathing the boys. I turn around and she's got my chinos in her hand.

'Your trousers,' she goes. 'They're covered in mud. Ross, what happened?'

I go, 'I don't know. I must have slipped.'

She's there, 'It looks like you were rolling around on the . . . Oh my God, Ross, were you with another woman?'

'No, I wasn't with another woman. Yeah, thanks for your trust, Sorcha.'

'So where did all this mud come from?'

'Look, if you must know, I was playing rugby.'

'Rugby? Ross, you're thirty-five.'

'I'm not thirty-five – I'm actually thirty-four.'

'You're thirty-five on Tuesday.'

'Do you know how old Mauro Bergamasco is?'

'I don't even know *who* Mauro Bergamasco is.'

'That says more about you than it does about me, Sorcha. Says more about you than me.'

She shakes her head, like this is all way beyond her understanding. She's there, 'Okay, assuming you're telling me the truth, who were you even playing rugby with?'

'Seapoint.'

'Seapoint?'

'I went for a trial yesterday – for the first team.'

'A trial? Oh my God, Ross, is this some kind of midlife thing?'

'No.'

'I'm saying it *sounds* like a midlife thing.'

'Well, you'll be happy to hear that I didn't get it. In fact, I made a complete focking orse of myself. Can you believe that not one single person there even knew who I was?'

'Ross, you'd really want to stort acting your age.'

'I'm going to throw you another name. Victor Matfield. Thirty-seven years of age. But you've probably never heard of him either.'

'Shit,' Leo goes – he's obviously learned a new word. 'Fock your focking shit.'

Sorcha bends down and picks Johnny out of the bath. I've still got Leo and Brian in there, sitting at either end.

'I think I'm going to talk to Honor,' Sorcha goes, as she towels Johnny dry, 'about this mystery boy of hers?'

I'm there, 'Okay, what happened to, "We don't want to be those kind of parents who have to know everything that's going on in their children's lives"?'

'I'm her *mother*, Ross. And, yes, I'm still a bit upset that this was something she felt she could talk to Erika about and not to me.'

'Sometimes it's easier to talk to people who *aren't* your old pair? I'm saying that as someone whose old pair are dicks.'

'Well, that's not the relationship I want with Honor. I've always dreamt of having a daughter who would think of me not just as a mother but as a best friend. In fact, a best, best friend – the way me and *my* mom are?'

'Focking shit!' Leo goes. 'Focking focker shit!'

I give him Splashy the Penguin, which he loves. He's like, 'Spashy Penguin! Spashy Penguin!' until Brian suddenly grabs it from him and focks it – we're talking, like, a heavy plastic toy? – right at Leo's head from, like, point-blank range. It misses by a millimetre.

Leo storts trying to kick Brian and of course that sets Johnny off. He's suddenly screaming hysterically. Sorcha's going, 'Ssshhh, ssshhh, ssshhh! It's okay, Johnny. Ssshhh, ssshhh, ssshhh!'

I decide to whip Brian out of the bath before he drowns Leo or Leo drowns him. I stort drying him off while he wriggles around like I don't know what.

'Anyway,' I go, 'this thing might not be going anywhere.'

Sorcha goes, 'What do you mean?'

'All we know is that she likes a boy. We don't know if he likes her.'

'Why wouldn't he like her?'

'Come on, Sorcha, don't pretend you haven't noticed. Honor's not exactly the prettiest of God's creatures, is she? She's actually kind of plain in terms of looks.'

Sorcha looks at me with her mouth slung open – *pretending* to be shocked? 'Oh! My God!' she goes. 'That is a terrible thing to say about your own flesh and blood.'

'Hey, I'm just stating it as a fact. I mean, she was a beautiful baby – don't get me wrong. But she's definitely disimproved. Jesus Christ, I don't know why you're looking so shocked. You've said it about her yourself – well, in so many words.'

'All I said was that she could possibly do more to make the most of herself.'

'See? That's just Passive Aggressive for the exact same thing that I'm saying.'

Sorcha sad-smiles me, then looks over her shoulder to make sure Honor isn't standing at the bathroom door, listening in.

'Okay,' she goes, 'I have to admit that, yes, sometimes I look at her and I'm disappointed for her sake that she's not prettier – you know, with your genes and my genes . . .'

She's ignoring the fact that her own mother is bet-down. I'm not pointing fingers. I'm stating it as a fact.

All of a sudden, Honor *does* appear at the bathroom door? She obviously didn't hear us calling her ugly, though, because she just goes, 'Are you having fun in the bath, Leo!' because she does actually *love* her brothers? 'Do you want me to give you a Mohican?'

Leo touches his head with both hands and goes, 'Hican!'

It's actually quite cute.

Honor crouches down to his level, then she sort of, like, teases his wet hair into a Mohican style.

'I want Hican!' Brian shouts then. They're unbelievably competitive with each other – it's something I'm definitely going to encourage. So Honor does the same for Brian, then the same for Johnny, who instantly calms down.

While this is all going on, Sorcha has this, like, look of resolve on her face that I recognize only too well.

'So, Honor,' she suddenly goes, 'how are things? As in, how are things with you?'

Honor's there, 'Fine,' and she says it a little bit defensively. 'What business is it of yours?'

'I'm only asking because I think it's very healthy for a mother and daughter to have regular catch-ups.'

'Yeah, spare me.'

'I'm just making the point that it'd be good to check in with each other from time to time – make sure we're up to date. Are there any, I don't know, boys that you're interested in at the moment?'

The woman is as subtle as a fart in a funeral home.

Honor looks suddenly sad – her eyes are all, I don't know, *disappointed*?

She goes, 'Erika told you.'

Sorcha's there, 'She only told us, Honor, because we were worried about you being off your food. But she didn't tell us anything else, except that you liked a boy.'

'And that he goes to Michael's,' I go. 'And thankfully not the other place.'

'We don't know anything else, I can promise you that. We don't even know his name.'

Honor goes, 'His name is Caleb – not that it's any of your focking business.'

'Caleb?' Sorcha goes, the delight written all over her face. 'Oh my God, you didn't even tell Erika his name!'

I'm there, 'So does Caleb play rugby?'

Honor goes, 'No, he doesn't play rugby.'

I'm like, 'Don't go rushing into anything would be my advice. Keep your options open.'

Sorcha decides to push it further, of course. 'So tell us a bit about him,' she goes. 'Where's he from, this Caleb?'

Honor sighs like the whole thing is just too much effort for her. 'Ulverton Road,' she goes. 'In Dalkey.'

'Well, he sounds lovely! So, am I allowed to ask, have you kissed him yet?'

'No, I haven't focking kissed him!'

'I'm not asking as a mother, Honor. I'm asking as a friend.'

'Nothing's happened between us. We're just, like, talking and texting, that's all.'

'Talking and texting! But you're obviously hoping that something *will* happen.'

'Oh my God, all these questions.'

'So how do you know him? Honor, I'm just showing an interest.'

'Look, if you must know, his sister's in my class – as in, Thea O'Halloran?'

I laugh. No choice.

I'm like, 'Her? The little dumpy one with the underbite and the swimmer's shoulders?'

She's one of Honor's regular bullying victims.

'She's actually okay,' Honor tries to go, 'when you get to know her.'

I'm there, 'Yeah, when you get to know her brother is what you really mean. I collected you from school a few weeks ago and you had the girl in a headlock for, like, twenty minutes. Her face was like a focking beetroot. It was hilarious.'

'So is he good-looking?' Sorcha goes. 'Caleb, I mean.'

There's, like, more eye-rolling and head-shaking. 'Yes,' Honor goes, 'he's good-looking.'

'Oh my God, do you want to invite him here?'

'Here?'

'You could invite him here – for, like, a play date.'

'A *play* date? How old do you think I am?'

'Well, whatever you want to call it. Invite him for tea, then. I could make some of my famous artisan macarons.'

Honor's face suddenly softens. She's like, 'Could I? As in, would that be okay?'

Sorcha's there, 'Oh my God, Honor, yes! I can't wait to actually meet him!' Sorcha smiles and claps her two hands together like a big idiot.

Honor goes, 'As long as you don't embarrass me.'

And I'm like, 'Yeah, we're *hordly* likely to embarrass you, Honor.'

Famous last words, of course.

*

How did I end up in Copper Face Jacks on a Sunday night? How does anyone end up in Copper Face Jacks on a Sunday night?

It was one of those nights out that didn't stort out as a night out. Oisinn rang to see did I fancy one or two quiet ones seeing as he's going away tomorrow and he doesn't know for how long.

I was like, 'Where are you going?'

He went, 'Qatar.'

'You're not taking the piss out of me, are you? That's definitely the name of a country?'

'It's the name of a country, yeah.'

'Because I wouldn't know if you *were* taking the piss – you know how thick I am.'

'It's where all the money is these days. I've got one or two meetings lined up. I might be meeting a dude who's a prince. Come on, Ross. Just one or two. I didn't get to talk to you for long on New Year's. And it's your birthday in two days.'

'Alright,' I went, 'I'll see you in Kielys – just one or two, though.'

Of course, you know how that generally goes.

It was Oisinn's idea to go country. Six or seven pints into the night, as they were calling last drinks, he went, 'Let's move on to Coppers – rip the piss. We haven't done that in ages.'

I laughed. I was like, 'There is no way in this world that I am going to Copper Face Jacks tonight.'

If there's one thing that everyone in this place has in common, it's that they have all uttered those exact words at some point this evening.

'By the way,' Oisinn goes, handing me a shot of Sambuca, 'you never told me how you got on yesterday.'

I'm like, 'Yesterday? What are you talking about?'

'Didn't you go for the trial? Seapoint?'

Shit.

I'm like, 'Er, yeah, no, I did, but I decided in the end it wasn't for me. I had, em, one or two issues with the playing surface.'

'It's a wet pitch,' he goes.

'Yeah, no, it's definitely that. It's definitely that.'

He knocks back his shot, then says he's going to the jacks. He doesn't make it that far, though. I'm actually getting the round in, wondering what's keeping the focker, when I suddenly look up to see him leaving with a bird who looks like Brodie Retallick in a GAA jersey and a stetson and she's hanging off him like a fur coat on a rapper.

I look at the time on my phone. What's the Golden Rule in Coppers? It's two – you'll do!

So now I'm on my Tobler, standing at the bor, listening to people from the Midlands try out their chat-up lines on each other – 'So what hospital do you work in yourself?' – and thinking that I never realized before how many hits Bon Jovi actually had.

I'm considering nearly calling it a night when I suddenly spot her across the room. It'd be hord to actually miss her. A good-looking girl will stand out in here like a shork at a pool porty. She's in – I'm guessing – her early twenties, with blonde hair and huge stonks. Gemma Merna is who I'd actually compare her to and that ends up being my opening line when I tip over to her.

She goes, 'Who?'

She's drinking a Fat Frog and she smells of *Shalimar by Guerlain*.

I'm there, 'She's actually an actress. As opening lines go, I just thought it was slightly more original than, "So what hospital do you work in yourself?"'

She ends up hearing only the *second* half of the sentence?

'The Rotunda,' she goes and I don't bother my hole explaining it.

Instead, I go, 'So who are you here with? Friends? Boyfriend?' trying to subtly smoke her out on the subject of her relationship status.

I'm a class act. I don't think anyone's denying that.

'Just the girls from work,' she goes, then she turns and introduces me to four women who happen to be standing next to her. Allow me to speak freely here. The last time I saw a collection of creatures this frightening, a focking ringmaster was cracking a whip at them.

'I'm Denise,' *my* one – the looker – goes, 'and this is Susan, Caoilfhionn, Attracta and Breege.'

'Okay,' I go, 'those are *all* lovely names.'

Get in with the mates and you're home and hosed.

Denise goes, 'It's Breege's leaving do. She's retiring after forty years working in the Rotunda!'

I'm like, 'Forty years? Jesus, you don't look old enough – and that's not me being sarcastic.'

It is me being sarcastic, by the way. She looks like she could have been one of the original staff. She's a big focking barrel of a woman, with orms like Cian Healy, hair like Lisa Dingle and a wart on her cheek so big it has its own focking Eircode.

She's actually *sound*, though? Not that personality is important, but she's the one who invites me to join them. She even buys me a pint of Heineken and tells me some of her funny A&E stories, a great many of which involve either lonely men or sexually frustrated women and their adventures with mustard jors or ketchup bottles.

I end up having a surprisingly enjoyable night. Denise is definitely keen and she's impressed with me for making an effort with her friends.

'Okay,' she even goes, 'why aren't there more guys out there like you?'

And I go, 'Because if there weren't bad ones, then the good ones wouldn't seem so special.'

You get nights like that – don't you? – where everything you say ends up being memorable.

The last song of the night ends up being 'I Don't Want to Miss a Thing' by Aerosmith, which people from the country seem to love in the same way they love going to Mass and eating coleslaw with a fry-up. When the music ends and the lights come on, Denise turns to me and goes, 'So this is going to sound maybe a little forward, but are you coming back?'

I'm like, 'Back? Back where?'

I've got a big, shit-eating grin on my face.

She laughs and goes, 'Back to ours!' like it's the most ridiculous question in the world.

I'm there, 'Are you saying I'm in?'

And she smiles and goes, 'You couldn't be that slow on the uptake! Yes, you're in.'

I like a girl who knows what she wants – especially when what she wants is me.

The whole lot of us end up getting a seven-seater taxi to Phibsboro. The whole way there, Denise keeps smiling at me and saying she can't believe that someone like me is still single.

But then suddenly one of the yolks – the hilariously named Attracta – throws a focking spanner in the works by going, 'Have you drink in, Denise?'

Denise goes, 'I've Bacardi Breezers in the fridge from Christmas.'

And Attracta's there, 'Let's carry on the party, so!'

The other girls all whoop and holler and I'm thinking, Okay, how do I subtly tell them to fock off without damaging the nice-goy rep I've built for myself here.

'Yeah, no, maybe we all should just call it a night,' I go.

Caoilfhionn's there, 'Oh my God, you're a total lightweight!' and they all laugh.

The taxi pulls up outside Denise's gaff and everyone hops out. I'm the one who ends up having to pay the driver, then I follow her and the focking circus freaks inside.

She turns to me when we're alone in the hallway and goes, 'I'm sorry about this. I should have said no to them.'

And I'm there, 'Hey, it's cool. But I wouldn't mind getting my head down – if you catch my drift.'

Oh, she catches my drift alright. Nurses are filthy.

She goes, 'Jesus, you don't believe in wasting time, do you?'

I'm there, 'I certainly don't. Which bedroom?'

'The one straight in front of you at the top of the stairs.'

I give her a little wink and I go, 'I'll head on up. Tell the rest of them I'm sorry to wuss out of the porty.'

I take the stairs two at a time, then into the room I go. It's a typical student nurse's room – a bed, a bike, a poster on the wall of a kitten clinging to a rope with the caption, *When life leaves you hanging – don't quit!*, and a giant, inflatable penis that's probably a souvenir from someone's hen.

I unbutton my shirt, then I step out of my Dubes and chinos, flick off the light and slip under the sheets. It's focking freezing in the bed. What is it about nurses that they don't feel the cold? They're like focking polar bears.

And of course you know what happens to the old vital organ when it's cold. That's right. It's like two walnuts and an empty popsock. Suddenly, I hear Denise coming up the stairs and I stort tugging on the old storter cord to try to heat the engine.

It ends up doing the trick. Years of practice, you could probably argue. A second or two later, the door opens and I'm suddenly blinded by the light coming from the landing behind her.

'Get into this bed right now!' I go. 'There's no more Mister Nice Goy. I'm going to ride you like AP McCoy!'

She leaps across the room and lands on the bed like an avalanche. She throws back the sheets and sits – I don't know – *astride* me, her two hands pressing down on my famous pectorals as she leans forward, her mouth trying to find mine.

And that's when my eyes suddenly adjust to the light and I notice that it's not Denise sitting on top of me at all.

It's focking Breege!

I actually scream. I'm like, 'What the fock!' as she storts sloppily kissing my mouth, her tongue all wet and throbbing, like something you'd find stuck to the hull of a ship at low tide.

I'm there, 'What the fock do you think you're doing?'

There are hundreds of stories out there about people who've found themselves suddenly capable of feats of superhuman strength in moments of, like, crisis or danger? I saw a thing on Sky News once about a woman whose son was trapped under the wheel of a bus and she lifted the focking thing clean off the ground with one hand and pulled the dude out with the other.

And that's basically what happens to *me* in that moment? From somewhere, I find the strength to throw Breege off me. She goes flying across the room as well and hits the floor like a focking rock slide, while I go chorging down the stairs – totally naked, bear in mind – screaming my head off, with a dong on me like a wok handle.

Denise and the rest of them come running out into the hall. I think it'd be fair to describe their reaction as surprised.

Denise goes, 'What's wrong?'

I'm there, 'It was horrible! Oh my God, it was focking horrible!'

She's like, 'What was?'

'She tried to hop me!' I go. 'The mad bitch tried to focking hop me!'

She looks at me with a confused expression on her face. 'Hop you?' she goes. 'I thought you liked her?'

I'm like, 'Breege? You must be focking shitting me!'

'So why did you come back with her?'

'I didn't come back with her – I came back here with *you*!'

'With me?'

'That's right. I pulled you.'

'No, you didn't.'

'Well, you certainly gave me the impression that I did. I asked you was I in and you said yes.'

'I meant in with Breege.'

It's terrible, roysh, because the woman herself suddenly arrives down the stairs and she has to listen to the conversation.

'Do you honestly think I'd be interested in that?' I go. 'Jesus Christ, look at the focking state of her.'

'But you spent half the night talking to her.'

'That was to try to get in with you. Get all the mates onside. Everyone knows that tactic.'

Breege has the cheek to turn around and go, 'You certainly gave me the impression that you were interested in me.'

'Yeah,' I go, 'you were focking dreaming. Jesus, no wonder you looked so focking happy leaving Coppers. It's all beginning to add up now. You were like a dog having its belly rubbed.'

Denise goes, 'I just presumed it was Breege you liked because you and her are, well, closer in age.'

'Closer in age? She's just focking retired! How old do you think I am?'

'I don't know. Fifty?'

'Fifty? I'm still technically thirty-four!'

'Well, I'm only twenty-two. I don't know why you thought I'd be interested in a man of your age.'

'Yeah, no,' I go, 'I'm beginning to wonder myself.'

I go back upstairs and I gather up my clothes with as much dignity as I can muster. It obviously isn't much.

Sorcha says I can't *not* celebrate my birthday. I tell her it's not that I don't want to celebrate it, it's just I don't want to make a massive deal of it, even though she obviously does, because she's booked dinner in Chapter One.

She goes, 'What would *you* prefer to do, Ross? And don't say you'd rather spend the night drinking pints in Kielys.'

I'm there, 'I'm a very uncomplicated man, Sorcha – that's all I'm saying in my defence.'

*She's* driving, by the way. It's, like, a Tuesday night and she doesn't want to be still half-cut on the school run tomorrow. It's Mount Anville, not Sion Hill.

'Oh, by the way,' she goes, 'guess who's coming over on Saturday?'

I'm there, 'Okay, please don't say your parents.'

'No, Ross, not my parents. I'm talking about this boy that Honor likes – as in, like, Caleb? Honor hates me calling it a play date, but I don't think I'm ready to call it a date date yet – that would mean admitting that our little girl is growing up!'

'Well, it doesn't affect me one way or the other because I'm not going to be around.'

'Excuse me?'

'I told Ronan I'd go and visit him in his *Love/Hate* caravan.'

'He goes there to study, Ross.'

'Yeah, no, I'll only stay a few hours.'

'Caleb isn't coming until three o'clock. Just make sure you're back by then. It's a huge day for Honor, especially if she really likes this boy.'

She suddenly pulls the cor over.

I'm like, 'What are you doing?'

She goes, 'I can't bear that look of longing on your face, Ross.'

We were just passing Kielys.

She's there, 'Do you *want* to go for a pint?'

I'm like, 'Would you mind?'

49

'It's *your* birthday, Ross. I can ring the restaurant and say we'll be half an hour late.'

'Yeah, no, I'll just have one or two. Or three.'

She porks outside Tesco Express, then thirty seconds later I'm practically running across the road, cors narrowly missing me, to reach the pub.

I push the door. The place is focking rammers, especially for a Tuesday night in January. Suddenly, there's this, like, humungous roar.

It's like: 'Happy birthday, Ross!'

And of course all I can do is laugh.

I turn to Sorcha and I'm like, 'I don't believe it! You organized all of this?'

She's goes, 'Happy birthday, my love!' and she gives me a kiss.

I'm saying this now and I mean every word of it. I am married to the most wonderful woman in the world. I'm going to make a genuine effort to try to stop cheating on her.

Pretty much everyone is there. Ronan and Honor. Christian and JP. The old man and Helen. Ryle Nugent and the great One F in Foley.

I end up having *the* most amazing night. I even manage to forget my age for a couple of hours – until just after ten o'clock when Helen produces a cake with thirty-five candles burning on it and Ronan shouts, 'Be careful the bleaten sprinklers don't come on!' which everyone finds hilarious.

The old man leads everyone in a chorus of 'Happy Birthday to You', then a couple of rounds of 'For He's a Jolly Good Fellow' for good measure, then everyone storts looking at me, going, 'Speech! Speech!'

I'm like, 'Fock off – you're not getting a speech!'

The old man goes, 'I'll say something, Ross, if you don't mind!' because he loves the sound of his own voice, of course.

'Thirty-five years ago today,' he goes, 'Ross O'Carroll-Kelly entered the world. His mother, who unfortunately can't be here with us tonight, came over funny in the National Gallery of Ireland whilst looking at some watercolours by Mr Joseph Mallord William Turner Esquire. She thought at first that it might have been a piece of Brie that didn't agree with her. That was until her waters broke all over the bloody well polished wooden floor!'

'Yeah, T.M.I.,' I shout. 'T.M. focking I.'

Everyone laughs.

He goes, 'His mother considered this an augury as to what course her son would take in life. In fact, he was very nearly christened Joseph Mallord William Turner O'Carroll-Kelly, so convinced was she that he was going to be an artist. "Stuff and nonsense!" insisted old Charles O'Carroll-Kelly here. "The chap will be a rugby player! Nothing surer!"

'Well, I'm happy to say that good sense prevailed and I was proved absolutely correct. Ross, as you all know, was one of the finest Irish players ever to play the game – brief as his career was. Hennessy Coghlan-O'Hara, his godfather and as shrewd a judge of rugby as I've ever known, would back me up, I think, in saying that it would be impossible to exaggerate how much potential he once possessed.'

For fock's sake – is this supposed to be making me feel good about myself?

'Sadly,' he goes, 'Ross didn't go on to play for Ireland like everyone was convinced he would. Neither did he win Heineken Cups nor captain the Lions nor score a record number of tries for his country. But he did something that was, well, almost on a par. He became a loyal and dutiful husband . . .'

That gets more than a few laughs.

He's there, 'A loyal and dutiful husband to a wonderful girl named Sorcha O'Carroll-Kelly, née Lalor, and without a shadow of a doubt *the* best father it has ever been my pleasure to watch in action. Ladies and gentleman, will you raise your glasses, please, in a toast to Ross O'Carroll-Kelly – thirty-five years young today!'

They all raise their glasses and there's, like, a big cheer.

I end up having a quiet little moment with Sorcha then. She goes, 'That was lovely what Chorles said!'

I'm like, 'Yeah, no, I thought he could have mentioned some of my other achievements, for instance coaching Andorra and playing three times for UCD.'

She's there, 'Oh, I have a present for you,' and she suddenly produces this humungous package, all wrapped up with a blue bow on it.

Blue for obviously Leinster.

I'm there, 'What is it? Inside, I mean.'

She's like, 'Open it and you'll see.'

Which is what I end up doing. I pull the bow loose, with everyone in Kielys watching, then I tear off the wrapping paper and it ends up being a huge, flat box with the words *Cole Haan* written on it. I lie it down flat on the bor, then I lift the lid and I pull aside the tissue paper.

It's a coat. I take the lapel between my thumb and my forefinger.

I'm like, 'Is that camel hair?'

Sorcha goes, 'Yes, it's camel hair. You see, I worry about you going to see that team of yours, standing in the freezing cold of the RDS. I've been saying for ages that you needed a good coat.'

'Well, I've got my famous Henri Lloyd sailing jacket, bear in mind.'

'I'm talking about a sensible coat, Ross. You're thirty-five now. You can't keep dressing like you're in UCD. Are you going to try it on?'

'What?'

'Go on, try it on.'

Literally everyone in Kielys is suddenly going, 'Put it on, Ross! Go on – put it on!'

So I end up having no choice in the matter. I whip off my famous sailing jacket and Sorcha takes the coat out of its box and she's like, 'You are going to be – oh my God – *so* warm in this!' as she holds it out for me to slip my orms into the sleeves. I pull it up over my shoulders, then Sorcha buttons it up and – again – everyone cheers. Ronan even wolf-whistles.

Sorcha's there, 'It looks amazing on you!'

It fits me like a focking shower cubicle.

I'm there, 'It's a bit, I don't know, roomy, isn't it?'

JP shouts, 'That's for the middle-age spread! You've got to plan for the future, Dude!'

Everyone gets a good laugh out of that.

Sorcha's there, 'Seriously, Ross, you look like an actual adult for once.'

That's when my old man tips over. He's there, 'You might as well open my present next. It's like you read my mind, Sorcha. I was thinking about the same thing – you could catch your death of cold in that RDS!'

He hands me a box. I stare at it for a few seconds, then I go, 'As long as it's not a focking hat like yours!'

I open the box.

It *is* a focking hat like his.

The old man picks it out of the box and presses it onto my head. Everyone cheers, then they're all suddenly taking pictures of me with their iPhones.

I happen to turn my head and I catch sight of my reflection in the mirror behind the bor, standing there in my camel-hair coat and hat. And I realize at that moment that it's happening. The process is underway.

I'm turning into my old man.


So it's, like, Saturday morning and – miracle of miracles – I'm up and about. Sorcha has taken Honor and the boys shopping – to get shit in for the visit of Caleb this afternoon. I don't know why she's going to so much trouble.

I'm enjoying a little bit of Ross Time, lying back on the sofa and scribbling a few notes in my notorious Tactics Book about how I see the forthcoming Six Nations panning out in terms of, like, *results*?

It's a genuine scandal that the IRFU has never found a role for me within the set-up. There's never a time when I'm *not* thinking about rugby?

I write out the names of the XV that I think should stort against Italy, then against France, then against England, then against Wales, then against Scotland, obviously injuries permitting. Then I write down the areas in which I think each opposition team is weak – 'Chris Robshaw: a focking dick' – and then I write down a few moves that I believe could unlock each team we're going to face.

And then I end up laughing because I'm suddenly picturing Joe Schmidt's reaction if he ever got his hands on this book. He'd read it, then he'd go straight to the IRFU and demand to know why someone who's still got this much to contribute is sitting at home in his boxer shorts, writing in a notebook and having a beer at eleven o'clock in the morning.

I couldn't swear to you that it's my first of the day either.

Joe wouldn't let them bullshit him, by the way. Especially not in a World Cup year. He'd be there, 'Why?'

And they'd be all, 'Why what?'

And he'd be like, 'Why isn't this goy part of the set-up?'

And they'd be there, 'Well, it's just the way he thinks about the game – the whole work hard, play hard thing – it doesn't fit in with our, I don't know, philosophy?'

And he'd go, 'I'd tell you what you can do with your philosophy if I wasn't such a lovely bloke. Actually, I *will* tell you – you can shove up it up your hole, you pack of useless focks. And it's very unlike me to swear. Have you looked through this book?'

And they'd be all, 'No, we're too busy with stuff, mostly bullshit.'

And he'd be there, 'Well, this morning, I want you to spend four or five hours absorbing what's in it, then I want you to clear out your desks. You're fired – every single one of you.'

I'm actually shaking my head and chuckling away to myself when I'm dragged from my fantasy by the sound of the phone in the kitchen ringing. Now, I generally never answer the house phone, but at the moment we're waiting for an oil delivery and I'm wondering is it possibly them ringing because they can't find where we are on the Vico Road.

I usually tell people it's the one that looks like Sleeping Beauty's gaff.

I lift the receiver. There's, like, a two- or three-second delay on the line, then I hear a voice – not an Irish voice either. I'm not going to say the woman is from India because that would be obviously racist. All I will say is that she's from one of those *types* of countries?

She goes, 'Hello, Sir.'

Again, you'll have to do the voice in your own heads because I don't want to be *accused* of shit?

I go, 'Okay, who's this?' wondering is it possibly Jerry Flannery ripping the piss, as he often does.

She goes, 'I am ringing because we have detected a problem with your computer.'

I laugh. I *actually* laugh? I'm there, 'Have you really?'

She goes, 'Yes, Sir.'

I'm like, 'A problem with my computer?' just reeling her in.

'That's right. You have a virus that is affecting your Microsoft Windows operating system. We can fix it for you.'

'That's focking great news,' I go. 'But listen, just before we get down to business, can I just say that you have a gorgeous voice. And gorgeous isn't a word I'd often use.'

She's a little bit *thrown* by that? She's there, 'Em, that is, em, very nice.'

'I could actually listen to you read the phone book,' I go. 'Have you ever worked for directory inquiries?'

'No, Sir, I have not.'

'Well, you could. Very easily.'

'Okay,' she goes, suddenly trying to be all business. 'We must repair this virus right now or it has the potential to destroy your computer.'

I'm there, 'What are you wearing?'

There's, like, five seconds of just silence, then she goes, 'I beg your pardon?'

'Describe what you're wearing. Underwear and everything.'

'Sir, it's not appropriate for you to speak to me this way.'

'I'm just trying to get a picture of you in my head. A wank in the bank, as they say.'

'Sir, I am asking you not to speak to me this way.'

'Say something filthy. Something really filthy that doesn't involve viruses. Tell me you're horny, for instance, then build up to something else.'

This ends up being the last straw for her. She's there, 'I am going to ask you to speak to my supervisor.'

I laugh. I'm like, 'Supervisor? Yeah, no, that's a good one. Stick him on there.'

I hear a lot of chatter in the background – it's all in Indian – then I end up being put onto some random dude. He's like, 'Hello?'

He's also from down that way – we'll call it India Direction just to keep the politically correct brigade happy.

I'm there, 'Okay, who have I got now?'

He goes, 'I am the supervisor. You have a virus that is affecting the Microsoft Windows operating system on your computer.'

'Yeah, no, we've been *through* all that?'

'It has the potential to destroy your hard drive.'

'Look, will you put that woman back on?'

'No, I will not. She is now on a different call.'

'It's just your voice is doing very little for me.'

The line suddenly goes dead. He's obviously put down the phone. I end up just cracking my hole laughing.

It's at that exact point that Sorcha suddenly arrives home from town with Honor and the boys.

I'm like, 'Hey, how'd you get on?'

She doesn't answer me. She's all business. 'Ross,' she goes, 'will you take the shopping bags from the boot, unpack them, then feed the boys. Oh my God, I've got *so* much baking to do this afternoon!'

I'm like, 'I don't know why you're bothering your orse,' then I turn to Honor and I go, 'One thing you definitely *don't* want to come across as is desperate.'

Sorcha's like, 'Ross, it's important to always project the best version of yourself.'

It's hord to tell which of them has a date this afternoon.

I go, 'I'm just questioning your tactics here, Honor. It never pays to come across as too keen. In my experience, goys are more interested in birds who are bitches, just as birds are more interested in goys who are bastards.'

Honor ends up letting me down, though. She turns to Sorcha and goes, 'Can you help me with something?'

And Sorcha's there, 'Sure, what is it?'

'I want to make myself look nice.'

I'm there, 'That's going to take some focking work.'

Actually, I don't say it. I just think it.

She goes, 'I was thinking, I might put on some make-up?'

Sorcha's face lights up like a box of firecrackers. She's like, 'Oh! *My* God! Charlotte Tilbury has this amazing YouTube video on how to use contouring to give your face more shape. She does Sienna Miller's make-up for the Oscars – and *she's* someone who definitely makes the most of herself.'

Honor goes, 'It's just, well, I want Caleb to think I'm pretty.'

Straight face, Rosser. Straight face.

Sorcha goes, 'There's, like, all sorts of things you can do using just bronzer and highlighter. Come on, let's look at that video.'

Then she suddenly stops, and that's when she says it.

She's like, 'Oh, Ross, speaking of which, did the shop ring about my computer?'

My blood goes cold. I'm there, 'Computer? Er, what computer?'

'Yeah, no, my laptop was running slow,' she goes. 'I dropped it into the Computer Laboratory in Sandyford. The lovely Indian lady in there thought it might have a virus.'

Oh! Focking! Shit!

Well, that's one laptop she won't be seeing again.

'Er,' I go, 'I'm heading out.'

Sorcha's there, 'Ross, I asked you to feed the boys – *and* unpack the shopping.'

'Yeah, no, I already told Ronan I was on the way over, Babes.'

'Oh my God, you are useless, Ross! Well, just make sure you're back here before Caleb arrives.'

The pit bull terriers have arrived, I notice. It'd be hord *not* to notice. The two of them take a run at me, snarling like focking tigers, when I stort walking across the field towards the caravan. If they weren't chained up, they'd be eating me for Saturday brunch right now.

I knock on the door. I hear Ronan inside go, 'Who is it?'

And I'm there, 'Yeah, no, it's me.'

He's like, 'Who's me?'

'It's Rosser. The Rossmeister.'

'Mon in, so. She's open.'

I pull the door, then in I go. It turns out that Ronan has company. His friends, Nudger and Buckets of Blood, are sitting around with him. Yeah, so much for studying. The three of them are drinking poitín, I notice, and looking at – believe it or not – a *map*?

I immediately fear the worst, presuming they're, I don't know, plotting the fastest possible escape from some jewellery shop, or checking out the route to the home of some bank employee. I just pretend I haven't seen it. In their world, it never pays to know too much.

I'm like, 'Alright, Buckets? What's the crack, Nudger?'

'All good,' Nudger goes. 'How's tings wit you, Rosser?'

'Things are pretty sensational, in fairness to them. What about you? Are you still with Blod?'

Blodwyn is this Welsh bird slash shoplifter who *I* actually introduced him to? I rode her over in Cordiff before a Six Nations match.

'Yeah,' he goes, 'we're habben a babby, so we eer.'

I'm there, 'That's great news. Hey, tell her I was asking for her,' and I give him a cheeky little wink – I don't *know* why? It's just me reminding him that I've been there, me being a wanker basically.

'I'll make shewer un to say that to her,' he goes. 'She'll gerra good laugh ourra that.'

I'm like, 'Why would she laugh?' immediately on the defensive.

'Just the memoddy of you over in Keerdiff,' he goes, 'throying to ride her wit your little mickey – she said it was like a child's sock.'

Ronan cracks up laughing. 'A child's sock!' he goes. 'He fooken got your there, Rosser!'

I'm like, 'He didn't get me. I had a lot to drink that day.'

'Addyhow,' Nudger goes, 'like I said to you, she's due addy day.'

'Well, one thing I will say about bringing children into the world – and I'm saying this as Ronan's old man – it's the best mistake you will ever make.'

He goes, 'Skeerdy, but – habben responsibidities all of a sutton. That's what this job is about,' and he sort of, like, nods at the map on the table in front of them.

I'm there, 'Look, I don't want to know anything about it.

Seriously, goys, I wouldn't last ten minutes in a police cell. I'd end up singing like the focking Dublin Gospel Choir.'

The three of them look at each other in, like, total silence. There's a definite change in the atmos in the caravan all of a sudden.

'The thing is,' Buckets of Blood goes, 'you alretty *do* know. You know we're arthur been pladden sumtin – a job.'

I'm there, 'I don't. I know fock-all. All I've seen is that map there.'

'Which makes you an access a doddy.'

'A what?'

'An access a doddy. Ine saying you're involved, Rosser. Ine saying you can't unsee what you're arthur witnessing hee-or today.'

'Like I said, all I've seen is a map. I don't know if it's the route to a bank, a jewellers, or whatever. As a matter of fact, Ro, I think I might head off. Honor's got this dude calling this afternoon and I said I'd give Sorcha a dig-out with the baking.'

'Sit thowen,' Nudger goes.

'I'll ring you later, Ro.'

'Sit the fook thowen!' Nudger roars at me.

I end up just doing what I'm told.

He goes, 'Why did you say jewellers?'

I'm like, 'What?'

'You joost said it was a jewellers. How did you know it was a jewellers?'

'I didn't. Dude, that was pure guesswork.'

I can hear the panic in my own voice now.

'The cops ardent going to suspect him of athin,' Ronan tries to go. 'I doubt thee'll pull him in, feddas.'

Nudger's there, 'We caddent take that risk, Ro. The man's arthur saying himself he caddent be thrusted. "I'll end up singing like a bleaten choir" was he's owen woords.'

I'm like, 'Whoa, whoa, whoah – you're not talking about, I don't know, whacking me, are you?' and there's, like, actual tears in my voice. It's suddenly got very serious in here. 'Ronan, talk to these goys, will you?'

Buckets shouts at me. 'Shut the fook up, will you, and let us think!' Then he stands up and steps over to the window.

'It's calt a loose end,' Nudger goes. 'We caddent have loose ends, feddas – I know he's your fadder, Ronan.'

After a few seconds, Buckets goes, 'Ro, get the JCB foyered up.'

I'm like, 'No! Please, I'm begging you, no!'

Ronan stands up. He goes, 'Ine soddy, Rosser.'

I close my eyes and put my two hands together in prayer. I'm actually bawling. I'm going, 'Goys, please! I'm begging you! I've got kids! I've got shit to live for!'

And that's when I hear the laughter. All focking three of them. I open my eyes.

Ronan goes, 'You're some bleaten flute, Rosser!'

I'm like, 'Bastards!'

'We fooken had you there! You were shitting yourself!'

'You focking bastards.'

They think it's genuinely hilarious.

Buckets goes, 'Is that what you think of everybothy on the Nort-soyud, Rosser – we're all just sitting arowunt, pladding robbedies and beddying people in the growunt?'

I *do* think that actually.

I'm there, 'No, of course I don't.'

Like I said, I focking do.

'Will we ted him what the job is?' Ronan goes.

Buckets shrugs. He's there, 'No heerm.'

Ro goes, 'We're pladding to set up a *Love/Hate* Toower of Dublin, Rosser.'

I'm like, 'A what?'

'A bus toower. We're gonna bring people arowunt all of the diffordent peerts of Dublin where diffordent scenes ourra *Love/Hate* was filummed.'

'Is that all?'

'That's alt.'

'So it's, like, fully legal?'

'Course it's fuddy legal,' Nudger goes. 'I've a bleaten babby on that way. Do you think Ine in a huddy to go back insoyut?'

'I suppose not.'

'I says it to Blod. Says I, "Ine making a promise to you – the

oatenly muddy Ine gonna be bringing into this house from heer-
don in is hodest muddy – muddy that's arthur being eerdened.'"

I've no focking idea what any of that meant.

I just nod and go, 'Fair focks, Nudger. Fair focking focks.'

Ronan pushes the map across the table to me. 'Look at all the bits
meerked, Rosser. This is alls where we're godda bring people. The
shop where Robbie Threacy got shot in the thrive-boy at the end of
the foorst episowid. The gaff that Nidge pipe-bobbemed and burdened Linda's face. The pub where Darden kiddled John Boy. The
exact geerden where Pathrick shot Shivodden and then moordered
Nidge as he lay on the growunt, the doorty fook – and that's not
saying athin against Thravellers.'

I'm there, 'You've put a serious amount of work into this,' looking at all the spots they've morked on the map. 'God, there was a lot
of drive-bys in that show, looking back, wasn't there? So, like, who's
going to go on this, like, tour?'

'Faddens of the show,' Buckets goes. 'People who enjoyt watching it and wanth a taste of that wurdled.'

Ronan nods. I can't tell you how impressed I am by all of this.

'Plus,' he goes, 'they're sedding the tedevision rights to *Love/Hate*
all ober the wurdled. There's gonna be a lorra toowerdists cubbin
to Arelunt wanthing to see the exact spot where their fabourite
scee-uns was fillumed.'

I'm there, 'So it's kind of like the *Sex and the City* tour that Sorcha
dragged me on when we were in New York once? Except with
swearing and shit clothes – focking tracksuit bottoms worn with
Christmas jumpers. No offence, Buckets.'

'That's the genoddle idea,' Nudger goes. 'Every toower will
woyunt up back hee-or – an exact reconsthructshidden of Fradden's
cadavan headquarthers, wha'?'

I'm like, 'So, like, how are you going to drive people around?'

Ronan's there, 'Buckets knows a fedda calt Muppet Burden – he
can lay he's haddens on an oawult dubba-decker bus. Lick of paint,
then off we go.'

I end up saying *the* weirdest thing then. I'm like, 'What about
school, Ro?'

I've some focking cheek, I know.

He goes, 'Buckets and Nudger hee-or are gonna run the show durden the week while Ine in school. I'll woork the weekends till arthur the Leabing Ceert, then I'll go full toyum in the subber.'

I'm there, 'And there's definitely no criminality involved? Again, that's not me being prejudiced against, well, your kind of people.'

'It's all abub boawurd,' Buckets goes.

I'm there, 'In that case, I'm going to have to say fair focks.'

Sorcha has put the boys down for their nap and now she's in, like, full air-hostess mode, giving me all the instructions and the announcements and the warnings and the dos and focking don'ts. It's all *make sure to use a napkin* and *try to make the conversation about something other than rugby* and *make sure to wipe the toilet seat if you happen to piss on it.*

I'm there, 'I honestly don't know why you're going to so much effort. This kid should have to take us as he finds us.'

Sorcha goes, 'He will not take us as he finds us, Ross. We want him to like our daughter.'

She pushes my feet off the coffee table, then she switches off the TV, even though I was watching it.

She's like, 'He'll be here any minute, Ross – get changed.'

I'm there, 'Changed?'

'Oh my God, you are *not* wearing that!'

*That* happens to be my Leinster thermal training top, which is the most comfortable item of clothing I own. It's like a permanent hug and I'm not giving it up for anyone.

Sorcha's like, 'Go upstairs and put a shirt on.'

I'm there, 'Hey, it's Honor who has a date, not us. I'm not getting dressed up just because someone's coming around to watch TV with her. I might if that someone happened to be Gigi Hadid – and even then, I think she'd genuinely love this top.'

Honor suddenly appears downstairs. She walks into the TV room and I actually laugh.

She's like, 'What the fock is so funny?'

I'm there, 'Yeah, no, nothing.'

It's just the first time I've ever seen her wearing make-up. Sorcha has basically drawn cheekbones on her with possibly a *mascara* pencil? Her face is like something off a focking pirate flag.

Then, suddenly, I notice that she's wearing – I shit you not – a *dress*.

It's hilarious, roysh, but at the same time it's *not*? One of the things I always loved about Honor was that she genuinely didn't give a fock what anyone thought of her. It was one of my favourite of all the qualities that she inherited from me. I never thought there'd come a day when she came off as desperate for anyone's approval, especially a boy's.

He'd better be a looker, that's all I can say.

The front doorbell rings.

Honor goes, 'Are you sure I look okay?'

I'm there, 'You look great, Honor.'

She doesn't – she looks focking ridiculous.

She takes a deep breath, then she goes out to answer the door.

Sorcha goes, 'Now, be nice, Ross.'

And I'm there, 'I can't guarantee anything. Except this – whatever he's like, he's not going to be good enough for my little girl.'

Sixty seconds later, Honor arrives back into the TV room, followed by this kid. I end up just staring at him with my mouth open. I take back what I said about him not being good enough for Honor. He is one handsome little bastard. If I had to say he looked like anyone, it'd be a young Justin Bieber.

I hate to say this about my own flesh and blood, but if she thinks a dude who looks like that is going to be interested in the likes of her, well, she's pissing into the wind.

'Mom, Dad,' she goes, 'this is Caleb. And Caleb, this is my mom and dad.'

He's there, 'Hello, Mrs O'Carroll-Kelly,' and we're talking full eye contact. He's obviously not short on confidence. 'Hello, Mr O'Carroll-Kelly.'

Sorcha goes, 'Oh, please! It's Sorcha and Ross!'

I'm like, 'I don't know. I think I'd prefer to keep it as Mr and Mrs for the time being,' just letting him know that not everyone in this house is a slave to his chorms.

God, he's a looker, though.

'So, Caleb,' I go, 'Honor tells me you're not a rugby man.'

Honor's like, 'Daaad!'

I'm there, 'I'm just making conversation, Honor – playing the protective father.'

He goes, 'They have rugby in my school,' and then he shrugs. 'But I've no interest.'

'Probably for the best,' I go. 'Michael's are hordly a superpower of the game. It'll save you a lot of disappointment down the line.'

He's got the Bieber hair and everything. Honor doesn't seem to realize how far out of her depth she is here. Still, the hort wants what the hort wants, even if the head is focking kidding itself.

Sorcha goes, 'I hope you're hungry, Caleb, because I've got sand-wiches, artisan macarons . . .'

He's there, 'Er, cool – thanks, Mrs O'Carroll-Kelly.'

'I told you to call me Sorcha!'

'So, Caleb,' I go, 'I met that sister of yours.'

He's there, 'Thea?'

I go, 'That's her name, isn't it, Honor? The one in your class?' and I give her a little wink. 'Is she adopted or something?'

He's like, 'What?'

'Or are *you* adopted?'

'What are you talking about?'

'It's just I don't see the resemblance, that's all.'

That's when the doorbell rings again. Sorcha goes, 'Ross, will you get that?'

I'm like, 'What's wrong with *your* legs?' because it never ends up being for me anyway.

Sorcha rolls her eyes, then she goes out to see who it is.

I go, 'So, Caleb, if you're not into rugby, what are you into?'

And that's when – totally unprovoked – he goes, 'Sorry, are you a focking simpleton or something?'

I'm like, 'Excuse me?' obviously a bit taken aback.

'I asked if you were a focking simpleton. You sound like a simpleton. All these dumb questions.'

Honor goes, 'Yeah, Dad,' letting me know where *her* loyalties lie, 'you're *such* an embarrassment!'

I'm there, 'I'm not trying to embarrass you, Honor. I'm just trying to get to know this boy who my daughter has taken a sudden interest in.'

He goes, 'Listen to the way you talk. *Muh, muh, muh, muh, muh.* Were you dropped on your head as a baby?'

Honor laughs – my own flesh and blood.

I'm there, 'No.'

He goes, 'Or was your cradle rocked too close to the wall?'

Honor laughs. She goes, 'Oh my God, Caleb, you are *so* funny!'

It's pretty obvious that she's one smitten kitten.

I decide that he needs to be taken down a peg or two. I'm there, 'So do you fancy yourself as a bit of a player, Caleb?'

He's there, 'I'm sorry, can you stop talking, please? Your voice is really starting to grate on me.'

'Look, we obviously haven't got off to the best of storts, me and you. You're going to find me tough but fair. And Honor will probably tell you that I have a tendency to call it. But I want to say this to you. If you even think about breaking my daughter's hort, I will snap you like a dry twig. My family is something I take pretty seriously and I will crush anyone who tries to hurt the people I love.'

And it's at that exact moment that Sorcha steps back into the room. She goes, 'Ross?' and there's a note of definite concern in her voice.

Then I suddenly notice – with a fright that almost causes me to shit my spleen – that she's holding her laptop and there's a man behind her, a man who could only really be described as an Indian dude.

And standing behind him, I really can't fail to notice, is an Indian woman.

I quickly go on the offensive. I'm there, 'I don't have time for this bullshit, whatever-the-fock this is supposedly about.'

Sorcha goes, 'Ross, this man said you made sexually suggestive remarks to his niece on the telephone.'

I watch Honor put her hand over her mouth. So much for not embarrassing her.

I'm there, 'She obviously got the wrong end of the stick, Babes. It might have been the language barrier.'

'I did not get the wrong end of the stick,' the niece goes. 'You asked me to talk filthy to you and you asked me what I was wearing. And now I would like an apology.'

The uncle goes, 'You asked her to describe her underwear?'

I'm there, 'Look, I'm just making the point that I wouldn't describe what I said as sexually *suggestive* as such?'

The woman then goes, 'You said I sounded like I had a pretty mouth and you said, "Say something filthy. Tell me you're horny and then build it up from there."'

'Yeah,' I go, 'it's going to sound bad if you're going to quote everything I said back word for word.'

The one good thing to come out of this is that it's shut Caleb up. He's watching this scene unfold in just, like, shock. I'm thinking, Welcome to the O'Carroll-Kelly house – like I said, take us as you find us.

But it's Honor's disappointed face that kills me. I can't bear to even look at it. So I decide to just come *clean*?

'Okay,' I go, 'if you must know, I was just, like, screwing with your head because I thought you were trying to fleece us.'

'Fleece you?' the Indian dude goes. 'Your wife asked us to remove a virus from her laptop.'

'Yeah, well, when you said you were ringing about the computer, I just presumed you were the same crowd that scammed Chloe's old pair.'

'What crowd?'

'Long story. Someone rang them and said, "Blah, blah, blah," and they somehow got into their computer and stole all their credit cord details. No offence, they were from out your way.'

'Sandyford?'

'No, not Sandyford. I'm going to just say it – India.'

'Okay, so everybody from India is a thief to you, yes?'

'Hey, I'm not pointing fingers.'

'A country of one point two billion people and we are all the same to you?'

'All I'm saying is that I jumped to the most obvious conclusion. And I thought I'd have a bit of fun with you – see where it led.'

Sorcha decides to land me even further in it then. She goes, 'I hope you know, Ross, that what you've just said is actually racist.'

I'm there, 'Everything is sort of racist these days, isn't it? I don't know if anyone else here finds that. It's like, if you don't get the regular updates, you find yourself suddenly saying something that used to be okay but is now a total no-no. It's something for us all to think about, I suppose.'

'Of all of the things you've ever done, Ross . . .'

'Ah, come on, Sorcha, this is way down the list.'

'It's, like, oh my God, what is *wrong* with you?'

'Hey, I said I was awesome. I never said I was perfect.'

It's a cracking line, one I've been saving up for a while. But it's the wrong line for this particular moment.

'Ross, I want you to leave,' she goes.

I'm there, 'Leave? Where am I going, Babes?'

'Anywhere. As long as it's out of my sight.'

I look around the room at all the faces. Sorcha is looking at me in anger, the Indians in disgust, Honor in utter humiliation and Caleb in complete contempt.

On my way out the door, I turn around to him and go, 'You'd better treat my daughter well, Player.'

He won't, of course. As soon as he finds out how handsome he is – if he doesn't know already – he'll drop her like a hot roasting dish.

He's like, 'Whatever!'

Sorcha just roars at me. She's there, 'Get out!'

The girl needs time to cool off, calm down, whatever you want to call it, so I decide to just drive around for a couple of hours.

My first instinct is obviously to turn left and drive up the Vico

Road towards Dalkey, but I end up turning right, which is Bally-brack direction – why, I don't *know*? In fact, I can't explain anything that happens in the next however many minutes. I don't remember deciding to do what I'm about to do. It just sort of, like, happens, as if my actions are being controlled by someone else.

Fifteen minutes later, I'm back on Churchview Road again, two wheels porked on the footpath this time, staring through the railings at two sets of players walking off the field. There's obviously just been a match. I recognize the blue, black and green of Seapoint. From the faces on the players, it's pretty clear they lost.

I shake my head and I go, 'What am I doing here? I can't do this, Father Fehily. I know you always had unbelievable faith in me, but it's a fact – the game *has* moved on. It's a lot tougher than you possibly remember it in terms of, like, physicality. I think I'll hit Ed's, grab a burger and hopefully Sorcha will have calmed down by the time I get home.'

Oh, fock it.

I've suddenly opened the door and I've got out of the cor. Before I know what I'm doing, I'm walking across the cor pork towards the clubhouse.

Some dude, who I take to be the coach of the team, sees me walking towards him. He's like, 'Are you alroyt, Moyte?' and I instantly pick up on the fact that he's a Kiwi.

He's, like, fat – I'm guessing mid-fifties.

'I want to play rugby,' I go. 'I want to play rugby for The Point.'

He's like, 'Unfortunateloy, we doyn't have a soyniors toym thus year. We've got a thirds toym – the Thirstoy Thirds. They troyn on Froydoys – that's uf enough of them shoy ap.'

I'm there, 'I'm not talking about playing with a team of drinkers. I'm talking about playing for this team here.'

He sort of, like, laughs. He can't actually *help* himself? He goes, 'Yoy can't just take up rugboy and expict toy . . .'

'I'm not just taking it up. I've played the game.'

'Whin?' he goes and I notice him not-too-subtly check out my waist. 'Whin did yoy ploy?'

'It was back in 1999.'

'The ninetoys?' he goes. 'Jees, Moyte, that was a long toym agoy.'

I'm there, 'I know it was a long time ago.'

'What posution dud yoy ploy?'

'Number ten. I captained Castlerock College the year they won the Leinster Schools Senior Cup.'

At this stage, the Seapoint players are storting to walk past us into the dressing room. Some of them are staring at me and it's pretty obvious that my face is storting to look vaguely familiar to one or two of them.

'Here,' one of them goes, 'it's that the dude who slipped on his focking orse a couple of weeks ago.'

All the other players laugh.

The coach looks over his shoulder and goes, 'Yeah, you're very voycal for a toym that's just lost at hoyme to Greystoynes by fortoy points.'

The dude remembers his manners and walks on.

I'm there, 'You're bottom of Division 2B.'

The coach is like, 'Soy?'

'So you need to do something. Otherwise, you're going down. All I'm looking for is a chance to prove to myself how good I could have been.'

'Unfortunatloy, Moyte, we doyn't ictually noyd a number tin.'

'Who's your ten?'

'Senan Torsney.'

'Never heard of him.'

'It was that goy who was just maathing off.'

'Right.'

'He just mussed aaht on the Leinster Acadamoy laahst year. He's hoyping to make ut thus year. He's only eightoyn. He *was* on the binch for Lansdaahn. Came to us because he noyds first team rugboy.'

'I'd still fancy my chances of dislodging him. That's the kind of competitor you're dealing with.'

He laughs. I can tell he likes me. 'Oy think Senny'll ploy for Oyerland one doy. You're looking at another Sixton in the moyking.'

I'm like, 'Fair enough. Just forget it, then.'

I'm just about to walk away when he goes, 'Oy doyn't noyd a tin, but Oy noyd someone whoy can doy a job for moy in the front roy.'

I'm like, 'The front row?'

He looks at my midriff again. I don't know why he's so obsessed with it. I would have said I was in pretty good shape.

'Our hookah,' he goes, 'Robbie Rowell – he broyk his toy aaht there todoy.'

'He broke his what?'

'His toy. His bug toy. Oy noyd to foynd a reploycement.'

'And you think I'm it?'

'Oy've noy idea whither you're ut. I've niver seen yoy ploy. Oy'm offering you a troy-aaht.'

'I don't actually have my gear with me. I was just driving around. My wife focked me out of the house.'

'We're troyning on Tuesday noyt. Eight o'clock. All Oy'm saying is Oy'll toyk a look at yoy.'

'Fair enough.'

'What's your noym, boy the woy?'

'It's Ross. It's Ross O'Carroll-Kelly.'

'Will, it's noyce to moyt yoy, Russ Akerell-Killoy. I'm Byrom Jones, the hid coych. I'll see yoy Tuesday noyt.'

And, just like that, I'm suddenly a rugby player again.

# 3. Once You Go Brack . . .

It's all spread out on the bed in front of me. Everything I need for tonight. We're talking training jersey, smock top, trackie bottoms. We're talking shorts, gum shield, jock strap. We're talking . . .

Boots!

Shit, I nearly forgot my boots. Imagine that. The Rossmeister's first night training with The Point and he turns up without his boots.

I grab the chair from Sorcha's vanity table, then I take it into the walk-in wardrobe and I stand on it to reach the box on the top shelf. I put it on the bed, open the lid and pull back the paper. There they suddenly are – my old Adidas Christophe Lamaison Pro Fly Eight-Studs.

The smell of leather and old mud brings a lot of memories flooding back.

I take them out of the box and I flip them over. There's actually a few clumps of grass still stuck to the studs and I'm suddenly wondering where they're from? Could be Belfield. Could be Castle Avenue. Could be Anglesea Road. Then – being deep – I'm suddenly thinking, What kind of hopes and dreams did I have when this mud first attached itself to the soles of these boots?

My eyes stort to fill up.

Maybe Sorcha's right. Maybe I am having some kind of, I don't know, mid-*life* thing?

I take the boots into the en-suite and I pick off the mud and flush it down the jacks. Then I grab Sorcha's black boot polish and a brush and I go at them for, like, fifteen minutes, until I can actually see my big ugly mug in them.

You could nearly mistake them for a brand-new pair of boots – except for the fact that Christophe Lamaison hasn't touched a focking rugby ball for more than a decade.

Well, that's something we definitely do have in common.

I sit down on the bed and I slip my feet into the things, first the left, then the right, just like the old days. I tie the laces, tight, and I stand up.

My chest feels suddenly heavy, and I realize that my breathing is, like, *short*? I'm thinking, Am I actually going to do this? *Can* I actually do it?

And my immediate answer is No. I don't know how to play hooker. All I really know about forward play is what I've learned from, like, watching matches.

But then I remember something that Father Fehily said to me back in 1999, when these boots were brand new and I was about to stort a rugby scholarship in UCD. 'Don't ever doubt yourself,' he went. 'There's plenty of people who'll do that job for you.'

I look in the mirror and I end up giving myself an unbelievable talking to. I'm there, 'I can do this thing!' and then I shout it: 'I CAN DO THIS THING!'

Ten seconds later, still buzzing on my words, I tip downstairs to show Sorcha. I'm kind of still in the doghouse for talking filth to that, again, Indian bird from the Computer Laboratory in Sandyford. But I think seeing me in my boots might bring back one or two happy memories for the girl.

I find her in the living room with Honor and – for fock's sake – Caleb, for the second time in, like, a week. He spends more time in this house these days than *I* even do? The little focking Bieber head on him.

The three of them are sitting on the sofa, watching something with Rachel McAdams in it.

I'm there, 'What's this?'

Caleb mutters something under his breath that sounds suspiciously like, 'Jesus Christ, this idiot again.'

Sorcha goes, 'We're watching *Midnight in Paris*. Oh my God, Ross, it's a gorgeous, gorgeous movie.'

I pick up on the vibe that Honor's not happy with Sorcha for being a gooseberry, because she goes, 'Mom, should the boys not be in bed? It's, like, half-six.'

Sorcha's like, 'Oh my God, I'm sorry. I just got so caught up in the movie. I'll go now and leave you two alone.'

But Caleb's there, 'No, don't. Please, Sorcha, stay – watch the end of it with us!' laying on the chorm.

'Okay,' she goes. 'There's not long left and – oh my God – I *so* love the ending!'

Brian comes chorging at me, head down, like I showed him, and I scoop him up in my orms. Johnny is sitting on Sorcha's lap, just staring at Leo, who is standing, like, six inches in front of the TV shouting, 'Fock this shit!' at Owen Wilson.

I'm there, 'I think I preferred Rachel McAdams in *Wedding Crashers*. Even though I've never seen this. Are you enjoying it, Honor?'

She's there, 'Yeah,' except she says it in a really, like, *defensive* way? 'It's really interesting – all about the different, like, writers from history.'

I laugh. The poor girl. I can see how much effort she's putting in. I'm there, 'Sorry, you've already lost me, Honor.'

Caleb pauses the movie – *he's* in chorge of the actual remote, yeah, in *my* focking house! – and he goes, 'Have you got anything to say that's actually worth hearing, because we're missing important parts of this.'

I don't get a chance to respond to that because Sorcha suddenly goes, 'Oh my God, Ross, *what* have you got on your feet?'

I laugh.

I'm there, 'I knew you'd eventually recognize the sound – my old rugby boots. I've got training tonight.'

'Training?'

'Yeah, no, it looks like I'm going to be playing for Seapoint after all.'

'Are you joking?'

'Rugby is the one subject I never joke about. You of all people should know that. Yeah, no, I've got training at seven. I'm going to meet my teammates properly for the first time.'

Sorcha – if you can believe this – goes, 'Ross, I don't want you wearing those boots in the house. It'll mork the wooden floor,' but I just, like, ignore this attempt to ruin my buzz.

'Rubby!' Brian shouts. 'Rubby!'

I'm there, 'That's right, Brian. Your dad's going off to play rugby – and one day, hopefully soon, you're going to see him line out for the famous Seapoint.'

Sorcha goes, 'Are you going out like that?'

I'm there, 'I'm hordly going to drive in my rugby boots, Sorcha. Yeah, no, I was going to change into my Dubes.'

'What I means is, are you not going to wear your coat?'

'Coat?'

'The coat I bought you for your birthday.'

I can't bring myself to tell her the truth – that it's an *old* dude's coat? And I'm not ready to wear it yet.

'Er, no,' I go, 'I thought I'd carry on wearing my sailing jacket and keep the Cole Haan for, like, special occasions.'

My focking seventieth birthday, for instance.

Caleb looks at me and goes, 'Okay, can we go back to watching this now?'

I'm there, 'Hey, I didn't ask you to pause it, Bieber.'

I put Brian back down on the ground.

Caleb presses Play and they all go back to watching their movie.

I'm there, 'Okay, everyone, wish me luck.'

No one says shit.

Sorcha goes, 'I could watch this movie, like, fifty times and never get bored with it. So many amazing, amazing lines in it.'

Caleb's there, 'I loved that word you used earlier to describe it, Sorcha. *Gorgeous.*'

And I end up just, like, chuckling to myself. Because I've suddenly copped something that Sorcha hasn't. And Honor hasn't either – yet. It's pretty obvious to me that the boy my daughter is supposedly in love with is head over heels in love with my wife.

The other players are checking me out in a big-time way. We're in the dressing room in – again, I'm saying it – Ballybrack and I can feel them all just, like, staring at me. It's like your first day at school. Or your first day in a new job, for people who have to work for a living.

They're all even younger than I thought they'd be – we're talking, like, late teens and early twenties.

I'm seriously feeling my age here.

The famous Byrom Jones goes, 'Alroyt iverybodoy, lusten up. I want to introjoyce yoy to someone whoyse goying to boy troyning with us tonoyt. I want yoy all to give a vurry spicial Seapoint will-come to this goy here.'

Someone goes, 'Who the fock is he?' just sending me a message that reputations count for very little out here.

'His noym,' Byrom goes, 'is Russ Akerell-Killoy. Naah I've talked to one or toy poyple in the goym and lit me till yoy this goy was a vurry bug doyl indoyd back in the ninetoys.'

'Yeah, so were his boots,' someone goes – he's a big dude, we're talking twenty-two, maybe twenty-three years old. I'm guessing he's either a loosehead or a tighthead prop? Everyone laughs. 'Sorry, Dude, but what the fock are you wearing on your feet?'

I look him straight in the eye. I go, 'They're Adidas Christophe Lamaison Pro Fly Eight-Studs,' and I say it in a real fock-you kind of way.

He's there, 'Christophe Lamaison? Who the fock is Christophe Lamaison?'

The worst thing is that he seems to *mean* it? I just look at him as if to say, You obviously know fock-all about history if you can ask a question like that.

Byrom's like, 'Guv hum a broyk, Bucky.'

The dude – Bucky, he's obviously called – goes, 'Look, as the captain of this team, I think I'm entitled to ask who the fock he is and why the fock he's training with us?'

Byrom goes, 'We noyd someone to full un for Rowellsoy. He's got a broyken toy.'

'Whoa, you're talking about putting this dude between me and Maho in the front row?'

'Thut's royt.'

'For fock's sake – he must be, like, forty.'

I'm there, 'I'm actually thirty-five.'

He laughs and he turns to the rest of the dressing room. 'Correction,' he goes, 'he's thirty-five!' like there's no real difference.

He's being a real dick.

He goes, 'Look, no offence, whatever your name is, but we can't afford to carry middle-aged men who are trying to rediscover the glory of their youth. This is Division 2B of the All Ireland League.'

'Correction,' I go, 'it's the *bottom* of Division 2B of the All Ireland League.'

Whoa! That's softened his focking cough. There's suddenly, like, deathly silence in the dressing room.

He goes, 'Repeat that.'

'I said it's the *bottom* of Division 2B of the All Ireland League,' I go. 'I've seen the table – ten matches, zero points.'

He goes, 'You've got a focking nerve,' and he makes a move towards me.

Some other humungous dude steps in between us, going, 'He's not worth it, Bucky. Save it for out there. Let's see how good he is.'

Bucky just glowers at me. I've pissed him off – there's no doubt about that.

So we all trot out onto the pitch. It's a dork, freezing cold night in January and it straightaway brings me back to my school days.

No one talks to me during the warm-up. I try to strike up a conversation with one or two of the younger players while we're doing our Dynamic Stretches, except they all just, like, blank me. I'm just some old fort to them. Then I just think, Fock it, I'm not here to make friends anyway and I get on with my lunges and my squats and my various other bits and pieces.

We do some ball-handling work – which I love – then Byrom splits us up into backs and forwards and, purely out of habit, I end up wandering over to where the backs are standing.

'Yeah,' this Bucky dude shouts at me, 'maybe ten focking years ago!' and I suddenly realize my mistake.

I walk over to where I'm supposed to be.

We do some work with the scrum machine. It turns out that Bucky is the tighthead and the dude who stopped us going at it in the dressing room – Maho – is the loosehead. As the three of us are doing the whole binding thing, Bucky squeezes my shoulder and goes, 'Jesus Christ, you've no muscle there. It's just focking fat.'

It's just, like, mind games. I ignore it.

'Crouch!' Byrom shouts and we all get into formation. 'Pause! Engage!'

Badoom!

We put our shoulders to the pads and we stort shunting the thing forwards.

The entire time, Bucky is in my ear, going, 'Are you not going to put any meat into it? You might as well sit on the focking thing and let us push you around!'

This goes on the entire time that we're scrummaging.

Twenty minutes, maybe half an hour later, Byrom says he wants us to switch to lineouts, which is what we do.

This is where I end up winning over possibly one or two of the doubters, because I've got an unbelievable throw and I always did. Even back in the day, my lineout throws were better than Oisinn's and he was our first-choice hooker.

I'm not good enough for Bucky, of course. Every time he goes up for the ball, he deliberately drops it. He goes, 'He's putting a wobble on it.'

I'm like, 'There's no wobble on these balls I'm throwing.'

He goes, 'What, you're saying I can't catch a ball cleanly in an uncontested lineout?' and he says it like his next line is going to be a punch.

I'm there, 'I don't know what you can and can't do, Bucky. All I do know is that, the way things stand, you're going to be doing it in Division 3B of the All Ireland League next season.'

He just, like, stares me out of it.

Byrom claps his hands together and goes, 'Alroyt, Oy think we've done enough work for tonoyt.'

I don't mind telling you that by the end of the session I'm focked. The old man was right. The game *has* moved on. These goys are just kids, but they tackle twice as hord as we did and they run for twice as long.

The session ends with what they call the Captain's Run? Basic-ally, the coach stands down and the entire team spends, like, ten or fifteen minutes running lengths of the field, passing the ball from man to man in two or three groups, just to shorpen up everyone's handling.

Byrom calls me to one side. He goes, 'Are yoy alroyt, Russ? Good work, Moyte. They were prutty haahd on yoy, thoy.'

I'm there, 'Hey, if I was Bucky and some total randomer was suddenly parachuted into my team, I'd probably react the same way. It's port and porcel.'

'Yoy stroyk moy as being a prutty strong goy – mintally, Oy moyn.'

I'm there, 'Yeah, no, not a lot would faze me – at least on the rugby field. I've seen most things.'

He nods. He goes, 'Bucky's a good bloyk. Uf he gits to loyk yoy, he'd walk throy a ployt-glass windoy for yoy.'

'Well, he doesn't seem to like me.'

'Oy'll till you something, thoy – what you sid to hum before, abaaht boying bottom of the All Oyerland Loyg, it shook hum aaht of hus comfort zoyne. Shook thum all. That's the bist they've troyned for a long toyme.'

I'm there, 'Well, I'm glad I helped, even if that ends up being my only contribution.'

'What do yoy moyn?'

'Look, it's pretty clear that I'm not welcome here. And maybe I have to also accept that the game *has* moved on? The intensity and blah, blah, blah.'

'What uf Oy told yoy I wanted yoy to ploy against Bictov at the woykend?'

'Bective?'

'Bictov. At hoym. Oy'd toytally understind if yoy thought it was beyond yoy. But Oy've soyn something here tonoyt. Yoy shook thungs up. Oy loyk that abaaht yoy. Ut's what this toym noyds.'

'I don't know. I think I just pissed a lot of people off.'

'Good, Moyte. That's what Oy want. Look, we're gitting relegoytud – nothing surer. We've got, like, eight mitches luft in the soyson. We need to wun foyve of them to have any hoype of stoying up. Loyk Oy sid, what's more likeloy to happen is that we goy throy the whoyl year without wunning a sungle mitch and we

80

drop daahn a divusion next year and moyst of these goys will just druft away from the goym.'

'I wouldn't want to see that. I was a major loss to the game myself.'

'Thin doyn't guv up naah. Moyte, Oy've soyn something in yoy and Oy'm a prutty good judge of a ployer. Alroyt, you're not twinty or twinty-toy loyk the rist of the goys. But yoy've got the toy moyst important attribyoots we're looking for . . .'

'Is one of them the option I offer as a back-up kicker?'

'Naah, what *Oy'm* talking abaaht is experience and goyle.'

'What was the second word?'

'Goyle.'

'Oh, guile.'

I've never really known what that even is. He can see I'm still in two minds.

And that's when he says the most unbelievable thing.

'Moyte,' he goes, 'Oy doyn't care uf yoy doyn't beloyve yoy can doy thus – Oy beloyve you caahn.'

Father Fehily used to say something similar to us: 'Of course there'll be times when you'll stop believing in yourself. In those moments, I'll just have to believe enough in you for both of us.'

So what else am I going to say in that moment, except, 'Okay, I'll see you Saturday.'

I join the Captain's Run then. I join the backs, rather than Bucky's group. So it's just, like, me and four or five of the goys running lengths of the pitch in formation, feeding the ball to each other.

Senny, the team's number ten, happens to be the player inside me. I was watching him practise his kicks earlier. I turn to him and I go, 'I was looking at you splitting the old chopsticks earlier on. I hope you don't mind me mentioning it, but I noticed one or two things you could improve on in terms of your technique.'

And that's when it happens. Someone hits me from behind. At first, I think someone has driven a van onto the pitch and knocked me focking down, because that's literally what it *feels* like? All of the wind goes out of my body and I hit the deck.

I swear to fock, for a good thirty seconds, I'm lying there on my back wondering am I actually dead.

I can feel this, like, heavy weight bearing down on me. When I finally dare to open my eyes, I discover that Bucky is on top of me, pinning me to the deck. He's a big dude as well. I genuinely feel like I'm trapped under rubble.

'We might be bottom of Division 2B of the All Ireland League,' he goes, 'but if you ever call me out like that again in front of my teammates, I will focking finish you. Do you understand me?'

I'm like, 'Yeah, fock, whatever.'

He gets up off me.

He goes, 'Okay, everyone – the Captain's Run is over.'

Everyone drifts off in the direction of the dressing room. I'm lying on the flat of my back in the middle of a field in, let's be honest, Ballybrack. I'm staring up at the stors, but at the same time, I'm still buzzing on what Byrom Jones said to me.

It takes me a good, like, thirty seconds to get back up, then I quite literally limp back to the cor. I'm beyond exhausted and in serious pain.

I haven't felt this happy in a long, long time.


The old dear is home from the States. She doesn't tell *me*, of course. She texts Sorcha and says she's back in Ireland and wants us all to meet her *fianthé* – that focking word again – and she wants to take us all out for dinner, we're talking me, we're talking Sorcha, we're talking Honor, we're talking the old man, we're talking Helen.

She tells us to meet them in l'Ecrivain at eight o'clock, then she does her usual thing of swanning in an hour late, pretending that she thought she said *nine*? So *we* all end up sitting at the table for an hour, basically storving while waiting for her to show her ridiculous, rubber face.

I'm there, 'Why don't we all just go ahead and eat?'

The old man jumps straight to her defence, of course. '*She's* invited *us* out to dinner,' he goes. 'We can't very well start without her!'

I'm there, 'We could always order for her. A bottle of Grey Goose and a slice of fennel bread to line her stomach – the focking drunk.'

Sorcha goes, 'Ross!'

'I'm sorry, Sorcha, but she always does this. I said it to you before we left the gaff. She does it for attention – so we're all just sitting here waiting for her to make her big entrance.'

Helen gives me a little smile over the top of her menu, just to let me know that she totally agrees with me. She knows the old dear is full of shit.

'Honor,' Sorcha goes, 'no phones at the table, please!'

She's been texting away for the last twenty minutes – no prizes for guessing who.

She goes, 'I'll put it away when I've finished this conversation.'

Sorcha goes, 'Did Honor tell you, Chorles, that she has a boyfriend?'

Honor's there, 'Oh my God, do you have to be so pathetic?'

'Okay, he's not her boyfriend. He's a boy and he's a friend and he's – oh my God – *so* nice, isn't he, Ross?'

'Yeah, no, I'm not a fan,' I go. 'He has no respect for his elders and no interest in rugby.'

I'm still the only one, by the way, who's copped that it's Sorcha he's *actually* interested in?

Honor goes, 'He wants to know can he come over on Friday?'

I'm like, 'What, again? Jesus Christ, is he homeless or something?'

Honor's there, 'Mom, he wants to know if he can see your Nelson Mandela letters?'

Sorcha goes, 'Oh! My God!' grinning like an idiot. 'You told him about my letters from Madiba?'

Honor shrugs. She's there, 'They're doing a project about heroes in school and he's thinking of doing Nelson Mandela. I mentioned that he wrote to you a load of times.'

The kid has a few moves, I'll give him that.

Sorcha goes, 'I think he really likes you, Honor!'

She's like, 'Do you think?'

I'm there, 'What you should do now, Honor, is tell him you're busy. Tell him he's been coming on a bit strong and you want to cool things.'

Sorcha's like, 'Don't you dare, Honor. He's a nice boy. If you mess him around, he might lose interest.'

'The alternative view is that you should be a bitch to him before he gets the chance to be a bastard to you. I'm giving you both sides here.'

Sorcha's like, 'Ross!'

'I'm giving her both sides, Babes.'

My wife doesn't always approve of my parenting methods. They're different – I'll accept that.

And that's when the picked chicken bone who calls herself my mother finally decides to show her blubber-filled face.

She makes her usual grand entrance.

'Oh, hello!' she goes. 'How long have you all been sitting here?'

And that's the first time I lay eyes on Ari. She's linking his orm. He looks like he's in his, I don't know, nineties. He's unbelievably small – we're talking five foot nothing – and he's also thin with grey hair and a look of permanent confusion on his face.

I go, 'We've been sitting here since eight o'clock – the exact time you told us to be here. The focking state of your face, by the way. You look like you've been beaten with a bag of limes.'

She decides to ignore this. Everyone does.

She goes, 'Everyone, this is Ari, my wonderful *fianthé*. Ari, this is my son, Ross, and his beautiful wife, Sorcha. This is their daughter, Honor. And this is my first husband, Charles – we're still terribly, terribly close – and the second wife, Helen.'

The second wife. The old dear really is a fockpig.

It ends up being handshakes and air-kisses and I've-heard-so-much-about-yous all round.

I go, 'Sit the fock down, you ridiculous-looking woman. Some of us need to eat.'

Sorcha goes, 'Congratulations on your engagement, Fionnuala! You too, Ari!'

My wife is such a crawler.

The old dear's there, 'Thank you, Sorcha,' and she holds up her left hand and there, on her ring finger, is a diamond so big you couldn't lift your orm to hail a taxi without running the risk of a hernia.

Sorcha's like, 'Oh! My *God*!'

The old dear takes it off – with some difficulty, I might add. She's got fingers like Hick's sausages.

Sorcha goes, 'Oh my God, I can't believe the weight of it!' as she slips it onto her own finger and twists it – I think birds do that for luck.

'I'm presuming that's a real diamond,' I go.

The old dear laughs. She's there, 'Of course it's real!'

Sorcha goes, 'What kind of a question is that, Ross?'

Helen's there, 'So have you set a date yet, Fionnuala?'

The old dear goes, 'Ari wants to do it on Saint Patrick's Day!'

Skanksgiving Day, as I call it.

'That's right,' he goes. 'We're going to do it on my boat.'

The old dear laughs. She goes, 'It's more than a boat, Ari!' and then she turns to the rest of us. 'Ari has a yacht. It once belonged to John D. Rockefeller.'

I'm like, 'Who?'

'He was, like, a really famous businessman,' Sorcha goes, 'and philanthropist.'

'Well, I've never heard of him, so I don't know where you're getting your information from.'

'He's going to have it brought up from Corsica,' the old dear tries to go. 'It's got thirty staterooms!'

Sorcha's like, 'Oh! My God! Thirty, Ross! That is, like, *so* romantic!'

'And we want you all to be there! Including you, Honor, and the boys – em . . .'

She doesn't know their names. She can't remember the names of her own grandsons.

'Huey, Dewey and Louie,' I go.

And she's like, 'Yes, that's it. Anyway, it's going to be the social event of the year!'

The waiter brings us menus. He also brings us finger bowls because we've been eating olives for the past hour, trying to keep the hunger at bay. I wash my fingers while the old man goes, 'So, Ari, Fionnuala tells me you're quite the entrepreneur.'

'Well,' the dude goes, 'I'm not sure if that's true, on account of the fact that I've never come up with an original idea in my entire life!'

Everyone laughs. I don't know why. It's not that funny. It's politeness, I suppose.

He goes, 'No, my talent – such as it is – is for spotting talent in others. For fifty years, people have been coming to me with their ideas for businesses and my job is to decide whether to finance them or not.'

As he's saying this, he picks up his spoon and – I swear to fock, I am *not* making this up – he storts eating the contents of my finger bowl like it's focking soup. The hilarious thing is that nobody even comments on it. We all just sit there watching the poor old focker drinking this lemony water that I just washed my hands in – and I won't even tell you what I was doing with my hands fifteen minutes before I left the house tonight.

'I made a lot of my money in hotels,' Ari is at the same time going. 'Hotels and spa resorts. Golf courses. But also in health insurance, automobiles, newspapers, phone companies, aluminium, radio stations, real estate – you name it . . . Excuse me, Sir.'

He collars this passing waiter. He goes, 'This consommé is lukewarm – at best.'

The waiter looks at the rest of us like he suspects this might be one of those, like, hidden-camera shows.

He's like, 'Consommé?'

Ari hands him the bowl. 'If I wanted cold soup,' he goes, 'I would have asked for vichyssoise, which I clearly did not. I'd like a fresh one, please – and I don't mean the same bowl heated up. You know what? Second thoughts, forget the consommé.'

'The thing is, Sir, that's not . . . actually consommé?'

'You're damn right it's not. It's not only cold, it's got no flavour. You're lucky I don't pour it over your head. Now get out of my sight. And don't let me see that on the bill.'

The waiter walks off with the bowl, looking totally bewildered.

I look at the old man and Helen as if to say, Jesus Christ, he's as nutty as a focking Snickers!

The old dear opens the wine menu and puts on her glasses to study it, like she's in any way fussy about what she drinks. I saw her make a Bloody Mary once by pouring vodka into a jor of

Dolmio spaghetti sauce. Drank it straight from the focking jor as well.

Sorcha goes, 'Your dress is fabulous, Fionnuala! Victoriana is so on-trend at the moment.'

I'm there, 'What my wife is trying to say is that you look like a corpse. You look like something Dr Marie Cassidy should be going at with rubber gloves and a bone saw.'

I even catch Honor smiling at that one.

And that's when *the* weirdest thing happens. Ari suddenly storts staring at the old man and Helen, as if he's seeing them for the first time.

'Fionnuala,' he goes, 'you didn't tell me we were having company.'

I look at Sorcha – one eyebrow orched.

'Yes, you met them a moment ago, Ari,' the old dear goes, in the same patient voice Sorcha uses when she's explaining to her grandmother how the Sky Box works. 'It's my ex-husband, his second wife, my son, Ross – remember? And his wife, Sorcha, and their lovely daughter, Honor?'

He goes, 'You have a son?'

'Yes, I have a son.'

'You're too young to have a son.'

The old dear doesn't even respond to this. She just goes back to reading the wine list while the rest of us are just, like, staring at each other in literally stunned silence.

The dude suddenly stands up then. He goes, 'I got to use the, er . . . I'm trying to think of the word you English use for it. Do you say the John?' and then off he heads.

He means shitter.

There's, like, ten seconds of silence at the table before the old man goes, 'Are you sure this chap of yours is, well, fully *compos mentis*, Fionnuala?'

She goes, 'Sorry, Charles?' pretending she has absolutely no idea what he's talking about.

'It's just he seems a tad, well, confused to me.'

'Oh, I know why that is. He had a Martini before we left the house. I told him not to drink on an empty stomach.'

Helen goes, 'Are you sure that's all it is, Fionnuala? He does seem a little, well, muddled.'

I actually laugh.

I'm there, 'He's not muddled. And he hasn't been drinking on an empty stomach either. He's bananas. He'd have to be, of course. I mean, why else would he want to marry you?'

'How dare you!' the old dear tries to go. 'He's old, that's all. I can assure you, Ross – I can assure you all – that he is in possession of his full mental faculties.'

It's at that exact point that we become aware of what would have to be described as a disturbance coming from the balcony looking down on the main restaurant floor.

Someone's going, 'Shush, shush, shush, shush, shush, shush, shush – can we have some shush, please?'

We all look up – and it turns out, of course, that it's Ari doing the shushing.

Silence, I don't know, *descends* on the restaurant? Every conversation in the place suddenly stops.

'Better,' he goes. 'That's much better. Ladies and gentlemen, tonight I would like to pay tribute to a very special lady. She is the most beautiful woman in the world and I am truly blessed to have her in my life. I want to take this opportunity to say thank you to my wonderful wife of fifty-three years, the lovely Avis. I know you enjoy very much the music of Cole Porter and I'd like to dedicate this next song to you.'

The old man goes, 'Good Lord, the chap's not going to sing, is he?'

Ari's there, 'It's called "Begin the Beguine".'

Then he launches into the song. You can see the staff looking at each other, wondering whether they should go up the stairs to stop him.

The old dear goes, 'He can be terribly romantic.'

I'm there, 'Romantic? He just called you Avis, you comical-looking pisshead. He thinks you're his *first* wife.'

I'm banjoed. And when I say banjoed, I mean *totally* banjoed? I thought training was going to get easier, but tonight was even horder than Tuesday and I can't believe we've got a match in, like, two days' time.

At the same time, I'm determined not to let it show. I feel like throwing my lunch up, then lying down on the floor of the dressing room to go to sleep, but I know Bucky and these other fockers would just love that, because it'd prove them right, that I'm just an old man trying to relive old glories.

I'm sitting there just leaning forward with a towel over my head and I'm listening to them talk about who's on what season of *Game of Thrones*, and their college essays that are due, and some bird who one of them scored in Everleigh who's supposed to be going out with someone on the Ireland U-20s team, and some tune by Kanye that's apparently the best thing he's ever done, and some place in the States where everyone is supposedly heading on their Jier this year, and a video of Conor McGregor knocking some dude basically unconscious with one punch that's got, like, two million hits on YouTube.

And no one's even talking to me. I'm what is known as a social piranha.

Byrom steps into the dressing room and he reads out the team for Bective on Saturday. Mine is the second name on the list. All I can hear after that is silence. I know I'm getting filthies from pretty much every player in the room, but I'm grinning from ear to ear under my towel. Fock knows how I'm going to recover in time to play, but in that moment I don't actually *care*? I'm about to make my All Ireland League debut at the age of thirty-five.

Byrom finishes reading the team, then turns around to Bucky and goes, 'Dud yoy talk to Russ abaaht the loyn-aaht coydes?'

Bucky's like, 'No, because I honestly didn't think you were going to go through with this.'

'Oy've just rid ahht the toym and he's pucked. So nah would boy a prutty good toym to guv hum the coydes, don't yoy thunk?'

I hear someone else go, 'Here, my old man played for Wanderers back in the seventies – he could definitely do a job for us at full-back.'

Everyone laughs.

I take the towel off my head. I look at Byrom and go, 'Thanks for believing in me. I won't let you down.'

89

He just nods and goes, 'Bucky's going to give yoy the loyn-ahht coydes – usn't thit royt, Bucky?'

Bucky just shakes his head and goes, 'This is a mistake. I'm saying that now. Okay, I make all the lineout calls. And we work off a simple code. Three options with the throw – front, middle or back. That's F, M and B.'

'Yeah, no,' I go, 'that sounds pretty straightforward.'

Everyone laughs.

'For fock's sake,' Bucky goes, 'I don't just shout F, M or B. How long do you think it'd take the opposition to work that out?'

If I got it straightaway, my guess would be not very long.

He goes, 'It has to be encrypted. So I'll shout the name of a country and then a number. For instance, it could be Colombia Three. So what you have to do is count back three letters. The third last letter of Colombia is B, which means the lifters are expecting you to throw the ball to the back. Germany Four means you need to throw the ball to the middle. France Six means it's going to the front. Also, you'll hear me throw in a third word, usually a colour or an animal, just to confuse the opposition. So I might shout Belgium Kangaroo One. Magnolia Namibia Three. Ignore the animal and the colour. It's just a decoy word. All you need to think about is the country and the number. Do you understand?'

Oh, fock. This shit is so far over my head, I couldn't reach it with a stepladder. Of course, I don't want to look stupid in front of everyone, so I go, 'Yeah, no, that's pretty basic actually.'

Byrom goes, 'Yoy definiteloy got thit, Russ, did yoy? Ut's just that ut looked loyk yoy moyt have zoyned aaht while Bucky was exployning ut.'

I should *say* something? I should just tell them that I didn't catch a focking word of what was said. Instead, I go, 'No, it's fine – all of that information has gone into my, I don't know, mind.'

And Bucky goes, 'Good. So there shouldn't be any fock-ups.'

I grab a shower then.

There's, like, seven or eight of the other goys in there with me, and, for the first time in my life, I feel – I'm just going to say it – body-conscious? I can't help but notice that they're all, like, seriously ripped – we're talking actual eight-packs here.

I'm, like, sucking my stomach in and clenching as I rub the shower gel over me, but I can feel them all having a good look at my Minka Kelly.

In my head, I go back over what Bucky just said. Is it the country or the colour that's the decoy word? Or is it the number? No, it couldn't be the number, because the whole point of it is using that number to, like, count backwards through the letters.

Jesus, I can't even spell going forwards, never mind backwards.

I get out of the shower, dry off and throw on the old threads. I hear someone go, 'I wonder how many points it was for a try when he last played the game?'

I just ignore it. I blank it out, like I used to blank out the haters when we played Blackrock or Clongowes or any of the others back in the glory days.

I grab my gear bag and I head out to the cor, feeling miserable but at the same time *happy*? Because I've got a chance to prove myself – and that's all I ever wanted.

Just as I'm throwing my bag into the boot, I hear the beep of a horn outside on Churchview Road, then I hear a voice go, 'Rosser, you transsexual!'

I just laugh. Ronan would put you in instant good form. I look up and I end up having to do a double-take. My son is sitting behind the wheel of a double-decker bus.

It's not an ordinary double-decker bus either. It's been painted black, roysh, and on the side there's a twelve-foot-high picture of Nidge pointing a gun and then, in massive letters, it says, 'The *Love/Hate* Tour of Dublin'.

'I calt out to the gaff,' he goes, 'and Sorcha said you were playing rubby for Ballybrack.'

I'm there, 'The team is actually Seapoint, Ro.'

He looks confused. He's like, 'You're a long way from the fooken sea, Rosser.'

I'm there, 'Yeah, no, I know we're technically *in* Ballybrack, but we don't *represent* Ballybrack? We represent Seapoint.'

'I gev up throying to wontherstand that game of yooers years ago. What do you think of me bus?'

I can't lie to him. I'm there, 'It's incredible. I'm going to have to say fair focks, Ro. I really am.'

'We're doing the foorst toower on Suttonday morden if you're arowunt. Ine arthur tedding your auld fedda alretty.'

I'm there, 'Yeah, no, I'll be there.'

'Hop in,' he goes. 'I'll bring you for an auld spin.'

So I lock the cor and I climb into the bus and Ronan closes the doors.

He goes, 'We're cheerching twenty euros for a two-hour toower – all the sites, Rosser.'

I'm there, 'Ro, I can't tell you how impressed I am by this,' as he takes the roundabout outside The Graduate and heads towards Dún Laoghaire.

'Hee-or,' he goes, 'you'd want to see the bleaten looks I was getting offa your neighbours – snobby bastards.'

I laugh. I'm like, 'Yeah, no, they wouldn't be used to seeing public transport on the Vico Road. They'll be on to Dublin Bus – terrified it's a new route!'

'Good one, Rosser.'

As he takes the Sallynoggin roundabout at, like, seventy Ks an hour, something suddenly occurs to me. 'Hang on,' I go, 'you don't even have a driving licence!'

He's there, 'Let me know if you see the Filth, then. If Ine gonna outrun a squad car, Ine gonna need a good head steeert.'

I'm, like, telling the boys a bedtime story. *Johnny Sexton and the Miracle of Cordiff* – again!

They're loving it as well.

'Ross,' Sorcha goes, 'could you not just tell them a regular night-night story like a normal parent?'

I'm there, 'They seem to love the rugby ones, Sorcha.'

'Fock Northampton!' Leo goes.

I'm there, 'Fock Northampton is right, Leo! Fock Northampton is right!'

Sorcha goes, 'Oh, by the way, Caleb's here!'

I'm like, 'Er – and this affects me how?'

'I'm going to show him my letters from Madiba.'

'I'm sorry but I'm struggling to give a fock right now – please try again later.'

She laughs.

'Men like you always end up being protective fathers,' she goes.

I'm there, 'What do you mean by men like me?'

'It's not a criticism, Ross. I think it's actually sweet.'

'Well, if you must know, I'm not actually *being* protective. I just happen to think that Honor is borking up the wrong tree.'

'What do you mean?'

Sometimes, my wife is the most intelligent person I've ever met. Other times, she's as focking thick as gutter mud.

I'm there, 'Are you genuinely that slow on the uptake? Caleb has a thing for you.'

She's like, 'For me?'

'Yes, you.'

'What do you mean by a thing?'

'A crush – whatever you want to call it.'

'Oh, Ross, don't be silly!'

'I'm not being silly.'

She's there, 'That's ridiculous!' although she ends up actually *blushing*?

'The way he acts around you,' I go. 'Then cracking on to be interested in those stupid letters. Trust me, Sorcha, one player recognizes another. And this kid is a definite player – he's years ahead of his time, in fact.'

She's there, 'You're being silly, Ross. He's just a lovely little boy with nice manners, that's all.'

She heads downstairs, clutching the letters.

I finish the story with the happy-ever-after ending of Johnny Sexton converting Nathan Hines's sixty-fourth-minute try. Then they all settle down to sleep. I might give them *Johnny Sexton Tames the Tigers* tomorrow night.

I tip down the stairs.

They're sitting in the living room. Honor and Caleb are both on the sofa and Sorcha is sitting next to them, on the orm. The letters are spread out on the coffee table and Caleb is throwing his eyes over them, going, 'You are so lucky to have these!'

I cop the smell straightaway. I actually *laugh*? I'm there, 'Are you wearing aftershave, Player?'

He gives me a look that you'd possibly describe as *withering*?

I'm there, 'It wouldn't happen to be *Spicebomb* by Viktor & Rolf, would it? Which just so happens to be my wife's favourite. I'm wondering did you hear her mention it or something?'

He goes, 'Yeah, we're kind of *busy* here?'

I'm like, 'Yeah, no, I can see that. You're some operator, I have to give it to you. Cracking on to be interested in those stupid letters.'

'It's for a project, if you must know.'

'About heroes. So I heard. And you couldn't have picked a rugby player, like presumably everyone else in your class? For instance, Keith Gleeson went to Michael's – although you've probably never even heard of him.'

'I hate rugby. I told you.'

'I know the dude personally and I can tell you it would kill him to hear you say that.'

Honor looks at me and goes, 'Rugby is only a stupid game,' and I'm giving it to you word for word. 'Madiba fought for, like, human rights – didn't he, Mom?'

Sorcha goes, 'Yes, he did, Honor.'

I'm there, 'Human rights are for, like, poor people – not the likes of us. As my old man says, you never hear rich people banging on about their human rights.'

Caleb goes, 'That's such an ignorant thing to say. Human rights are the only thing that separates us from the animals.'

Sorcha's there, 'I've been a member of Amnesty International since I was about your age, Caleb. Actually, Honor's a member, too – aren't you, Honor?'

Honor goes, 'Yeah, my mom renews my membership every year for my birthday.'

I'm there, 'And Honor always goes, "What a waste of focking money – do you have any *actual* presents for me?"'

God, I'm storting to miss that girl.

'Anyway,' I go, 'I can't stand around talking about focking Mafusa all night – I've got shit to do,' and I tip down to the kitchen to grab a Nespresso and my Tactics Book and do some work on the lineout calls for the match against Bective tomorrow. And when I say 'do some work on the lineout calls', I mean try to work out what the fock Bucky was talking about last night.

So I'm sitting there, five minutes later, scribbling away in my book, trying to remember what the whole point of the colour and the animal was, when all of a sudden I look up and notice Caleb standing there, staring at me.

I actually *laugh* when I see him?

I go, 'That's some focking effort you're putting in, Bieber. Although I think you should tell Honor the truth. I don't like the way you're stringing her along.'

He goes, 'Those letters are fake.'

He says it just like that – out of the blue.

I'm there, 'What are you talking about?', trying to *not* look guilty?

'Nelson Mandela didn't write those letters,' he goes. 'That's not his handwriting – I've *seen* his handwriting – and also the word peace is spelled P, I, E, C, E.'

I'm there, 'Okay – and how would you have spelled it?'

He laughs. He goes, 'You wrote those letters, didn't you?'

I'm like, 'You're full of shit,' because it was actually Oisinn.

He goes, 'You definitely wrote them. All that stuff about, "This Ross chap you told me about sounds like a genuinely good guy with a big future ahead of him in the game of rugby."'

'He loved the sport,' I go. 'There's a famous photograph of him with Francois Pienaar.'

'Don't worry. I'm not going to tell her.'

'I wasn't worried. I'm not worried.'

'I'm not going to tell her because I don't want to hurt her.'

'She wouldn't believe you anyway. She'd think you were full of shit – just like I do.'

He ends up saying *the* most unbelievable thing to me then. He goes, 'I don't like the way you treat Sorcha.'

I'm like, 'Is that right?'

'Yes, it is. You don't respect her and you don't love her the way she deserves to be loved. You're not even interested in any of the things that she's interested in.'

'That's because a lot of them are boring.'

'You're not worthy of her.'

Seriously, he's got more front than Brittas Bay.

I'm there, 'Not worthy of her? You don't know shit! You're nine.'

'I'm ten. And one day, I'll be eighteen. And by then, Sorcha will have got sense and she'll have divorced you.'

Okay, this is one creepy focking kid.

I'm there, 'You seem to have it all worked out, Bieber.'

And he goes, 'When that day comes, I think it's only fair to warn you, *I'm* going to marry her.'

Byrom reminds us of the job we're facing.

'Bictuv or noybodoy's fools,' he goes, 'and we'd be croyzoy to under-istimoyte them. But at the staaht of the soyson, Oy've got to till yoy, this is one of the mitches Oy maahked daahn as a hoym wun. We're bitter thin Bictuv – Oy royly doy beloyve that, despoyte our posution in the toyble. We've got eight goyms lift. We're gonna noyd at loyst foyve wuns to have inny realustic hoype of remoyning in Divusion Toy Boy. Lit's git the first of thoyse wuns todoy!'

He claps his two hands together and everyone just, like, cheers. At the top of their voices, everyone suddenly storts shouting, 'Come on, The Point! Let's do this!'

We're each handed a jersey. I lay mine flat on my lap and I look at it. It's not the red and black of Castlerock College. It's the black, blue and green of Seapoint Rugby Club. It feels weird – of course it does – but I look at the crest and I think about that Mortello Tower, wherever the fock it even is, and I'm suddenly filled with pride.

''Mon, The Point!' the shouts go up again.

I stand up and I pull the jersey over my head, then down over my belly. Then I go to pop the collar and I realize that it doesn't have one. It's yet another way in which the game has changed.

The players stort to file out of the dressing room and onto the field. I've got, like, serious focking butterflies. But then nerves are good. It's all about channelling that energy in a positive way.

Eat nerves, shit results is just another way of saying that.

On the way out of the dressing room, I sidle up to Bucky and I go, 'Can I just run through the lineout codes with you again?'

He's like, 'I focking told you the lineout codes.'

'Yeah, no, I wouldn't mind doing just a quick recap.'

'What, have you got Alzheimer's or something?'

'No, I don't have Alzheimer's. I just wouldn't mind you telling me again so it's, like, fresh in my head. There was something about a colour and an animal and a country.'

He goes, 'For fock's sake,' like it's a massive, I don't know, imposition. 'The colour and the animal are irrelevant.'

'You were the one who mentioned them.'

'Because they're a focking *decoy*. If I mention a colour or an animal, just focking ignore it, okay? The only relevant pieces of the code are the country and the number.'

'Okay.'

'So if I say Denmark Giraffe Four . . .'

'The first thing I do is drop the Giraffe – the Giraffe is gone.'

'Yes, the Giraffe is gone. It's the fourth last letter of the word Denmark. Which is M. Which means we're expecting the ball to be thrown to the middle.'

'Yeah, no, that's, em, pretty straightforward alright.'

'Just make sure you get it right. And make sure you put your focking weight in at scrum time. We're not here to indulge your focking midlife crisis.'

Anyway, the game storts and we end up scoring a try after, like, two minutes. Davy Dardis, our scrum-half – the smallest man on the field – gets over the line and Senny adds the points.

But I'm getting a serious sledging in the scrum. The Bective hooker is going, 'Jesus, the last time I saw a body like that, ten Japanese fishermen were chasing it in a trawler!'

Either side of me, Bucky and Maho actually laugh – my own focking teammates. And I end up doing something that I've never done before on a rugby pitch – I fall to pieces. I end up giving away two stupid penalties, one after the other, and the Bective number ten kicks his team back to within a point of us with only, like, ten minutes gone.

I've cost us six points. I'm having a mare. I don't mind admitting that.

Bucky keeps looking over at Byrom on the bench, asking him to do something – presumably he means take me off. He goes, 'We're playing with a focking seven-man pack.'

Byrom does nothing, though. At least he's determined to give me a proper chance to prove myself.

Bucky just keeps bollocking me out of it. He goes, 'You're in the wrong focking place every focking time!'

I'm there, 'I'm doing my best, Dude.'

And he's like, 'Your best is going to get us relegated. If Byrom's not going to do anything about this, I focking will!'

The match is, like, twenty minutes old when we win our first lineout. The players line up as I grab the ball in my two hands, pull it back over my head and wait for the call.

Bucky goes, 'Azerbaijan Six Deep Maroon.'

It's, like, *what the fock?* Which one of those words is a country? It's got to be Abrakebab, doesn't it? So how many letters back – did he say six? Jesus, how do you even spell it?

I end up thinking about it for too long. Bucky and the others are screaming at me. They're going, 'Throw the ball! Throw the focking ball!'

I end up panicking and I just fock the thing into the air. Bective win the lineout, then five phases later, they score a try, which ends up getting converted, to put them, like, six points ahead.

There's no doubt who my teammates blame.

The next time there's a break in play, Bucky gives me a shove in the chest. He's like, 'I told you the focking code.'

I'm there, 'Abrakebab? Are you taking the focking piss?'

'I said Azerbaijan. It's a focking country.'

'That's a debate for another day. You couldn't have thought of an easier one to spell, no?'

'It was B for Back. It couldn't have been anything else. There's no F or M in it.'

'And how the fock was I supposed to know that? I didn't even know it existed until five seconds ago.'

We end up having to be separated by Maho and the rest of the pack.

From the sideline, Byrom shouts, 'Goys, yoy're suppoysed to boy on the soym soyd.'

The Bective goys are loving it, of course.

We end up conceding a second try – this one, *not* my fault? – but then we somehow manage to break downfield. Maho drags one of their players into touch while in possession and we suddenly have another lineout ten yords from the Bective try line.

I pick up the ball again and wait for Bucky's call.

He goes, 'Federated States of Micronesia Amazonian manatee twenty-seven.'

You're taking! The focking! Piss!

Which he is. It's a sad state of affairs when your team captain is prepared to basically throw the match just to prove a point about one of his teammates.

He shouts it again. He's like, 'Federated States of Micronesia Amazonian manatee twenty-seven. Hurry up this time, for fock's sake!'

I think to myself, okay, the manatee thing must be the animal. So the country must be the first thing he said. Microfantasia. There's definitely no B in there, because there's no, like, *buh* sound? There's definitely an F and it sounds very much to me like there might be an M. So it's one or the other – we're talking 50–50.

In the end, they get fed up waiting. The referee warns me about time-wasting and they all stort shouting, 'It's the front! Throw it to the focking front!'

Which I do – and Bective end up stealing it again.

It gets quite heated when we go in at half-time. We're, like, 26–7 down and I'm already out on my feet. I'm tired and beaten up and I feel like I've just played two matches back-to-back.

Bucky's going, 'Isn't this what I predicted? Isn't this what I said would happen?'

Byrom ends up actually defending me. He goes, 'You're suppoysed to boy toym moytes. You're bloody well not behoving loyk ut.'

Our inside centre – I don't even know his name – goes, 'He's out of his depth,' and of course I can't offer anything in my own defence, except threats to deck various people in the dressing room.

We go back out for the second half. The Bective goys have obviously picked up on the fact that we're a divided team.

They're, like, focusing on me, going, 'Where's your focking Zimmer frame, old man?' and laughing.

None of them seem to know who I am or what I achieved in the game. I might as well have never played it before.

Five, maybe ten minutes into the second half, we win another lineout, this time inside our own half. I'm determined to figure out the lineout call, even though Bucky is obviously deliberately trying to fock me over. I decide to try to, like, think faster.

He goes, 'Goitered gazelle Bosnia and Herzegovina twenty!'

I'm thinking, Bosnia, Bosnia, Bosnia – okay, that's got to be B for Back. Which means the ball has to go to the back!

I launch it into the air. It ends up being a beautiful throw as well. But Bective end up stealing it and they score another try from it and it's basically game over.

Our two second rows – I don't even know their names – end up seriously losing it with me.

I'm there, 'It's not my fault they guessed right.'

One of them goes, 'They didn't guess. You announced it.'

'What?'

'You said the word back.'

'No, I didn't.'

Bucky goes, 'You focking did. Unbelievable. Not only can you not focking scrummage, you can't figure out lineout codes without moving your lips.'

Shit.

All in all, I would definitely have to be considered one of Ireland's thickest people.

We end losing by something ridiculous. I'm pretty sure it's 45–7, but the only people who are still counting at the end are the referee and whoever's covering the match for the papers.

And then, as we're walking off the pitch, Bucky gives me a seriously hord shove in the back and goes, 'Congratulations. You've just played your first and last game for Seapoint.'

# 4. *The Daahk Aahts*

'So,' the old man goes, 'what do you make of Lucinda Creighton's latest move?'

I'm like, 'Who?' and I genuinely mean it.

'Oh, there's talk of a new political party!' he tries to go. 'About to launch any day. I said to Hennessy, "Ross will have a line on this. And it'll be something suitably acerbic – better put the old hard hat on, old scout!"'

I'm there, 'I don't know what you're talking about and neither do I *give* a fock?'

He suddenly bursts out laughing. 'Oh, I can't wait to report back to your godfather! Acerbic is the word alright! I just hope I can remember it word for word.'

'I said I don't know what you're talking about and neither do I *give* a fock?'

'That was it! Oh, it'd take a brave man to steer you onto the subject of politics, Kicker! Although brave or foolhardy, I'm not sure which! I think I would have been on safer ground bringing up Ireland's Six Nations victory over Italy yesterday!'

This conversation, by the way, is taking place upstairs on Ronan's brand-new, second-hand, double-decker bus. We're hurtling along the south Dublin quays in the general direction of Heuston Station, the two of us freezing our nuts off. It's the first day of the *Love/Hate* Tour of Dublin and from where I'm sitting, Ronan is totally nailing it.

'Cubben up on the left,' he's going, into his little headset microphone, 'is the pub where Real IRA gang boss Git was moordered by Tommy arthur Git raped he's boord, Shivodden, in the foorst episode of Seerdies Tree.'

Fifty heads instantly turn. Everyone has their camera phones out and they're pointing them at the building.

'The moorder of Git, arthur a thrink and thrugs binge on Patty's Day, kicked off the toorf war that was to clayum meddy, meddy lives before the seerdies ended.'

He's really hamming up the Dublin accent. Give the punters what they want. I suppose that's what you have to do in this day and age. I turn to the old man. I'm like, 'Are you catching any of this?'

'The occasional word,' he goes. 'Murder seems to be a recurring theme. I've picked up on that much. You must be so proud of him, Kicker. He's a go-getter – not unlike you, of course.'

I'm like, 'Me? I'm not a go-getter. I've done fock-all with my life.'

He goes, 'I think you're being rather hard on yourself there, Ross,' and then there's a moment of silence when he tries to come up with something worth mentioning. In the end, he just changes the subject. He goes, 'By the way, isn't it wonderful to see your mother so happy with this new chap of hers?'

I actually laugh.

I'm there, 'Er, why *wouldn't* she be happy? She's about to marry a billionaire who happens to be gaga.'

He goes, 'I'm not sure I'd use the word gaga, Ross.'

'Er, were you *in* the restaurant? You saw and heard what happened.'

'Your mother seems to think it was an issue with his medication – shouldn't have been drinking with it, by all accounts.'

'And you buy that, do you?'

'Ross, you're not suggesting that your mother is taking advantage of this chap, are you?'

'Seriously – how could you be married to that woman for thirty-whatever years and not know the first thing about her?'

Buckets of Blood, I'm relieved to say, is driving the bus. I know for a fact that the old man has promised to pay his wages for twelve months until the business is properly up and running.

He can be alright, my old man, when he's not being a knob.

'Next,' Ronan goes, 'we're gonna see the newsachunt shop where Dadden's brother, Robbie, got shot in the foorst episode of Seerdies One. Robbie was just arthur being released from Cloverhill Prison

and Tommy was apposed to pick him up, except he was late, because he was arthur been giving Dadden and Robbie's sister, Meerdy, the royud . . .'

Buckets swings the bus right and over, I don't know, whichever Liffey bridge it actually is. I've already got pretty much hypothermia. Fock knows how cold it's going to be on this side of the city. The old man hands me his hip flask. A whack of XO is just what I need.

He goes, 'Do you mind my saying, Ross, you don't seem your usual jovial self today?'

I end up just blurting it out. 'You might as well know,' I go. 'I went back playing rugby in the end. For Seapoint.'

He's there, 'You should have told me! I wouldn't have missed that for the world!'

'Well, you'll be happy to hear you were right. I made a complete focking tit of myself against Bective.'

'Look, Ross, I probably could have been a little more supportive when you mentioned that you were considering making a comeback.'

'Are you listening to me? I'm saying you were right. Rugby *has* moved on. It's a young man's game now.'

'You'll be wonderful, Ross, once you adjust to the pace of it.'

'I won't, because I'm not going back. I've been a lot of things in my life. But one thing I've never been is a laughing stock. That's what I was against Bective.'

'I'm sure that's not true, Kicker.'

'You weren't there. I was playing hooker.'

'Hooker? Good Lord!'

'I couldn't work out the lineout calls without moving my lips and giving the game away. We ended up taking a serious tonking and it was all down to me and my stupid brain.'

'What, so you're just going to give up?'

'That's the plan, yeah. I must have been mad to think I could still hack it in Division 2B of the All Ireland League.'

'Oh, so you're a quitter now, are you? That's interesting.'

'I'm not a quitter. I just couldn't show my face in, let's be honest, Ballybrack again.'

'All I'm saying is that, well, it's not what Denis Fehily taught you. *If at first you don't succeed, you're running about average*. That was one of his, wasn't it?'

'Stop.'

'What?'

'You're pushing all kinds of buttons there and you know it.'

'All I was trying to say was –'

I end up shouting at him then. I'm like, 'You're pushing all kinds of buttons – end of story!'

We sit there in silence then, listening to Ronan's running commentary. He's holding up a T-shirt for everyone on the bus to see.

'These are avaidable in tree sizes for €15.99,' he goes. 'Each T-shoort caddies a lifelike depiction of John Boy's famous Last Supper mewerdle from Seerdies Two, featuring Bob Merely, Michael Cottons, Boppy Saddens and Tupac Shikewer . . .'

The old man sort of, like, chuckles to himself. 'And to think,' he goes, 'we all worried about the future that we were bequeathing to young Ronan's generation. After the whole economic meltdown business, I mean. I'm looking at him there and I'm thinking, Well, we needn't have worried at all. Never underestimate a man's ability to turn a bad hand into a better one.'

I'm there, 'Is there a lesson in there for me or something?'

'There's a bloody well miracle going on around you, Ross. Ireland is on the up and up again. Who would have thought that even possible a few years ago? We were an economic basket-case. Now look at us! The skyline is full of cranes again. They're saying that within the next twenty years, houses in Dublin could be worth what people are actually paying for them!

'That hasn't happened by accident, Ross. And it had nothing to do with our so-called political leaders – your friend Lucinda, and the rest of them. No, it's happened because of the unique spirit of the Irish people – evidenced by your son, there. You see, we're a bloody hardheaded race of people, the Irish. We don't know when we're beaten. And that's one thing you were famous for, Ross, when you played rugby and Denis instilled it in you. You never, ever gave in.'

★

Byrom actually laughs when he sees me sitting there, changing into my training gear.

He goes, 'Oy dudn't thunk yoy'd come beck,' and then, before I get a chance to say a word, he goes, 'Oy'm glad yoy dud, Moyt.'

There's not too many in the dressing room who feel the same way – that's judging from the *looks* I'm getting? I can see the likes of Senny and Maho and even little Dordo staring at me in just, like, shock. They genuinely can't believe I'd show my face around here again after what happened at the weekend.

I tie the laces of my famous Christophe Lamaison's and I think of something else Father Fehily used to say: 'Cowards never start. The weak never finish. Winners never quit.'

There's still no sign of Bucky, I notice. I wonder is he even coming tonight.

I do some stretches while they all continue to just stare at me.

I look at Senny and I try to reach out to him – what's the phrase, expand the olive branch?

'I thought you kicked very well against Bective,' I go. 'It was one of the upsides for us – especially the conversion. It was a pretty tough angle.'

He looks at me like I've just offered to braid his hair. He goes, 'Do you honestly think I need compliments from you?'

I found out, by the way, through Googling him, that Senny won a Leinster Schools Senior Cup runners-up medal with Clongowes last year. Of course now he thinks he knows it all.

A runners-up medal. I can't stress that enough.

I'm there, 'I'm actually saying fair focks to you, Senny.'

He goes, 'And I'm saying that means nothing to me. You can't even think without moving your lips – and, what, you're going to tell me how to play number ten?'

That's when Bucky arrives. He sees me standing there and he laughs – except not in a good way. He shakes his head.

Byrom goes, 'You're loyte. Hurry up and choynge.'

Then out into the February wind and rain we go.

I end up putting in an unbelievable shift, determined not to let them break my spirit. I throw myself at the scrum machine like a bull at a gate and I manage to correctly guess most of the lineout calls and my throws end up being pretty much perfect.

There ends up being a moment just before the Captain's Run when Bucky tries to give me a shoulder nudge, except I actually *anticipate* it? I just horden my shoulder and he ends up coming off worse. It's like he's walked into a wall.

I'm happy with my evening's work, as is Byrom, who puts his orm around my shoulder as I'm leaving the pitch and goes, 'What yoy just dud took character. Good on yoy, Moyte.'

It's just what I need to hear. But when we get back to the dressing room, it ends up all kicking off again.

I'm actually throwing on my civvies when I notice that Bucky is holding several sheets of paper in his hand. I have no idea what the fock they are, but from the way he's looking at me, I suspect that I'm about to find out.

'Coach,' he goes, 'can I talk to you about something?'

Byrom's like, 'What's on your moynd, Bucky?'

'It's actually something I found on the Internet. Something I think should be of interest to everyone in this dressing room.'

'So what us ut? Put us aaht of our musery.'

'Well, the headline is *Former Schools Cup Hero Guilty of Doping.*'

Fock.

I shake my head and I pull a face to suggest that this is as much a mystery to me as it is to everyone else in the room. I could always claim it's a different Ross O'Carroll-Kelly.

The dude then storts reading out the piece.

He's there, 'South Dublin school Castlerock College are to be stripped of the Leinster Schools Senior Cup title they won in 1999 after an admission by their former captain that the school had a doping programme. Ross O'Carroll-Kelly, who was once tipped as a future Ireland number ten, recently admitted in an interview that he had used performance-enhancing drugs extensively in the lead-up to the school's only schools cup triumph on St Patrick's Day 1999. Newbridge College, who finished as runners-up, will now be awarded the title.'

There's a lot of, like, headshaking and all the rest of it.

I'm getting ready to get my excuses in. It's a pretty common name, nothing was actually proven – blah, blah blah. But that's when Byrom goes, 'Oy knoy all abaht ut. Oy can use the Internut as will, you knoy?'

Bucky's like, 'So you know he's a drug cheat and you're still happy to have him in the team?'

I still haven't said a word, bear in mind.

Byrom goes, 'Ut was a long toym agoy. He was just a kud.'

Bucky looks at me then. He's like, 'Do you have anything to say? I mean, are you on drugs now?'

I'm there, 'No, I'm not on drugs now.'

He goes, 'And we're supposed to just believe that, are we?'

I'm like, 'Hey, it was a few methamphetamine injections and then something unpronounceable that they use on racehorses. I've never made any secret of what I did – well, not once my solicitor advised me to change my plea from not guilty to guilty.'

'So you're a cheat – you're admitting that?'

'I suppose you *could* make the argument that what I did was cheating. But I would have still been great – with or without drugs.'

It's actually Senny who throws in his Fiddy Cent's worth then.

'We're bottom of the table,' he goes, 'and we're facing relegation to Division 2C. But I'd rather go down fighting honestly than stay up doing it some other way. At least I can put my hand on my hort and say that I've deserved everything I've achieved in the game.'

There's, like, applause from the rest of the team.

'Which is what exactly?' I hear myself go.

He's like, 'What did you just say?'

'I'm asking you what exactly you think you've achieved in the game. You're the kicker on a team that hasn't won a match all season. Apparently, you *nearly* made the Leinster Academy last year, just like you *nearly* made the first team in Lansdowne. Oh, and you've got a Leinster Schools Senior Cup medal – a focking *runners-up* medal!'

Everyone goes, 'Whooooaaahhh!' because I'm dissing not only him but two or three others in this dressing room who were on the same Clongowes team.

I'm there, 'For all your talent, you're the ultimate nearly man, aren't you?'

He tries to go, 'There's a lot of current Irish internationals who don't have a Leinster Schools Senior Cup medal of any colour,' which is a weak comeback, it has to be said.

I'm there, 'I won a runners-up medal myself back in 1998 – the year before I won the real thing. Do you want to know what I did with it?'

He goes, 'You better not say what I think you're about to say.'

'I used it to pick the mud off my boots, then I focked it in the Dodder. I just figured it was the best place for it. What with it being a medal for focking losers.'

He stares at me for a good ten seconds, seething.

I'm there, 'If you had any self-respect, you'd do exactly the same thing with yours.'

He suddenly makes a run at me, except three or four of the goys grab him and hold him back. They're going, 'He's not worth it, Senny. He's a fat focker and he's finished.'

I grab my gear bag and I go, 'Thanks for the session, goys,' just letting them know that I'm mentally strong enough to take whatever gets thrown at me from here on in. 'I'll see you on Thursday night.'

I head out to the cor. Byrom follows me outside. He's like, 'Russ?' and I turn around. He goes, 'Well done, Moyt.'

I'm there, 'I'm not sure it was. I think I've just succeeded in pissing them off even more.'

'Ut's what Sinnoy noyds to hear. Yes, he's got begs of potintial, but you're toytally royt – he's achoyved nothing. He has a hibit of bloying ut on the bug occasions. He noyds to hear ut. Look, Oy want to puck yoy for the goym aginst Hoyfoyld.'

'Highfield? When are we talking?'

'A woyk on Saturdoy. Ut's in Cork.'

'I don't know, Byrom. Look, I'm really glad I came back tonight – especially after what happened at the weekend. I think I proved one or two doubters wrong. I may have even proved a thing or two to myself. But I can't see these goys ever accepting me.'

'Trust moy – they wull. Yoy're gonna wun them oyver.'

'And how am I going to do that?'

'Boy maahstering the daahk aahts.'

'The what?'

'The daahk aahts.'

'Are you trying to say dork orts?'

'Exictloy. The daahk aahts. Look, Oy knoy that yoy ployed at number tin, but yoy must remimber some of the trucks poyple got up toy in the scrum back in the doy.'

'Yeah, no, I suppose I do.'

'Well, that's what Oy want from yoy. Thoyse ployers, Russ, they're all incridibloy strong and fut, but they're toy facken soft. They ploy boy the royles. Do yoy knoy what Oy moyn?'

'Not really, no.'

'A lot of thoyse referoys we're coming up aginst in the A.I.L. are boying faahst-tricked by the IRFU. They're young – unexperienced. Yoy can royly troy it on wuth them. Do you git moy?'

'I think I do now.'

'That's what Oy want to see from yoy aginst Hoyfoyld nixt woyk. These opposition pecks – they're kicking the shut aaht of us. We noyd to haahden up. Thut's what Oy thunk yoy can bring toy the toym.'

'Look, Dude, I'm very flattered that you'd think that about me. But it's a different game to the one I played.'

'Lit moy aahsk yoy something. Since yoy funushed ploying the goym, did yoy ivver git the sinse thut moyboy yoy dudn't fulfill your potintial?'

'Every day of my life.'

'That moyboy yoy had unfunushed business? That moyboy yoy stull had something toy offer?'

'Like I said, I feel like that all the time.'

'Well, woyk up, Moyte, because your toym has come. Ut's here. Ut's naah.'


It's, like, Saturday morning and I arrive home from reading Gerry Thornley's Ireland v France preview over brunch in Dalkey to find

Sorcha standing in the hallway, grinning at me like a focking chimp with lockjaw.

I go, 'Is everything alright, Babes?' because I know from past experience that, when a woman smiles at you, it's not necessarily an indication of happiness. It *often* is? But there are no guarantees – that's the point I'm trying to make.

A smile from Sorcha could mean a million different things. So the key is to take nothing for granted.

'If this is about the toilet in the en-suite,' I go, 'I tried to flush it twice before I went out.'

She walks over to me, puts her two orms around my neck and kisses me full on the mouth, the way she used to kiss me when we were, like, first going *out* together? I've kissed a lot of girls in my time, but no one does it as well as Sorcha – when she's on her game.

Okay, I'm thinking, so it's definitely not the dancing bear in the upstairs jacks.

'I'm going to repeat the question,' I go. 'Is everything okay?'

She laughs. 'Everything is fine,' she goes. 'I'm just the luckiest girl in the world, that's all.'

I'm there, 'Is this about me being back playing rugby? Because I'm definitely in the team to play Highfield next weekend.'

'It's nothing to do with rugby. I'm just letting you know that I appreciate what an amazing, amazing husband you are.'

Oh my God, I think we're about to have sex.

'Listen,' she goes.

I do.

I'm there, 'I can't hear anything.'

She goes, 'Exactly. I dropped Honor down to Caleb's house and my mom and dad have taken the boys to Imaginosity!'

I stort unbuttoning my shirt before another word is even spoken.

She grabs me by the hand and we race up the stairs. We kiss on the landing, then I pick her up, carry her into the bedroom and throw her down on the bed.

We're all over each other like DNA.

I reach for the drawer. I'm there, 'Hang on. I just need to throw on a scrumcap.'

'No, you don't,' she goes. 'Er, you had a *vasectomy*, remember?'

And I'm like, 'Oh, er, yeah, that's right!'

My wife thinks I had a vasectomy. It's well over a year ago now. I possibly should tell her that I didn't go through with it, except it only seems to occur to me when we're about to have sex, and it's the kind of detail that I always feel might possibly *spoil* the moment?

So we stort going at each other like crazy people, tearing at each other's clothes, mouths snapping away, promises and threats exchanged in the heat of the moment. And there I'm going to draw a discreet veil on proceedings out of respect for all the participants involved. Some people like to advertise what goes on in the bedroom. Not me. That's not how the Rossmeister rolls.

It's probably enough just to say that everyone ends up having a fun day at the fair. Especially her. At one point – I think it's fair to call it the climax of the action for hopefully *both* porties? – I'm standing in the doorway and Sorcha has her legs wrapped around my waist and she's bobbing up and down like she's on a baby door bouncer and she's bleating madly like a sheep caught in a borbed-wire fence.

But then, like I said, I'm a gentleman.

Afterwards, we lie on the bed to try to get our breath back. Sorcha discusses various ways in which we could improve the experience for her next time – our old friend Duration gets its usual mench – while I nod off mid-conversation and sleep for what feels like two hours.

When I wake again, I remember that I'm supposed to be meeting the goys for one or two lunchtime scoops before we head to the Aviva.

I throw on my T-shirt and my boxers and I tip downstairs to the kitchen, thinking to myself, Do you know what would make this *the* perfect day – aport from obviously a win against France? If Sorcha's old man walked through the front door right now and saw me in my jockeys, with a dirty grin on my face, stinking of sex with his daughter!

Unfortunately, that doesn't happen.

I open the fridge. The first thing I do is pull the leg off the cooked chicken that Sorcha bought for tonight's dinner. That's going to be my storter. I horse into it, close the fridge and sit down on one of the high stools.

And that's when I suddenly see the flowers on the island in front of me. I recognize them straightaway as roses.

I count them.

One, two, three, four, five, six, seven, eight, nine, ten, eleven – and that one there makes twelve.

I find the little cord in among them. It's just like, 'To Sorcha. With all my love. Happy Valentine's Day xxx.'

I put the cord back and I pick the rest of the chicken leg clean. If there's one lesson I've learned today, it's that you can never under-estimate how happy a girl will be to receive a bunch of flowers. They totally focking love them.

But I can tell you something else – with my hand on my hort. I didn't actually send these to my wife. As a matter of fact, I didn't even know it was Valentine's Day.

Leo has learned a new word. It's not 'train' or 'banana' or even 'please' or 'thank you'.

It's 'bastard'.

He tries it out for the first time while we're in the gorden, throw-ing the ball around. I make the mistake of laughing and of course that really gets him going.

'Bastard!' he's going, at the top of his voice now. 'Bastard! Bas-tard! Fock! Shit! Bastard!'

I go, 'Shush, shush, shush,' and I throw him the ball. He catches it – he's already got unbelievable hands – but then Brian absolutely creams him with a tackle. Leo ends up spilling the ball and then him and Brian end up rolling around on the ground, scratching and smacking and trying to bite each other.

I think to myself, Actually – do you know what? – let them at it. It'll horden the two of them up.

Of course, Johnny suddenly bursts into tears watching them go at each other – I'm storting to wonder is he going to be into soccer – and that's when Sorcha steps out into the gorden and goes, 'Ross, I can't believe you have them out in this cold!'

I'm there, 'It's a winter game, Sorcha. It's best that they get acclimatized to it now.'

'Come on,' she goes, picking Johnny up, 'let's get them indoors.'

I grab Brian and Leo and bring them inside to the kitchen.

Sorcha goes, 'I've made some of my Jamie Oliver butternut squash soup – will you ask Honor does she want some?'

So I tip upstairs to her bedroom. And that's when, standing outside her door, I end up hearing it. The sound of my daughter sobbing.

Now, I could count on one hand the number of times I've heard Honor cry and still have enough fingers left over to let Dan Biggar know what I think of his focking OCD, pre-kick ritual. The point I'm trying to make is that Honor has never been a crier. Even as a baby, she considered it a sign of weakness. Which is why it upsets me way more than it would if it was, say, Sorcha, who'll cry at literally anything – Ed Sheeran lyrics, roadkill, anything with Gerard Butler in it.

I push the door. I'm like, 'Hey, Honor, are you okay?'

She's sitting on her bed with her back to me. She storts wiping her face with her hand, trying to clean up her tears before I can actually see them. She's like, 'I'm fine.'

I walk over to her and I sit down on the bed beside her. Her eyes are all red and her face is still wet.

I'm there, 'Do you want to talk about it? And, hey, it's cool if you don't. It might be easier to talk to your old dear.'

She doesn't say anything for ages. Then she goes, 'Caleb wants us to be just friends.'

I'm there, 'Oh . . . right.'

'I sent him a cord for Valentine's Day and he didn't send me one and then he didn't reply to any of my text messages and then he rang me and I asked him why didn't he send me a cord and he said he didn't like me in *that* way?'

She's sobbing her little hort out. I put my orm around her and I pull her close to me and she just, like, melts into my chest.

See, she spends so much of her life doing evil that you forget sometimes that she's still just a little girl with feelings, the same as everyone else.

'If you ask me,' I go, 'he needs his head focking examined.'

She goes, 'But how can I make him like me, Dad? How can I make him like me in *that* way?'

My hort breaks.

I'm there, 'I don't know, Honor. I genuinely don't know the answer to that question. You could try getting off with one of his friends. I'm just thinking out loud here.'

'I don't like any of his friends.'

'You don't have to like them, Honor. The whole point is to piss him off or make him jealous.'

'Mum always said that if I was a nice girl, then boys would like me.'

'Look, your mother's got a lot of shite going on in her head. The thing is, Honor, you can't *make* people like you. Everyone has their own taste. Some people like strawberry jam. Some people like marmalade. Strawberry jam can't do anything to make me want to eat it. All strawberry jam can do is just carry on being strawberry jam, happy in the knowledge that at least *someone* out there is going to like it. It's the same with people, Honor. Not everyone is going to feel the way about you that you feel about them. That's a fact of life. All you can do is just be yourself.'

'I don't want to be myself. I want to be pretty.'

'You are pretty.'

'I'm not. I know I'm not. I'm really plain and I have horrible hair and disgusting teeth.'

'Those are things we can fix, Honor. Your mother's going to bring you to the orthodontist – do you remember that conversation?'

'He likes someone else.'

'Who are we talking about?'

'Caleb. He likes another girl.'

'How do you know that?'

'He told me. He told me when he said that he just wanted us to be friends. He said he was in love with someone.'

Shit.

She goes, 'What?'

I'm there, 'I didn't say anything.'

'You did. You said, "Shit." Oh my God, you know something!'

'I don't know anything – I'm giving you my word.'

'You do know something. I can see it in your face.'

'Honor, I've just given you my word. That has to count for something.'

'Tell me! Tell me what you know!'

'Okay, then. Look, you're not going to like this, but I'm going to have to tell you because you caught me lying.'

'What?'

'He's in love with your mother.'

'What?'

'He loves Sorcha. Now, she hasn't led him on – I want to say that in her defence. She's actually still in denial about the whole thing. But he sent her flowers.'

'He sent *her* flowers?'

'Yeah, no, for Vally's Day. Keep that to yourself, by the way. Your old dear somehow got it into her head that they were from me and, well, I'd like to keep it that way.'

She goes suddenly quiet.

I'm there, 'I actually copped it pretty much from the stort – the day you were watching that movie with Rachel McAdams in it. I could see he had a thing for her.'

'It's because *she's* pretty and I'm not.'

'I disagree with that analysis.'

'It's true.'

'Again, I see it differently. Looks are obviously important, Honor, but they're not the be-all and end-all. Have you ever heard the phrase, "It's personality that counts"?'

'No.'

'Yeah, no, you don't hear it mentioned much anymore. I think Irish people were genuinely a lot more ugly back in the 1990s. Something to do with our diet probably. The point I'm trying to make is that one day, Honor, you're going to meet someone who thinks you're the greatest thing that was ever born, who'll just have to think about you and, seriously, his hort will be focking raving.

Someone is going to fall for you very, very hord, and you'll fall for him, and you won't even think twice about this so-called Caleb.'

'You have to say that because you're my dad.'

'I also have to say it because it's a fact. Honor, I wish you could see what I see when I look at you.'

'Which is what? I'm not good-looking. I don't even have a nice personality. I'm horrible.'

'You're far from horrible, Honor. I shouldn't say this, but you're actually my favourite of all my kids.'

'No, I'm not. What about Brian and Johnny and Leo?'

'Don't get me wrong, I love them – of course I do. We've got rugby and all the rest of it ahead of us. But I don't have the bond with them that I have with you. Hey, do you remember we burned all your granddad's books? Do you remember he had a complete shit-fit? And do you remember we had to send you to a child psychiatrist?'

She laughs through her tears. I think, deep down, she realizes that what I'm talking here is *sense*?

She dries her eyes and goes, 'Fock him. Fock Caleb.'

I'm there, 'That's the spirit. He's not even that good-looking. Well, he is – but that whole Bieber thing is going to get old.'

'If he doesn't like me,' she goes, 'he's not worthy of me.'

'Exactly. The only thing in this world that's worth being, Honor, is yourself.'

Oisinn answers the phone on the fourth ring.

He's like, 'Hello?' and it sounds like he's asleep.

I'm there, 'Hey, Dude, how are things in Guitar?'

He goes, 'It's pronounced Qatar, Ross.'

'Yeah, no,' I go, 'that's the only way I'm going to remember it. By saying Guitar. How are things either way?'

He's there, 'Yeah, they're good. Some good meetings.'

'Where are you? You sound like you're in bed.'

'I am in bed. It's, like, three o'clock in the morning over here.'

I laugh. I've never really gotten my head around that whole

different time-zones thing. When someone in, say, Australia or the States tells me that it's night-time there when it's daytime here, there's a little bit of me that doesn't believe them.

I'm there, 'Yeah, no, the reason I wanted to talk to you was, well, do you remember I mentioned that I was thinking about going back playing rugby?'

He's like, 'Yeah?'

'Okay, I haven't told many people this. I wanted to keep it below the radar. Sorcha knows and obviously the old man – the knob. Dude, I played for Seapoint the weekend before last. I made my All Ireland League debut after fifteen years out of the game.'

He laughs, but not in a *bad* way? 'Jesus!' he goes. 'How did you get on?'

I'm there, 'Well, let's just say the game *has* moved on a bit since me and you played. I accept that now.'

'I presume your kicking game is still as good as it was.'

'That's the thing, Dude. I know this is going to sound totally random, but I'm not playing outhalf. I'm playing in *your* old position?'

'What?'

'I'm a hooker.'

He laughs. 'Hang on,' he goes, 'I think I'm still dreaming here! Are you serious?'

I'm there, 'How many times have you ever heard me joke about rugby?'

'Point taken. So what happened?'

'Well, let's just say that the rest of the team aren't too happy with the idea of an old-stager – albeit a legend of the schools game – coming back to play for them. I need to win them over, Dude.'

'How are you going to do that?'

'You need to tell me what went on, Oisinn, in the scrum? I'm talking about back in the day.'

He's quiet for a long time – to the point that I think he might have actually hung *up*?

Eventually, he goes, 'It was a long time ago, Ross.'

I'm there, 'I never knew what happened in there. I mean, as far as I was concerned, it was your job to put your bodies on the line so that the pretty boys like me and JP and Christian could do our stuff.'

'Like I said, Ross, it was another age.'

'Oisinn, all I'm looking for is a few tips.'

'You don't need tips from me. You know your rugby.'

'I love hearing you say that. I've got goosebumps here.'

'You know what the position involves. You know what you have to do after the put-in?'

'Pretty much.'

'Try to push their front row back and don't let your opposite number hook the ball.'

'Yeah, I know all that.'

'And you know how to throw a lineout ball. Your lineout throw was better than mine.'

'This is doing unbelievable things for my confidence. But, Dude, what I'm actually looking for here is something that might give me an advantage – you know what I mean?'

'Are you talking about drugs?'

'No, I'm not talking about drugs. I'm determined to do it clean this time – prove the critics wrong once and for all. Dude, I'm talking about, you know, the rough stuff.'

'Ah,' he goes, at the same time laughing, 'you're asking me about the secrets of the scrum – what the Kiwis call the Daahk Aahts.'

'The Dork Orts. That's exactly it.'

He thinks about this for a good ten seconds, then he goes, 'When is your next match?'

I'm there, 'We're playing Highfield on Saturday.'

'Okay, don't shave between now and then.'

'Don't shave? I like to look my best, Oisinn, whether I'm a forward or not.'

'Well, from now on, that's no longer your priority. The front row is no beauty contest.'

'I love that quote. I might write that somewhere.'

'You want about a week's worth of stubble. Then when you go cheek to cheek with their number two, give him a good rub with it – it's like sandpaper.'

'That's it?'

'After twenty minutes, his face will be red raw and – trust me – it'll be the only thing he can think about. The beauty of it is, these young goys you're going to be playing against, they're all just muscle. They think the game is about lifting weights and being big. Your opposite number is going to be, what, twenty, twenty-one?'

'They're all definitely young alright.'

'He won't have had anyone do that to him before. Then you stort sledging him. Get in his ear. Give him dog's abuse.'

'About being from Cork? Because I can think of loads of shit to throw at Cork people.'

'You'll need something better than that, Ross. The thing is, people from Cork actually *like* being from Cork?'

'What then?'

'That's your job, Ross. That's what scrummaging is all about. You've got to find your opponent's breaking-point.'

I'm like, 'Dude, thanks – I owe you big-time.'

It's, like, just after ten o'clock on the day of the match and I'm awoken by the sound of voices downstairs in the kitchen. I check my phone. It's, like, one hour before the bus leaves for Cork.

Sorcha's talking to someone – it sounds like another woman.

Yeah, no, but who?

I throw on my clothes, then I tip downstairs to investigate. I walk into the kitchen to find my wife sitting at the island, drinking cappuccinos from the good Denby cups, with a woman, who is, I'm guessing, in her forties, with – and this is going to sound weird, but bear with me – a skinhead. We're talking a blade four all over. It's not everyone suits tight hair. It *can* make a woman look like a focking thug. But this woman has the features to carry it off – especially the eyes. I literally can't stop looking at her.

I'm like, 'Hello, there,' laying it on like Nutella.

'Ross,' Sorcha goes, 'this is Flidais – as in, Caleb's mom!'

I'm all, 'Hello, Flidais as in Caleb's mom,' in my seductive voice. 'It's lovely to meet you.'

She goes, 'It's nice to meet you, too.'

Her head is, like, perfectly focking round. She's one of the most beautiful women I've ever seen in my life. And I've been around a few corners.

I look around me. The kitchen is the usual scene of chaos. There are toys strewn all over the floor. Brian is in his chair, eating his breakfast slash lunch. Leo is sitting on his mat, shouting 'Focking bastard!' at his mother, while Johnny is sitting on the floor a few feet away, sucking on a Flash Wipe.

I take it from him and I pick him up. I look at Flidais and I go, 'God, I'm supposed to be playing a rugby match today – in Cork of all places.'

Sorcha can see that I'm flirting, so she tries to, like, drag my attention away. She goes, 'Speaking of which, you'd better get going. What time does the bus leave?'

I'm there, 'Eleven o'clock. It's, like, a 3.30 kick-off. Plenty of time. Where's Honor, by the way?'

Sorcha goes, 'She and Caleb are in the living room, watching *The Life of Pi.*'

Jesus Christ, a week ago she said she was done with him. Oh, well. Such is the female mind. There's focking geniuses who couldn't get to the bottom of it. What chance have I got?

I'm there, 'I didn't think she was a fan of that film. She walked out of the cinema after, like, twenty minutes.'

'Well,' Sorcha goes, 'I was the one who said she'd love it if she gave it an actual chance!'

That's when Flidais, totally out of the blue, goes, 'So, em, can I talk to you guys about something that's a little bit, well, delicate?'

'Oh my God,' Sorcha goes. 'What is it, Flidais?'

The woman goes, 'Okay, well, I don't know if you're aware of this, but Caleb has told Honor that he doesn't want them to be, you know, boyfriend-girlfriend?'

Sorcha's there, 'I know, it's *such* a shame. But I think they're going to be – oh my God – *such* good friends. Which is lovely, because Honor's never really had many friends, has she, Ross?'

Correction. Honor's never really had *any* friends.

'Well,' Flidais goes, 'I know Honor's a lovely girl, but I think

Caleb may have, well, an ulterior motive in wanting to spend so much time in this house.'

Sorcha's like, 'Go on.'

She's slower than Lent.

Flidais goes, 'I think Caleb may have a bit of a crush on you, Sorcha.'

Of course, Sorcha acts all shocked, even though I called it right from the stort.

I'm there, 'A bit of a crush? He told me that when he turned eighteen he was going to take her off me. He said it to my face as well. He said he was going to marry her.'

Sorcha tries to laugh. 'But they're just silly things you say when you're young,' she goes, 'even though I've always believed that children's emotions are just as valid as those of adults.'

I don't think I'm far off the mork in saying that there's a little bit of Sorcha that's actually *flattered* by all of this?

'Well,' Flidais goes, 'I just wanted to mention it, just so you were aware of it. I mean, he talks about you *all* the time! As in, like, *constantly*?'

'That's kind of sweet.'

'He wanted to phone you the other night. He'd read something on the Internet about – was it about Nelson Mandela?'

'Madiba, yes. I showed him my letters.'

'Yes, he mentioned that. But I had to have a chat with him about boundaries and what was and wasn't appropriate contact. I mean, I hated doing it, but he was about to phone you at, like, eleven o'clock at night.'

I've been so focused on her boat race and her beautiful baldy head that I didn't notice her incredible mushmellons.

She goes, 'I mean, I agree with you, Sorcha, I do think it's just a harmless crush. But, well, let's just say we've been down this road before.'

I'm there, 'Oh?'

She's like, 'Well, last year, it was Miss Dubois, his French teacher – I know she became a little bit uncomfortable with it in the end. Before that, it was Brandusa, our cleaner.'

Hey, I'm in no position to judge the kid. As an occasional visitor to Howl at the Moon back in the day, I've had my hands on more old ladies than Massey's Funeral Home. But still.

'It really storted happening after my husband and I broke up,' she goes.

Whoa, I'm thinking – plot twist!

I'm there, 'I'm sorry to hear that, Flidais. That's, um, shit.'

She goes, 'Oh, it's okay. It's three years ago now. Davin was a cheater.'

'Why do men have to be that way?' I go. 'It's the kind of thing that gives the rest of us a bad name.'

Sorcha doesn't pull me up on it, even though there's shit she could say. She goes, 'And what, Flidais, this is his way of acting out?'

'Well,' she goes, 'I took him to a counsellor, who reckoned his interest in older women was his attempt to create a surrogate marriage to replace his parents' marriage. It's complicated.'

Sorcha goes, 'Well, as long as you don't think it's a problem, Flidais, I'm happy to just ignore it and let it hopefully run its course.'

It's at that exact point that the little focking weirdo shows his face in the kitchen. He goes, 'Mum, can I sleep here tonight?'

Flidais goes, 'What? No, of course you can't sleep here!'

'Honor said I could.'

'Well, maybe it's not Honor's place to tell you that.'

'If I ask Sorcha and Sorcha says yes, then can I sleep here?'

The little blond head on him – he really is full of himself.

'Caleb,' Flidais goes, 'how many times have I had the conversation with you about what is and isn't appropriate behaviour?'

Caleb's there, 'Is it because *he* doesn't want me to stay?'

*He*, by the way, is me. He flicks his thumb in my general postcode.

'I'll answer that,' I go. 'I definitely don't want you staying here. I'm with your French teacher on this one – Miss *Bleu Bleu Bleu* – I find the whole thing a bit creepy.'

Sorcha's like, 'Ross!'

I'm there, 'I call as I see, Sorcha. I call as I see.'

I walk out of the kitchen and I tip up to the living room, where Honor is sitting with the movie paused.

'What's it like?' I go. 'Is it a steaming pile of shit like you said before?'

She's like, 'No – it's actually a really good movie if you give it a chance.'

'I remember, just before you walked out of the cinema, you were cheering for the tiger to eat the kid. It was very funny.'

In her eyes, I'm sure I can see a faint flicker of the old Honor.

I'm there, 'You shouted, "Eat the focking kid, already – he's been pissing me off since the opening credits!" It was one of my favourite of all your quotes. Do you know who else loved that quote?'

She goes, 'Who?'

'Your Auntie Erika.'

'Did she?'

'And she's a *real* bitch. The genuine orticle. She laughed for a good ten minutes when Sorcha told her.'

After a few seconds, she goes, 'Well, that was before. It's actually a good movie. Can Caleb sleep here tonight?'

I'm like, 'No, he can't.'

'Why not?'

'Honor, look, he's told you he's not interested. Not in that way.'

'I know he doesn't want to go out with me, but we can still be friends.'

'Men and women can't be friends, Honor. It's never worked and it never will.'

'Well, I've decided that I'd rather have him in my life as a friend than not have him in my life at all.'

It kills me to hear my daughter talking like that. She's going to get dicked around her entire life if that's what she genuinely believes.

'Honor,' I go, 'take it from me, this thing isn't going anywhere. He has a thing for older women because there's something wrong with him. Right now it happens to be your mother. As soon as it wears off, you're not going to have him in your life either way.'

'That's not true.'

'I'm saying this out of concern for you. Get out now, Honor, before you get hurt.'

But Honor gives it the full theatrics. She bursts into tears and runs out of the room, going, 'I can't get out! I can't get out! I'm too in love with him!'

The Highfield players are singing whatever that focking song is called – 'The Banks of My Own Lovely Lee'. This is before they even go out on the pitch. One thing is for sure – their mothers didn't raise many singers.

'Lusten to thet,' Byrom goes. 'Thut's called pession. They want to wun. If woy doyn't at loyst mitch thet pession, woy moyt as will goy hoyme naah. They sing thut song to troy to intumidoyt us. Are woy gonna boy intumidoyted?'

We're all like, 'No!'

'Oy sid, are woy gonna boy intumidoyted?'

We're all there, 'NO!' except even *louder* this time?

He goes, 'Thet's good to hear. Because a lot of toyms come here and they're boyten before thoy oyven stip ontoy the foyld of ploy. That's whoy they're singing in there – abaaht thet fuckun river. Ut's their woy of litting yoy goys knoy thut they're unoytud – they have a collivtuv identitoy. They're from Cork – and thut moyns something to them.'

'Fock Cork!' Maho shouts. 'Fock them and their English Morket and their Jazz Festival and their ridiculous up-and-downy way of talking.'

From the reaction, it's obvious he speaks for everyone here.

Dordo goes, 'Yeah, if they want to talk like that, why don't they just go and *live* in focking Wales.'

There's no doubt we're pumped for this one.

'Alroyt,' Bucky goes, 'lit moy soy some of thet attitoyde aaht on the putch.'

As we're leaving the dressing room, he pulls Bucky to one side and I hear him go, 'Oy hoype your luttle strop is oyver, Moyte, because you pull inny of thut shut you dud the laahst doy with the loyn-ahht calls, Oy'm toyking yoy off – captain or not. Do yoy understaahnd moy?'

I don't actually hear Bucky's answer because I'm already walking out onto the pitch.

Highfield make us wait before they come out. It's all port of their game plan, I'm sure. Then out they trot. Again, they're young – they're basically kids to me, we're talking twenty-two, maybe twenty-three years old.

They don't think much of us, judging from the way they're looking at us.

I hear their loosehead turn to their tighthead and go, 'Aren't they a fine clutch! Oh, tis mighty fun we'll have this day, swatting them away like harvest midges dying for the want of a bite!'

Or maybe that's just what *I* hear when people from the country talk.

I'm looking for their hooker and then I suddenly cop him with the number two on his back. He's a big focker – we're talking fifteen, maybe sixteen stone of pure muscle. He's got, like, a proper gym body, which he's obviously proud of, judging from the way he carries himself. But he's younger than the others – we're talking nineteen or twenty at the most, with a handsome, tanned face.

He catches my eye and goes, 'God welcome you! If a finger was in your eye, you wouldn't see it for the thrubble that's coming your road this day! You may ask the Lord Himself for His Mercy, for tis known He prefers prayers to tears!'

The other Highfield players seem to find this hilarious.

I rub my hand over my stubbly face, then we suddenly kick off.

From what I can gather from the shouts of his teammates, his name seems to be Con. And it doesn't take long before I come literally face to face with him when we're awarded a scrum right on their twenty-two-metre line with only, like, three or four minutes gone.

We bind, Bucky to my right, Maho to my left, then we engage. Badoom! Two tonnes of bone and muscle colliding. As I'm coming in, I give this Con focker a good rub with my stubble, right on his focking cheekbone. I hear him go, 'The devil mend you!' but it only increases his determination to hook the ball, which he does and they end up winning the scrum.

But a couple of minutes later, there ends up being another one – this time, it's *their* put-in? I do the same shit. I hit him on the exact same spot with my chin – an even *horder* rub this time?

He goes, 'The crow's curse on you!' and I end up shunting him back a good ten metres, showing unbelievable strength, before their scrum just collapses like a detonated building and we're awarded a penalty right in front of the chopsticks.

As I'm climbing to my feet again, Con gives me a shove in the chest. 'Upon my word, you're a polished trickster!' he goes. 'And you laughing from the teeth out!'

One of his teammates ends up having to drag him away, going, 'Fret not, you'll have your own back, for it is true for you as it's true for me – there's no cure for misfortune than to kill it with patience!'

Bucky slaps me on the back and goes, 'Well done, Rossi!' Not Ross, or Rosser, or even the Rossmeister General. He calls me Rossi. It's a new one. But then this is a new me, so I don't bother correcting him. I just go, 'Thanks, Dude,' then I pick up the ball, throw it to Senny and I go, 'Now you do *your* thing.'

Which he does. He slots it over to put us 3–0 up.

The Highfield players stort complaining to the referee. Their captain goes, 'You haven't the eyes to see a bull nor a thimbleful of sense, for tis obvious their hooker is the very devil for causing thrubble – and him still waiting for you to give him a bar of your tongue!'

But the referee looks a good five years younger than I am. I look at him and I'm there, 'There's fock-all in the rules about having to have a shave before a match. It's like Nigel Owens always says – it's not soccer.'

The referee seems to accept this explanation and he tells the Highfield players that I haven't broken any laws.

It storts to rain, then – as in, like, *really* pissing down? The pitch quickly turns wet and slippery. It's already obvious that this isn't going to be a day for free-flowing rugby with lots of pretty tries. It's one of those days when you could nearly tell players eleven-to-fifteen to get back on the bus now. They have no business being here. Today is going to be all about the forwards.

Still buzzing on my early success in the scrum, I end up throwing myself into tackles. I'm sore all over from about the tenth minute. After a short while, I stort to become aware of a familiar voice calling from the sideline, going, 'That's it, Seapoint! It's a day for the proverbial boot, bite and bollock!'

I actually laugh. He came all the way down to Cork to see me play. He's un-focking-believable. I know I give him a hord time, but he's always there to support me, no matter what I'm doing.

'Who's that annoying focker?' Maho goes as we're binding for another scrum.

I'm there, 'I don't know. I've never seen him before in my life.'

Bucky goes, 'Must be one of the alickadoos. His voice is focking irritating, isn't it?'

It's instantly one of my favourite all-time quotes.

The two scrums engage again. I give Con another good rub of my chin and this time I end up drawing actual blood. I can feel, like, wet on my face as we shove their scrum back five metres, then ten metres, before they go down again.

The referee blows the whistle. Another penalty. Maho and Bucky both slap me on the upper orm. They're like, 'Well done, Rossi! Well done!'

Con jumps to his feet, blood pouring down his face, the skin around his cheekbone all torn, and he storts pointing at me in, like, a threatening way. He goes, 'Bad cess to you! May your crop be tall and your *meitheal* small and may there never be enough of your people to make a half-set!'

The referee tells him to calm down.

Con goes, 'He's putting the roguery across on us all. Haven't you eyes in your head to see he had the face torn off me with his beard?'

I just happen to go, 'Yeah, no, I'm surprised you don't like it – your focking girlfriend loves it when I do it to her.'

It's just a throwaway line, roysh – the kind of shit you throw at each other the entire time on the rugby field – but the dude reacts like I've said something way worse than I actually have.

He grabs a fistful of my shirt and there ends up being a shoving match involving all fifteen players from each side.

When the referee finally restores order, Senny kicks us into a six-point lead.

I can tell that I'm slowly gaining the trust and the respect of my teammates, because when we win our first lineout midway through the half, Bucky makes the code easy for me to crack by using a short country name and an animal that I've actually heard of.

He goes, 'Cuba two dog.'

I cover my mouth with the ball while I reason it out. I go, 'Okay, so you drop the dog. Then it's, like, two, which means it's the second-last letter of the country name, which is Cuba, which I'm guessing is spelt Q, U, B, A, which means the letter is B, which means the ball has to go to the . . . hang on . . . *back* of the lineout.'

I throw the ball and it finds its torget. Maho catches it and we get a rolling maul going. Teamwork makes the dream work – that's another one of Father Fehily's phrases.

It's a seriously shit game of rugby, from a spectator's point of view. But we make it to half-time six points to the good.

I hear the old man shouting, 'A masterclass in scrummaging from the Seapoint number two!' like he thinks the whole world is his audience. 'Why isn't anyone from the IRFU here to see this? Fifteen years on, I'm forced to ask the question yet again!'

I look over and I spot him, standing next to K . . . K . . . K . . . K . . . Kennet, who obviously drove him down here. I give him a nod to say hello and he goes, 'Whither, Joe Schmidt – eh, Ross? You've already given him much to ponder here this afternoon!'

We get back to the dressing room. The forwards look like they've played eighty minutes instead of forty, while most of the backs have barely got a lick of mud on them. Another forty minutes like that and they won't even need to wash their gear.

Bucky holds his hand out to me. He's like, 'Mark Buck.'

He's actually introducing himself.

I shake his hand. I'm like, 'It's good to meet you, Dude.'

He storts pointing out goys to me – mainly the forwards. 'Barry O'Mahony, loosehead. Behind you, in the second row, that's Gilly over there – Graham Gilligan – and that's Dilly – Rob Dillon – with the big focking ears.'

I'm just, like, nodding at these goys and they're all, like, nodding at me.

'Back row,' Bucky goes, 'blindside flanker, Eddie Wynne. Openside flanker, Andy Walpole. Number eight is Goffo – Stephen Godfrey. Scrum-half – Davy Dardis. Outhalf – Senan Torsney. You can meet the rest of the goys some other day.'

Like I said, they might as well throw their civvies back on.

Byrom tells us to keep the intensity going in the second half, because Highfield will come back at us – we can count on that much.

Then he has a private word with me as I'm about to walk back out onto the pitch. He goes, 'Whativah ut us you're doying aaht there, koyp ut up.'

Bucky claps his hands together and goes, 'Come on, The Point!' and everyone's, like, kicking the walls and clenching their fists, actually storting to believe that we could get our first win of the season here today.

As both teams are walking out onto the field again, I tip over to the Highfield captain – who's their number ten – and I go, 'Dude, I'm sorry it all kicked off earlier. That was down to me. I was bang out of order.'

He's actually surprised that I'm apologizing to him, though shocked is possibly *more* the word? He goes, 'Bad scran to you, you blackguard!'

I'm there, 'Yeah, no, I genuinely mean it. Look, one thing you're guaranteed when you come to Munster is a tough, tough match. But Munster players are famous for another thing – and that's playing by the rules.'

It's utter horseshit, of course, but he seems to be buying it. Munster people love being told they're great.

I'm there, 'Sledging has no port to play in the modern game. The words just came out of my mouth and, you know, I wasn't expecting that reaction.'

'Lookit,' he goes, 'give a sharp ear to me now. Poor Con is senseless after a woman he lost and neither God nor Mary nor St Patrick can ease his suffering!'

I'm there, 'A woman? Is that why he reacted the way he did when I mentioned his girlfriend?'

'Indeed and indeed! And a finer-looking woman never stood in shoe leather – and she with skin as white as a swan! But, my sorrow, didn't she leave him for his brother and it's keening for her his heart is still! The cries out of him could be heard equally well in Kilcrohane as in Youghal!'

His brother? Jesus. I'm tempted to say, That's Cork for you.

Instead, I go, 'God, that's genuinely shit for him. Anyway, I'll definitely watch what I say in the second half. At the end of the day, it's only a nothing match, isn't it? You're mid-table and we're heading for relegation either way. It's not like there's anything at stake.'

The game restorts and Highfield do come back at us. For the first, like, fifteen minutes of the half, they end up throwing everything at us. There's some unbelievable hits going in. They stort gaining territory, hord yord by hord yord. Eventually, they make it to within five metres of our line.

Their number eight gets the ball in his hands and drives for the line, but I tackle him hord and he manages to spill it and Maho kicks it downfield and suddenly the siege is lifted. We all go haring after it and we spend the next five minutes pushing Highfield further and further back.

One of their players knocks the ball on and we suddenly have a scrum just inside their twenty-two. As the two front rows are doing the whole binding thing, I look at poor Con's face. One side of it is like a focking pizza – all red and raw.

'Engage!' the referee shouts.

We do.

As I'm coming at him, I give his face another quick sanding.

'Aaarrrggghhh!' he goes. 'My sharp grief!'

Then, as Dordo puts the ball in, I whisper in Con's ear, 'Yeah, no, I'd say that's the same noise your girlfriend makes when your brother's riding her!'

Suddenly, it's like pushing a revolving door – as in, there's no real resistance coming back. We gain about five yords – me, with the ball under my feet – until Con eventually gets over the shock and storts pushing back.

He storts trying to hook the ball. He almost manages it as well. He puts his foot on it. Then, again into his ear, I go, 'I'd say he's stuffing her right now! Saturday afternoon? Nothing focking surer! I'd say the headboard is knocking lumps of plaster off the wall!'

He's gone. We know it and they know it. It's suddenly eight of us pushing seven of them. We're pushing them further and further back. Dordo is standing at the back of the scrum, going, 'Give it, give it, give it!', looking for the ball so that he, or one of the backs, can finish the move.

But I keep rolling the ball forward under my studs and we keep pushing them back and back and back. It's going to happen. It has to happen. We've got the momentum. My head is down and I can see the line five yords in front of me.

Con makes one last effort to hold us back. He's a strong focker, in fairness to him.

He's going, 'May there be guinea-fowl crying at the birth of your child!' because I'm rubbing my chin against his cheek again and at the same time I'm going, 'I'd say they're lashing each other out of it, Con. They've been hord at it since they woke up this morning and they'll be hord at it till they fall asleep tonight.'

We move two more steps forward, then I reach down for the ball. Their tighthead makes a move to stop me, but he can't, because I'm too focking quick for him. I pull the ball tight to my chest and I fall face-first over the line.

The referee blows his whistle.

Gilly and Dilly – our two locks – grab a hold of my shirt and they just lift me to my feet, then I end up getting just, like, mobbed by my teammates. They're all, like, hugging me and telling me I'm a legend and calling me Rossi.

Senny adds the points and there's no way back for Highfield. We end up winning 13–0.

To see our reaction at the final whistle, you'd swear we'd just gained promotion to Division 2A. We're talking high-fives, we're talking hugs, we're talking chest-bumps. We even slide on our bellies through the mud, while the Highfield players end up having to drag Con off the pitch. He's, like, totally lost it. He's roaring curses at me, going, 'May you have little for your skillet! May your obituary be written in weasel's piss!! May the Lamb of God stir His hoof through the roof of Heaven and kick you in the arse down to Hell!'

Bucky grabs me by the shoulders and goes, 'A pushover try? We've never scored one before!'

I'm there, 'Hey, I sensed a weakness and I went for it.'

'What were you saying to that dude? I couldn't hear.'

'Nothing. It was just a bit of old-fashioned what-we-used-to-call mind games.'

The old man is shouting, 'Highfield undone by a peerless display of old-school front-row play! As it was in the days of Noah, so shall it be until the Coming of the Son of Man! Exclamation mark, new paragraph!'

I give him a big smile and I mouth the words, 'Shut the fock up, you big dick,' at him.

He smiles back.

'Greatness has the quality of permanence!' he goes. 'Age shall not wither it, nor the years condemn it! Quote-unquote!'

I slip into the dressing room. There's no singing next door. No one's banging on about the Lee. Instead, it's suddenly *us* making all the noise?

We're giving it:

> *Everywhere we go! (Everywhere we go!)*
> *People always ask us! (People always ask us!)*
> *Who we are! (Who we are!)*
> *And where do we come from? (And where do we come from?)*
> *And we tell them! (And we tell them!)*
> *We're from Seapoint! (The mighty, mighty Seapoint!)*
> *And if they can't find us! (And if they can't find us!)*
> *It's cos we're in The Brack! (We play in Ballybrack!)*

It's pretty heady stuff, it has to be said. But the best is yet to come. Byrom steps into the dressing room and Bucky shushes everyone to let him speak. But when the dude opens his mouth, he discovers that he can't.

He just goes, 'Oy want to soy . . .' and then he breaks down and everyone just cheers.

Eventually, he gets his shit together and he goes, 'Oy knoy ut's oynloy one wun. But if we ploy loyk thut iveroy woyk between naah and the ind of the soyson, there usn't a toym in the world who'll boyt us.'

# 5. The Booby Trap

The old dear decides to ring just as I'm getting out of the cor. 'Not a good time,' I go. 'I'm back playing rugby. And Monday night is Strength and Conditioning night.'

She just goes, 'Well, keep Friday week free, Ross, because Ari and I are having a party to celebrate our engagement! It's going to be here in the house.'

I'm there, 'Did you not just hear what I said? I played against Highfield last weekend and I was the main difference between the two teams. You can ask the old man.'

She just goes, 'Oh, well, how nice.'

That's an exact quote. She's so wrapped up in herself, it's unbelievable. I just hang up on her, grab my gear from the boot, then into the clubhouse I go.

Most of the goys are already in the gym. The music is blasting out. It's 'Club Can't Handle Me' – fittingly enough.

When the goys see me, they all stop warming up and they just stort clapping. It's an incredible moment for me – a sign that I've finally been accepted into the team, having shown them what I can actually do.

Bucky even goes, 'Look, I'm sorry again, Rossi – for being a dick to you.'

'If the roles were reversed,' I go, 'I probably would have been the same way. I mightn't have screwed you over in terms of the lineout calls, but I might have taken a shit in one of your shoes.'

This seems to shock him.

'Seriously?' he goes. 'You'd have done a dump in one of my shoes?'

It's obviously not a thing anymore.

I'm like, 'Hey, it's yet another example of how rugby has changed.'

Whether it's changed for the better or not, I don't comment either way. I just leave it hanging in the air between us.

He introduces me to the goys – except *properly* this time? – and also to the four or five I didn't really meet the last day. Inside centre is Rob Fortune, outside centre is Johnny Bliss, right wing is Mark Dwyer, left wing is Frank Hugo and full-back is Ollie Lysaght.

As we do our stretches, I'm listening to the banter between them and it reminds me so much of me and the goys back in the day. Johnny Bliss – or Blissy – is obviously the ladies' man on the team. I suppose you could call him Seapoint's *me*? He's telling Ollie – as in, Ollie Lysaght – that he joined the UCD Students' Union Campaign to Free Ibrahim Halawa, even though he hasn't a clue who Ibrahim Halawa even is, and he morched on the Egyptian Embassy on Clyde Road, just so he could get close to Eabha MacAmhlaoibh, who's apparently into the whole, like, *Amnesty* thing?

He's so like me, I end up having a little chuckle to myself. I morched on so many embassies with Sorcha, I'd be shocked if I'm not on an official Gorda list of shit-stirrers somewhere.

Eabha MacAmhlaoibh is apparently hot. Except these goys don't say 'hot', they say 'wet' – as in, 'Eabha MacAmhlaoibh is wet, but her friend, Leesha Byrne – second-year Planning, Geography & Environment – is even wetter!'

In my day, that would have meant they were a couple of focking knobs.

And they don't shout, 'Affluence!' like *our* generation did? They have their own equivalent, which I discover when Rob Fortune asks little Davy Dardis – in other words, Dordo – where his new girlfriend is actually from and Dordo makes the mistake of going, 'Technically, Foxrock.'

Rob is on it like an Easter Bonnet. He goes, 'Technically, Foxrock? You mean Chavinteely?'

And Dilly – one of our second rows – shouts, 'Wealth gag!'

When someone shouts, 'Wealth gag!' everyone has to stop whatever it is they're doing – no excuses – and shout, 'Wealth gag!' before high-fiving every teammate who happens to be in the immediate vicinity.

I go, 'We used to shout, "Affluence!" – as in just, "Affluence!"'
and Bucky just nods and smiles patiently at me, like I do when Sorcha's granny storts reminiscing about tuberculosis and the Latin
Mass.

It's sad, of course, to see the old ways dying out, but every generation has its own thing. It's called the circle of life. I decide to just
go with it.

So I go, 'Wealth gag!' along with all the others, then everyone in
that dressing room gets a high-five from me.

Suddenly, it's time to work. Derek Duddy, our Strength and
Conditioning coach – the famous Dudser who I've heard a bit
about – walks in. He's supposedly a serious ball-buster. There's no
pleasantries. He's like, 'What the fock are you all sitting around
gossiping for? It's like a focking hockey dressing room in here!'

We get down to business. The training ends up being unbelievably
hord. Dudser is a seriously intense goy – ex-Ormy, apparently – and
he drives us relentlessly. There's a lot of work with, like, weights
and kettlebells and blah, blah, blah, but it's a lot more scientific than
it was when I last played. We did a lot of work to build up our abs,
pecs and biceps, whereas Dudser's more into the idea of training
movements rather than, like, *muscles*?

We end up being divided into two groups – we're talking backs,
we're talking forwards. The backs do their thing and we do ours,
which involves using the weights to practise the basic movements
you use in scrummaging, rucking and mauling – squat, bend, push,
pull, twist and single leg.

The penalty for slackers is the dreaded Three Minute Death
Run – you have to sprint to Ballybrack Shopping Centre and back
in 180 seconds. If you're even a fraction of a second over, you have
to do it again.

Anyway, by the end of the session, I'm seriously focked, but at
the same time – whether it's a word or not – *exhilarated*?

I grab a quick Jack Bauer. Bucky tells me that I put in one hell of
a session and we talk about City of Derry, who we're apparently
playing at home on Saturday.

'They've probably got the best pack in Division 2B,' he goes.

'They destroyed us earlier in the season. We're talking, like, pure brute force. By the way, Rossi, what are you doing Wednesday night?'

Sitting at home with my wife and kids is the answer. I don't say that, though, because it'll only make me sound old.

Instead, I'm like, 'Wednesday night? I don't know. That remains to be seen.'

'It's just because Wednesday night is Cinema Night,' he goes. 'We all go as a team.'

'Yeah, no, cool.'

'We're going to see *Taken 3*. Liam Neeson?'

'Jesus, he's done a third one, has he?'

'They're saying it's the best of the trilogy.'

'Well, I loved the other two, so I'm definitely in.'

He says he'd better hit the road because he's about to pull an all-nighter. He's a got a Jurisprudence essay to write about the Prosecution of Twitter Trolls as an Example of how Societal Morals Shape Law. See, that's another way in which young people have changed. I wouldn't have bothered my hole writing – I would have told the lecturer to go fock himself.

Like I said, rugby is a totally different game.

It's, like, Tuesday afternoon and I call in to see the old man – just, like, randomly. Like I said, he can be alright when he's not trying too hord to be my bezzy mate.

He opens the door and before I get a chance to even open my mouth, he goes, 'Here he comes!' at the top of his focking voice. 'The man who revolutionized the way the outhalf position is played and is now rolling back the years as the spearhead of the Seapoint pack!'

You could hear his focking voice at both ends of Ailesbury Road. Somehow, I manage to bite my tongue.

I go, 'Yeah, whatever – look, I just called in to say, you know, thanks for coming down to Cork to support me. It was good having you there.'

He's there, 'It was just like old times, eh?'

'Just keep a focking lid on it, will you? And keep your focking voice down as well.'

'The only question for me now is do I call you Kicker or do I call you Hooker?'

'Definitely don't call me Hooker.'

'Well, that's the position in which you're playing, Ross – the role in which you will soon no doubt be receiving mentions in dispatches!'

'I'm serious – don't call me Hooker.'

'Righty-ho! We shall stick with Kicker, then!'

There's something different about him, even though I can't quite put my finger on it.

He goes, 'I say, Ross, what are you doing now?'

I'm there, 'I'm standing on your doorstep wondering why the fock you haven't asked me in.'

'I was going to say I've got the famous Kennet inside. I was about to let him go for the day. What say, on his way home, I get him to drop the two of us into town? We could go to The Shelbourne. Order a bottle of something outrageously expensive to toast your comeback.'

'I've got training tonight. But if you're paying, I suppose I could have one or two.'

So five minutes later, we're in the back of the Merc. We're on, like, Lower Leeson Street and I'm looking sideways at him. It's, like, *bothering* me now?

I'm there, 'Okay, what is it? What's different about you?'

He laughs. He goes, 'You've noticed, have you?'

I'm like, 'Yeah, but I don't know what the fock it is – as in, I can't put my actual finger on it? But you're definitely different – somehow.'

He goes, 'Say nothing, Kennet! See how long it takes for Ross's famous brain to work it out!'

'Have you lost weight?'

'No, no – it's not that.'

'Then you've put on weight. Yeah, no, that's it – you're definitely fatter.'

'I'm the same weight now as I was twelve months ago.'

I just stop guessing.

The old man goes, 'I'm sure the proverbial penny will what's-it before too long!'

Kennet catches my eye in the rearview mirror. He goes, 'Meant to say f . . . f . . . feer fooks to you, Rosser. The rubby, Ine talking about. You p . . . p . . . p . . . p . . . playut veddy well, so you did.'

I'm there, 'You wouldn't know the first focking thing about the game. But thanks for saying it anyway.'

There's a port of me that will never forgive Kennet for the way he treated Ronan.

He pulls up outside The Shelly. Me and the old man get out of the cor.

'Are you sure you're not fatter?' I go. 'Your orse definitely looks fatter.'

The old man goes, 'Fourteen stone on the button! Same as I was a year ago! Keep guessing, Ross!'

I don't get a chance to, roysh, because the weirdest thing suddenly happens. The doorman sees the old man and his face lights up. He goes, 'Oh, hello! It's great to see you! Really great to see you!'

The thing is, I always thought the staff in The Shelbourne thought my old man was a dick.

'Thank you,' the old man goes. 'It's very nice to see you, too.'

We go through the revolving door, then into the No. 27 bor. The place is rammers. There must be, like, a *conference* on or some shit? One of the staff – a woman – comes up to us and goes, 'Oh, hello! It's lovely to see you! If you give me just one moment, I'll find a table for you!'

I turn to the old man and I go, 'Why are they being so nice to you?' and that's when I all of a sudden cop it – as in, what's actually different with him. 'Oh my God,' I hear myself go, 'you've got hair!'

He laughs. He's there, 'That's right – I knew you'd get it in the end!'

It's obviously a wig. It has to be a wig because the focker is as bald as a cricket ball. 'It's focking incredible,' I go, grabbing him by the shoulders and turning him around. 'It doesn't even look like a wig. I mean, that's why it took so long for the penny to drop. It looks like actual hair. I'm trying to think of something negative to say, but I'm actually struggling here, in fairness to you.'

He's there, 'That's terribly kind of you, Ross.'

'So where did you get it?'

He goes, 'Would you believe me if I told you I found it?'

'Found it?'

'Found it! Yesterday! In Helen's attic! We were having a bit of a clear-out.'

'Whoa, whoa, whoa,' I go, at the same time laughing. 'You found a wig in the attic and, what, you just put it on your focking head?'

'Well, Helen thought it rather suited me. So I thought I'd wear it for the day – just to see who noticed.'

'Whose wig even is it?'

'I've no idea. Helen thinks it may have been there since before she moved in. And that was almost thirty years ago.'

'You look different with hair. Younger. No, not younger – more, I don't know, important or something.'

'I'm glad you said that, Ross. It really is the strangest thing. Since I put it on yesterday, people have been, well, different towards me.'

'Different in what way?'

'Well, you saw the reception we got when we walked in. It was all smiles and "Lovely to see you!" and "I'll get you a table!" This morning, Kennet pulled into the Topaz on the Donnybrook Road to fill up the car. I got out to stretch my legs and pick up a copy of *The Times*. The next thing I knew, a chap had appeared on the forecourt – one of the staff. He said, "It's great to see you!" and he started filling up the tank for us.'

'Random.'

'Oh, that's the word for it alright! Random! It's the strangest bloody thing. Since I put this thing on my head, the world suddenly seems like, well, a more accommodating place.'

He storts to touch it then – as in, sort of, like, patting it down with his hands. The woman who promised to find us a table signals to us from the other side of the bor. She's got one for us. So we tip over to her. And that's when some dude I've never seen before steps up to the old man and thrusts out his hand.

'Put it there!' the dude goes. He's, like, my age, except dressed in a suit.

The old man takes a step backwards. He automatically assumes that a stranger in a suit sticking out his hand and smiling is about to serve him a writ.

That's what a guilty conscience will do for you.

'People say a lot of things about you,' the dude goes, 'but I just wanted to say, thank you for bringing Johnny Sexton home.'

'Oh!' the old man goes. 'Yes! Oh, that's quite alright! It was my pleasure, in fact!'

When the dude walks off, I turn around to the old man and I go, 'Bringing Johnny Sexton home? What the fock was all that about?'

And he laughs – like someone has just said something hilarious – and goes, 'I know what it is, Ross! I finally know why people are different towards me!'

I'm like, 'Why?'

He smoothes down his brand-new head of hair with his hands and he goes, 'They think I'm *him*, Kicker! They think I'm Denis O'Brien!'

So it's, like, seven o'clock on Wednesday evening. I'm sitting in the cor pork of Dundrum Town Centre, checking myself out in the rearview mirror. I rub my hand over my still stubbly face. I have to admit that I'm looking well. I get out of the cor and stort making my way through the cor pork and into the actual shopping centre. That's when my phone rings. It ends up being Bucky.

'Rossi,' he goes, 'where are you?'

I'm there, 'Yeah, no, I've just porked. I'll be there in five.'

He goes, 'Dude, you have to rip the piss out of Goffo when you get here!'

Goffo is our number eight. He's third-year Orts in UCD.

I'm like, 'Why, what's he done?' already laughing along with him.

Bucky goes, 'Yeah, no, it's more what he's *wearing*? The dude's turned up in – I swear to fock – a Ralph Lauren polo shirt!'

I hear all this, like, laughter in the background.

Fock it, I think, because *I'm* wearing a Ralph Lauren polo shirt as well.

I make sure to laugh, though. I'm there, 'No focking way!'

Okay, what the fock is wrong with a Ralph Lauren polo shirt?

He goes, 'Yes focking way! I said to him, "What year do you think this is, Goffo – 2005?"'

I'm there, 'Focking ridiculous. No one wears Ralph anymore. These days it's all . . .'

I'm about to say Abercrombie.

'Hollister!' he goes. 'Exactly!'

I'm there, 'I've a good mind to give him a wedgy when I get there! That's what would have happened back in the day. One thing would have automatically followed the other.'

'Well, we're ripping him here in a major way. Do us a favour, Rossi. Pretend we haven't spoken to each other. Then when you rock up, you just look at him and go, "Ralph Lauren? Jesus, Goffo, I haven't seen anyone wear that for about ten years!"'

'I'll do it. I'm going to definitely do it.'

'It'd be hilarious coming from you.'

I suddenly remember that there's, like, a Hollister store on Level 2. Up the escalators I go.

I'm like, 'Bucky, I've just realized that I've forgotten something. I have to go back to the cor.'

He goes, 'Cool. But don't forget to rip him when you get here!'

I'm there, 'Oh, I'll be ripping him alright! Don't you worry about that!'

I hang up, then into the store I go. I *say* store, but the place is more like a nightclub. It's, like, pitch dork in there, with spotlights dotted around the place, flashing red, white and green, and a dance version of 'Can You Feel the Love Tonight?' blaring out at a volume loud enough to make your brain bleed.

Some teenager with no top on and abs like an upturned egg tray comes dancing over to me, all enthusiasm.

I'm suddenly feeling my age again.

He goes, 'Are you alright for sizes?'

I hate fockers who ask you that question before you've even looked at anything. I generally go, 'Yeah, I'm looking for a medium, please?'

And they're like, 'A medium? In what, though?'

And then I go, 'Yeah, that's what I'm here to decide. Now fock off and let me have a proper look around.'

I don't say that this time, though. Instead, I go, 'I'm just, er, having a general mooch.'

He goes, 'I'm Marcus. Are you looking for anything specific?'

The dude is still focking dancing, by the way, shaking his hips and doing the whole *Saturday Night Fever* finger-dance thing.

'I don't know,' I go, 'just some kind of top.'

He's like, 'A T-shirt?'

'Yeah, no, a T-shirt would probably do the trick alright.'

'The T-shirts are over here!'

He leads the way, dancing with his two hands held above shoulder-height in a sort of, like, raise the *roof* kind of way? Then he stops. In case I'm in any doubt as to where I should be looking, the dude storts doing this dance where it's like he's thumbing a lift – except he's using his thumb to point over his shoulder at a display of different-coloured T-shirts, all perfectly folded and arranged in neat piles on the table.

'Yeah, no,' I go, 'I think I've got this now.'

I pick up a blue polo shirt with the word 'Hollister' written across the chest in massive capital letters.

The dude goes, 'You like that one? What's your size?'

I'm there, 'Yeah, I think I'm either a medium or a lorge.'

He looks at my midriff in a Scooby Dubious way, then he goes, 'Yeah, maybe in Ralph Lauren you are – I'm going to give you this one in XXL.'

I'm there, 'XXL? You've got to be shitting me.'

He hands me the T-shirt in XXL. He's like, 'Here you go! The fitting rooms are just over there.'

I tip over, with the T-shirt in my hand, convinced that it's going to be swimming on me. In I go. I whip off the Ralph and pull the Hollister on over my head.

Holy fock, it's a snug fit. I end up having to breathe in and hold it to pull the thing down over my Ned. This is supposedly XXL! I'm thinking, Who focking decides these things? And who the fock would Small fit? People with only hours to live, presumably.

I step out of the changing room. The track has changed. It's now a really souped-up cover of 'Feels Like I'm in Love'. Marcus dances over to me with a look of horror on his face. 'I think we're going to need a bigger size,' he goes.

I'm there, 'Dude, I'm not wearing XXXL.'

'It's just this size is very tight on you.'

'I'm not wearing XXXL, Marcus – end of conversation. This is going to have to focking do.'

I hand him my balled-up Ralph. I'm there, 'Stick that in the bin, would you? I'm going to wear this now.'

He goes, 'Gladly!' and he dances over to the cash desk. I follow him, just walking, like a normal person.

He tells me it's sixty yoyos and I hand him my plastic. He sticks it in the machine and while I'm waiting for my receipt he storts singing. He's going, *'My knees are shaking, Baby – my heart it beats like a drum,'* and then he storts slapping his bare chest, going, *'Boo-boo! Boo-boo! Boo-boo! Boo-boo! It feels like – it feels like I'm in love.'*

I eventually get out of there, blinking in the suddenly bright light of the shopping centre. I look down. It turns out that my blue T-shirt is actually a green T-shirt.

I think, Fock it – there's no way I'm going back in there.

I head into the cinema. I spot the goys straight away. They're over at the counter, getting popcorn and drinks and whatever else.

They're all delighted to see me. It's amazing what a pushover try can do for your reputation.

They're like, 'Rossi!' and it ends up being hugs all round. They're very huggy, I've noticed, young goys today. Back in my day, we could say everything we had to say with a high-five – or, if you were feeling particularly emotional, a chest-bump.

I just go with it. I think I'm already becoming a big hero to them.

I can see one or two of them checking out my T-shirt. They're obviously big label heads. It's nice that some traditions survive. Or maybe they're looking at my gut, which the cut of this T-shirt seems to actually *emphasize*?

I'm like, 'Where's Goffo?'

Maho goes, 'He's in the jacks. Hammer him when he comes back, Rossi. Focking Ralph Lauren!'

I shake my head and I go, 'He's out of order. I stopped wearing Ralph years ago!'

I order a lorge popcorn and Coke, then I step out of the queue and that's when I suddenly spot – oh, shit! – JP and Chloe walking in.

Obviously, I don't want them seeing me hanging out with a bunch of – let's be honest here – kids, so I try to hide my face from them, but JP ends up copping me.

He's like, 'Ross! Ross! Ross!'

I turn around to the goys and I'm like, 'Hang on a second – this dude over here has just recognized me, probably from my Senior Cup days.'

I tip over to him. JP goes, 'What the fock are you wearing?'

I'm there, 'It's just a T-shirt – what's your focking issue?'

He's like, 'It's February, Ross. Are you not freezing?'

'Hollister,' Chloe goes, like it's a new one on her. 'It's very tight on you, isn't it?'

I'm there, 'What are you, a fashion critic now? What movie are you going to see anyway?'

'*The Theory of Everything*,' she goes. 'It's, like, the Stephen *Hawking* story? What about you?'

'*Taken 3*. Liam Neeson.'

I might as well have said animal porn. She's like, 'Oh my God, have they *made* a third one?'

'It's supposedly the best of the trilogy,' I go. 'That's what everyone seems to be saying.'

JP laughs. He's there, 'How the fock did you persuade Sorcha to go and see that?'

'Yeah, no,' I go, 'I'm not here with Sorcha. I'm here with the, em, goys.'

'Oisinn and Christian?' he goes, looking over my shoulder. 'I thought Oisinn was still in Qatar.'

I'm like, 'No, not those goys. Okay, look, I might as well tell you, I'm with those goys over there,' and I flick my thumb in the direction of Ollie, who's demonstrating on Blissy, in slow motion, another Conor McGregor knockout he saw on YouTube.

JP goes, 'Who are you talking about, Ross? All I can see is a bunch of muscly boys in tight T-shirts and hoodies.'

He stops. He looks at my big Minka Kelly, sticking out of my T-shirt like it's maternity wear. He has suddenly copped it.

He laughs. 'Okay,' he goes, 'what the fock are you doing hanging out with them? What are they – twenty, twenty-one?'

I'm like, 'They're my teammates.'

Behind me, I hear someone – I'm pretty sure it's Dordo – shout, 'Wealth gag!' and that kicks off a round of high-fives.

I'm raging that I'm missing it.

JP goes, 'So you went back after all?'

I'm there, 'That's right. You're talking to Seapoint Rugby Club's new hooker.'

He laughs in my actual face.

I'm like, 'Yeah, fock you, JP – thanks for your support. You spent ten years of your life walking around this town with a Leinster Schools Senior Cup medal around your neck because of me – can I just remind you of that fact?'

He goes, 'Don't get sore with me, Ross. It's just, I don't know, I'm in shock here. It's the T-shirt and these kids you're suddenly going to the cinema with . . . I'm worried about you.'

I suddenly hear Bucky shout, 'Rossi! Rossi!'

Goffo is obviously back from the jacks.

Chloe goes, 'Rossi?' at the same time putting her hand over her mouth. 'Oh my God, is that what they call you? Rossi?'

I'm like, 'Yeah, no, it's their equivalent of Rosser. Or Rossmeister.'

The two of them consider this, for some reason, *hilarious*?

I'm there, 'Look, I knew I was going to have my critics – coming back after however many years out of the game, to try to keep Seapoint in Division 2B. But I didn't think the doubters would be among my supposed friends.'

'Ross,' JP tries go, 'look –'

And I'm there, 'No, forget it, Dude. I don't want to hear your apologies. I'd rather spend my time around people who actually idolize me.'

'I was just going to say,' he goes, 'you left the tag on your T-shirt.'


Oisinn finally rings me back. This is, like, fifteen minutes before kick-off. I go, 'You're cutting it focking fine, aren't you?'

He's there, 'Sorry, Dude. I've been in meetings all morning. I genuinely think Doha is going to be the new Dubai.'

I'm there, 'Good for focking Doha. Did you get my message?'

'I didn't listen to it – what's up?'

'We're about to play City of Derry in, like, fifteen minutes and I need more of your wisdom slash dirty tricks.'

'What?'

'That shit you told me the last day worked a dream.'

'You beat Highfield?'

'We destroyed them. And it was all down to your advice. So I need more.'

'Who did you say you were playing?'

'City of Derry – quick, Oisinn.'

'Okay, well, Ulster packs tend to be pretty formidable.'

'Is that where City of Derry are from? Ulster?'

There's, like, five seconds of silence on the other end of the phone. Even after all these years, it still comes as a genuine shock to Oisinn how thick I can be.

'That's right,' he goes. 'Their front row is going to be tight.'

I'm there, 'Pure brute force was the expression that was used to describe them.'

'Okay, I've got one.'

'Go on.'

'We used to do this thing with the bind. Who's your tighthead?'

'A dude called Bucky. He's the captain of the team.'

'Okay, get this Bucky dude to bind over you instead of you over him.'

'Okay, what does that do?'

'It allows him to press down on their hooker's neck when the ball is put in and keep him bent double. He won't be able to move his legs.'

'That's focking brilliant.'

I thank him, hang up, then peg it back into the dressing room just as Byrom is finishing his team talk.

'Oy've got a lust here of all the toyms in Division Toy C,' he goes, waving a piece of paper at us. 'Thoyse are the ployces you'll boy ploying your rugboy nixt soyson if yoy git rilligoytud ... Boyne ... Dundawk ... Muddletun ... Kanturk ... Nevun ... Sloygoy ...'

'They won't make us go to Sligo,' Ollie goes. 'There's no focking way.'

'Sloygoy is on the lust ... Tullamore ... Bruff ... Rossi, have you ivver ployed in Bruff?'

'Yeah, I've played in Bruff,' I go. 'We used to say the B was silent.'

He goes, 'Lusten to Rossi. He's boyn there, he's seen ut, he's done ut. Oy'm gonna pun thus lust to the wall of thus drissing roym as a permanent remoynder of why yoy've got toy stoy in Division Toy Boy. Yoy all remimbaah, Oy hoype, what happened the laahst toym we ployed these goys in Dirroy – thoy moyd shut of us. Lit's not lit thet happen agin. Lit's buld on what hippened laahst woyk and moyk ut throy more poynts!'

Bucky claps his two hands together and goes, 'Come on, goys, you heard the man! Come on, The Point!'

We're all like, 'Come on, The Point! Come on, The focking Point!' and then out onto the pitch we go.

I turn around to Bucky and I tell him the plan. He looks at me – I'm going to take a chance that this is a word – *incredulously*?

'Is that legal?' he goes.

I'm there, 'Dude, you're supposedly studying law. Everything's legal – until the moment you're caught.'

He laughs. He loves that quote. It's one of my old man's. And speak of the devil.

'Come on, Seapoint!' I hear him go. *'Palma non sine pulvere, sapiens qui prospicit* and whatever you're having yourself!'

Bucky squints his eyes in the old man's direction. He's like, 'Is that Denis O'Brien shouting his mouth off over there?'

I don't want to admit that it's my old man, so I go, 'Yeah, no, it certainly looks like him.'

'I didn't know he was a Point fan.'

'I didn't either.'

We kick off. City of Derry end up being every bit as tough as Bucky said they were likely to be. Their forwards are all, like, two or three inches taller than us and at least two stone heavier. Our scrum is no match for theirs in terms of, like, physicality, which we discover in the first five minutes, when they manage to win two against the head.

I've told Bucky to hold off on the illegal-bind thing until I give him the signal. I spend the first ten minutes getting in the referee's ear, going, 'Watch the bind, ref. They're binding illegally.'

It's all port of the psychology. He eventually turns around to me and goes, 'I'm refereeing this game, not you.'

He's a bit of a dick. Which suits me.

So then we end up winning a scrum just inside the City of Derry twenty-two. There's, like, ten or fifteen minutes gone and they're, like, 3–0 up. I give Bucky the nod and we do the illegal-bind thing, getting on top of their hooker and forcing our combined weight down on his neck, so that he's basically staring through his legs, unable to move his feet.

It puts the brake on their scrum, I discover. And the added beauty of it is that their hooker can't complain to the referee about it because at that moment his head is almost literally up his own hole.

We eventually produce the ball for Dordo, who feeds Senny, who beats three players to score under the posts and make the conversion easy for himself. As he's adding the two, I hear their hooker turn around to the referee and go, 'Raf – chack ite the baind!'

Which is Ulster for check out the bind.

But this is where my earlier work pays off. It was always a tactic of ours back in the day to complain to the referee that the other team was doing something that *we* were *actually* doing? Then when the other side complains, the referee thinks, 'Yeah, no, the two of them are obviously at it,' and you tend to get away with it.

What's the famous phrase? Six of one and half-a-dozen of the other one?

Anyway, the point I'm trying to make is that it ends up working. The referee tells their hooker the same thing he told me. In fact, he goes, 'If you want to referee this game, we'll have to swap jerseys first. Do you want to do that?'

On the sideline, the old man is going, 'Observe the sons of Ulster – showing the famous ill-discipline that has long been a blight on the game in the North!'

Of course the trick is not to tear the orse out of it. We only do it every second or third scrum. The next time we do it, their scrum ends up collapsing – I think the dude's legs are focked – and we win a penalty, which Senny kicks to put us 10–3 ahead. Then, just before half-time, we repeat the dose. Another pen. Another three points.

The referee eventually cops what's happening, of course. As we're walking in at half-time, he turns around to me and goes, 'I've just seen what you're doing.'

And I'm like, 'Yeah? What do you think you saw?'

'Don't be clever with me. I see you do that in the second half and I'm sending you to the bin.'

But there's no need to do it again. Because we've got, like, a ten-point cushion. And possibly because of that, *the* most incredible thing happens when we come out for the second half. Well, first we get a fluky try in the first minute when Ollie Lysaght chorges down a City of Derry kick, gets the bounce and sprints, like, eighty yords to deposit the ball under the posts. Then Senny adds the old Twix after dinner and suddenly the gap is, like, seventeen points.

We're definitely not seventeen points better than City of Derry, but for the first time, presumably this season, we stort playing with actual confidence. The goys have stopped thinking of themselves as just fodder for the bigger teams and they're suddenly thinking, Er, we can actually *win* matches.

At the stort of the second half, in fact, you can sense that the City of Derry goys already know the game is up. Then it becomes all about the backs and I finally discover why Senny is on the verge of being accepted into the Leinster Academy. He has an unbelievable forty minutes of rugby, grabbing a second try for himself and doing all the work to create one for Johnny Bliss, who crosses the line, already kissing his badge to demonstrate his loyalty to the twenty or thirty fans who've shown up.

We end up destroying them. In the last five minutes, me and Bucky end up doing the bind trick again. Their scrum collapses and it's, like, high-fives all round. Maho and Bucky especially are like, 'Well done, Rossi!'

As Senny is shaping up to take the penalty, the old man shouts, 'The Seapoint number ten will take away all the plaudits, but the number two is the real power behind the throne today!'

Maho turns to me and goes, 'Jesus, that Denis O'Brien seems to be a massive fan of yours, Rossi.'

I'm like, 'Yeah, no, he does alright.'

We end up winning 47–3.

The final whistle is the trigger for, like, wild celebrations. Byrom walks around the pitch and puts his orm around each and every one of our shoulders and he tells us he's proud. But he tells me he's especially proud of me.

Bucky says we're going out tonight to celebrate – and we're going to celebrate in a major way. So I trot over to Denis O'Brien and I tell him that I need €500 in cash.

Old habits die hord.

Sorcha asks me if I'm excited about tonight.

I'm like, 'Tonight? What's tonight?'

She's there, 'It's your mom and Ari's engagement porty!'

'Oh, that?' I go. 'Yeah, no, I'm not going.'

'What do you mean you're not going?'

'I couldn't be focking orsed.'

'Ross, your mom is getting remarried and I think you need to stort getting your head around that idea. Either way, we're going to her engagement porty tonight.'

I'm there, 'I probably will end up going, but hopefully just to rip the piss.'

I decide that if I'm going to have to put myself through it, I'm going to have to go to bed for a couple of hours, so I stort climbing the stairs. 'Here,' I go, 'where's Honor, by the way?'

Sorcha's there, 'She's upstairs in her room, doing her homework.'

This is, like, five o'clock on a Friday afternoon, by the way.

I'm like, 'Homework?' understandably worried. 'Is that not something she usually does on Monday morning in the cor on the way to school?'

'It used to be,' Sorcha goes. 'But that's Caleb's influence. They're actually studying together!'

'Studying? She's in focking primary school.'

'Well, Caleb told her she didn't want to find herself going into secondary school in a few years and discovering that she was behind everyone else in terms of her educational development.'

'I don't like the sound of that one little bit. Hang on, are you saying Caleb is upstairs with her?'

'Now, don't stort doing the whole protective father routine, Ross. Nothing's going to happen.'

'Of course nothing's going to happen. He's already Friend Zoned the girl. It's you he actually wants.'

'Don't be silly, Ross. His mother has already had a talk with him about it.'

'Well, either way, I'm sick of him being here all the time.'

I head upstairs. I think about sticking my head around Honor's door, just to let Caleb know that not everyone under this roof is a slave to his chorms. In the end, I don't bother.

I tip into the bedroom, lie down on the bed and close my eyes. And that's when I get the sudden sense that there's, like, someone in the room with me.

I open my eyes and at the same time I sit up. He's standing at the end of the bed.

I'm talking about Caleb.

I'm like, 'What the fock?' because I get a genuine fright.

He keeps looking over his left shoulder in a sort of, like, *shifty* way? Somehow, I get the impression that he's just stepped out of Sorcha's walk-in wardrobe.

I'm there, 'I asked you a question. What the fock?'

He's like, 'What do you mean by that?' trying to brazen it out. But his face is all flushed.

I'm there, 'What the fock are you doing in my bedroom? What were you doing in the wardrobe?'

He goes, 'Honor asked me to get her something.'

'I call bullshit on that.'

'It's not bullshit.'

'So what were you getting?'

'It's none of your business.' He slips out of the room and out onto the landing.

I shout after him.

I go, 'Don't let me catch you poking around in this room again, you little focking psychopath.'

The old dear is loving being the centre of attention. I'm sure you can picture the scene.

'Oh my God,' Sorcha goes, 'she looks amazing!'

I'm there, 'No, she doesn't. She looks like exactly what she is – a scarecrow in a Versace gown, with a painted-on smile to hide the fact that she's shitfaced and painted-on eyebrows to make it look like she's actually interested in what other people have to say and –'

Sorcha's there, 'Ross!'

'Hang on, Babes, I'm not done yet . . . who's then been repeatedly smashed in the face with a snow shovel. Okay, now I'm done.'

'Like I said to you earlier,' Sorcha goes, 'do you not think it's about time you did something about your mother issues?'

I'm there, 'I wasn't aware that I *had* mother issues?'

There must be, like, two hundred people in the gaff in Foxrock. I swear to fock, it's bigger than our actual wedding.

'Fionnuala is getting married,' Sorcha goes, 'and she's content for the first time in – oh my God – *so* long? Why can't you be happy for her?'

I'm there, 'Because she's about to marry someone who's not in his right mind. And even though that's the second most important quality she looks for in a man – after obviously money – I actually feel sorry for the poor focker. I seem to be the only one who does.'

'You shouldn't feel sorry for him.'

'Er, he was in l'Ecrivain singing Broadway focking show tunes to his first wife – who died nearly thirty years ago.'

'But saying you feel sorry for him is patronizing and can only serve to stigmatize people with impaired reasoning and memory.'

'Oh, so you're agreeing with me that there is something wrong with him?'

'No, I'm saying I think we should take Fionnuala's explanation at face value – that he drank on an empty stomach and the combination of that and his blood pressure medication –'

The old dear is suddenly waving at us across the crowded room, going, 'Sorcha! Ross! Yoohoo!'

We end up having to go over to her, of course, to congratulate her again and have yet another look at the ring and generally feed her need to be the centre of absolutely everything, the fat, plunger-faced, attention junkie.

'Sorcha!' she tries to go. 'You look fab-a-lous! I was just telling the girls about the wedding plans!'

She's chatting to Delma and some woman I vaguely recognize from the campaign to stop the Luas coming to Foxrock. They're both, like, nodding away and doing their best to come across as happy for the old dear. I always think Delma is like one of those people who had a chance to kill Hitler back in the early days, then spent their whole lives basically kicking themselves that they didn't.

'The yacht we're getting married on has six floors,' the old dear tries to go, 'each with its own deck – teak-finished, naturally. Every stateroom has a walk-in wardrobe and a His and Hers bathroom and every deck has its own hot tub, sauna and steam room. It has six fully stocked bars, including the one in the underwater observation room, where you can enjoy a Gin Mule, or a Caipirinha, or a Mai Tai, or a Daiquiri, while enjoying the wonderful, wonderful sea life.'

I decide to put a stop to her gallop.

'What if a whale happens to see you looking out at it,' I go, 'and notices that you've got half of its mother's fat injected into your focking lips and forehead?'

Sorcha goes, 'Ross! Apologize to your mom this minute!'

But I just wander off, having made my point. I overhear someone say that they just saw Denis O'Brien horsing into the mango and crayfish canapés, so I head for the buffet, where I find the old man, of course, stuffing his face.

I'm there, 'I can't believe you've still got that focking thing on your head. Is this going to become, like, a permanent thing?'

'No,' he goes, 'I'm just having a bit of fun with it. You know, I bumped into poor Gavin O'Reilly coming out of Peterson of Dublin yesterday? I was popping in for a box of my cigars. Well, he got such a fright when he saw me, he almost walked out in front of the Viking Splash bus! I must tell Denis that! I have to say, Ross, I'm rather enjoying the experience of *being* him. I feel, well, not to put too fine a point on it, positively virile!'

'Okay, too much information.'

'Oh, it's one thing that even his fiercest critics – Sam Smyth, Eamon Dunphy, Vincent Browne, *et al.* – would have to admit about Denis. His hair is bloody magnificent. Hennessy has been saying it for years. That's the real source of his wealth. You don't need a tribunal of inquiry to tell you that. It's all in the hair – that lustrous, lustrous mane of his. He let me touch it once. One of only about six people to have ever touched it. It was in Quinta do Lago. He was at the absolute peak of his powers.'

I grab a glass of Champagne from a passing waiter, then Ari storts walking around, trying to herd everyone into the drawing room, where he's apparently going to make a speech.

I wander in there, not because I want to hear what he has to say but because I see a pretty girl walk in ahead of me. If I had to say she looked like someone, that someone would be Alana Blanchard and she has the biggest pair of tartugas that I have ever seen. I sidle up to her.

What can I say? I'm a social animal.

'Hey,' I go, 'I don't think we've ever met. I'm pretty sure I'd remember if we did.'

She's there, '*Excuse* me?'

From her accent, I'd say she's either American or from somewhere around here.

I'm there, 'I'm just wondering what your connection is to the supposedly happy couple? I'm Ross, just to let you know. It's actually my mother who's getting married.'

She looks me up and down – not in a good way – and goes, 'Fionnuala O'Carroll-Kelly is your mother?'

I'm like, 'Unfortunately, yeah. So, like, how do you know her?'

'I was in rehab with her. In Malibu. She never mentioned that she had a son, by the way.'

The woman is un-focking-believable.

'Well,' I go, 'I'm not making it up. So, what, you became, like, friends with her, did you?'

'Oh, we are *far* from friends – that's my grandpa she's taking advantage of.'

There's, like, a buzz in the room. Thirty conversations going on at the same time. Ari is trying to shush everyone. He wants to make this speech. Or maybe he's going to focking sing again – nothing would surprise me after l'Ecrivain. He's going, 'Quiet, please! I got something important to say! It's important! Goddamn it, I said quiet!'

There suddenly *is* quiet. After a long pause, he goes, 'Yesterday, December seven, nineteen forty-one – a date that will live in infamy – the United States of America was suddenly and deliberately attacked by naval and air forces of the Empire of Japan. The United States was at peace with that nation and, at the solicitation of Japan, was still in conversation with its government and its emperor looking toward the maintenance of peace in the Pacific . . .'

Everyone – including all of the old dear's friends – is looking at each other as if to say, 'Okay, what the fock?'

I turn to Ari's granddaughter and I go, 'My old dear is trying to claim it's a problem with his medication.'

'It has nothing to do with his medication,' she goes. 'He's got senile dementia.'

I'm like, 'Definitely?'

She goes, 'Are you even listening to this?'

Ari's there, 'It will be recorded that the distance of Hawaii from Japan makes it obvious that the attack was deliberately planned many days or even weeks ago. During the intervening time, the Japanese government had deliberately sought to deceive the United States by false statements and expressions of hope for continued peace.'

The old dear, who's obviously embarrassed – a rare enough event in itself – walks up to him and tries to stop him making a total orse of himself, but mostly of her.

She's like, 'Ari, I really think –'

But he ends up going, 'Fionnuala, it's difficult to hear it, I know, but it still has to be said. The attack yesterday on the Hawaiian Islands has caused severe damage to American naval and military forces. Very many American lives have been lost.'

I turn around to his granddaughter and I'm like, 'So what are you going to do?'

And she's there, 'Everything I can to stop this charade going ahead.'

'No matter how long it may take us to overcome this premeditated invasion,' Ari goes, 'the American people in their righteous might will win through to absolute victory. I believe I interpret the will of the Congress and of the people when I assert that we will not only defend ourselves to the utmost but will make very certain that this form of treachery shall never endanger us again.'

That's when the girl – I might have already mentioned that she's an absolute lasher with a fantastic set of Mungo Jerrys – storts pushing her way through the crowd over to where Ari is ranting and raving. I follow, sensing that there might be some kind of fireworks.

Ari obviously has no idea that his granddaughter is here – that's judging by his surprised reaction when he sees her. But it's nothing compared to the old dear's shock.

She goes, 'Tiffany Blue?' and I'm thinking, holy shit, is that her actual name? 'What the hell are you doing here?'

'Oh,' this Tiffany Blue one goes, 'I can see how it's kind of inconvenient for you, me turning up like this. But I'm here to take my grandpa home.'

God, she's a ride.

Ari's like, 'Take me home? Are you crazy? I'm getting married!'

'You can't get married because you're not capable of understanding what that means.'

Ari's obviously hurt by that because he actually staggers *backwards* a step or two? He's like, 'You say that to me. My own flesh and . . .'

'You have senile dementia!' Tiffany Blue just goes.

Everyone gasps, and I give Sorcha a look across the room that's meant to get across the point that I focking told her so!

Ari's like, 'I got a problem with my meds, is all.'

Tiffany Blue goes, 'We both know that's not true.'

'It's true! I never felt better in my life! I'm marrying your grandma and there's nothing you can do about it.'

'Grandma's dead. She died in 1987. Don't you remember?'

I decide to weigh in to the debate. I'm there, 'You have definitely convinced me. It should have been obvious from day one. There'd have to be something wrong with any man who wanted to marry that drunken boxtroll.'

Sorcha tries to get involved then. She goes, 'Why don't we sit down and discuss this like adults?' because she's always keen to use whatever skills she picked up when she did that Certificate in Mediation course in the Smurfit Business School.

'I'm not sitting down,' Tiffany Blue goes, 'and I don't feel the need to discuss anything with you, whoever you are. I'm here to stop my grandpa being shaken down by this cold-blooded, scheming, morally bankrupt woman.'

Seriously, I'd knock the orse off her.

'You have a nerve!' the old dear all of a sudden roars. '*You* accuse *me* of being a gold-digger? You don't care about Ari – all you care about is his money. That's all you've ever cared about. He raised you when your parents died. And how did you repay him? You broke his bloody heart! You stole from him – for what? To fill your body with drugs!'

I'm there, 'Whoa! You're on thin ice talking about drugs – I just want to point that out. Continue.'

'Oh, she's on thin ice alright,' Tiffany Blue goes. 'You know what she told me when we were in rehab? She said when she got out, she was going to find a rich, old man to marry – someone who was right on the verge of falling off the perch.'

'I don't think I would ever use such a phrase,' the old dear tries to go.

'That's a direct quote.'

'Well, I wasn't in my right mind,' she goes, looking around the room for support. 'Neither of us was. We were in rehab, for heaven's sake.'

'Except she didn't need to wait till she got out,' Tiffany Blue goes. 'Grandpa came to visit that afternoon. As soon as she found out what he was worth, she had her hooks in.'

'You don't know the first thing about it!' the old dear tries to go. 'You don't know how Ari and I feel about each other!'

'I can't believe I actually introduced you. Your face lit up when you heard two billion. I caught you Googling him. Do you remember that? In the computer room.'

'I was interested in him. He was a gentleman and there aren't too many of those left in the world.'

'You got the life you wanted – restaurants, clothes, jewellery . . .'

I'm there, 'Gin,' just letting the girl know whose side I'm on.

She goes, 'Okay, I'm not the most perfect person in the world. I've made mistakes and, yes, I've hurt Grandpa. But I am not going to stand back and watch you steal his money.'

'*Your* money!' the old dear roars. 'That's what you really mean, isn't it?'

Sorcha goes, 'Sometimes it helps, Fionnuala, to let what the opposite side has just said land for a moment before you respond.'

She totally blanks her.

'Because that's what this is really about,' the old dear goes – her face has gone all, I don't know, lizardy? She hasn't had anything to drink for six or seven minutes. 'The money that you thought was coming to you! Well, here's the news – your inheritance is perfectly safe!'

Tiffany Blue goes, 'Excuse me?' obviously surprised by this news.

Ari goes, 'That's right. Fionnuala wants to sign a prenup. I didn't ask her. She insisted. I said no – ain't no way. But she didn't want people questioning her motives. So she said to me, no prenup, no wedding.'

There are a lot of surprised faces in the room. It's hilarious how all my old dear's friends think the worst of her.

Tiffany Blue ends up being more shocked than anyone. She looks at the old dear and goes, 'So you . . . get nothing?'

'Correction,' the old dear goes, all delighted with herself, 'I get to share my life with this wonderful, wonderful man. But as for money, no, I won't get a cent when he dies. I hope that puts everyone's mind at rest – including yours, Ross. Now, if you don't mind, I would like to get on with celebrating my engagement!'

Sorcha is sitting at the vanity table, taking off her make-up. I'm trying to decide if I should make a move on her or just go to sleep.

I'm very pissed, but very horny, and I'm trying to figure out which is the stronger – I don't know – emotion?

'Oh my God,' she goes. 'What an amazing night!'

I'm there, 'I thought it was a bit of an anti-climax in the end.'

'A prenup, Ross! Oh my God, how romantic!'

'I still think Tiffany Blue accepted it too easily.'

'Well, she's going back to California tomorrow with her tail well and truly between her legs.'

'I still say the old dear's up to something. That's my analysis. There's no way she'd be marrying this dude if he was poor.'

Sorcha steps into the walk-in wardrobe to take off her clothes.

She's there, 'By the way, Lauren is home from France for a week. She said she had lunch in town with her dad yesterday and her sandwich came served on a table-tennis bat with the rubber torn off it.'

'God,' I go, 'that takes me back.'

'That's what I mean. It's got to be a sign that things are returning to the way they were. The next thing we know, it'll be . . . Oh! My God!'

She suddenly appears at the door of the walk-in wardrobe with a look of shock on her face and also no top on – her garbos hanging there for all the world to see.

I think horny is going to win out.

I'm like, 'What's wrong? Is there a spider in there?'

Her actual response is something I'm definitely not expecting.

'Ross,' she goes, 'where have all my bras gone?'

I actually laugh. I'm like, 'What the fock are you talking about?'

'I just went to put my bra away and the drawer is practically empty. All my good ones are missing, including the ones you let me put on your credit cord as a Christmas present.'

Oh, holy shit. I suddenly remember Caleb being in the room this afternoon. I knew he was acting shifty and it looked like he'd come from the direction of the walk-in wardrobe.

She goes, 'Who's been stealing my bras, Ross?'

And I'm there, 'Come on, Sorcha, is it not obvious? I found him poking around in here this afternoon.'

'Who are you talking about?'

'I'm talking about your little boyfriend.'

'Caleb?'

'Yes, Caleb. You heard what his mother said – he's got the big-time hots for you. Even she agreed that he was weird.'

'Why do you always think the worst of people, Ross? Your mother? Caleb?'

'Are you sure you're not just saying that out of guilt?'

'Guilt? What do I have to feel guilty about?'

'Look, I'm not saying you led the kid on, but you could have made it clearer to him that you weren't interested.'

'Excuse me?'

'I told you from nearly day one that he was into you. He thought he had a shot at the title and you should have told him in no uncertain terms that he didn't. Except I think a little bit of you was flattered by the attention.'

'Okay, I'm a huge believer in non-violence, Ross – my heroes are the likes of Aung San Suu Kyi, Sophie Scholl and obviously Anna Politskovskaya – but I have never wanted to slap someone across the face so hord in my life.'

I pick up the bedside phone and I dial 911.

Sorcha goes, 'What are you doing?'

I'm there, 'What do you think I'm doing? I'm ringing the Feds.'

'Yeah, I don't think we *need* to get the Gords involved?'

'Are you shitting me? How much were those bras worth?'

'I don't know – a few hundred euros. But Caleb is just a child, Ross. This could ruin his life.'

'Good. It'll hopefully teach him a lesson – like not to be a creepy little focker who steals women's underwear. By the way, that's exactly how serial killers get storted. Okay, why isn't 911 working?'

'Because that's the number for emergencies in the States. Seriously, Ross, you watch far too much TV.'

'Okay, well, what's the equivalent of 911 in Ireland then? There must be an equivalent.'

'I'm not telling you the equivalent.'

'Why won't you tell me the equivalent?'

'Because,' she goes, 'I don't want the police involved. He's a ten-year-old boy, Ross. And, anyway, we still don't know for sure that he took them.'

'I can't believe you're still defending him.'

'I'm not defending him. I'm just saying there might be another explanation as to what happened to my bras. Like, for instance, I did that big clear-out of my wardrobe last week – do you remember the clothes appeal for the victims of Typhoon Hagupit?'

'No, but continue.'

'I sent seven bags of clothes. I could easily have –'

'What, accidentally put all of your good bras into one of the bags?'

'It's possible. Ross, my mind is all over the place with the job of raising four children.'

'That still doesn't explain why I caught him in our bedroom looking shifty.'

'He told you that Honor asked him to get something.'

'Sorcha, you always want to believe the best of people. You're a complete sucker and I mean that in an almost nice way.'

'All I'm saying is that we can't go accusing him without any proof.'

'Okay, you want proof? We'll get proof.'

'And how are you going to do that?'

'The next time he's here, we'll leave him on his own for a while and see what he does.'

'But would that not constitute entrapment?'

'You can call it entrapment if you want. I'm going to call it catching the little focker in the act.'

# 6. *Netflix and Chill*

It's, like, three o'clock on Wednesday afternoon and I'm in UCD. It's actually worth repeating that, given that I barely set foot in the place when I was supposedly enrolled here.

I'm in UCD.

I'm playing pool, though, so there's nothing to panic about.

I drove up to have a bit of lunch with a few of the goys, we're talking Dilly and Gilly, our two second rows, who are both doing Engineering, we're talking Rob Fortune and Johnny Bliss, our two centres, who are both doing Commerce, and we're talking Senny, obviously our number ten, who's doing Orts.

Lunch turned into a few pints of the Lovely Bubbly in The Clubhouse in the Student Centre, which then turned into a winner-keeps-table pool competition.

Which I happen to be winning hands-down.

'This place has changed so much,' I go, as I sink the black, then take yet another ten yoyos – this time from Rob Fortune. 'When I was here, there were a lot more people drinking during the day. People used to be half-shitfaced going into lectures. Does anyone want another one? I feel guilty taking all this money from you.'

Dilly and Gilly are like, 'Actually, we'd better head off. We've got a Functional Anatomy and Kinesiology lecture at three o'clock.'

I look at the other goys as if to say, 'See what I mean?'

A third-level education is wasted on some people.

Blissy storts racking the balls up again and goes, 'So, Rossi, what do you, em, do? I'm talking *actually* do?'

He's obviously wondering how I'm free to be hanging around UCD with a bunch of young goys on a weekday afternoon.

'Yeah, no, pretty much nothing,' I go. 'Well, *actually* nothing – fock-all, to be more specific.'

They've obviously been talking about this among themselves, because Rob goes, 'So, like, do you have a girlfriend or are you married or what?'

I laugh. I'm there, 'Okay, this is going to make me sound really old, I realize, but I'm actually married with five kids.'

'Five kids?' all three of them go at exactly the same time. *'Five?'*

'I've got, like, four kids with my wife, including triplets, and I had a son with a woman – she was a bit of a skank – when I was, like, sixteen. He's a great kid. He's doing his Leaving in June. He'll possibly end up coming here. Or even Trinners. I might actually have other kids, but those are the known cases.'

I break, sending the balls everywhere and a stripe into the bottom-corner pocket.

Senny goes, 'So, like, what do you do for money?'

I'm there, 'Absolutely nothing, to be fair to me. I inherited a gaff. It's a not-too-shabby pile of bricks on the old Vico Road. No mortgage. My old man pays all the other bills and gives me ten grand a month to keep things ticking over. Yeah, no, he's loaded.'

They all shake their heads like I'm the luckiest man in the world. I sink a second ball, then a third, before missing an easy enough pot over the middle pocket.

'So what about this weekend?' I go, because we're playing Barnhall on Friday night. 'How are you feeling about the match?'

It's Blissy's turn at the table.

'Barnhall are good,' he goes. 'I mean, they kicked the shit out of us before Christmas. They scored, I don't know, forty-something points.'

He sinks a spot but manages to also pocket the cue ball.

I'm like, 'Forty-something? That's ridiculous.'

He goes, 'They're a pretty physical team. And by the way, their number two is as wide as he is tall.'

'Really?'

'Seriously, Rossi, he's, like, eighteen or nineteen stone, but it's pure muscle.'

I nod. Then I sink a long ball. I'm like, 'That's good to know. It's good information for me to have.'

I clean up the table. Blissy hands me my tenner, then him and Rob end up having to head off, leaving me and Senny on our ownio.

I'm there, 'What about you, Dude – have you got a lecture this afternoon? Because I actually don't mind. I could hang around here until you're finished.'

He shakes his head as he racks up again. 'It's like I told my old pair,' he goes. 'There's no point in me breaking my balls this year. If things work out the way I'm expecting them to, I'm going to be joining the Leinster Academy next year. I'll be dropping out of college anyway.'

I'm there, 'Can I say something to you, Senny? I really love your attitude.'

'Thanks.'

'You remind me so much of myself at that age. I was the exact same. I never went to a single lecture.'

'Hey, I'm just focused on becoming a professional rugby player. I know a lot of people might consider that arrogant.'

'It's not arrogance if you've got the talent to back it up. I used to always say that.'

'Playing rugby is all I've ever wanted to do – since I was, like, six years old.'

'Seriously, this is like history repeating itself. What I would say, in terms of advice, is don't be afraid to enjoy the lifestyle.'

And as I'm saying it, two birds walk into the bor. One of them is disgraceful-looking, but the other one, I can't help but notice, is an absolute ringer for Kacey Barnfield.

'What do you mean by the lifestyle?' Senny goes, obviously a bit slow on the uptake.

'I'm talking about everything that comes with being a number ten,' I go, studying Kacey's orse as she strides confidently up to the bor. 'Don't get serious with just one bird.'

'Too late.'

'What?'

'Yeah, no, I'm with this girl called Torah.'

'Torah?'

'We've been together since we were, like, fifteen.'

'The same bird? What the fock are you thinking?'

He laughs. He goes, 'We're really happy, Rossi. She's actually really good for me.'

'Yeah, so is focking broccoli,' I go, 'but you couldn't eat it for every meal. I presume you're still doing little bits and pieces on the side, though?' and, as I say it, I flick my head in the direction of Kacey Barnfield. 'A bit of extra-curricular. I used to call it cardio!'

He's there, 'No, no interest. I mean, we're practically living together.'

'What?'

'Yeah, no, I live on campus and Torah stays over pretty much four nights a week. She's doing Orts.'

'Well, whatever makes you happy. Personally, I think you're mad.'

I break. I don't pot anything.

'Hey, Rossi,' he goes, 'do you like Drake?'

I'm there, 'I've never had it. My old dear usually does a goose on Christmas Eve. She's an unbelievable cook, the ugly focking sow.'

This answer causes Senny to totally miscue and not hit anything. He laughs, then goes, 'I'm talking about the music – that tune that's on. You've never heard of Drake?'

'Yeah, no, I think I have. Where are they from again?'

'Drake is a *he*, Ross, not a *they*. He's from Canada.'

'Yeah, I did actually know that. I've, em, fallen a bit behind in terms of my knowledge of the music scene and blah, blah, blah. I might borrow the CD from you.'

'CD? Seriously, Rossi, you're focking hilarious.'

Kacey Barnfield keeps looking over. I've got what they call peripheral vision. She's interested in one of us and I'm guessing it's me.

I pot a long ball into an end pocket, then I say something to Senny that's been on my mind. 'Look, Dude,' I go, 'I was possibly out of order saying that your Leinster Schools Senior Cup runners-up medal wasn't worth shit. A Leinster Schools Senior Cup medal is a Leinster Schools Senior Cup medal – doesn't matter what the colour is.'

It's horseshit. I know it even as I'm saying it.

He goes, 'No, you were right, Rossi. A runners-up medal isn't worth a fock.'

'Okay,' I go, 'have it your way.'

'In fact, you were right in all the things you said to me that day. Nearly won a senior cup medal. Nearly made the academy. Nearly made the team at Lansdowne. By the way, I *nearly* made the Irish schools team as well.'

'You played unbelievably well against City of Derry. Your second-half performance especially – I just hope someone from the Leinster branch was either there or saw what you did on YouTube if anyone recorded it on their phone.'

'A lot of that performance was down to you. You woke me up to myself. When you said that shit to me that day, it really struck a chord.'

'I presume that's why you tried to deck me.'

'I got home that night and I told Torah the entire conversation. And as I was telling her what you said, I realized that the reason it got to me was that you were right. I've proved nothing in the game.'

'You've got time on your side.'

'The problem is, Rossi, I've always bottled it at the vital moment. Schools Cup final – missed an easy kick with, like, a minute left that would have won it for us. Academy trial – same shit. Had a total mare. I think that's why I never made the first team at Lansdowne. They don't think I have the big-match temperament.'

And I'm like, 'Well, Dude, keeping Seapoint in Division 2B of the All Ireland League is your chance to prove that you do.'

I clear up the table, then I tell Senny that it's my round and I tip up to the bor.

'Two pints of the Hydrogen,' I go.

The bor dude sets them up.

I look to my left and Kacey is smiling in my direction. The ugly mate doesn't look happy – but then ugly mates never do. It must be a lonely life.

'Hey,' I go, laying it on good and thick. 'How the hell are you?'

Kasey goes, 'Oh, hi,' a little bit giddy. 'I'm fine. Thank you.'

'So what's your name?'

'I'm Hannah and this is Ava.'

Yeah, I don't remember asking about the other one. I don't say that, even though I'm tempted.

'Hannah's one of my favourite names,' I go.

She's like, 'Thank you.'

'Oh, it's right up there on the list – believe me!'

'That's, er, great news.'

Shit, I'm losing her, so I decide to hit her with something cheesy – girls love a cheesy line, no matter how much they pretend they don't.

'So,' I go, 'where have you been all my life?'

And Kasey bursts out laughing and she goes, 'I wouldn't say I was born for most of it!'

That even puts a smile on the ugly mate's face. I pay the borman, pick up the two pints and head back over to Senny.

I'm in town, buying a new gumshield, when Oisinn decides to finally return my call. I'm actually stepping out of Elvery's on Stephen's Green when my phone all of a sudden rings.

He's there, 'Ross, were you looking for me?'

I'm like, 'Yeah, two focking hours ago. What's that noise in the background?'

'It's the call to prayer.'

'Whoa, heavy! How are things going out there?'

'Great. I just had a very productive meeting with an Irish goy. He was in property. Lost nearly everything he had – and I'm talking five or six hundred million yoyos – in the crash. Two years ago, he storted buying up non-performing loan portfolios. Now he's worth five or six hundred million again.'

'God, it'd bring tears to your eyes, wouldn't it, a story like that? There's definitely a movie in it.'

'Hey, I got a text from JP. He said he saw you in the cinema with a bunch of muscly boys who were calling you Rossi.'

'That focker would want to remember the rugby player that I helped him become, instead of ripping the piss out of someone who's proving that he still has a lot to contribute to the game at the age of thirty-five.'

'He was only having a laugh . . . Rossi!'

'Yeah, whatever.'

'Hey, did you hear his old man is reopening Hook, Lyon and Sinker?'

'I heard a rumour.'

'It's true. Property prices in Dublin are up 15%.'

'There's so many signs that the whole recession thing was just a blip. Anyway, look, we're playing Barnhall tomorrow night.'

He laughs. He's like, 'Seriously?'

I'm there, 'Dude, everything you've told me so far has been spot-on. We beat City of Derry out the gate. We destroyed their front row.'

'Barnhall,' he goes, obviously thinking deeply.

I'm there, 'I'm pretty sure it's Trevor Brennan's old club.'

'Oh, *it's* Trevor Brennan's old club alright. They're a very hord team to beat.'

'I don't know if that's true. They're only three places ahead of us and we're bottom of the focking table.'

'Okay, have you ever heard of pulling forward?'

'Dude, *all* this shit is new to me. What's pulling forward?'

'Okay, here's how it works. You bind, then you come together with the opposition pack.'

'Okay.'

'Then just before the ball is put in –'

'Our put-in or theirs?'

'Either, doesn't matter – you pull the opposition pack towards you.'

'What does that do?'

'It makes the referee think that they're driving before the ball is played.'

I laugh.

I'm there, 'I focking love it!'

'It's a guaranteed penalty,' he goes.

'I'm smelling what you're stepping in and I'm enjoying that smell.'

'Again, don't tear the orse out of it. You'll get away with it twice, maybe three times in a match before the referee realizes he's being had. But it could be worth nine points to you. Anyway, Rossi, I've got to go.'

'Yeah, no, thanks, Dude.'

He hangs up.

I head back to the Stephen's Green Shopping Centre, where I porked the cor. I notice I have a text message from Sorcha. Apparently, Caleb is coming over on Saturday. Happy focking days. I've got Sorcha to agree to the idea of laying a trap for him, while noting for the record her concerns about – and I'm actually quoting her here – the possible infringement of his civil liberties.

You couldn't make my wife up.

As I'm walking into the shopping centre, I end up running straight into Lauren. Like Sorcha said, she's home from France for the week.

I'm like, 'Hey, Lauren, how the hell are you?'

She just goes, 'Hi, Ross,' no joy at all in the girl. She actually stiffens when I try to give her a hug.

She's pushing little Oliver in his stroller and beside her is little Ross Junior, who I can't help but notice is wearing an Elsa from *Frozen* costume – a focking *dress*, in other words?

He's all, 'Hi, Roth!'

And I'm like, 'Yeah, no, hey, Ross.'

What is he now, six?

'Roth,' he goes, 'I've been shopping with my mom! She bought thoo thopth in thitrus colourth and a pair of palatho panth. She lookth *tho* cute in them.'

Here's another kid who needs to learn about boundaries.

I go, 'Does she?' trying to sound like I give a shit, because Lauren thinks children are like porking tickets – they have to be validated. 'I'd love to see her in those pants.'

He's like, 'She lookth *tho* cute in them!'

See, people are encouraged these days to say every little thing that's on their minds. You hear it constantly, don't you? People going, 'I think it's time we started talking about this thing' or,

'I think it's all time we had a national conversation about that thing.'

I think it's time we all shut the fock up about a lot of things. But that's just me calling it.

I turn to Lauren and I go, 'So have you any plans to move back to Ireland?' just making conversation with the girl. 'Oisinn's just been telling me about this dude who was doing shit and now he's doing well again. It's all definitely coming back again. I heard you had a sandwich on a table-tennis bat?'

She doesn't even acknowledge my point. She just goes, 'What's going on with Christian?' and she says it in, like, an *accusing* way?

I'm there, 'Christian? I don't know, I haven't seen a lot of him lately. Mainly because I'm back playing rugby.'

Shit like that never impressed Lauren like it did other girls. She actually turns on me.

'I saw him today,' she goes, 'and I barely even recognized him. He was drunk out of his head. At lunchtime.'

Ireland is becoming like America. You have three or four beers for breakfast and suddenly everyone's telling you that you've got a problem.

I'm there, 'He's definitely hitting it hord – I'll give him that.'

She goes, 'I asked you a question, Ross – what the hell is going on?'

I'm like, 'Hey, why are you asking me?' suddenly feeling like I'm on the back foot here. 'He's *your* husband, Lauren.'

'*We're* separated. But *you're* still his best friend – or so you've always claimed.'

'That claim still stands.'

'Oh, does it?'

'We played rugby together. There's a bond.'

'But you're still happy to stand by and watch while he drinks himself to death, are you?'

'That's a bit dramatic, Lauren. I know bigger dipsos than Christian – way worse, in fact.'

'You're no friend, Ross. You're no friend at all.'

It's that comment that tips me over the edge.

'Whoa,' I go, 'it's hordly my fault, Lauren,' and I'm actually shouting at her – this is just outside Benetton, bear in mind, in front of a crowd. 'The dude is drinking because you walked out on him. You took his kids and you focked off to France. And now you're having a go at me, why? Because you feel guilty?'

She has no answer to that. She just goes, 'I need to get away from you, because if I don't, I will *actually* hurt you.'

I'm there, 'Hey, it sounds to me like I've touched a nerve!'

'Come on,' she goes to little Ross Junior, 'let's go to the Disney Store,' and she storts pushing the stroller. She walks a few feet, then she turns back and goes, 'You have a bond, huh? I wish Christian had never played rugby.'

I'm there, 'You're upset, Lauren. You're lashing out.'

'Because then he never would have met you. That stupid game brought him nothing, just a bunch of friends who held him back and dragged him down, then abandoned him when he needed them most.'

The Barnhall hooker is a monster and we're talking pretty much *literally*? Imagine a Portaloo with a headband and you'll get the general idea. I'm not actually exaggerating here. If you crashed in the Andes with this dude, you and the crew could be corving steaks off him for a month before the focker even noticed.

He is the biggest thing I have ever seen on a rugby field and they call him The Grip.

He's apparently a coalman around these ports – meaning Leixlip, of all places – and that I can well believe, because he's throwing us around the place like we're sacks of Black Diamond Premium Polish, we're talking backs *and* forwards. It's all the same to him.

The old man is on the sideline, shouting, 'The key is to stop number two!' stating the focking obvious. 'Stop number two and you stop Barnhall!'

Which of course is like trying to hold back the dawn.

Ten minutes into the second half, the dude scores his third try of the afternoon. I'm clinging onto his left leg as he crosses the line – being literally carried along – and he acts like I'm only a mild irritation to him, like a pebble in his shoe or something.

He grounds the ball, then sort of, like, ruffles my hair, like I'm a little kid.

At this stage, Barnhall should be out of sight. And they would be, except for two things. Firstly, their kicker couldn't hit a urinal wall with a stream of piss after a feed of pints. He's kicked, like, two conversions but missed four penalties. It turns out he's actually a Gaelic footballer – thick as a plate of frozen shite – and he's standing in for their regular ten, who's doing exams.

Secondly, the trick Oisinn taught me about pulling their scrum forward before the ball is put in has gifted us four penalties, all of which Senny has managed to stick between the posts.

'They're chorging,' I make sure to tell the referee very early on. He's only in, like, his late twenties – promoted too early and way out of his depth. 'They're notorious for it as well. They've been doing it all season.'

This doesn't go down well with the Barnhall players. Their number eight actually gives me a shove in the chest at one point and goes, 'You cheating fucker!'

The Barnhall captain ends up having to drag the dude away from me, going, 'Don't let him get inside your head. Don't give him the pleasure.'

I look at the referee and I go, 'This is what they do. They try to intimidate everyone. It's just that they've never come up against a referee who was strong enough to stop them.'

This, of course, appeals to the focking dope's ego and he storts giving us shots at goal that we have no actual right to – two in the first half, then two in the second, which explains why it's only, like, 19–12, and we're still within a score of levelling the match with fifteen minutes to go.

We're focked, though. Let's just say there are a lot of broken bodies on the battlefield. I think I've put in more tackles tonight than I did in my entire Senior Cup career. It's like the Battle of the Blackwater out there.

We're getting the shit kicked out of us in the physical stakes, but I'm clapping my hands together and telling the goys, 'Come on, The Point! We can get something out of this!'

I think Bucky is the first to actually believe it – and that's because he sees that *I* believe it? He knows I've probably been in this position before.

While Rob Fortune, our inside centre, is being treated for a dead leg, I'm walking around the goys as they're taking a breather and I'm giving them one of Father Fehily's old lines. 'When opportunity knocks,' I'm telling them, 'you better make sure you recognize it – because sometimes it comes dressed as hord work.'

They're all blown away by that quote.

Bucky's suddenly going, 'Rossi's right. We're only a converted try behind. There's a point in this for us! We need to keep putting the tackles in and make sure we don't lose our discipline!'

Five minutes from the end, Barnhall are putting pressure on us again, trying to close the game out, when the ball unexpectedly squirts sideways out of a ruck and Johnny Bliss – the famous Blissy – just swings his foot at it. It travels, like, thirty metres towards *their* try line and suddenly Senny is involved in a foot race with the Barnhall full-back to be the first to reach it. Senny is a flier. He ends up burning the dude for pace, bends down and scoops up the ball with one hand without even slowing up.

We're all screaming at him, going, 'Go on, Senny! Go on!'

He heads for the line and puts the ball down under the posts to make the conversion a piece of piss.

We end up going totally ballistic.

The Barnhall players are all just looking at each other, wondering how the fock we're suddenly level here.

We end up getting a bit complacent as the game moves into injury time. They have possession and we, for some reason, go to sleep. We miss a couple of tackles and suddenly The Grip gets a hold of the rugby ball, tucks it into one of the folds in his belly and storts heading for our line like a runaway something or other.

Goffo, Maho and Dilly all try to put in tackles, except he swats them away with, like, total contempt. He actually laughs, because he knows there's suddenly no one standing between him and the winning try.

One or two of the Barnhall players are already celebrating. But, as he thunders towards the line and a certain try, the Rossmeister suddenly appears out of nowhere.

I'm, like, twenty feet behind him. Then it's, like, ten feet. Then it's, like, six feet. I realize there's no point launching myself at him, because he'll end up just carrying me over the line with him, wearing me like a focking hula-hoop.

So I throw myself down on the ground, then I reach out my right hand and, with the tips of my fingers, I give his ankle just the tiniest of little taps.

He goes down like an overturned lorry – and like an overturned lorry, he ends up shedding his load. The ball spills and Maho is the first to reach it.

Of course, the question on his mind is obviously, do we kick for touch and take the draw or do we play on and see can we get the win?

Senny, Blissy and Mark Dwyer, our right wing, are all screaming for the ball, but Bucky goes, 'Kick it out, Maho!' deciding to settle for the point.

He kicks it into touch and the referee blows up.

The Barnhall players are sick. They were better than us, so it's very much a point won for us. But instead of celebrating, there ends up being a massive row between our backs and our forwards over the decision to settle for a draw. Goys like Gilly, Dilly, Bucky, Maho and Andy Walpole have been taking punishment all night and they're happy to be leaving Barnhall with something other than heavy bruising and tinnitus. But Senny, Blissy and especially Dordo, our scrum-half, think we should have just gone for it. I kind of agree with them – being a back at hort – except I stay out of it while they're debating the issue at the top of their voices, with a bit of pushing and shoving thrown in.

I look over at the old man. He's rubbing his hand through his hair, going, 'Lost for superlatives, Ross! One is simply lost for superlatives to describe it!'

Byrom Jones actually claps me off the field. 'Thut's one of the moyst incridible tickles Oy've ivver soyn,' he goes.

I shrug, all modesty, and I give him another one of Father Fehily's lines: 'No tree is too tall for a short dog to piss on it.'

He laughs. He loves it.

'Rossoy,' he goes, 'have a look beyond yoy?'

I look back over my shoulder. Senny and Bucky are having a serious borney. Senny is stabbing his finger into Bucky's chest to give, like, extra emphasis to the point he's making.

I'm there, 'Shit, that's not good.'

Byrom goes, 'Are yoy kidding moy? Sux woyks agoy, they dudn't get thut upsit abaaht loysing. They've just toyken a point from a mitch thoy had noy businuss tayking a point from and they're upsit that ut wasn't all throy. Have yoy inny oydea what a turnaraahnd that us?'

'Yeah, no,' I go, 'I suppose they showed a lot of desire out there.'

'Yoy've got them beloyving, Rossoy.'

'Do you think?'

'Moyte, you've got *moy* beloyving. Which Oy dudn't before. What you sid to them abaaht opportunitoy knocking and ut coming drissed as haahd work. Oy was watching them aahfter yoy sid ut. Oy could soy them groy in stature. You're a facking loyder, Rossoy. A born loyder.'

'That's, er, good to hear.'

'Will I till yoy the even bitter noys?'

'Yeah, no, go ahead.'

'Bictive lost to Groystoynes tonoyt. Which moyns, for the first toym thus soyson, we're off the bottom of the toyble.'

I call Honor outside to the gorden, giving it, 'Honnnorrr!!! Honnnorrr!!! Honnorrr!!!' at the top of my voice.

Sixty seconds later, she steps outside wearing a look of confusion mixed with suspicion.

She goes, 'Okay, what the fock's wrong?'

And I'm there, 'Yeah, no, nothing's wrong. I just wanted to show you – look how many daffodils there are in the gorden. Loads, huh?'

I can see her little nose twitching, wondering have I been drinking.

I'm there, 'I'm totally sober, Honor. I'm just saying, it's very colourful, isn't it?'

Of course, I've got about as much interest in Sorcha's flowerbeds as Honor probably does. The plan is just to get her away from Caleb for ten minutes to see does he pop upstairs to grab some more of my wife's Jack McGraths.

She's like, 'Okay, this is *so* random. Me and Caleb are watching *Mr Magorium's Wonder Emporium*.'

'Yeah, no,' I go, 'I'm just remembering the day your old dear planted all these flowers. You told her that as soon as they came up, you were going to kick the heads off every single one of them. Do you remember that?'

'Are you having a nervous breakdown?'

'No, I'm just reminiscing, that's all. It's just you all of a sudden seem so grown up. Flowers are nice, though, aren't they? I'm talking about flowers generally.'

'Oh my God, you are *such* a sap.'

Yeah, I'm not the one watching *Mr Magorium's Wonder Emporium*.

I'm there, 'I've never given a massive amount of thought to flowers before now. I'm going to stort, though – as in, I must find out more about them. All the different kinds. Blah, blah, bah.'

She definitely thinks I'm pissed. 'Are you, like, deliberately wasting my time?'

I'm there, 'Will we try to name as many as we can think of?'

'Excuse me?'

'Okay, there's tulips. There's roses. They're the obvious ones. Then there's, em . . . help me out here.'

'Did you pick up a focking brain injury playing rugby?'

'Dandelions,' I go. 'Let's see how many we can come up with without actually Googling it.'

She storts walking back to the house.

I'm there, 'Hang on, Honor, I wanted to say something else to you.'

She turns around. She's like, 'What? What the fock do you want?'

I'm there, 'We, er, drew last night. Against Barnhall. We possibly deserved more out of the game, but I'd still consider it a point won rather than two dropped.'

'You must be confusing me with someone who gives a shit.'

'Just let me finish the point I'm trying to make. We need to get back to winning games, though. We've got Sunday's Well at home next weekend. Would you be interested in coming along to see your old man in action?'

'I'd rather eat my own colon.'

'I'm just thinking, you've never seen me play rugby, have you?'

'And that's the way I intend to keep it.'

I'm there, 'Yeah, no, go back inside so,' because I suddenly spot Sorcha standing at the back door, with her orms folded, looking sad.

Honor goes back inside and Sorcha walks down the gorden to me.

I'm like, 'Well?'

She doesn't say anything for a good thirty seconds, then she goes, 'I feel sick.'

I'm there, 'What happened?'

She sighs. Then she goes, 'He tiptoed up the stairs the second Honor went outside. I stood on the landing. I heard him opening and closing drawers in the wardrobe.'

'Hey,' I go, 'I hate saying I told you so – so instead I'm just going to say, I was the one who called it.'

I stort walking back towards the house. Sorcha trots after me, going, 'What are you going to do?'

I'm there, 'What do you think I'm going to do? I'm going to search his coat.'

'Just remember, Ross, he has a right to be present if you're going to search his property.'

'Come on, Sorcha, you don't believe in that human rights guff any more than I do.'

His jacket is hanging on the back of a chair in the kitchen. I pick it up and I check the pockets.

They're empty.

I'm there, 'Where else could he have hidden them?'

Sorcha goes, 'He had a bag when he arrived.'

'Did he?'

'Yeah, he brought his schoolbag with him for some reason.'

'Yeah, no, I think I can guess the reason.'

So then I burst into the living room, with Sorcha following behind me, quoting the Geneva Convention. Honor and Caleb look up from the TV – they both get a fright. Dustin Hoffman is on the screen, acting the focking dope.

I look at Caleb and I go, 'What were you doing upstairs?'

He tries to go, 'I wasn't upstairs.'

And even Honor goes, 'He hasn't left this room. I swear.'

Then I notice the bag at his feet. I make a grab for it. I'm like, 'Let's see what you've been up to?'

He's like, 'Give me that! You've no right!' but I unzip it anyway.

Sorcha goes, 'Caleb, we're just trying to understand the reason you went upstairs to our –'

She suddenly stops talking when she sees me pulling two bras, three pairs of knickers and one bikini bottom out of the bag.

Again, he tries to deny it. He's there, 'I don't know how they got in there.'

I actually laugh. I'm there, 'Yeah, no, I'm sure you don't. Sorcha, phone his old dear.'

Honor just bursts into tears.

Caleb goes, 'No! Please don't ring my mom! She'll send me back to see that therapist!'

But Sorcha whips out her phone, her face all business now, and goes, 'Caleb, it's for your own good – you'll see that in the long run.'

She phones Flidais and asks her to come to the house – she mentions that it's, like, *urgent*?

Honor is, like, really sobbing her hort out now.

Caleb turns to her and goes, 'Honor, they must have, like, fallen in there somehow. *You* believe me, don't you, Honor? We're friends, remember?'

I go, 'Friends don't steal knickers and bras from each other's mothers,' even though I'm on pretty shaky ground there. I've still

185

got one of Christian's old dear's black thongs that I keep as a screwvenir of our time together.

This is very different, of course. This is, like, weird shit.

Eventually, Caleb's old dear shows up. Sorcha goes, 'Flidais, I'm very sorry to ask you to come here like this, but something very, very serious has happened this morning.'

Flidais is like, 'Oh?' looking from Sorcha to me, then back to Sorcha again.

God, I love her perfectly round golf-ball head.

I go, 'We caught your son with his hand literally in Sorcha's underwear drawer,' seeing no point in sugar-coating it for the woman. 'He's a bra robber and a knicker thief.'

She's in, like, shock. She tries to go, 'What?' except the actual word won't come out.

Sorcha goes, 'It's true, Flidais. Ross just opened his bag and found, well, those five or six items you see there on the coffee table.'

'Bras and knickers,' I go. 'Bras. And. Knickers.'

Honor has her face in her hands, sobbing her little hort out.

Caleb turns nasty then. He points at me and he goes, '*He* did it. *He* put them in there, Honor.'

I'm like, 'And why would I do that?'

'Because I told you I was in love with your wife. But I didn't steal anything. The only thing I did was send her flowers on Valentine's Day.'

Sorcha's like, 'Flowers?'

I quickly go, 'Let's stick to the point here, can we? You can't blame your way out of this one, Caleb. Sorcha heard you rooting around in our wardrobe. And I caught you in there last week.'

Flidais sighs, like she's – I don't know – suddenly *resigned* to something? She goes, 'Not again, Caleb.'

I'm like, 'Excuse me? Are you saying he has previous for this kind of shit?'

'With Ainukka.'

'Who the fock is Ainukka?'

'She was our nanny. From Finland. I should have possibly said something the last day.'

It's actually Sorcha who ends up having the conniption fit. She actually roars at Flidais. She's like, 'Yes, you should have said something! I can't believe you would keep something like that from us!'

Flidais goes, 'I fully understand why you're angry.'

Caleb goes, 'I swear. I didn't do it this time. Honor asked me to get something from the bedroom – didn't you, Honor? Remember the chocolate, Honor? Your mom keeps a bor of Galaxy at the bottom of her underwear drawer.'

Through her tears, Honor goes, 'I did! Mom, please! I sent him upstairs to your room to get chocolate! You've got to believe me!'

Sorcha sad-smiles Flidais and goes, 'Flidais, I don't even like Galaxy chocolate.'

'Dad!' Honor goes. 'Please don't send him away!'

Flidais shakes her head and goes, 'Ross, Sorcha, I'm sorry I didn't tell you everything. All I can do is apologize to you again,' then she sort of, like, frog-morches the famous Caleb with his big Bieber head outside to her Audi TT.

Honor's screaming like a focking banshee, going, 'Nooooooo! Caleb! Come back! Pleeeaaassseee!'

Into the cor they jump, then twenty seconds later, they're gone.

Honor spends the next fifteen minutes just, like, sobbing her hort out, going, 'I hate my life! I hate my life and I hate myself!'

I try to console her by going, 'He was a weirdo, Honor. I said it from day one.'

But it's no good.

She goes, 'What you did was entrapment. I can't believe you had the whole thing planned. To get me out of the house, so he could go upstairs.'

Sorcha's there, 'You've had your hort broken, Honor, and you're going to feel sad for a while. But you'll get over this and one day you'll meet someone else.'

'I don't want someone else. I want to be with Caleb.'

'He's not right for you, Honor.'

I go, 'He's not right at all.'

Honor whips out her phone and goes, 'I need to ring him. I need to talk to him.'

But Sorcha snatches the phone out of her hand. 'You are not ringing him, Honor, and that's the end of it.'

Sorcha goes into Honor's contacts and she deletes Caleb's name and number.

Honor suddenly roars at her. 'You bitch!' she goes. 'You had no right to delete his number!'

Sorcha goes, 'I'm thinking of you, Honor. I'm thinking about your welfare.'

'You're thinking about yourself! You were jealous, that's all. You were throwing yourself at him right from the stort.'

'That's ridiculous!' Sorcha goes.

I don't comment either way.

'*You're* ridiculous!' Honor goes. 'And you're a focking bitch and a focking slut! And you might be pretty, but your orse is focking huge!'

She stomps up the stairs to her room.

Sorcha shouts up after her. She goes, 'What happened to that beautiful little girl who let me show her how to do contouring a couple of weeks ago?'

Honor leans over the top banister and goes, 'She's focking dead!'

Honor is refusing meals and calling her mother a fat, peroxide blonde heifer through her locked bedroom door. It's good to see that things are finally returning to normal around here.

I'm downstairs in the gym, doing an unbelievable number of sit-ups, especially for a man who's basically bruised from the neck down after the Barnhall match.

As I'm doing my sit-ups, I stort for some reason thinking about Christian and I stort to feel suddenly guilty. Lauren might have had a point when she said I've possibly abandoned him. I've just been, I don't know, doing my own thing, following my dream of playing rugby again, while he's been out there, drinking himself to an early death.

As I switch from sit-ups and bicep curls, I stort to get this weird feeling in my head that I recognize straightaway as my conscience. And that's when I come up with the idea of doing maybe an intervention with him. It's apparently a big thing in, like, the *States*? You sit down with someone in a safe and comfortable environment and you tell them straight out that you're worried about them and you're concerned about the way they're living their life.

Kielys wouldn't be a bad call in terms of a venue, I'm thinking. Somewhere he feels at home. If I was being a little bit selfish, I'd point out that it's a Saturday night and I wouldn't mind going out for a few pints, especially after the drama of this morning.

I finish up and I give the dude a ring while I'm, like, towelling myself off. It goes straight to his voicemail. I leave him a message. It's just like, 'Hey, Christian – how's it going, Dude? Just wondered how you were. Wanted to see did you maybe want to catch up, have a few sensible pints? Give me a shout back. It's Ross, by the way.'

Then, just as I'm hanging up, the phone rings in my hand. I can see from the screen that it's not Christian – it's actually Senny?

I answer by going, 'Not a great time, Dude – I'm in the gym.'

He laughs and goes, 'I've just come from the gym. How are you feeling after last night?'

'Bit sore,' I go. 'Bit bashed up. But I'm working through it. You played unbelievably well, by the way.'

He goes, 'In terms of?'

I smile to myself. I think I'm becoming a bit of a guru to him.

'In terms of your kicking,' I go, 'in terms of your decision-making, in terms of the way you ran the match.'

He's there, 'We didn't get the result, though.'

'We got *a* result.'

'Yeah, but we need wins. I can't believe Bucky decided to just take the point.'

'Your worst enemy is your memory.'

'What's that?'

'Yeah, no, it was one of Father Fehily's sayings.'

'Your worst enemy is your memory?'

'Yeah, no, it means don't be always looking back and regretting shit.'

'Your worst enemy is your memory.'

'He always used to say it to me when I'd be replaying old games, even just moves that didn't come off, in my head.'

'You're actually right. You know, I think I'm going to make that quote the cover photo on my Facebook page.'

'Yeah, no, you do that. Actually, Johnny loves it as well – that quote.'

'Johnny Bliss?'

'No, not Johnny Bliss. Johnny Sexton.'

'Johnny Sexton?'

I can tell he's surprised to hear me drop his name.

'And that's not just me name-dropping,' I go.

He's there, 'You're actually mates with Johnny Sexton?'

I laugh.

I'm there, 'You could say that, yeah. I think if you asked him, he'd say he possibly sees me more as a mentor.'

He's like, 'Really?'

'I text him on the morning of every match he plays. First thing. Same message – eat nerves, shit results. It's become an actual port of his routine. Even when he left Leinster for Racing, I still did it. I said it to him: "You're still getting the focking texts, Dude. They're nailed on."'

'I actually did a training camp with him when I was, like, eleven or twelve.'

'Well, if things had been different, I could have been giving that training camp. Another kicker who admires me, of course, is Mads?'

'You know Ian Madigan as well?'

'Know him? Jesus, I practically raised him. Yeah, no, he's been coming to me for advice since he was a kid. He's acknowledged that in interviews – the role I played in his development. He says he wouldn't have become the player he is today if he hadn't seen me totally fock things up for myself before him. Words to that effect. I think what he's trying to say is that I showed the likes of him, Johnny and even Ian Keatley where the landmines lay. And I did that by walking on every focking one of them.'

'Hey, but you're back now, Rossi. Imagine how you'll feel if we manage to stay up. We were gone before you arrived. We'd given up.'

'Yeah, no, I know that, but sometimes . . . ah, look, I envy you, Senny, that's all. Being twenty-one, twenty-two . . .'

'I'm actually twenty.'

'Twenty? Jesus, you've got it all ahead of you. Like I once did. What I wouldn't give to be in your position again. I'd do everything differently.'

He goes, 'Your worst enemy is your memory.'

And I end up having to laugh. I'm like, 'Yeah, I could do with taking my own advice once in a while! By the way, what are you up to now?'

'I'm heading home.'

'Yeah, no, I'm talking about *after* that? It's been a pretty emotional day here today. My daughter got her hort broken for the first time. I was wondering did you fancy hooking up for a few pints?'

He goes, 'I was actually thinking of having a quiet one tonight, Rossi.'

I'm there, 'You mean staying in?'

'Netflix and Chill,' he goes. 'Know what I'm saying?'

I laugh. I'm there, 'Oh, I hear you, Dude. I know *exactly* what you're saying!'

I hang up, then I tip down to the kitchen.

'I'm heading out,' I go.

Sorcha's like, 'What? Where?'

'I'm going to pop around to Senny's gaff,' I go. 'We're just going to watch a box set and relax.'

She's there, 'Who's Senny? It better not be a girl, is it?'

'Sorcha, you wouldn't have to ask me that question if you actually listened when I talked about rugby. He's our kicker. You've got to come and see us against Sunday's Well next week. I want you to bring the boys as well.'

She's just put them to bed and she's sitting at the island, having a glass of Sancerre and reading, literally, a book.

She goes, 'So how old is this – what did you say his name was?'

I'm there, 'Senan Torsney. We call him Senny. I don't know – twenty.

But I think I'm becoming a bit of a hero to him. It's nice. I've always seen myself as a role model.'

'So, what, you're hanging out with him, are you?'

'Yeah, so what?'

'Nothing. I just think it's, I don't know, random, that's all.'

'No more random than you and your book club. A living room full of angry-looking women drinking Pinot Grigio on the third Tuesday of every month. Pack of focking weirdos.'

'Why are you being so defensive, Ross? All I said was that it was random. So you're leaving me here with Honor, are you?'

'I can't see her coming out of her room for a day or two. She's not going to forgive you easily.'

'Forgive *me*?'

'*Us* – she's not going to forgive *us*.'

'We had no choice, Ross. Caleb's obviously very disturbed.'

'Hey, you're preaching to the choir.'

'I knocked on Honor's door about a half an hour ago, asked if she wanted to make brownies with me. She called me horrible names, Ross.'

'As in?'

'The W word.'

'Wanker?'

'No, not wanker. The other one.'

'I'm not sure I know the other one. Any hints going?'

'Whore, Ross.'

'Whore? Does that begin with a W?'

'Yes, it begins with a W.'

'See, *that*, to me, is random. Anyway, I better hit the road. Like I said, we're going to watch something on Netflix. Senny's probably keen to get it on. I'll see you in the morning.'

I point the cor in the direction of Belfield. Fifteen minutes later, I'm driving through the main gate of UCD when my phone all of a sudden rings. I check the screen and it ends up being Christian, ringing me back.

His timing couldn't be focking worse.

I stare at the screen for, like, twenty seconds, wondering should I even answer it. In the end, it just rings out. I feel shit about it, but I'll bell him back tomorrow, or possibly sometime next week.

I pull up outside Senny's aportment block. I ring his mobile, except there ends up being no answer. I ring it, like, three times, but it just rings out.

So I wander up to the door of the building. I key in the aportment numbers, then I press the little button with the bell on it. I wait a good, like, thirty seconds and nothing happens, so I give it another ring – a longer one this time. Still nothing.

I think to myself, Fock it, he might have changed his mind. Maybe I'll ring Christian back after all – see if he fancies going for a few pints.

But then I think, Hang on, maybe Senny's fallen asleep. He must be wrecked if he said he wanted to just crash. I wander around the back of his building, because he mentioned that he lives on the ground floor.

There's, like, a little deck at the back of his gaff. He's definitely home because the curtains are open and the light is on. I duck between the top and bottom rail and step onto the deck. Then I go up to the French doors and I stort peering through the window into the gaff.

And that's when I get a fright that nearly turns my hair grey.

Senny and some bird are hord at it. They're coming towards the end of the transaction, from what I can make out. Senny's about to, well, let's just say, bring the curtain down on proceedings the way people having sex on the Internet tend to do.

They can't see me, of course, because it's dork outside and I end up sort of, like, forgetting myself, standing there, staring through the window at them, going at it like porn stors.

That's when I suddenly feel something hit me across the back of the head. I end up stumbling forward and walloping my forehead off the French doors.

Senny and, I'm presuming, Torah get a fright. She gets up off her knees. I turn around and there's, like, a dude standing there. It turns out he's cracked me across the head with a focking wok.

He holds it up, like he's ready to clobber me with it again. 'What the fock are you doing looking in that window?' he goes.

He must be, like, Senny's next-door neighbour.

I'm there, 'Dude, it's not what you think?'

I look over my shoulder and I notice Senny walking towards the door to investigate the kerfuffle outside. I only have, like, a second or two to act. So I point to something over the neighbour's left hammer and I go, 'The reason I'm here is that thing behind you?'

He looks over his shoulder. His reward for falling for such an obvious trick is an unmerciful kick in the balls, which causes him to drop the wok and keel over in pain, allowing me to make a run for it. I peg it back to the cor and I manage to get into it and get the engine storted and I'm out of there like Sebastian focking Vettel.

Jesus, my head, though!

I drive back to Killiney, obviously thinking, What the fock. Why would Senny tell me to call over if he was home with Torah?

Into the house I go. Sorcha hears the front door open and close, then she goes, 'Ross?' poking her head out of the kitchen. 'What are you doing back so early?'

I'm there, 'Yeah, no, we couldn't decide on a box set, so we decided not to bother in the end.'

'What are you talking about? Oh my God, Ross, you're bleeding.'

She walks up the hallway towards me.

I'm like, 'What?'

She goes, 'Your head, Ross.'

I put my hand where it's sore – right on the crown – and it's, like, wet to the touch. I look at my fingers then and they're, like, covered in blood.

'What the hell happened?' she goes, inspecting it closely. 'Did you two have a fight?'

I'm there, 'No.'

'A fight over what box set to watch?'

'Don't be ridiculous. We're mates.'

'So why are you bleeding?'

I decide to just tell her the truth. I've got nothing to hide – for once in my life.

'Yeah, no,' I go, 'I called to Senny's gaff and there was, like, no answer. He wasn't answering his mobile either. So I tipped around the back of the building and he was, well, hord at it.'

She's like, 'Hord at it? Hord at what?'

'Do you really want me to spell it out for you, Sorcha? Him and his girlfriend were in the middle of . . . stuff. I believe the phrase for what they were actually doing is finishing off. Anyway, the dude next door caught me watching them through the window and he smashed me across the back of the head with a wok. There really isn't any more to it than that, Sorcha.'

'But why would he invite you around to his place if he knew his girlfriend was coming over?'

'That's what I keep asking myself.'

'Did he definitely invite you, Ross? As in, what did he actually say?'

'Yes, he invited me, Sorcha. I asked him if he wanted to go for scoops and he said he'd prefer to have a night in. He said he was thinking in terms of Netflix and Chill.'

Sorcha's mouth forms a little O, then she has to slap her hand over it to stop herself from laughing in my face. 'Oh! My God!' she goes. 'Oh! My! God!'

I'm like, 'What?'

'You've never heard of Netflix and Chill?'

'I've heard of Netflix. And I've heard of chill.'

'It's slang, Ross!'

'Slang? Slang for what?'

'What do you think, Ross? Slang for sex!'

'Okay, you're shitting me.'

'He wasn't inviting you over to watch, I don't know, *Homeland* or something. He was telling you that his girlfriend was coming over for sex!'

I don't focking believe this.

'Jesus Christ,' I go, 'why can't young people just say what they mean? It's like they speak a whole different language to the one we use to speak – as in, they have their own words. And it's not only words. They like different music to us. They like different labels to us. And they have sex like they're doing it for an online audience.'

She goes, 'This is what comes from not acting your actual age, Ross.'

And she storts laughing so hord, I think she's going to have a focking prolapse.

'Sorcha,' I go, 'I'd be pretty certain that the Gords are out there right now searching for a man who matches my description. I would suggest we keep this story very much to ourselves.'

I'm pushing the three boys up Westmoreland Street in their big, triple stroller, with people having to step onto the road to let us pass. All the *wans* are going, 'Ah, would ya lookit – de tree babbies, look!' and 'They're oately goergeous, so thee eer!' to which Leo's answer, to one and all, is, 'Shit fock bastard! Focking shit fock bastard!'

All I can hear behind me then is, like, howls of laughter and then people repeating what he just said, as if they've never heard a baby use the F-word, or the B-word, or the S-word before for that matter.

'Focking shit!' he goes. 'Focking shitting focks.'

I'm like, 'You tell them, Leo. You tell –' and I suddenly stop, because that's when I realize that it's not actually Leo swearing at all. Not this time. It's Brian.

I'm wondering how long we can go on ignoring it, especially now that there's a focking pair of them at it.

'Focking shit,' Leo goes, as if responding to the point Brian just made. 'Shitting shitting focker.'

I just keep pushing the stroller. It's, like, Sunday afternoon and we're on our way to see Ronan at work. I actually wanted to take the boys on the *Love/Hate* Tour of Dublin, although with the mouths on them, people will probably think they're port of the focking attraction.

'Shush, shush, shush,' I go, as we're about to take the turn onto Aston Quay. 'You love buses, don't you, Leo?'

He's like, 'Shitting bastard. Shitting bastard.'

I check my phone. We're just in time for the two o'clock tour.

I'm there, 'Like I said, goys, get ready, because you're in for a big surprise!'

I'm the one who ends up getting the surprise, though. As we take the turn at the bottom of Westmoreland Street onto the quays, I spot the *Love/Hate* tour bus straightaway. It'd actually be impossible to miss it.

The thing is on fire.

My first thought is obviously for Ronan. I'm hoping to fock he's not trapped inside. I'm actually building myself up to yank the door open and drag him out when I suddenly spot him in the doorway of Caddles Irish Gifts – him, Nudger and Buckets of Blood, the three of them standing there in a tight little circle, smoking and talking to each other out of the corners of their mouths while waiting for the fire brigade to arrive.

There must be, like, two or three hundred people just hanging around, watching the bus – my son's pride and you'd have to say joy – go up in flames.

I push the stroller over to where they're standing and I go, 'Ronan, what the fock?'

Brian goes, 'Focking fock.'

Ronan is surprised to see me there. He's like, 'Alreet, Rosser?'

I go, 'No, I'm not alright. What the fock happened? Why is your bus on fire?'

He's there, 'Leeb it, Rosser – you're out of yisser depth.'

'No, I won't leave it. Please tell me it's just an insurance scam?'

I'm looking at poor Tom Vaughan-Lawlor's face just melting, along with the windows and the tyres and everything else.

Jesus, the heat off the focking thing.

'You myrus well teddum,' Buckets goes. 'Utterwise, he's gonna keep on aston you.'

Ronan takes a long pull on one of his rollies, blows smoke out the side of his mouth, then goes, 'It was a fedda from Coolock did it.'

I'm like, 'Coolock? Is that the name of a place?'

'Yeah, it's the nayum of a place. Doatunt woody, Rosser, he'll be got.'

'Who'll be got? Who are we talking about here?'

'He's calt Scum.'

'Scum? His parents actually named him Scum?'

'No, that's he's nickname, Rosser. He's real name is Deddick Tattan.'

'Derek Tattan?'

'Deddick Tattan. He dudn't like it, but. He prefeers Scum.'

'So, what, he burned out your bus?'

It's Buckets who actually tells me the truth. He goes, 'It's a row over teddy toddy.'

It's mad to think that I grew up half an hour up the M50 from Buckets of Blood and I might as well be talking to a focking Wookie.

I'm there, 'Are you trying to say territory?'

'That's what I bleaten did say,' he goes. 'Teddy toddy. Scum is operdating a *Love/Hate* toower heself. *Love/Hate*: The Toower.'

'Hang on, are *you* not *Love/Hate*: The Tour?'

'No,' Nudger goes, 'we're The *Love/Hate* Toower of Dublin. Addyhow, he's arthur accusing us of muscling in on he's patch.'

'Eeben though they're two veddy diffordent toowers,' Ronan goes. 'Scum brings you to the apeertment where John Boy lived in Seerdies Two and you get to howult the izact sayum gun that Hughie used to accidentally blow he's own berrains out. I says it to Scum. Says I, "There's room for boat toowers."'

I'm there, 'I'm taking it this Scum dude didn't agree?'

Ronan looks at the blazing bus and goes, 'You catch on fast, Rosser. You catch on fast.'

Nudger goes, 'We throyed to reason wirrum. But Scum says to us, "Eeder clowiz dowyn yooer toower or supper the consequences." Says I, "Ast me bleaten bollix, you doorty fooken Coolock pox."'

'Focking pox,' Brian suddenly goes. 'Focking shitting pox.'

Ronan goes, 'We turdened up for woork thus morden. Did the foorst toower of the day – norra botter. Lunch toyum, we goes into the Londis arowunt the corder there for the chicken dippers.'

Chicken dippers. It really is a different world.

'We come out,' he goes, 'and the bleaten thing is on foyer.'

The sound of fire-engine sirens suddenly fills the air. Two come haring around the corner from, presumably, Pearse Street.

Of course the bus is beyond saving at this point.

I'm there, 'So what are you going to do? I'm presuming you're not insured?'

'We're inshewered alreet,' Nudger goes. 'And we can hab a temper doddy bus delibered by the ent of the arthur noon.'

Ronan's there, 'I think Rosser's aston what we're gonna do about Scum. We're gonna retadiate, Rosser.'

'Re –?'

'– tadiate. Means we're gonna hirrum back – eeben heerder.'

Leo and Johnny stort coughing and spluttering. They're obviously breathing in smoke. I probably should move on, though not without at least *trying* to talk some sense into their brother first?

I'm there, 'Can I suggest an alternative to the whole retaliation thing? Would you maybe think about switching from a *Love/Hate* tour to a *Fair City* one?'

Ronan goes, '*Feer City:* The Toower?'

'I don't think anyone's doing one. I mean, there's as much human focking misery in *Fair City* as there is in *Love/Hate*. All tight leather jackets and people being annoyed with each other. Plus, like I said, you'd have the field to yourselves. It's worth thinking about from a business POV.'

'Ast me bleaten bollocks, Rosser.'

'Ro, this dude just burned your bus.'

'And he'll be got – thrust me.'

I swear to fock, the way he says it, he actually *sounds* like Nidge?

'Ro,' I go, 'you've got to remember, it's just a TV show.'

'It's not joost a TV show, Rosser. It's how *we* lib eer loyuvs.'

Nudger and Buckets both nod.

I'm there, 'Think again about the *Fair City* idea. I think the entire thing is pretty much filmed in the RTÉ cor pork – probably for safety reasons.'

'Fook *Feer City*,' Ronan goes. 'This is all-out bleaten war.'

*

I'm watching Honor through the kitchen window. She's kicking the heads off Sorcha's daffodils. One by one, slowly and clinically. Three steps backwards, two to the side – I can't say enough good things about the girl's execution.

The apple doesn't fall far from the tree.

I fix myself a cup of coffee, then I go back to the living room to watch *Midday* – or, as I call it, breakfast television. I have a serious thing for Elaine Crowley and it's never going away.

I actually love the show as well because you end up finding out a lot about women – as in what they want, why they sometimes act the way they do and how their minds can sometimes work.

And it's as I'm sitting there, thinking about the complicated nature of the female mind, that a thought suddenly hits me like a focking diesel train.

Jesus Christ.

No.

I jump up off the sofa and I literally sprint out of the room, then out to the gorden, where Honor is swinging her foot at the last daffodil standing.

She catches me just staring at her with my mouth open and she goes, 'What the fock is your problem?'

I'm there, 'Honor, I figured it out.'

She's like, 'What are you crapping on about now?'

'It was you! Oh my God, you set Caleb up!'

She stares at me for a long time without saying a basic word. She's possibly trying to, like, gauge how I *feel* about it? I actually don't *give* a fock. I'm glad the little focker is out of our lives.

'He got what he deserved,' she eventually goes. 'He thought he could use me to get to her.'

'So Sorcha's knickers and bras. *You* took them – and you planted them in his bag?'

She just shrugs. Doesn't admit it, doesn't deny it. I think she's learned a lot from watching me over the years.

I'm there, 'So when he said you sent him into our room to look for chocolate . . .'

Honor suddenly produces a bor of Galaxy from her pocket. She moves over to the swing bench and sits down. I do the same. I sit down beside her. She breaks off a chunk and offers it to me. I take it and pop it into my mouth.

She's like, 'How did you figure it out?'

I'm there, 'I don't know. I was in there watching *Midday* and it just hit me. I mean, when I pulled those bits and pieces out of his bag, he did seem genuinely surprised. So either he's an incredible actor or he was stitched up. So when did you decide, like, to do it?'

'That very first night he was here.'

'That long ago?'

'He was, like, all over her – and she was loving it, of course. Then every time he texted me after that, it was, *Sorcha this* and *Sorcha that* and, *I'd love to see your mom's letters from Nelson Mandela.*'

'Any excuse to get close to her, huh?'

'And I just said to myself, Nobody focking treats me like that.'

'So stealing her underwear – where did that come from?'

'He'd already told me what happened with the nanny from Finland. So I just thought, "Okay, getting you is actually going to be *easy*?"'

'I'm in genuine awe of you here, Honor. It's kind of like something I'd do. I think that's the other reason it suddenly dawned on me. You know, you and I are so similar, it actually frightens me.'

'I'm nothing like you.'

'I definitely disagree with you. So all that pretending to be a sap. All that, "I'd rather be his friend than not have him in my life at all." That was all an act?'

'Do you honestly think I'd let a boy make a fool of me?'

'He fancied himself as a serious player and *you* ended up playing *him*! I'm so proud of you, Honor.'

'Are you going to tell *her*?'

'I am in my focking hole. The thing is – look, between us – I actually agree with you. I think she kind of encouraged Caleb by not putting him wise earlier.'

'That's because she's a bitch.'

'Well, she's also your mother, Honor.'

'So-called.'

Sometimes, we look at our children, and we hope to see the best of ourselves reflected back at us. But sometimes, we look at them and we see the worst of ourselves. And do you know what? That can be every bit as wonderful.

'Can I tell you something else?' I go. 'I love the way the old Honor seems to be very much back.'

And she goes, 'I hope you break your focking neck playing rugby.'

I missed her.

# 7. Nidge's Heir

It's an incredible sight. For a minute, I wonder am I even imagining it, but no, it's there alright, three or four doors down from Crowes in Ballsbridge, a humungous window with, like, pictures of gaffs in it, then above the door, in big, shining capital letters, the words HOOK, LYON AND SINKER.

I laugh. It's, like, an *automatic* thing? JP and his old man really are back in business.

I push the door, then in I go. The porty is in full swing. It's, like, a Friday night. The office is full of well-wishers, all skulling the free booze – we're talking friends of JP's old man, we're talking politicians, we're talking the local business community. I recognize five or six former members of staff who worked there when I worked there and are now presumably back on the payroll.

It finally feels like 2002 again.

The office is fitted out just like it was in the old days.

There's, like, ten or fifteen desks squeezed into the tiny floor space, with computers and telephone headsets. JP's old man's voice comes booming across the office floor, like it used to back in the day, when he was giving one of his famous Monday-morning pep talks – the ones that always ended with the words, 'Let's get on the phones – this economy's not going to overheat itself!'

I tip over to where JP is standing. He's milling into the old Veuve Clicquot.

'I never thought I'd hear myself say this again,' he goes, 'but I'm actually getting sick of the taste of Champagne!'

We all laugh.

I automatically go, 'Wealth gag!' and I hold up my hand for a high-five.

JP leaves me hanging. He looks at me *blankly* in fact? I'm like, 'As in, you know . . . wealth!'

He's there, 'What the fock are you talking about, Ross?'

I'm like, 'It doesn't matter. It's what people are saying these days instead of, *Affluence!*'

'Of course,' he goes, deciding to be a dick, 'you're down with the kids these days, aren't you, Rossi? Here, are you not wearing your belly-top tonight?'

He laughs.

I just go, 'Yeah, Seapoint are off the bottom of Division 2B of the All Ireland League for the first time this season because of me, JP – proving once and for all that there's still a lot of rugby left in me.'

He's there, 'I'm only ripping the piss, Ross.'

He ends up getting shushed then, because his old man is about to make a speech.

'Boys and girls,' he goes, 'pardon me if I get a little emotional here, because I'm remembering the last time that most of us were gathered together like this. It was the Christmas party in 2009. A dark year in all of our lives, you will remember. At the end of the night, I broke the news to you that Hook, Lyon and Sinker was going into voluntary liquidation and some of you were a little sore with me when I told you that I'd been using your weekly PRSI contributions to try to keep the business afloat. A lot of things were said in anger that I've thankfully forgotten now.

'The following day, as you cleared out your desks, then went off to spend your statutory redundancy money, I made each and every one of you a promise. I told you that it wasn't goodbye. Because I knew there was a future for people like us – even as our so-called politicians promised that never again would they allow the property market to become so vital to our economic well-being that something as simple as a collapse in house prices could bring about the financial ruin of an entire country.

'They said it was over for people like us. They said we were dead. I want everyone in this room to check their pulse. Go on, do it, right now – check your pulse.'

Everyone automatically does it.

'Now, let me ask you a question,' he goes. 'Do you feel dead?'

I look over to my left and I spot Christian leaning up against the wall – completely and utterly shitfaced. This is at, like, nine o'clock in the evening.

'I said, do you feel dead?' JP's old man goes, except even *louder* this time?

At the top of our voices, we're all there, 'No!'

Then he smiles.

'We're alive,' he goes. 'We got through this thing. So here's to the next period of temporary economic buoyancy.'

It's pretty inspirational stuff, it has to be said. There's, like, a collective whoop from the staff and even the odd high-five. I feel like nearly pulling up a chair and snapping on a headset myself.

And that's when I hear what could only be described as a crash coming from the direction where Christian is standing, followed by a lot of people going, 'Whooooaaa!!!' and that's when I realize that Christian has fallen face-first – oh, holy shit! – through a glass coffee table.

A huge space clears around him – people turning away, their hands over their mouths, not wanting to look. Me and JP sprint over to him and we lift him to his feet.

Oh, fock!

His face is covered in blood and there's, like, splinters of glass – Jesus Christ! – embedded into his actual forehead.

The good news is that he's not aware of any of this. He's out cold.

JP's there, 'Jesus, how long's he been drinking?'

And I go, 'About eight months solid,' at the same time remembering my conversation with Lauren outside Benetton and feeling instantly guilty for not doing anything about it.

Me and JP each take an orm and we put it around our shoulders and we help him over to a sofa. We sit him down and I stort pulling the bits of glass out of his head. Someone hands JP a wet cloth and he storts to clean the blood from the dude's face.

'Christian,' I'm going, 'can you hear me?'

Jesus, he's also pissed his chinos.

I'm going, 'Christian? Christian, can you hear me?'

He half opens his eyes, but I can tell he's struggling to actually focus on me.

'It's not as bad as it looked,' JP goes – as in, there's a lot of blood, but there's only, like, three or four cuts on his forehead and none of them looks deep enough to need stitches.

Someone else grabs a cupful of water from the cooler and I hold it up to Christian's lips to try to get him to take a sip.

JP's old man decides that the show is over.

'Okay,' he goes, 'let's not forget the real reason we're here, which is to celebrate the return of Hook, Lyon and Sinker,' and everyone goes back to portying.

I feel like the biggest prick in the world. Lauren was right to ask. Where was I when he needed me?

I go, 'Help me get him up,' which JP does. We help him outside and we hail a passing taxi. The driver doesn't want to take him but two fifty-yoyo notes does wonders for his attitude.

I'm there, 'I'll go with him this time,' as I put him in the back of the taxi. I get in the other side.

As we drive off, Christian storts waking up. From the expression on his face, it's obvious that he can feel the pain in his forehead.

'Where am I?' he goes.

And I'm like, 'In safe hands – now. Dude, I'm sorry I let you down.'

'Okay,' Sorcha goes, 'someone's nappy needs changing!'

She picks up Leo, then Brian and has a sniff of them both. I do the same with Johnny.

'Okay,' I go, 'it's this little dude. Jesus, I don't think I'll ever get used to that smell.'

Sorcha's there, 'I'll change him,' and she lays a towel down on the kitchen table.

'Prick!' Johnny suddenly shouts. 'Focking prick!'

Sorcha puts her hand over her mouth. At the same time, she goes, 'Okay, don't respond, Ross. Don't give him any reaction.'

I'm there, 'Yeah, no, I'm beginning to wonder is that definitely the right way to go, Sorcha? That's, like, all three of them at it now – they're swearing like focking Talbot Street. Maybe we should stort telling them that it's wrong.'

'I'm the one who read a book on this subject, remember?'

I've no answer to that. I've read six books in my entire life – and five of them were Johnny Sexton's autobiography.

Sorcha goes, 'What are you doing up anyway?'

It's, like, half-ten on a Saturday morning.

I'm there, 'I'm calling over to see Christian.'

She goes, 'Christian? Oh my God, how is he?'

'Not good. He fell through a glass coffee table at the reopening of Hook, Lyon and Sinker last night. Pissed himself as well. Lauren said some shit to me that's finally hit home – about possibly being a better friend to him? I'm going to go and talk to him about hope-fully cleaning up his act.'

'That's a lovely thing to do, Ross.'

'I know. I'm already patting myself on the back for it.'

'Well, I'm going to spend the day trying to pick out a dress for the wedding.'

'What wedding?'

'Er, your *mother's* wedding?'

'Oh, that sham? Yeah, no, I still haven't decided if I'm even going.'

'We've been through this, Ross. You *are* going.'

'Whatever. Look, I'll see you in a few hours.'

'Focking prick!' Johnny goes.

I hop into the cor and I point it in the direction of Carrickmines. I actually swing into Costa on my way there and I grab Christian an Americano, a freshly squeezed orange juice and a bacon toastie, although I end up eating the bacon toastie before I reach the gaff because it smells so focking good.

Christian answers the door of his tiny aportment in his boxer shorts, his big, white belly hanging over the waistband like a baker's hat. He hasn't even opened his eyes properly yet and he's already cracking open the first can of the day.

Well, I can only presume it's the first.

The blood on his forehead has dried. He looks seriously wretched.

I whip the can out of his hand, step past him into the hall, then into the kitchen and I pour it down the sink.

Good Heineken as well.

He's like, 'It was just a focking beer.'

I'm there, 'I meant what I said last night, Christian. It stops now.'

He's like, 'What?'

He clearly has no memory of me putting him to bed.

I'm there, 'Have you looked in the mirror this morning?'

He goes, 'No.'

'Have you seen your forehead, for instance?'

He puts his hand up to it, then he goes into the bathroom, presumably to get a look at himself. A few seconds later, he steps out again.

He's like, 'What happened?'

I'm there, 'You fell face-first through a glass table. You were lucky not to lose your eyes.'

'Shit. Where did it happen?'

'Ballsbridge.'

'What was I doing in Ballsbridge?'

'You don't remember? You were at the reopening of Hook, Lyon and Sinker. For fock's sake, Christian, you need to sort your shit.'

He goes, 'Yeah? What's the point?' and he actually turns his head away from me.

'The point,' I go, 'is staying alive.'

'Okay, what have I got to live for, Ross? If you're such an expert. What have I got to live for? My marriage is gone. My kids are gone –'

He suddenly sits down at the kitchen table and puts his head in his hands. Shit, he storts crying.

I'm there, 'Maybe if you stop drinking, you can get Lauren and the kids back.'

'She doesn't want me back,' he goes. 'She doesn't want me back. And I haven't got a single thing to live for.'

And it's hearing him say that – and sounding like he genuinely means it – that leads me to say what I say next.

I go, 'Lauren does want you back, Christian. That's the good news.'

He looks up, surprised. He's there, 'What are you talking about?'

I'm like, 'Yeah, no, I saw her when she was home for the week.'

'And she told you she wanted to get back with me?'

'Absolutely. She said she'd love to give your marriage another try – but only if you cleaned up your act first.'

He nods. It's like he's suddenly filled with, I don't know, *resolve*? He wipes away his tears with an open palm. I push the little cordboard tray across the table to him, with the coffee and the orange juice in it.

'Get those into you,' I go.

He's there, 'My head is killing me. I don't suppose you brought any food with you, did you?'

'I bought you a bacon sandwich, but I scoffed it. The smell just got to me. Anyway, this is only the stort of it, Christian. I'm taking you to training with me from next week.'

'Training? Training where?'

'See, you've been so hammered lately, you probably don't even know that I'm back playing rugby. For Seapoint.'

'Seapoint in Ballybrack?'

'Seapoint in Ballybrack. Let's be honest. You're coming to training with me next week and you're going to stort using the gym to get in shape. I'll square it with the club. Now, go and grab your Cantos, your Leinster jersey and your Nikes. I'll be waiting in the cor.'

He's like, 'What? Where are we going?'

And I'm there, 'We're going running, my friend.'


'How much further?' Christian wants to know.

We've been pounding the roads around Killiney Hill for the best port of, like, an hour.

I laugh.

I'm there, 'What did Father Fehily used to do if we asked that question? He'd throw on another mile!'

He stops outside Enya's gaff, bent over double, one hand on the wall, looking like he might puke any second. 'Please,' he goes, between breaths, 'don't make me run another mile.'

I stop as well, but I'm, like, jogging on the *spot*?

'That shit you're feeling,' I go, 'it's just the poison leaving your body.'

He's there, 'I think I'm going to have a hort attack.'

He looks focked, in fairness to him. His face is, like, beetroot red and he's sweating – I'm presuming – pure alcohol. His forehead has storted bleeding again and the blood is, like, dribbling down his face.

I'm thinking, Wait till Dudser gets a hold of him at Strength and Conditioning.

I'm like, 'You're not going to have a hort attack. I'll tell you what, one last hill before home. Then I'll get Sorcha to do us a couple of whatevers in the NutriBullet and we'll watch Ireland do a job on Wales in the Six Nations.'

I'm not even going to drink in front of him. That's how determined I am to get him back to the way he used to be – although I'll probably nip out to the kitchen for the odd sly can.

He goes, 'She definitely, definitely said she'd come back? I'm talking about Lauren.'

Now is possibly the time to tell him the truth, except I end up bottling it.

'Like I said, they were her words,' I go. 'She said she wanted your marriage to work and hopefully if you stopped drinking and got your shit together in a general way, then she was ready to give it another go.'

'She'd come home from France?'

'She loves you, Christian.'

'She said that as well?'

'It was obvious from the conversation. Focking obvious.'

He suddenly closes his eyes and puts his hand up to his mouth. Jesus Christ, he's about to leave a pizza for Enya with everything on it.

'Bllleeeuuuggghhh!!!' he goes, spewing his ring all over the pavement. 'Bllleeeuuuggghhh!!!'

I'm patting his back, going, 'Better out than in. You know today is Johnny Sexton's fiftieth cap for Ireland. I texted him the usual this morning but I put it in capital letters. I wonder did he notice.'

It's at that exact point that my phone rings. I check the screen and it ends up being Ronan's Shadden.

It's pretty unusual for her to ring me, which is the reason I end up actually answering it. I'm like, 'Hey, Shadden, what's the Jack?'

'Rosser, Ine woodied,' she goes and I can tell she's been crying.

It's all go today.

I'm like, 'Worried? About what?'

She's there, 'Ine woodied about Ronan.'

I straightaway go, 'In terms of?' like any father would if he thought his son was in trouble.

'He came home thudder night with a barroken ardum. Except he woatunt tell me who done it. He came home with a full cast on it and says I to him, "Happened your ardum?" and says he, "The less you know, the bethor!"'

I'm there, 'It must have been Scum!'

She's like, 'Which Scum?' because it seems there's more than one of them. 'Coolock Scum, Ballybough Scum or Artane Scum?'

'Coolock Scum,' I go. 'That's what I'm presuming. He's the dude who burned out the bus.'

She's more than a bit surprised by this news. She's like, 'The bus was burdened out?'

She obviously didn't know.

I'm like, 'Look, is he giving a tour today?'

She goes, 'Yeah, he's in towun, so he is.'

And I'm there, 'Okay, Shadden, leave it to me.'

I hang up, then I tell Christian that I'm going to run on ahead. I need to grab the cor and head into town. He raises his hand between hurls to tell me it's cool.


Shadden wasn't exaggerating. When I hop on the new replacement *Love/Hate* bus, just past the Ha'penny Bridge, I notice that Ronan's got, like, a full plaster cast on his orm, from his wrist to his shoulder.

Of course, he won't tell me how it happened.

He goes, 'I fell, Rosser – playing rubby.'

I'm there, 'I wish that was true, Ro. I really do.'

'Rosser,' he goes, 'Ine in the middle of gibbon a toower hee-or. So eeder take yisser seat along with evoddy body else, or get off the bleaten bus. The choice is yooers.'

I stare at him for a long time. Then I go, 'Okay, I'm going to sit down. But I'm going to get the truth out of you, one way or the other.'

He stays standing at the front of the upper deck of the bus while I take my seat. He picks up the microphone and all of the chatter on the bus comes to an end.

'Ladies and jettlemen,' he goes, 'I hope yiz are enjoying the toower so feer and that yiz all enjoyet seeing Ado's actual flat. Like I said to yiz eerdier, that was where the lovable dealer and shooting gallody proprietor got kneecapped at the steert of Seerdies Tree. It's also where John Boy's geerlfrent, Debbie, used to go to scowur gear behoyunt John Boy's back in Seerdies Two.'

The people on the bus are all just nodding, totally – I suppose – *captivated* by him? He definitely has a way with people. I suppose he's not unlike *me* in that regord?

'Now,' he goes, 'in a half an hour or so, we're gonna be heading up the mountains, so we eer, to visit a cadavan that's an izact replica of the cadavan that was owunt by one of me own personiddle favourite cadickters offa the show – the dog lubber, cigadette smoogler and loan sheerk, Fradden, who became one of Nidge's most thrusted henchmen in Seerdies Tree, even though Nidge maimed he's boord wirra pipe bomb after riding her in an eardier episowut.

'Theer, you'll get the chaddence to walk arowunt a cadavan joost like Fradden's and to howult the actual golf club that Nidge used to smash Tommy's head open when he fowunt out that Tommy was arthur been riding Dano's wife, Georcheena.'

We're, like, flying down the quays. Buckets of Blood really has his foot down.

'But foorst,' Ronan goes, 'we're gonna grab an ould bit of lunch. Ine gonna bring yiz now to a chipper in Christchoorch that's owunt by a toord cousint of the actor Tom Vodden-Lawdor. Thee do the best chips addywhere in towun, so thee do, and if you mention that you're on the *Love/Hate* Tewer of Dublin, you'll get a free can of minner doddle with orders over foyuv euros.

'And if you're *reedy* hungry, I can veddy much recommend the

Soorf and Toorf – smoked cod *and* a spice boorger with chips and a minner doddle for a tedder. Thrust me, it'll sort you out for the day, so it will. So we're just pudding up outside it theer now – it's on yisser left – and I'll see yiz all back on the bus in a harp an hour.'

He's good. There's no denying that. But I'm not letting the issue of that broken orm go. I follow him down the stairs of the bus, going, 'Shadden rang me. She's worried about you.'

He's there, 'I toalt her not to be woodied.'

'But you won't tell me how it happened?'

'Hab I ebber been a tout, Rosser?'

'Telling your old man hordly counts as touting, Ro.'

'Yeah and you'll go sthraight to the Garda Shickaloneys and tell them ebbedy bleaten woord.'

We pass Buckets, who's still sitting in the driver's seat. Ronan goes, 'I'll get the loonches, Buckets – you moyunt the bus.'

Buckets nods.

I follow Ro into the chipper.

'Look,' I go, 'if you're in over your head, Ro, you can tell me.'

'Ine nowhere near ober me head,' he goes. 'Doatunt you woody about that.'

He's so proud.

He approaches the counter. 'Two Soorf and Toorfs,' he goes to the bird. 'Rosser, do you want a Soorf and Toorf?'

I'm there, 'No, I've got a match tomorrow. We're at home to Sunday's Well.'

He rolls his eyes like that's no kind of answer, then he goes, 'Just the two Soorf and Toorfs, so, Love. And lowuts of salt and videgar.'

She's like, 'What minner doddle?'

'I'll hab a Coke and Buckets will hab a Sebben-Up.'

She turns around to put the order together. I'm as determined to get the truth as Ronan is determined to get Type 2 Diabetes.

I'm like, 'Ro, whatever trouble you're in, I'm sure we can pay someone some money to sort it out.'

He goes, 'No one's paying addyone athin.'

'It wouldn't be coming from me. I'd get it from my old man.'

'We're at war, Rosser.'

'Is that not a bit over the top, though, Ro?'

'Thee burdened eer bus out, so we burdened theers out.'

'Jesus Christ.'

'Top of O'Coddle Street. Nudger knows what to do wirra a can of petro doddle and a lyrer.'

'So, what, I'm presuming this Scum came back at you? A revenge attack and blah, blah, blah?'

'I was woorking yesterdee. We'd no skewill – peerdent-teacher meeting –'

'I didn't hear anything about a parent-teacher meeting.'

'Do you want to hear this stordee or not, Rosser? It was ford o'clock in the arthur noon and I was upsteers counting the take. Buckets had gone arowunt to Supermacs for a slash.'

Supermacs. Jesus, it's like an actual *storyline* out of *Love/Hate*.

'Ine sitting upsteers on the bus, up the veddy fronth. Like I says, Ine counting what we're arthur eerdning. The next thing I hear is footsteps cubbing up the bleaten steers. Foorst, I thought it was Buckets cubbing back arthur he's slash. Then I look oaber me shoulter and what do I see? Scum and two udder shams cheerging towarts me – all tree of them with bleaten machetes.'

I'm like, 'Machetes? Are we talking *actual* machetes?'

'We're not thalken inflatable ones, Rosser. Bleaten pox bottles. I jumped up on the seat and threw meself oaber the soyut of the bus. Off the top deck, Rosser. Lanthed on me ardum – which is how I broke it. Then the filth arroyved on the scene. I ditn't call them – I want to fooken emphasoyuz that.'

'No one thinks you're a tout, Ro.'

'Thee just happened to be going by. Scum and the boys legged it. I was lying theer, bleaten howlin with the payun. Thee took me to James Zuzz, then thee questioned me for tree or four hours arthur I gorrout. I nebber breathed a woord.'

I'm there, 'Ro, you have to end this.'

He goes, 'Doataunt woody, Rosser – we're *gonna* end it.'

'By doing what?'

'That's for us to know and Scum to foyunt out.'

'Ro, I think I'd prefer you to just concentrate on your Leaving Cert before someone gets actually murdered.'

Jesus, talk about sentences you never thought you'd hear yourself say.

The bird behind the counter hands him his order.

Ro just goes, 'Pay the woman, Rosser.'

Between psyching myself up for the old dear's wedding, trying to save the lives of my best friend and my son and then Ireland's defeat to Wales in the Six Nations, Saturday ends up getting away from me and I totally forget to ring Oisinn to ask him for some more dirty tricks to use in the scrum.

I don't even think about it, in fact, until we're walking out onto the pitch to face Sunday's Well, with Byrom's shout of, 'Lit's git beck to wunning woys,' still ringing in our ears.

It's going to be a tight game. According to Bucky, it nearly always is when Seapoint and Sunday's Well come together. The scoreboard tends to turn over only three clicks at a time. A lot is obviously going to depend on Senny's accuracy with the boot, so I make sure to have a word with him while we're walking out.

I'm there, 'We need a massive game from you today, Dude.'

He looks at me with a look of worry on his face. He goes, 'Apparently, there's one or two goys from the Leinster Academy here to watch me.'

'Then show them what you can do,' I go. 'Are you feeling okay?'

He looks like shit, it has to be said. I'm presuming it's, like, *nerves*?

'Yeah, I'm fine,' he goes. 'Just not sleeping great. Well, it's Torah really. I don't know if I said it to you during the week but we've got a prowler.'

Uh-oh.

'A prowler?' I go. 'Is that not a bit random?'

He's like, 'It was last weekend, just after I was talking to you. We were in my gaff, you know, doing stuff and there was some focking weirdo looking in the window at us.'

'Did they get a good description of the dude?'

'No, it was actually my neighbour who saw him. He hit him over

217

the head with a wok or something, but the focker managed to over-power him. Of course, Torah's barely slept since. Every little noise outside, she thinks it's him back again.'

'Dude, the best thing you can do is put this so-called prowler out of your mind, not just for today but for good. It sounds to me like there's probably a totally innocent explanation for it. You need to just concentrate on your game.'

'Maybe you're right.'

We high-five. And that's the moment when I realize that I've totally forgotten to talk to Oisinn. It's too late to go back to the dressing room for my phone because we're about to kick off, so I decide to just wing it for today.

Sunday's Well are another shower from Cork and no sooner are we out on the pitch than they stort sledging us in that strange yokel language they speak down there.

Their hooker is *easily* the worst offender? He tries to get inside Senny's head from the first minute, trying to basically soften him up. He's practically in his face, going, 'I own to God and the world, would you look at the measure of this fella! The whole country is wild with the news that you're the one they've come to see! Well, you may cut the sign of the cross on yourself, for you'll get nothing easy out of us this day, only torment!'

None of the other Seapoint players does anything. But I'm not having anyone talking to one of my teammates like that, even though I only understand about a quarter of what he actually said. I walk over to the dude. I put my hand on his chest and I shove him backwards.

He tries to go, 'What ails you at all?'

I'm there, 'Back the fock up or you'll be decked.'

'Oh, you're a class of plucky and no mistake. The will of my breast and soul, I'll warm your shins and you'll be better off with the sense that'll come of it!'

'I'm not going to say it again. Back the fock up, you focking broc-coli rapist.'

*He* goes to shove *me* then? And we end up having a bit of a scuffle. Maho, Bucky, Dilly and Gilly run over and they help pull us aport – this is before a ball has even been kicked, bear in mind – and at the same time they're going, 'Fair focks to you, Rossi!'

And I'm going, 'What the fock were the rest of you doing? It's *our* job to protect him.'

But this focker keeps up his tirade against Senny, even when Senny is shaping up to kick a penalty in the fifth minute. Showing disrespect for a kicker is something I've never tolerated – no matter who that kicker happens to be. I took Sorcha to see Ireland versus France at the Aviva once and she booed Morgan Parra as he shaped up to take a penalty. I couldn't have sex with her for about three months afterwards – and no one hates Morgan Parra more than me.

So this focker watches Senny do his little pre-kick dance and – at the top of his voice – storts going, 'Man dear, tis queer behaviour to be sure! The heart in my breast but you've notions!'

So I wait until the third or fourth scrum to fix the focker. He's giving *us* loads as well, by the way? The same kind of shit and it's, like, constant. We're, like, binding and we're getting ready to engage. He turns to his own teammates and he storts going, 'God spare you the health, fellas, isn't that the prettiest front row you've ever put eyes on? Twas often I said that before my bones were laid under the green sod, I wanted to see a ladyboy with mine own eyes – and my word to you if there aren't three of them standing before me this very night!'

In Cork, a ladyboy is any man who sits down to take a shit.

We crouch and he's still giving it loads. He's going, 'My sorrow, you'll not leave here today without the taste of blood on your teeth.'

As we're getting ready to engage, I decide to go early and I use the top of my head to crack the focker right on the bridge of his nose. It's a trick I remember Oisinn using once or twice back in the day to soften up front rows who had ideas about themselves.

So I hit him with my head and there's, like, a sickening crunch and down their scrum goes.

'Penalty, Seapoint!' the old man shouts from the sideline. 'Deliberate collapsing!'

The dude stands up, blood streaming from his nose.

The Sunday's Well players are trying to tell the referee that it was a straight decking. But he seems happy to accept my explanation that it was an accidental clash of heads.

He even makes their captain apologize to him after he goes, 'Yerrah, there's no bigger fool under the bright sun than you, referee!'

The referee orders a reset, but the Sunday's Well hooker ends up having to go off so they can try to fix his face. He's gone for maybe five minutes. When he arrives back, his nose is completely strapped, with tape all over his face, holding the bandage in place.

He's a hell of a lot quieter now. Anytime he storts sledging, I just give his nose a rub with my head when the two front rows come together and that softens the focker's cough.

Senny ends up having one of those matches that every outhalf dreams about, with scouts from the academy watching. He directs the play like – and I say this in all modesty – me in my prime. Early in the second half he's kicked five from five and we're, like, 15–3 ahead and fully in control.

And that's when I end up doing something stupid.

Their inside centre is an absolute flier. He gets the ball in his hands and he attacks our twenty-two-metre line. He beats two players, three players, four players – he absolutely burns them for pace. There's no doubt he's going to get over for a try.

Until I clothesline the focker.

I hang a forearm out there and he runs straight into it. He hits the deck. The Sunday's Well players are immediately surrounding the referee, going, 'He's the very devil for causing trouble – Old Nick himself would be in fear of him!' and 'God direct you to do what's right, referee!'

I know I'm in serious shit here. The ref reaches inside his pocket. The cord he produces is thankfully yellow, but it still means I'm going to be missing for ten vital minutes of the second half.

The Sunday's Well players are shouting, 'Long life to you!' and 'God's blessing on your road!' as I walk off the field with my head down.

I apologize to Byrom, but he's cool with it. He just goes, 'Stay warm,' and he throws me an ankle-length coat.

Their number ten kicks the penalty, then Goffo – rattled now, because we're down to fourteen men – immediately concedes another, which they *also* kick? Suddenly it's, like, 15–9 and Sunday's Well are only one score from taking a lead they definitely don't deserve.

I end up taking out my frustration on the giant recycling bins in the cor pork, kicking the shit out of the one for aluminium cans.

Those ten minutes end up being among the longest of my life. By the time I'm allowed back onto the field, Sunday's Well have pulled level and I'm apologizing to Bucky, going, 'I let you down.'

We all know that another draw is fock-all use to us.

But he just goes, 'There's twenty minutes left. We've won this match once, Rossi. Let's win it again.'

It's exactly what I need to hear.

My return manages to shore things up and we stop conceding silly points. Then, five minutes from time, our full-back, Ollie Lysaght, kicks a long ball deep into the Sunday's Well half, but fails to find touch with it. Their full-back sprints over to get it and something, I don't know, maybe some little voice inside my head, tells me to go after it, which I do.

The dude reaches the ball and the most incredible thing happens. It's what every player who's ever chased a lost cause dreams about.

The focker snots himself.

He slips on a patch of wet grass and up in the air he goes, screaming, 'Aroo!' before landing on his orse.

By the time he does, I've scooped up the ball and I'm heading for the line with the sound of Sunday's Well players behind me, their feet eating up the ground, so that it sounds like I'm about to be run over by a stampede of horses.

Our goys are going, 'Keep going, Rossi! You're nearly there! You've got the pace, Rossi! You've got the pace!'

The truth is, I don't have the pace. I'm thirty-five years old and the oldest player on the field by a good decade. But I do have one thing, and that's just the right amount of field in front of me.

I'm tackled around the waist just as I reach the line. I fall sideways to my right. But as I do, I manage to twist my orm and ground the ball.

'May bad luck melt you!' one of the Sunday's Well players goes to me.

Seconds later, I find myself lying at the bottom of a pile of my tearful teammates.

Sorcha still hasn't decided what she's going to wear to this so-called wedding tomorrow, despite the fact that we're already on Ari's yacht and we're moored five miles off the Dalkey coast.

'I was thinking I might wear my Roland Mouret Henderson metallic organza gown with my strappy gold Jimmy Choos,' she goes – this is at, like, the meet-and-greet porty the night before the wedding. 'Either that or my Oscar de la Renta turquoise embellished silk-chiffon gown with just, like, *wedges*? But then, when I was packing last night, I was thinking, Oh my God, it's still, like, the middle of Morch – am I mad even *considering* wearing silk, especially on a boat? So that's why I also packed my Temperly London Sahara pleated chiffon maxi dress with my Nicholas Kirkwood laser-cut sandals.'

'Oh my God,' Honor goes, 'you're so self-obsessed. It's not even you who's getting married. It's someone *else's* big day?'

She still hasn't forgiven her for giving Caleb the come-on.

Sorcha goes, 'Don't be like that, Honor! Why don't you and I make a really concerted effort to become friends again during this little break?'

Honor calls her a sad sack, then wanders off, while Sorcha smiles at me sadly. She goes, 'I'm still detecting a lot of hostility from her.'

I'm there, 'Really?' just ripping the piss. 'I'm not getting that at all.'

'She still blames me for the way things ended with Caleb. Ross, he was stealing my underwear!'

'Yeah, I'm well aware of that, Babes.'

I still haven't told Sorcha what actually happened – and I doubt if I ever will.

'Anyway,' she goes, 'I'm going to go and talk to your mom's

friend Delma, because her daughter, Aodhnait, was in UCD with me studying languages and I haven't seen her since her Erasmus year in Izmir.'

Off she focks.

I have another glass of the old bubbly – no Heineken onboard, by the way – then I tip over to the old dear, who's loving being the centre of attention, of course.

The meet-and-greet is a typically over-the-top affair. It happens on the deck of the yacht, under the stors, and it's, like, a white-tie ball – we're talking tuxes, we're talking a seafood buffet, we're talking an actual thirty-piece orchestra, we're talking the works.

There's, like, a hundred or so guests, we're talking *her* friends and then *his* crew – old farts, most of them – who've flown over from the States.

'Fionnuala, I can't believe you arranged all of this!' the old man goes, at the same time handing me a Cohiba. 'You've always had class, of course!'

She hasn't, by the way. He's talking out of his hole.

She goes, 'It's wonderful that you came, Charles. You know, you and I remaining friends remains my proudest achievement in life – and that includes all of the books I've written and the hundreds upon hundreds of lives I've saved in the Third World.'

He's there, 'I could say the same thing, Fionnuala. Better than all the business deals I landed and all the homes I built thanks to material contraventions of the County Development Plan.'

I'm like, 'Seriously, you two – get a focking room.'

He lights my cigor for me.

And that's when I spot her – Ari's granddaughter, Tiffany Blue. I didn't think she was going to show her face, although I'm happy she did. I think I already mentioned that Tiffany Blue is a ringer for Alana Blanchard. If I didn't, I'm saying it now.

The old dear goes, 'Oh, hello!' all fake teeth and pretend sincerity.

The old man reintroduces himself to her. 'Charles O'Carroll-Kelly,' he goes, offering her his hand. 'We met at the engagement party. Fionnuala's erstwhile consort *und* partner in crime!'

That's what he says – word for word. You'd seriously have to wonder where I got my famous silver tongue from. People are entitled to ask.

'Looking well!' I go, just to let her know that the O'Carroll-Kelly men aren't *all* pathetic saps. 'Looking very well indeed! Are you having a good night so far?'

She ignores this.

The old dear goes, 'There's a full cocktail bar. Oh, Tiffany Blue, they have a list of mocktails, too!' presumably because the girl has a problem with the sauce.

They did meet in rehab.

Tiffany Blue just, like, stares her out of it. I'm picking up on the vibe that she's still Scooby Dubious about the whole prenup thing.

'So you're very welcome,' the old dear tries to go. 'Relax and enjoy the party!'

Tiffany Blue goes, 'I've spent holidays on this boat since I was a little girl. I don't need your permission to enjoy myself.'

Something happens then. Something very subtle. The old dear switches her Champagne glass from her left to her right hand. She puts it to her lips and Tiffany Blue's eyes go suddenly wide.

'Oh my God,' she goes, 'what is that?'

'It's the Krug Clos d'Ambonnay,' the old dear goes. 'It's a pity you can't have any, Tiffany Blue. It's made with Pinot Noir.'

'I'm not talking about your drink. What is that on your finger?'

It's a diamond, by the way. The second biggest one I've ever laid eyes on. The biggest one is on her other hand.

'Oh, this?' the old dear goes, with a big fock-you smile on her face. 'It was a gift from your grandfather. A celebration ring – it sort of balances out my engagement ring, doesn't it? My other hand was beginning to feel a little light!'

Tiffany Blue goes, 'That was Grandma's ring.'

'I beg your pardon?'

'I said that was Grandma's engagement ring. Grandpa promised it to me.'

'Oh, I had no idea! He didn't mention it!'

It's almost like she's *trying* to provoke her?

'That's because he doesn't know what day it is,' Tiffany Blue goes. 'Give me that ring.'

My old man tries to act as, like, peacemaker. He's there, 'Could I humbly suggest that this is neither the time nor the place to argue about the whos, the whats, the whys and the what-nots?'

Tiffany Blue just, like, stares the old dear out of it. She goes, 'Don't think for one minute this is over!' and off she goes in the direction of the bor.

The old man goes, 'I'm going to go and see what Helen and Sorcha are up to,' then off he heads as well, leaving me alone with the old dear, the hog.

I'm there, 'You did that on purpose.'

She's like, 'I beg your pardon?'

'You flashed the ring so she'd see it. I watched you do it.'

'Oh, please, Ross – this is supposed to be a happy occasion.'

She smiles. She has a face like a busted zip.

She goes, 'I'm so pleased that it's you who's going to give me away tomorrow.'

I'm there, 'I still can't believe you've found someone mad enough to want to marry you.'

'Oh, look, I know what people are thinking, Ross. I'd probably think the same thing myself if I heard about someone else in her fifties marrying a man in his nineties.'

Fifties? She's got some focking cheek. I'm letting an awful lot go here.

She's there, 'That's why I insisted on the prenup, so no one can impugn my motives. When Ari dies, I won't inherit a cent. Everything will go to Tiffany Blue.'

'She still doesn't seem to trust you.'

'I try not to judge her too harshly. She's had a tough life. She lost her parents when she was just a little girl. An awful, awful car crash. Or maybe it was a house fire. Something. Ari's the closest thing to a father she's ever had.'

'Er, yeah, no, bummer.'

'She's a nice girl. She's just got a lot of problems. The drink and the drugs and, well, the other thing.'

'What other thing?'

'Oh, she's one of these – what are they called – sex addicts?'

I feel my face break into a smile. I can't help it. It's automatic.

I'm like, 'You're shitting me.'

She goes, 'That's if you believe in that kind of thing.'

'I thought I noticed her checking me out. I thought it was just because I look well in a suit.'

'When we were in that place – rehab, whatever you want to call it – she claimed to have slept with a thousand men.'

'A thousand is a decent number. I'm saying that as a player myself.'

'Well, apparently, when she's drunk, she turns into a complete nymphomaniac.'

I turn my head, my eyes suddenly seeking her out. She's up at the bor.

'Anyway,' I go, 'I can't sit around here listening to you gab on all night, you focking moose. I need to go and mingle.'

'I'm on your side,' I go. 'I hate her more than anyone. She's my mother, bear in mind.'

Tiffany Blue is drinking just, like, water. I ask the borman for a bottle of Champagne.

She goes, 'Grandpa promised me that ring. I can't believe he gave it to that . . . woman!'

I'm there, 'You don't know that he *did* give it to her?'

'Excuse me?'

'I'm just saying, we've only got her word for that, haven't we? She might have just taken the ring, then told him that he gave it to her. You were the one who said he was senile – he wouldn't know his orse from a hole in the forest floor.'

Tiffany Blue turns around and stares at the old dear, who gives her a smile and a little wave. She's like, 'What a sick . . . bitch.'

I'm there, 'Hey, if you want to talk about it, I just want you to know that I'm here for you.'

I've always been a good listener when it comes to women. When I say a good listener I mean that I'm very good at just sitting there and not interrupting while they bullshit on.

I'm there, 'You don't know the half of it. I could tell you stories about her that'd make you lose your faith in the human race. Will you have a glass of this shit with me?'

'No,' she quickly goes. 'I'm supposed to be on the wagon.'

I'm like, 'Fair enough. Whatever you're into. I'm just trying to be a friend to you here.'

'I should have done more to stop this thing happening.'

'I take it you're not convinced by the whole prenup thing? She definitely signed it. I can tell you that for a fact.'

'I still don't trust it. She's up to something.'

'You'd be right to think that. Like I said, I've got stories about the woman that'd make your eyeballs bleed. She's definitely up to something – you just don't know what it is yet. If we both put our heads together, we might be able to figure out what it is, though. Come on, have a drink with me.'

She thinks about this for a few seconds, then her face just, like, visibly relaxes? 'You know what?' she goes. 'I don't think I can get through this weekend sober.'

I get another glass from the borman and I pour her a glass of bubbles. Then I go, 'Like I said, I'm on your side. As a matter of fact, when I look at your grandfather, I automatically think of Alma Goad.'

She's like, 'Okay, who the hell is Alma Goad?'

'I'm actually glad you asked me that question. Alma Goad was this woman the old dear worked for. She had a florist shop in Stillorgan – this was, like, back in the day. She was about the same age as your grandfather. Half-blind, losing her morbles, same as him. Here, let me top you up there.'

'So what happened?'

'Yeah, no, the old dear worked for her for a couple of years – in this – like I said – flower shop. Anyway, the whole time she was there, she was thieving from her. Her hand was never out of the till, the hideous-looking troglodyte.'

Honor suddenly arrives over to us. She goes, 'Can I ask you a question?'

I'm there, 'It's a bit difficult at the moment, Honor. I'm just telling Tiffany Blue here one or two funny anecdotes about the woman who's marrying her grandfather tomorrow.'

'Can I have Champagne?'

'I don't know. Did you ask your mother?'

'No, because she'll only say no. That's why I'm asking you.'

In other words, the cool one! I actually laugh. She knows how to get around her old man alright.

'Here,' I go, handing her what's left of our bottle. 'There's probably a glass and a half in that. I'm going to get another one anyway.'

Off she goes with it. Champagne, I think to myself. She's going to grow up with some expensive tastes!

I nod to the borman to get us another bottle, which he does.

'I don't think the two things are the same at all,' Tiffany Blue goes. 'One is stealing money from a store. Jesus, we've all done that. This is, like, marrying an old man to steal the money he spent his whole life earning.'

I'm there, 'If you'd let me finish, I could tell you just how deeply evil the woman is. You see, she wasn't just dipping into the till for the sheer joy of robbing. I mean, that kind of thievery she's always associated with the poorest of the poor. Yeah, no, *she* was robbing the till to make it look like the business was going down the tubes. She did it for, like, a year or two – every week, helping herself to a little bit more of the take, until poor Alma couldn't pay the electricity anymore, never mind the repayments on a bank loan my old dear persuaded her to take out.'

She necks her second glass in one go, then pours herself a third. I'm wondering how many it'll take before she storts getting slutty.

She's there, 'Keep talking.'

'Well,' I go, 'eventually the bank called Alma in and told her she'd have to sell the business. Oh, did I mention that the bank manager was actually my old dear's father?'

She's suddenly, like, goggle-eyed listening to this.

I'm there, 'And guess who bought the shop at a knockdown price? That's right – *her*! Within, like, two or three years, she had a whole chain of flower shops, which she ended up selling for an absolute mint.'

'And what happened to this old lady she screwed over?'

She's throwing back the Champagne like it's shots now. It doesn't seem to be making her any more amorous, though.

I'm there, 'What do you think? She died a broken woman. She had two daughters. They hadn't a clue what was going on. It was only after Alma died they found out that she'd sold her home to one of these equity release companies – on my old dear's advice, by the way. So there was no gaff. They got nothing from the will. As in, there *wasn't* anything?'

She doesn't say anything for a long time. Eventually, she turns and looks at me. Her eyes are pissed. She goes, 'So are we going then?'

I'm like, 'Going? Going where?'

She rolls her eyes, like I'm slow on the uptake. I am, of course.

She's there, 'To my room. I presume you want to have sex with me?'

I'm like, 'Errr,' because I literally haven't used any of the chat-up lines I prepared. 'That'd be nice, yeah.'

At the same time, I'm looking over my shoulder to make sure Sorcha isn't watching. She's isn't. No one's watching. They're all too busy fussing over my old dear.

Tiffany Blues slips away from the bor. Ten seconds later, I follow. As I'm catching up with her in the corridor, I tell her she looks genuinely well tonight. A compliment often gets the ball rolling – that's something I've learned with women.

But Tiffany Blue isn't interested in my observations.

As soon as we get into her room, she shoves me backwards onto the bed, then kicks off her shoes. She unzips her dress at the back, takes it off over her head and sits astride me, then she tears open the fly of my tux trousers like an Irish emigrant with a bag of focking Tayto.

She goes, 'Hey, before we do this, maybe we should get some coke.'

I laugh. I'm there, 'We're at an old people's wedding. Where are we going to get coke? It's not 2002.'

'I heard the barman say he could get some.'

'I've never really been into it, to be honest. My life's a natural high.'

Like I said, she's sitting astride me. She reaches back and has a rummage around in the old toy box and finds what she's looking for. It's hord to tell from her reaction whether she's impressed by it or not.

'You better not disappoint me,' she just goes.

And I'm thinking, I almost certainly will – but it'll be a testament to how turned on I am by you.

Anyway, the usual rules apply. Mister Discretion and blah, blah, blah. All I will say is that the girl knows a few moves and I'll leave it at that. She twists herself into all sorts of shapes over the next, well, however long it lasts. She bites my earlobes and she mutters instructions and threats and she slaps my thighs like she's up on a chorger with the Indians giving chase.

I give a pretty good account of myself, and I say that in all modesty. I bend her this way and that way and the whole sweaty business comes to a glorious end with her pulling various rollercoaster faces, whacking her head repeatedly off the headboard and honking like a kicked pig.

I've possibly said too much.

When the transaction is completed, I do my usual thing of drifting off. I don't know how long I end up being out for, but it feels like several hours. In that dozy period between being asleep and being awake I'm suddenly aware of, like, *voices* in the room?

'Did you get it?' one voice goes – it's Tiffany Blue.

'Yeah,' a man's voice goes. 'I've got it here.'

Without even opening my eyes, I instantly know it's the borman.

Thirty seconds later, I hear this, like, long, snorting sound and I realize that they're doing lines of coke off the vanity unit.

'How was he?' the borman goes, in a slightly mocking voice, obviously referring to me.

Tiffany Blue just laughs – *cruelly*, I would have said?

She goes, 'He kept shouting, *"Allez les Bleus!"*'

'*Allez les Bleus?* What's that?'

I wouldn't mind, roysh, but the dude sounds like he's local. Learn about your focking heritage, I feel like nearly telling him.

Tiffany Blue goes, 'Who knows what weird shit goes on in you men's heads when you're doing it . . . [*sniff*] . . . Whoa, this is good shit . . . Hey, I should wake him up. Asshole. I should wake him up and demand that he fucks me properly.'

Fock that, I think. I've got nothing left to give. I'll have to pretend to be asleep. I make a kind of snoring noise and that seems to do the trick.

'Hey, I've got a better idea,' the dude goes. 'We could go to my cabin . . . [*sniff*] . . . we could take this shit with us . . . [*sniff*] . . . carry the party on there . . . Jesus, my brain feels like it's on fire.'

'I should try to keep a clear head . . . [*sniff*] . . . my grandpa is getting married in a few hours.'

'Your Grandpa? Who's he marrying?'

'That asshole's mother. Bitch. She's trying to steal my inheritance . . . [*sniff*] . . . he's not in his right mind. He's got senile dementia.'

'Shit – so what are you gonna do about it?'

'What can I do?'

'I don't know,' he goes, suddenly talking ninety to the dozen, 'you could put a lawyer on the case to stop him getting married on the grounds that he's mentally something or other not capable uncapable incapable.'

'It's a bit late for that maybe I'll just stay up snorting coke and having sex with you then I'll show up at the wedding and stab her in the heart.'

'Hey I can give you an ice pick from the bar come on let's go to my room.'

'Okay let me put some clothes on hey what are we gonna do with this guy will we shave him useless motherfucker maybe cut his dick off . . .'

'Forget about him he's not worth it but hey let's take his trousers throw them in the sea . . .'

Ten seconds later, I hear the door close and they're gone. I open my eyes and I hop out of the bed.

Shit, what time is it?

I check my phone. Fock, it's seven o'clock in the morning and I've got, like, nineteen missed calls from Sorcha. Okay, I need to get my shit together here.

I search the floor for my trousers. Fock, she took them. Hell hath no fury like whatever the actual phrase is.

I throw on my jacket and shirt, then my boxers and socks, and I'm thinking, Okay, all I've got to do here is get back to the room before Sorcha has hopefully woken up, slip into the bed beside her and pretend I've been there for hours. Come on, I think – you've done this a hundred times before, even though it's the first time without actual trousers.

I pick up my shoes and I slip out of the room. Fock, it's already bright out.

I tiptoe along the passageway to Room 14, which is, like, *our* room? I reach for my key and I think, Oh, shit, it's just my luck. It was in my focking trouser pocket.

I try the handle, hoping against hope that Sorcha has left the door unlocked, but then it flies open and she's suddenly standing in front of me with a face as angry as loads of wasps.

I make sure to get my defence in first. 'Sorcha,' I go, 'I know how this looks. But I can guarantee you nothing happened.'

She's like, 'Nothing happened?'

I'm there, 'I swear on my mother's life.'

She just, like, shakes her head. She goes, 'Of all the things you've ever done, Ross, this is definitely the worst.'

I'm thinking, Steady on – what about riding your sister? Obviously I don't say that.

Instead, I go, 'Sorcha, all I'm guilty of here is trying to be a friend to a girl who was upset.'

She's there, 'So you plied her with drink?'

'I wouldn't say I plied her with it. I offered her a glass of Champagne because I thought it might help her chill out. Then she was suddenly throwing it into her. The girl has got a serious problem, by the way.'

'How much did she drink?'

'I don't know. Eight or nine glasses?'

'*Eight or nine glasses?*'

'Minimum. And she had a couple of shorts as well. Tequila and then something else. Why the big concern, Sorcha?'

I shouldn't complain, but she's so focused on the drink aspect of the evening that she hasn't even noticed that I'm standing there in my jockeys.

'Why the big concern?' she goes, as mad as I've ever seen her.

I'm like, 'Yeah, no, why is it such a big deal if the girl has a few drinks? I don't give a fock either way – neither should you.'

She goes, 'Our nine-year-old daughter is drunk, Ross! She's so drunk she can't even stand!'

A wave of relief washes over me.

I'm like, 'Honor's drunk?'

She goes, 'Do you think this is funny?'

'No.'

'Then why are you laughing?'

'It's just, I don't know, possibly *nerves*? So Honor's drunk – that's who we were talking about just there.'

'She's also been sick everywhere.'

'Okay, where is she now?'

'In the bathroom. I'm still trying to sober her up.'

She turns around and storts walking towards the bathroom. I step into our bedroom. The smell of vom hits me straightaway. Jesus, she wasn't wrong. It's all over the bed, the floor, the vanity unit.

But Sorcha ends up not even noticing the whole no-pants thing. I'm, like, punching the air – quite literally.

Johnny, Leo and Brian are all awake and screaming their lungs out.

'Ross,' Sorcha goes, 'will you come in here to the bathroom and help me? I've been ringing you all night!'

I go, 'Hang on, I'm just taking my trousers off so I don't get puke on them.'

I'm a genius. I'm going to use that word.

I give it a few seconds, then into the bathroom I go. Honor is sitting on the floor with her back against the wall and her eyes sort of, like, half closed. We've all been that soldier.

She sees me and goes, 'Look at this . . . focking asshole.'

I'm there, 'I'm going to let that go, Honor, because you've had a few too many.'

She looks at Sorcha then. 'And you . . . you focking . . . whore.'

Sorcha goes, 'I will not tolerate you speaking to me like that, Honor, drunk or not.'

Jesus, I thought we'd have to wait until she was at least fourteen before we had this kind of conversation.

Honor goes, 'You *are* a focking . . . whore . . . couldn't let me . . . be happy . . . you were all over him . . . like a . . . whore . . .'

'I am not having another conversation with you about Caleb,' Sorcha goes. 'Certainly not until you sober up. And then, by the way, you're going to have a very sore head indeed and I hope it scares you off ever drinking again.'

'No chance of that,' I go. 'This is actually good preparation for us.'

'What do you mean?'

'For when she's a teenager. It's all ahead of us. Wesley. Blah, blah, blah.'

'Ross, I can't even talk to you right now.'

'Am I to take it that I'm being blamed for this?'

'You gave our daughter alcohol!'

I stare at Honor, trying to gauge just how hammered she actually is and whether she'll remember this conversation when she sobers up.

I'm there, 'I didn't give her alcohol!'

Sorcha's like, 'Excuse me?'

'*I* didn't give her alcohol,' I go, all wounded innocence.

Shit, Honor ends up being more sober than I imagined because she goes, 'You did! You said I could drink!'

I'm there, 'Honor, I don't know why you'd make up something like that about me.'

She goes, 'You liar!' practically spitting the words at me.

She's going to be a bad drunk. That much is obvious, even at this age.

Sorcha goes, 'But you admitted it, Ross. You said you told her it might chill her out. She had eight or nine glasses of Champagne, you said – and some spirits.'

I laugh.

I'm there, 'You must have got your wires crossed, Babes. I was actually talking about . . . someone else.'

Honor goes, 'You focking said I could . . . you're a focking liar.'

'She's possibly blaming me,' I go, 'because I'm the cool dad. That makes me an easy torget.'

Sorcha smiles at me, her head tilted to the side, and she goes, 'I'm sorry I accused you, Ross.'

I'm like, 'Hey, ain't no thing but Gustavo Fring. It'd be nice if you had faith in me the occasional time, though.'

'I really am sorry, Ross.'

It genuinely shocks me how easily taken in she is sometimes. The girl shouldn't be allowed out of the house.

'Focking liar!' Honor shouts.

I'm there, 'That's just the drink talking.'

Sorcha goes, 'Well, that's me out of the wedding then, isn't it?'

I'm like, 'Why?'

'Ross, she's still drunk. Then we've got the hangover to come. You'll have to tell your mother I'm sorry. I'm going to have to miss her big day.'

'Sorcha's not coming,' I go. 'She sends her apologies and blah, blah, blah.'

The old dear has to make a big song and dance of it, of course. She's like, 'Sorcha's not coming? Is she sick?'

I'm there, 'Yeah, no, Honor is. She's spewing her ring up. She's actually still pissed from last night.'

'Your *daughter* Honor? You're saying she was drinking alcohol?'

'I don't know why you sound so surprised. She has your genes, you focking soak.'

She pulls a face as if to say that she's not going to let what I say today affect her. She's rising above it.

She goes, 'How do I look?'

I'm there, 'Like someone sat on Bruce Jenner's head.'

'Ross,' she goes, 'you're about to walk me up the aisle. Can't you be nice to me – just for one day?'

I get famously emotional at weddings. It kind of sneaks up on me, which is probably the reason I end up going, 'Okay, fine, you look well – genuinely well.'

She smiles. She goes, 'That's a lovely thing to say, Ross.'

I'm there, 'Hey, I only said *well*. You know, don't go quoting me down the line, saying I said this, that and the other.'

'*Well* is good enough for me.'

'So you're definitely going to do this then?'

'Oh, Ross, I can't remember the last time I was this happy.'

So I nod at the conductor of the orchestra and the music storts up – we're talking something by Vivaldi.

The old dear links my orm and we step out onto the deck of the boat. There's, like, an aisle in front of us with seventy or eighty chairs set out in rows on either side. We walk slowly, one step at a time, the old dear giving me instructions out of the corner of her mouth, like, 'Slower, Ross!' without ever breaking her smile.

I spot the boat's captain, who's apparently going to perform the necessary, standing at the top of the aisle in a blazer and a white hat and a humungous, grey walrus moustache.

And in front of him, with his back to us, is the groom. When we're, like, halfway up the aisle, he looks over his shoulder. He's grinning from ear to ear, but he's also, like, gibbering away to himself. When we reach the top, I can hear what he's saying. He's going, 'As chairwoman of the reception committee, I extend the wishes of every man, woman and child of Freedonia. Never mind that stuff. Take a card. Card? What will I do with the card? You can keep it. I've got fifty-one left. Now what were you saying?'

I go, 'She's all yours, Ari. Do what you want with her.'

'As chairwoman of the reception committee, I extend the wishes of every man, woman and child of Freedonia . . .'

'Ssshhh,' the old dear goes, which seems to quieten the dude down. 'This is it, Ari – we're getting married!'

I take my seat, next to the old man. I take Johnny onto my knee. The old man has Brian and Helen has Leo.

'Wonderful job,' the old man goes, wiping away an actual tear.

I'm looking around. I notice that there's no sign of Tiffany Blue. I'm wondering is she sleeping off her coke hangover?

We sit through the whole thing. There's, like, a Mass-type thing – it might even *be* Mass.

It storts during the exchange of vows. Johnny is the first. 'Focking motherfocker!' he shouts. 'Motherfocking focker!'

That sets Leo off. He's like, 'Shitting motherfocker! Focking shitting bastard! Shitting shit!'

And then Brian decides to have his say. He's there, 'Fock off! Fock off, focking bastard!'

People are turning around and staring at me, expecting me to do something, including the old dear.

'Focking pricks!' Johnny shouts.

I'm thinking, Yeah, no, I couldn't have put it better myself, Johnny.

People turn back and face the front again. The old dear and Ari do the necessary, then they sign some paperwork to say that they're actually married, then they kiss and we all clap. And then that's that.

Or should I say that *should* be that?

I'm sitting there thinking, Thank fock that's over, I could do with a drink to take the edge off this hangover – I might even bring one to the room for Honor. Might get me out of her bad books!

That's when a voice behind us goes, 'You . . . bitch!'

I turn around. Everyone turns around. It's Tiffany Blue. There's more than a few gasps from the congregation – especially when they see the state of her. It's pretty obvious that the girl hasn't been to bed yet. She's been up all night and all morning snorting coke and drinking fock knows what and now she's looking for a fight.

'You're drunk,' the old dear goes, grinning at her. 'And God knows what else.'

Tiffany Blue goes, 'Step away from my grandpa!'

It's actually comical the way she says it.

'You're too late,' the old dear goes. 'The deed is done.'

And that's when I notice the flash of metal in Tiffany Blue's hand. Shit, she has an ice pick – and suddenly she's stomping up the aisle, holding the thing like a dagger.

One or two people make a grab for her, but the girl is not about to be stopped. She slips two or three attempted tackles and suddenly she's standing in front of my old dear, getting ready to plunge the thing into her chest.

And that's when, suddenly, Tiffany Blue is tackled around the waist and wrestled to the deck of the boat. It happens so fast that no one knows who the hero of the hour happens to be. It takes a few seconds for them to realize that the old dear's saviour is none other than me.

Delma, one of the old dear's knob friends, manages to pull the ice pick out of Tiffany Blue's hand.

'Ross!' the old dear goes. 'You saved my life!'

'Stop it!' a voice suddenly roars.

Everyone looks up. It's Ari. He stares at his granddaughter and goes, 'You should be ashamed yourself!'

She's there, 'I'm not!'

'Well, *I'm* ashamed of you! And I'm ashamed enough for both of us! I thought I raised you better than that!'

Yeah, she's in and out of rehab like Chorlie focking Sheen, by the sounds of it – I wouldn't go throwing bouquets at yourself, Ari.

She's like, 'I can't believe you married that woman!'

'That woman,' Ari goes, 'has a name,' and then he goes quiet for a few seconds. It's pretty obvious that he's trying to remember it.

Tiffany Blue goes, 'She's just about the money and you can't see it!'

'She's not about the money,' he tries to go, 'because I already told you she signed a piece of paper that . . . Hey, you know what?'

He reaches into his jacket and pulls out a wad of pages. I'm presuming it's the actual prenup. 'Fionnuala – that's it! – she suggested, as a demonstration of her love for me, that she sign this bullshit piece of paper, cutting her out of everything in the event of my death. You know what I'm going to do now?'

'Don't you dare!' Tiffany Blue screams. 'It'll be the biggest mistake of your life!'

Ari takes the pages and he rips them up. Everyone genuinely gasps.

'Ari,' the old dear goes, 'that really wasn't necessary!'

At the same time, I notice a huge smile on the old dear's

lips – and that's when I realize that she played me. She played me, she played Tiffany Blue, she played Ari – she played us all.

She knew that if she flashed that ring around, she'd get Tiffany Blue riled. She knew that if she told me that Tiffany Blue got slutty with drink on her that I'd try to get her back on the booze. She knew that if Tiffany Blue was shitfaced, she'd look for coke and then she'd kick off in a major way. And she knew that if Tiffany Blue kicked off, Ari would tear up the prenup and she could look like it was all a major shock to her.

You can say I'm possibly *reaching* here? But then I know how her mind works as well as I know my own.

Ari stares at Tiffany Blue and goes, 'You're worried about Fionnuala getting everything when I die? Well, you can stop worrying because I'm putting you out of your misery. She's *getting* everything. I'm cutting you out and I'm cutting you off.'

Tiffany Blue's jaw hits the – literally – deck. 'You don't mean that,' she goes.

He's like, 'Hey, it just happened. You're dead to me.'

He takes the torn-up prenup and he throws the pieces in the air and they suddenly rain down on us.

'Oh, look,' the old dear goes, 'it's just like confetti!'

# 8. Club Can't Even Handle Me Right Now

Dudser is letting fly in a serious way. We're, like, five minutes from the end of Strength and Conditioning, but there's no let-up in the intensity. We're doing, like, one-leg squats and he's going, 'Deeper! Go deeper, you pack of wimps!'

Christian's sweating like a menopausal woman. I'm like, 'This is Dudser in a good mood, by the way!'

Christian laughs in a sort of, like, bitter kind of way.

'Gilly,' Dudser shouts, 'Blissy, Ollie Lysaght. Tesco and back – three minutes. I'm timing you.'

Blissy has a go back at him. 'I'm *doing* the focking exercises,' he goes.

Dudser's like, 'You're not. You're checking out your hair in the mirror. Ballybrack Shopping Centre and back. The rest of you can keep doing one-leg squats until they get back!'

We're all like, 'You better hurry the fock up!'

Anyway, the torture eventually ends. Dudser goes, 'That's it, ladies. See you next week. Same time.'

He always calls us ladies. He's one of those people who's sound but *also* a wanker? I'd like to think I'm a bit like that myself.

Christian goes, 'Thanks, Dudser – for letting me do the session.'

Dudser seems amused by him. 'So run this by me again,' he goes. 'You're not playing for the actual team – but you want go through the same suffering that they do?'

I'm there, 'Yeah, no, he's trying to win back his wife.'

Dudser reacts like this is the funniest thing he's ever heard.

'I thought there might be a woman involved,' he goes. 'I didn't think it was going to be your own wife!'

He walks away, still laughing.

I'm there, 'Dudser's far too young to be that cynical.'

Christian goes, 'I was talking to her today. Lauren, I mean. It was just about money for Ross and Oliver – maintenance, whatever you want to call it – but we had a really civil conversation. She said I sounded well.'

'Did you tell her that a lot of that was down to me?'

'I mentioned that you'd been helping me get my shit together, yeah.'

'Well, hopefully I'll get the credit next time I see her.'

I grab a quick Jack Bauer. As I'm towelling myself off, I notice that Senny's now lifting weights while listening to his iPhone.

'Who's that?' I go.

He pulls the buds out of his ears. He's like, 'What was that, Rossi?'

I'm there, 'Yeah, no, I was just wondering who are you listening to? A bit of Drake, is it?'

I'm trying to learn as much as I can about all this new music that there suddenly seems to be.

He goes, 'It's actually Nicki Minaj.'

Nicki Minaj? Jesus Christ, Honor listens to Nicki Minaj. I suddenly realize that my daughter is closer in age to Senny than I am.

He's about to put the buds back in, then he remembers something. He's like, 'Hey, by the way, were you talking to Bucky?'

I'm there, 'Er, not tonight, no.'

He goes, 'We were just wondering, have you ever surfed?'

I laugh.

I'm like, 'Have I ever surfed? I'm sorry for laughing, Dude. Yes, you could safely say that I have surfed.'

I've never focking surfed. I can't even swim.

He goes, 'It's just Bucky was saying we might all go away for the night. After we play Rainey Old Boys. Bundoran is only a ninety-minute drive from Derry.'

I'm there, 'Is that where Rainey Old Boys are based? Bundoran?'

He laughs. 'No,' he goes, 'Rainey Old Boys are from Derry. The surfing is in Bundoran.'

'Okay,' I go, 'I think I've got it now.'

'We could do the drive as soon as the match is over. Have a Saturday night in Bundoran, then spend Sunday surfing. Turn it into a bit of a guyatus.'

'A what?'

'It's what we call a night away for the boys – a guyatus?'

'Yeah, no, it sounds good to me. Like I said, I love surfing in the, em, sea.'

He goes, 'Mint!', which I'm presuming is what young people say instead of 'Cool!'

He puts the buds back in his ears and I think to myself, Oh, fock! What have I just talked myself into?

There's, like, no answer from Ronan's mobile, so instead I ring his gaff. It's Shadden who ends up answering.

I'm like, 'Hey, Shadden, is Ronan there?' because it's a Wednesday afternoon and he usually gets a half-day from school.

She goes, 'He's not hee-or, Rosser. He's in he's cadavan up in whatever it's calt.'

I'm there, 'Ticknock.'

'Ticknock – that's it. He's studying theer for the arthur noon. Foyunts it eadier to concenthrate.'

In the background, I can hear little Rihanna-Brogan practising for her school's Easter Recital, singing some piece of shit song from *Frozen* in her half-and-half accent. She's all:

> *Lerrit go, lerrit go,*
> *Cawn't haild it back anymoyer,*
> *Lerrit go, Lerrit go,*
> *Turn away and slam the doyer.*

It's pretty focking hilarious, it has to be said.

'Yeah, no, I'm not too far from Ticknock,' I go. 'I'll swing up there and see him.'

She goes, 'Feer denuff, Rosser.'

I turn the music back on and I point the cor in the direction of Ticknock. I borrowed Honor's iPod and I'm listening to a bit of Nicki Minaj. It turns out the woman has got a filthy focking mouth on her. It's bitch-this and motherfocker-that.

It reminds me of mealtimes in our gaff.

I pull up on the road outside Ronan's field. I listen out for the dogs, except I don't hear any borking. I open the door of the cor and the first thing that hits me is the smell of burning.

I look up, above the trees, and I can see black smoke and I straightaway fear the worst.

I run all the way to the entrance of the field. I pull open the heavy gate and I'm suddenly standing there, just rooted to the spot. Ronan's caravan has been burned to the ground. All I can see is this, like, twisted mass of blackened metal, which still has smoke pouring from it.

There's, like, no sign of my son anywhere.

I walk closer. As I do, certain things become clearer to my eyes. I can make out the fridge where Ro kept his poitín chilled – black, but still intact – then the springs from what was once the sofa. The smell is horrendous.

And then, for some reason, I happen to look to my left, over to where the JCB is porked and I see this, like, mound of freshly turned soil. There's something on top of it, which at first I don't recognize. It's only when I walk over to it that I cop what it actually is.

It's Ronan's Dublin GAA baseball cap. I pick it up and I just, like, stare at it, the little crest on the front with the castle and the Viking ship. It still smells of *Instinct by David Beckham*, which Sorcha bought him for Christmas.

I'm like, 'No!'

I actually scream it.

I'm like, 'Nooooooo!!!'

Then I get down on my hands and knees and I stort clawing at the dirt with my bare hands, dreading what I'm going to find under it, yet still digging. And at the exact same time, I'm sobbing, going, 'Jesus, it was only a bus tour! Why did I let it go this far?'

I manage to move thirty or forty handfuls of dirt, but I'm making slow progress. But then I look at the JCB and I have an idea.

I climb into the cab. The keys are actually still in it. I stort her up and I stort fiddling about with the various gear sticks and levers to try to figure out how to drive the thing and move the orm up and down.

It only takes me a minute or two to master it. Then I drive it over on its tracks to the edge of the mound and I stort digging up the earth, pulling up maybe a tonne of soil at a time, then spinning the orm around and dropping it a few feet away. Then I jump out of the cab and I search the pile for my son's body.

When it's not there, I feel instant relief. But it doesn't last long. I jump back into the cab and I dig up another tonne of earth and repeat the process.

Soon, I've dug up about eight tonnes and there's still no sign of Ro or his remains. I'm suddenly beating the ground, crying and going, 'I should have stopped it! I should have stopped it when I had the chance!'

And that's when I hear a voice go, 'You're some fooken can of piss, Rosser.'

I look up.

Ronan is suddenly standing over me with Nudger and Buckets of Blood.

I'm there, 'Ro! Oh, thank God! I thought Scum had killed you and buried you using your own Fran from *Love/Hate* mechanical digger!'

He goes, 'Where'd you foyunt me cap? Gimme that, you fooken clowin.'

He snaps it out of my hands.

I stand up. I'm like, 'Ro, what the fock happened here? I'm presuming this was, like, Scum's work?'

'You're presuming reet,' he goes. 'He burdened me base or operashiddens – he's arthur oberstepping the meerk.'

I'm there, 'Ro, surely you both overstepped the mork the moment you storted burning each other's buses? Ro, think about your daughter. She's at home practising for her Easter Recital while you're out here, playing at being a gangster. Would you not think of possibly calling a truce?'

He's like, 'A throoce? A fooken throoce, is it?'

It's only then I notice the change in Ronan's appearance. He's had his head totally shaved and he's wearing a jacket zipped right

244

up to the neck so that he *looks* like actual Nidge? He's all, like, nervy and jittery like him as well.

He goes, 'Feddas like Scum ardent inthordested in throoces, Rosser. Thee wontherstand oately one thing.'

I'm there, 'Ro, do you want to end up like all your heroes in that show – either dead or, worse, walking crooked with a snooker cue up your orse?'

He turns to Nudger and Buckets and goes, 'Toyum to turden up the heat on eer friend.'

Nudger's like, 'The job's alretty in the woorks, Ro.'

And Ronan goes, 'Coola fooken boola.'

'Oh! My God!' Sorcha goes. 'Look at the colour of you, Fionnuala!'

She has some Peter Pan alright. She goes, 'Thank you, Sorcha. You know, I was walking along College Green today and someone tried to hand me a leaflet for the Viking Splash.'

I'm supposed to just sit there and listen to this bullshit.

She goes, 'You see, they thought I was one of these foreign nationals!'

'Yeah,' I go, 'we all know the point you're trying to make. The girl just complimented you on your tan. I don't know why you have to turn everything into a focking anecdote. It's ridiculous at this stage.'

She blanks me and goes, 'Would anyone like more of the venison casserole.'

I'm there, 'I'll have some – even if it's just so I don't hurt your feelings.'

I help myself to another plate of it. It's incredible, by the way.

'Although I'll probably be bent over the toilet all night,' I go, 'throwing it back up.'

Sorcha goes, 'What about you, Ari, did you enjoy the honeymoon?'

They arrived home last night. Of course, the old dear couldn't wait to invite us over to show us their photos.

Ari's like, 'Me? Oh, yes, I had a fine time. Quite fine.'

A week in his villa in Sardinia. You wouldn't blame them.

The old dear goes, 'So who's looking after, em . . .'

'Crouch, bind and set,' I go.

'Yes, that's it – those lovely children.'

Sorcha's like, 'My mom and dad are babysitting Honor and the boys. Oh my God, Ross, I forgot to tell you – and Fionnuala, I know you'll be interested in hearing this because you've raised *so* much money for charity yourself – but I might be setting up, like, a foundation!'

I'm there, 'A what?'

'A foundation, Ross. It's something that's been on my To Do list – oh my God – since I was at school. So then today, I was trying to manoeuvre the stroller out of Caviston's and who did I meet? I mean, it has to be, like, fate. Muirgheal Massey? Do you remember Muirgheal Massey, Ross? She was in Mount Anville with me. She went for Head Girl the year I got it, even though she was genuinely, genuinely delighted for me when I won.'

I'm there, 'Keep talking, Sorcha. It might come back to me.'

I'm not really listening anyway.

She goes, 'Muirgheal just so happened to mention that she's looking around for something to do. She and her husband just broke up. I don't know if you remember Tchaik Coffey, Ross, who was in the Institute with me? A total bastard to women. Anyway, she thinks that thing might be charity work! And I was like, "Oh! My God! I've been saying for years that I would love to do, I don't know, *something* for maybe a country in Africa?" '

The old dear goes, 'What a wonderful idea, Sorcha!'

'Well, everything suddenly snowballed. We ended up going for lunch and we actually decided there and then to set up a foundation called The Mount Anville Africa Fund.'

I'm there, 'And what are they going to supposedly do?'

She goes, 'Well, hopefully raise awareness of the issues affecting Africa among pupils and past pupils of Mount Anville.'

'Something like that has been long needed,' the old dear goes. 'Long, long needed.'

'Well,' Sorcha goes, 'I posted something about it on the Mount Anville Matters Facebook page at, like, four o'clock and – oh my

God – I couldn't believe the reaction. It got, like, forty-seven likes and thirteen comments and that was in, like, three hours. So anyway there's going to be, like, a meeting about it in our house on Friday night, Ross.'

'Yeah, no,' I go, 'I think I remember Muirgheal now. JP might have been with her once or twice. She used to make this slurping noise with her mouth whenever you kissed her – that's if it's the same girl I'm thinking about.'

'What Muirgheal and I would love to do is to try to raise enough money every year to send, like, the entire of Transition Year to Africa for a week – although obviously not one of the dangerous countries – to see the kind of challenges that the people face there every day of their lives.'

'It was like she was eating hot chips. *Ssshhhlllluuuppp. Ssshhhlllluuuppp.* Ask her does she still make that noise?'

'I'm not going to ask her does she still make that noise, Ross.'

'Well, *I'm* pretty sure it was definitely her.'

Suddenly – this is, like, totally out of the blue – Ari goes, 'Well, I got a message for *your* Mister Hitler! If he *is* planning to use these Olympic Games as a demonstration of Arian supremacy over the rest of the world, he's in for quite a shock. For I – and hundreds of black athletes like me – intend to train as hard as God will allow me to ensure that the Führer's athletic will-to-power comes to nothing!'

Jesus Christ.

The old dear puts her hand down on top of his hand to try to, like, calm him down.

'I'll see you in Berlin!' he shouts.

But she just goes, 'Ari, it's okay. We're in Ireland, Ari, remember? Ssshhh . . . Ssshhh . . .'

And he's like, 'Fionnuala?' as if he's suddenly back in the present day

'That's right,' she goes. 'It's Fionnuala. I'm here with you. In March 2015. We just got married, Ari,' and that's when *the* weirdest thing suddenly happens. I see something in the old dear's eyes – something I've never actually *seen* before? This is going to sound focked up, but I'm pretty sure the word is, like, compassion?

In that moment, I can suddenly see what I probably haven't wanted to see up until now, which is that my old dear does actually love this man – even if he is losing his mind, even if she did, I don't know, conspire to get his granddaughter cut out of his will – and she loves him in a way that she never loved my old man and she certainly never loved me.

I watch Sorcha wipe away a tear with the back of her hand. I can feel one or two building up in my own eyes and I end up having to say something just to bring some semblance of normality back to the situation.

'I can only imagine the damage that this dinner is doing to my focking insides,' I go. 'What's the bets I'm on the jacks all day tomorrow, shitting baby food?'

Suddenly, there ends up being a ring on the doorbell.

'Who on Earth could that be,' the old dear goes, 'at this time of night?'

She goes outside to answer it.

I hear all this, like, kerfuffle outside in the hallway, then, about ten seconds later, the dining-room door flies open and in she bursts – we're talking Tiffany Blue.

Easy on the eye though she is, I genuinely hoped I'd never set eyes on her again.

The old dear goes, 'You haven't been invited and you are intruding. Kindly leave this instant or I shall be forced to phone the Gords.'

She's like, 'The what?' because she's from the States, bear in mind.

'The Gords,' the old dear goes. 'The Irish police force.'

Tiffany Blue's there, 'You think I'm scared of the police?'

It's pretty obvious from looking at her that she's off her tits on coke or booze or both.

I'm like, 'Yeah, no, maybe you should do what she says, though, and head off.'

She looks at me with, like, *real* contempt? 'Hey, look,' she goes, 'it's the three-minute wonder!'

Sorcha looks at me, confused. She's there, 'What's she talking about, Ross?'

I'm like, 'I've no idea, Sorcha. Let's just forget about it.'

'What I'm talking about,' Tiffany Blue goes, 'is I had sex with your husband on the boat. And let me tell you, I've had sneezing fits that lasted longer.'

I'm going to give you a little bit of advice now that's worth printing out and pinning to your bathroom mirror – Never Make Mental Your Mistress.

'Ross?' Sorcha goes, about as hurt as I've ever seen her. 'Is this true?'

And that's when something else incredible happens – the old dear, for whatever reason, saves my hide. I don't *know* why? Possibly because she was the one who put the idea of riding the girl into my head?

She goes, 'Of course it isn't true! Sorcha, don't believe it for an instant! She's trying to poison everyone's happiness – it's what she does!'

Sorcha looks instantly relieved. She goes, 'I'm sorry, Ross.'

I'm there, 'Hey, it's fine, Sorcha. Give a dog a bad name.'

'You believe what you want,' Tiffany Blue goes. 'I'm just here to tell you something.'

The old dear's like, 'Say your piece and then leave.'

'Okay, here's my piece. I got a lawyer.'

'Oh, a lawyer!' the old dear goes. 'I've got lawyers. I've got all sorts of lawyers.'

'Well, this one thinks I have a very good case to have this so-called marriage declared invalid.'

'It doesn't matter what you do. You won't change the way I feel about your grandfather or the way your grandfather feels about me. You won't have that declared invalid.'

'You might as well know, I'm going to your High Court. This lawyer I got is going to seek an injunction, forcing Grandpa to submit to tests to establish his state of mind. That's word for word. And when they find out his true mental state, I can promise you this, Fionnuala – you won't be getting shit.'

Me and Christian run from, let's call a spade a spade, Ballybrack all the way back to the Vico Road – we're talking, what, three Ks?

Except he's not tossing chowder in Enya's entranceway this time. He's actually in proper shape.

It's, like, ten o'clock when we arrive back at the gaff. There's, like, eight or nine cors in the driveway – we're talking Toyota Rav4s, we're talking Volvo S40s, we're talking Volkswagen EOSs, we're talking Honda CR-Vs.

Honor, I notice, is outside, rooting around in the dashboard of my cor. She's like, 'Er, *why* do you have this?' and she produces her iPod.

I'm there, 'I was, em, listening to something.'

She presses the button in the middle of the click wheel. 'Okay, *why* were you listening to Nicki Minaj?'

'I don't know. I just wanted to see what all the fuss was about.'

'Oh my God, you're so sad!'

'Who owns all these cors, by the way? It's not Sorcha's book club tonight, is it?'

Honor rolls her eyes. She goes, 'No, she's hosting a meeting – so-called – to set up The Mount Anville Africa Fund.'

'Yeah, no, I forgot that was tonight.'

Christian says he's going to head back to Carrickmines and I tell him not before I fix us a couple of protein shakes he's not. I put my key in the door and in we go. Through the living-room door I get the whiff of quiche and *Tom Ford White Patchouli* and I hear raised voices going, 'Oh! My God!', all the usual giveaways that your house is infested with Mounties.

I turn around to Christian and I go, 'Hang on a second,' and then I stick my head around the door of the living room to see who else Sorcha and Muirgheal have managed to rope into this thing.

The first girl I spot is actually Carolyn Fusco, a bird I got off with once or twice back in the day. She's saying she took the liberty of ringing the Deportment of Foreign Affairs today to ask for a list of countries in Africa that would be, like, really, really poor, but still safe to visit for, like, Transition Year students.

She says they mentioned Botswana.

Muirgheal goes, 'Oh my God, I spoke to Sister Obadiah at the school today and she also mentioned Botswana. She said it's, like, one of *the* safest places in Africa. But the good news is it's also got, like, Aids, storvation, blah, blah, blah. And the other thing that it's got going for it is that it has some amazing, amazing safori tours!'

Muirgheal, by the way, *is* the same Muirgheal that JP used to score, because I recognize her. The noises were hilarious – *ssshhhlllluuurrrppp, ssshhhlllluuurrrppp, ssshhhlllluuurrrppp* – like a fat kid eating his way out of an ice-cream maze.

No one notices me until I suddenly go, 'Hey, there! I'll tell you something – there's one or two faces from the past in this room.'

I do the same mental inventory I always do when I walk into a room of women. I've ridden one, two, three, four of them – five, if you want to include Sorcha.

Sorcha's there, 'You all remember my husband, Ross, I presume?' and they all go, 'Yes,' with – it has to be said – varying degrees of enthusiasm.

'Okay,' she goes, bringing the meeting to an end, 'everyone knows their duties, yes?'

And everyone's like, 'Yes!'

'Okay, we'll stort a What's App group, but we'll also meet back here, when, two weeks from tonight?'

That seems to suit everyone. Off they go into the night, while I take Christian down to the kitchen to make him that drink.

'I was actually dubious about the NutriBullet when Sorcha first bought it,' I go. 'I said to her, "I'll take my meals in liquid form when I'm in a coma and not before then." But I've actually got into it.'

Sorcha has waved off all her Mountie friends, except Muirgheal, who's obviously sticking around for coffee, because Sorcha turns on the Nespresso. 'Oh my God,' she goes, 'I am *so* excited about this thing!'

Muirgheal's like, 'Me, too. I mean, I'm in two book clubs and I have my Bikram and my Reformer Pilates, but I'd forgotten how much I enjoy having an actual *project*?'

I'm like, 'Fair focks to both of you. I'd be the first one to say it.'

'By the way, where even *is* Botswana?' Muirgheal goes. 'As in, like, where in Africa?'

Sorcha doesn't know. I think it goes without saying that I don't either. It's actually Christian who comes up with the answer. 'It's towards the bottom,' he goes. 'Just above South Africa.'

Muirgheal goes, 'Oh my God! Brainiac, much?'

Christian laughs. 'I only know,' he goes, 'because Father Fehily spent a lot of time there when he was younger. He used to talk about it all the time.'

It's lovely to hear him talk about Father Fehily. I really feel that something of the old Christian is storting to return.

Muirgheal obviously Googles 'Botswana' on her phone because she's suddenly looking at her screen, going, 'Okay, it's got the second-highest prevalence of HIV slash Aids in the world! We're talking twenty-four point eight per cent of adults between the ages of fifteen and forty-nine!'

I'm there, 'That sounds great.'

'In fact,' she goes, 'the only country with a worse HIV slash Aids epidemic is Swaziland! Should that say Switzerland?'

Sorcha's like, 'I don't know.'

'I've never heard of Swaziland.'

'It does sound wrong. How are they spelling it?'

'S, W, A, Z, I, L, A, N, D.'

'That *is* random.'

'It must mean Switzerland. Okay, epic fail, Wikipedia! Actually, Switzerland wouldn't be a bad place to send kids either, even though it's not in Africa. My cousin goes skiing there – oh my God, she always brings back amazing chocolate.'

I finish making the shakes. I hand one to Christian. He takes a sip out of his, then goes, 'So, like, how much money do you need to raise?'

Sorcha's there, 'Enough to hopefully send the whole of Transition Year to Africa next year – I'm thinking initially, like, €100,000?' and then her face all of a sudden changes, like she's suddenly had an idea. 'Oh my God!' she goes. 'Oh! My! Literally? God!'

Muirgheal's like, 'What is it?'

Sorcha's there, 'I'm actually blaming you, Christian, for mentioning South Africa! I've had an *amazing* idea how we can raise money!'

'Is it a charity *Strictly Come Dancing*?' Muirgheal goes. 'Because that was going to be one of my suggestions. We could call it Strictly Botswana.'

'This is even better. I'm going to put my letters from Nelson Mandela up for auction.'

Fock! Off!

Actually, I say that out loud.

I go, 'Fock! Off!' and they all look at me. 'Yeah, no, what I mean is, you know, why would you want to get rid of them? And I'm only asking that because I know how much they mean to you.'

'Yes, I loved receiving them, Ross. And my correspondence with Madiba is one of the most – oh my God – amazing, amazing things that has ever happened to me. But now I have an opportunity to use my good fortune to open the eyes of future generations of Mount Anville students to the problems that Africa faces on a daily basis.'

'Okay,' I go, 'I'll phrase that a different way. Who the fock would want them? They're *to* you. They're all about you potentially switching to European Environmental Law. Who's going to be interested in that?'

She's there, 'He also talked about himself, Ross. I mean, those letters are an amazing, amazing insight into Madiba's state of mind at a very delicate stage of South Africa's transition to a multi-porty democracy.'

'I'm disagreeing with you. I think they're boring. I was actually bored reading them.'

'Well, I still think they'd be worth something.'

Christian goes, 'You know what, I could actually see, like, a university or someone like that buying them.'

I wish he'd stay the fock out of it. He's obviously forgotten that Oisinn wrote the things.

Muirgheal goes, 'I totally agree! Especially if, like Sorcha said, they shine a light on his thinking at a particular moment in, I don't know, *history*?'

She can keep her focking hooter to herself as well.

Christian drinks his shake, then says he's going to hit the road.

Muirgheal knocks back her coffee and says she'll have to do the same because she's got Pilates in the morning.

Off the two of them fock.

Sorcha smiles at me. She goes, 'By the way, Ross, I think it's an amazing thing that you're doing. Christian looks so well.'

I'm there, 'Hey, I just hope Lauren appreciates it.'

Sorcha looks at me, all concern. 'Ross,' she goes, 'you didn't tell Christian that Lauren was going to come back to him, did you?'

I'm there, 'If he cleans up his act – yeah, no, I possibly implied that she would. To give him an incentive as much as anything else.'

'Ross,' she goes, 'Lauren's met someone. In France. His name is Loic and he's a cinematographer.'

It feels like I've suddenly been kicked in the stomach. All I can think to say is, 'Okay, what the fock is a cinematographer? It sounds like another makey-uppy thing. Like Human Resources.'

'I don't know what exactly he does,' Sorcha goes, 'but he's made, like, thirty movies.'

'I think what I'm actually trying to say is, what the fock is Lauren playing at? She's a married woman.'

'Ross, she's separated. The marriage is over. She told me that when she was home. She doesn't love Christian anymore.'

'She didn't say that to me. She never mentioned any cinema-whatever-the-fock-he-is either. What kind of name is Loic anyway? He doesn't sound like a rugby goy.'

'I don't know if he's a rugby goy.'

'He doesn't sound like one. In which case I'm doubly disgusted with the girl.'

'Ross, you've got to tell Christian the truth.'

'I can't now, can I? It'd set him back.'

'Ross, it's wrong to give him false hope. I really think you should tell him the truth.'

'I'm actually going to do the opposite. I'm going to keep lying to him and hope that he never finds out.'

It's, like, Friday night, the night before we play Rainey Old Boys, and I'm just in the gym, lifting weights with the rest of the goys, listening to a bit of Calvin Harris – I thought he was a fashion designer – and talking about what an achievement it will be if we do manage to stay up. Two wins from our last three matches could even be enough.

Bucky goes, 'It'd be one of the greatest comebacks of all time. We had, like, zero points. Now we're unbeaten in, what, four matches?'

Senny's like, 'I said it to Torah last night. No matter what I go on to achieve in the game – be it European Cups, Six Nations championships, hopefully playing for the Lions – keeping Seapoint up would always rank right up there.'

Seriously, it's like having a conversation with my twenty-year-old self.

I'm there, 'Let's not get ahead of ourselves. We've got to beat Rainey Old Boys first. Let's all just stay focused on the next match.'

And that's when my phone all of a sudden rings. I check the screen and it ends up being Shadden again. I get this sudden feeling of – I *think* it's a word? – *forbodery*?

I answer by going, 'Shadden? What's the Jack?'

She's there, 'Rosser?' and I can straightaway tell that she's crying. 'Rosser, Ine skeered.'

I'm there, 'Scared? Scared of what? What's going on?'

'Someone's arthur thrown a brick troo Rihatta-Barrogan's bedroom window. I ren up the steers and her bed was all cubbered in glass.'

I'm like, 'Jesus Christ!' because that's my granddaughter she's talking about. 'Is she hurt?'

'No,' she goes, 'she's croying, but.'

'Where's Ronan?'

'I don't know where he is.'

'What about your old man, focking K . . . K . . . K . . . Kennet?'

'Him and me ma are out. Ine woodied about Ronan. This war he's arthur getting mixed up in – Ine woodied where it's going.'

'Don't worry, Shadden. It's not going anywhere because it's ending tonight. Where would I find this Scum who's running the rival *Love/Hate* tour?'

'If it's Coolock Scum, it's Deddick Tattan.'

'Derek Tattan. That's the dude. Shadden, where would I find this focking scumbag?'

'I doatunt know.'

'Shadden, think. I need to go and sort this – before someone is killed.'

After a few seconds, she goes, 'I know he thrinks in The Tipsy Wagon.'

I'm there, 'The Tipsy Wagon?'

'It's in Coolock.'

'Okay, good. What does he look like? Shadden, I need to know what he looks like.'

'Ine throyen to think, Rosser. He's a skiddy fedda . . .'

'Keep going.'

' . . . red heer. Galasses and rotten teet – that's alls I know.'

I'm there, 'Okay, you did good, Shadden.'

'What are you gonna do?' she goes.

'I'm going to pay our friend a little visit. Now, what you're going to do is take Rihanna-Brogan and go to your sister's.'

'Kadden's in Tederife. I'll go to Dadden's.'

'Go to Dadden's then. And if Ronan rings, tell him it's sorted.'

I go outside and I hop into the cor. Forty minutes later, I'm pulling into the cor pork of The Tipsy Wagon pub in Coolock.

Straight into the actual boozer I morch.

I spot him straightaway, even though the place is rammers. Shadden's description ends up being pretty much spot-on. He's sitting in a corner, drinking a pint and watching the nine o'clock news on RTÉ.

He's, like, mid-to-late forties and – like Shadden said – skinny, with red hair and freckles, glasses that have got, like, a dork tint, and a mouth like a sink full of broken dishes. Oh, and a Christmas jumper with tracksuit bottoms.

I straightaway hate him, if I didn't already. I feel my blood stort to boil, like it used to whenever I saw photographs of Rory McIlroy with Caroline Wozniacki.

I walk over to him and I'm like, 'Scum?'

'All depends,' he goes. 'Who's aston?'

I go, '*I'm* asking.'

'And who the fook are you?'

'Let's just say I'm an associate of Ronan's. Ronan who runs the *Love/Hate* Tour of Dublin?'

'So?'

I'm there, 'I hear you've got a problem with him.'

'I've no probem with him,' he goes, then he laughs. 'Not addy mower. The problem has been sorthed – did he not tell you what happent?'

'Oh, what, you think just because you attacked his home – threw a brick through his daughter's actual bedroom window – that that's going to be the end of it?'

'I nebber troo a brick troo addyone's window.'

'Do you expect me to believe that? You already burned out his bus and his caravan. You and your scumbag mates went for him with machetes.'

'Did you just say scumbag?'

'That's all they are. That's all you are.'

He goes, 'You've some bleaten balls cubbing in hee-or and saying that. Take my advice, pal – turden arowunt and get the fook ourra hee-or.'

I'm there, 'I'm not focking scared of you, Scum. If I have to deck you, I will. I'm here to end this thing.'

He goes to grab something out of his inside pocket – I'm presuming a knife – but I'm too quick for him. I grab him by the front of his jumper and I lift him off his stool. It doesn't take a lot of strength. There's not a lot of meat on his bones. I hold him steady with my left hand and I punch him full in the face with my right, breaking his glasses and sending him sprawling across the deck, furniture falling everywhere.

'Ah, hee-or!' the borman goes.

Scum ends up just lying on the ground with his back against the bor, his glasses broken and hanging from one ear.

People are looking around and they're *also* going, 'Ah, hee-or!'

I'm there, 'Don't you ever – and I mean *ever*! – threaten Ronan or his family again. If you do, I won't hestitate to come back here and deck you a second time if that's what I end up *having* to do?'

Scum takes off his broken glasses, then touches his nose and stares at the blood on his fingers with a look of, like, disbelief – like he's never seen his own blood before and he's surprised at the colour. He looks at me then and laughs.

I sense that the atmosphere in the pub is storting to dorken. I stort making my way towards the door. 'You're gonna be soddy for that,' Scum goes.

And suddenly this sick feeling washes over me, the sense that I might live to regret what I just did – and that's only if I'm very, very lucky.


Sorcha's got, like, tears in her eyes as she gives her Nelson Mandela letters one last read.

'It's not too late to change your mind,' I go. 'I still say you should keep them. I mean, fock Africa.'

She goes, 'I told you what the woman in Sotheby's said when I rang. They could be worth up to €100,000! Maybe even more!'

Honor suddenly looks up from her phone. This is at, like, the *breakfast* table?

'A hundred grand?' she goes, snatching one of them out of Sorcha's hand. 'Seriously? For these?'

Sorcha's there, 'Be careful with them Honor. Madiba said a lot of things in these letters that he never said publicly before, especially in relation to finding common ground between Inkatha and the ANC.'

'Oh my God,' Honor goes, laughing, 'look at the way he spells peace! Er – P, I, E, C, E?'

Sorcha's there, 'The spelling doesn't matter, Honor. As my dad said at the time, all it does is show how committed he was to his work, that he didn't have time to read back over every single word he wrote. I think it actually *adds* to their authenticity?'

Sorcha carefully puts the other letters into a hord-backed envelope and I realize that I'm running out of time here.

I'm there, 'The other thing I was going to say was that I think Honor should maybe have them. They're, like, her birthright? They should be passed down through the generations and blah, blah, blah.'

Honor goes, 'I don't focking want them.'

'They were written by Nelson Mandela, Honor,' I go. 'Mindimba.'

'So focking what?'

'Okay, I'll put it to you another way. They're worth a hundred grand!'

With my eyes I'm subtly trying to encourage her to say that she's changed her mind, that she actually *does* want them? Except she's not going to say it, because she's picked up on the fact that it's what I *want* her to say? And she's determined to fock me over for denying that I gave her alcohol.

'One hundred Ks,' I try to go. 'Imagine the amount of shit you could buy for that, Honor? You'd probably be the youngest customer in the history of Brown Thomas ever to go platinum.'

Honor looks at Sorcha and goes, 'Just to let you know, if you ever did give me those letters, the first thing I'd do would be to rip them up in front of your face and put them in the bin – and I'd do it out of pure spite. In fact, the only reason I haven't ripped this one up is that I'm dying to find out why *he's* so keen for you not to sell them.'

I'm there, 'I just think they should be kept within the family. And they're boring.'

Honor hands the letter back and Sorcha sticks it in with the others.

I watch Sorcha seal the envelope. I'm there, 'I'll post that for you this morning, Babes. I'll be passing the post office in Ballybrack.'

Sorcha laughs and goes, 'You don't *post* something this valuable, Ross! I'm sending it by international courier! Where are you going, by the way? You don't have another match, do you?'

'We've one every week, Sorcha. It's a league. I've explained that to you.'

'And where are you playing?'

'A place called Derry.'

'Derry in the North?'

'I'm not much of a geography buff, Sorcha, but that's the talk, yeah.'

'But you're coming home tonight, I presume?'

'Yeah, no, that's the thing I meant to mention. We're heading to Bundoran for the night.'

'Excuse me?'

'It's a bit of a guyatus.'

Honor goes, 'He's definitely having a nervous breakdown.'

I'm there, 'I'm not having a nervous breakdown. We're going to have a few drinks tonight, then tomorrow we're going to hopefully catch a few waves.'

Sorcha's like, 'Waves? What are you talking about?'

'I'm talking about surfing, Sorcha.'

'Surfing? Ross, you can't even swim.'

'I'll cross that bridge when I come to it. Is my Hollister T-shirt out of the wash, by the way?'

It's at that exact moment that the buzzer at the front gate sounds. Sorcha goes, 'That'll be DHL!'

Shit, the letters. This is my last chance to actually do something. I suddenly act – totally on impulse. I knock over the coffee pot. I don't even make it look like an accident. I just do it and the coffee spills across the island. Except Honor very focking helpfully manages to whip the envelope up a split second before the spillage reaches it.

She's like, 'Oh my God, you're such a klutz!', delighted with herself.

And Sorcha goes, 'Ross, can you please be more careful? This could be The Mount Anville Africa Fund's operating costs for its entire first year!'

I'm there, 'Yeah, no, I'm sorry,' and she gets up from the island and tells me to mop up the mess while she brings the envelope down to the front gate.

Honor's just, like, looking at me with a grin spreading across her face, the exact same expression she uses when she's staring into the fish tank in Daniel's of Glasthule, deciding which lobster she wants killed and plated up.

'I'm going to find out the truth about those letters,' she goes.

And of course I know that she won't rest until she does.


Rainey Old Boys doesn't sound like a rugby team. Rainey Old Boys sounds like a group of elderly dudes who play Dominoes together on wet winter nights for the want of company.

Never was a team so wrongly named.

They're not old boys. Neither are they Dominoes players. That much is obvious sitting in our dressing room, listening to them shouting and roaring next door.

I turn to Maho and I go, 'What even language is that?'

They sound like focking Vikings.

He laughs. He goes, 'You're Up North now, Rossi.'

Which means fock-all to me. In my mind, Drumcondra is Up North.

I look around the dressing room. There's a lot of nervous faces.

'Yoy noyd to shoy these goys that you're not skeered,' Byrom goes.'

One of their players steps into our dressing room. He's a big dude with a shaven head and biceps like Galias. He's old as well – older than even me.

He goes, 'Ay just wanted to see, on behalf of the taim, welcome tee Lonhon Tarry.'

I haven't a focking clue what he's saying. It's kind of like when I run into Paddy Jackson. I usually just nod at him, not a focking clue what he's trying to even say to me.

All the goys are like, 'Yeah, no, thanks – nice of you to say it. Have a good game.'

The dude goes to leave, but then he suddenly sticks his head through the door again. 'Och,' he goes, 'Ay forgat tee ask yee, who's your nomber tan?'

I think he's asking who our number ten happens to be, because Senny instantly goes, 'It's me.'

And that's when the atmosphere suddenly changes.

'Yee're a morked mawn,' he goes. 'Ay'm gonney fockun breek yee up, so Ay awm.'

I might only recognize the occasional word, but I know a threat when I hear one. I happen to be sitting right behind the door at the time. I kick the door with the sole of my left boot and it hits the dude smack in the face.

Then I pull the door back to find him wiping blood from his nose and I go, 'You'll have to come through me first.'

My reward for trying to protect Senny is eighty minutes of war with this focker. It turns out that the dude is *their* hooker? And he knows all the same tricks as me. Collapsing. Pulling down. Wheel and shoe. The fake chorge.

He rips my cheek with his stubble just like I rip his. He sledges me and I sledge him back. And we tackle each other as if the intent is to kill.

I can hear the old man going, 'Watch the Rainey scrum, referee! There's skullduggery afoot!'

By half-time, with the scores tied at 6–6, I feel like I've been in a cor crash rather than a rugby match.

And then the strangest thing happens as we're walking back to the dressing room. The dude puts his orm around my shoulder and goes, 'Och, this is greet, isn't ut?'

I laugh.

I'm there, 'Great? What are you, some kind of masochist?'

'Ay most bay,' he goes, 'stull pleeing rogbay at forty-five! Hay old are yee?'

'If you're asking me how old I am, the answer is thirty-five.'

'Och, yee're good, Ay'll guv it to yee. Have yee always pleed in the front roy?'

'No, I used to be a ten. I hadn't even played rugby in years. I just wanted to come back for one year to prove that I could.'

'One more yurr? Ay've been seeing the seem sunce abite 2002!'

That's when I cop it. He's *their* version of me.

He's there, 'The neem's Griggsy, bay the wee.'

And I go, 'I'm Ross. They call me Rossi.'

'Nace to meet yee, Rossay. Yee're fockun dayud in the sacond hawf, bay the wee.'

I laugh and I'm like, 'Yeah, no, you're focking dead, too.'

Byrom's half-time team talk is basic enough. He tells us to keep our discipline. If we do, he says, we'll get a chance – he's sure of it. 'Goyms loyk thus,' he goes, 'are abaaht whoy blunks first.'

As a spectacle, it's even worse than 6–6 suggests. In the second half, it doesn't get any better. Me and Griggsy go back to war, but we avoid doing anything stupid – or rather we avoid getting caught doing anything stupid – and for the first half an hour of the second half, there ends up being no scores, just a lot of heavy tackles and a lot of desperate defending, mostly by us.

They need the win to stay on top of the table and they stort upping the intensity.

'Lat's keep the prassure on them,' their number eight shouts, between the, I don't know, twentieth and the twenty-first phases. 'These gorls are abite tee crack, so thee are.'

And that's when it happens.

He gets the ball in his hands and he tries to make some yordage. I go in low and I go in hord. Mathieu Bastareaud would be proud of this tackle. It's the kind of hit that'd change the direction of your bloodflow.

The dude goes, 'Hhhnnnggghhh!' as the air leaves his lungs.

The ball gets turned over.

'Och,' their goys are all shouting, 'yee drapped it, so yee dud.'

Dordo feeds Senny from the ruck and Senny sets off on an unbelievable run. He beats one player, then another, then he crosses into the opposition half and he has eyes only for the line.

The Rainey players are going, 'Stap hum! Someboday stap hum!', but they have no one who can match him for pace.

He covers the ground like Usain Bolt chasing the man who mugged him. He grounds the ball under the posts, then adds the two to give us the win.

'Yee were fockun steeped,' Griggsy tells me as we walk back to the dressing room after the final whistle. 'But Ay hope yee stay op – after thot, yee desorve ut, so yee doy.'

He ends up being actually sound.

Back in the dressing room, everyone's just, like, sitting around, too tired and too sore to even take their clothes off and get into the shower.

Outside, I can hear the old man going, 'A victory fashioned in the smithy on the scrum! First rate! Bravo to both teams for a wonderful display of old-fashioned forward play!'

I actually chuckle to myself as I sit down and pull off my boots without even opening the laces. I'm tired and I'm bashed up, but I feel great. Of course, the only thing I have to worry about now is the fact that I'm almost certainly going to drown tomorrow.


She's a ringer for Georgia May Foote. I'm not the only one who says it either. Little Davy Dardis is convinced that it's *actually* her?

Ollie Lysaght goes, 'What the fock would Georgia May Foote be doing drinking in The Kicking Donkey in Bundoran?'

Dordo's there, 'Same thing as us. She could be over here on holidays.'

She's with a group of about six or seven other birds – some of them nice, some of them hogs.

Dordo goes, 'I'd nearly be tempted to go over and talk to her.'

Bucky laughs. He's like, 'There's only one man in this pub who's up to the job of pulling that kind of quality.'

I lift my pint glass to my lips, smiling modestly, at the same time thinking, These goys actually idolize me.

But then he goes, 'Johnny Bliss.'

My hort for some reason sinks. I think I mentioned already that Blissy is a bit of a looker and the closest thing the team has to an actual ladies' man.

He looks over at the birds and goes, 'I presume we're talking about the one with the black hair,' obviously sizing up the job.

I go, 'Hey, do you mind if I have a crack first?'

All the goys laugh. They've never seen me in action, of course.

Blissy's there, 'Yeah, no, you fire ahead, Rossi!' like it's a challenge.

Senny goes, 'Are you not married, though, Rossi?'

Seriously, sometimes I wonder is it the same sport that I played at all.

I go, 'I'll give you a wave as we're leaving!'

I tip over to where the girl is standing, with her mates, drinking pints of cider. I'd say she's in, like, her twenties.

I'm there, 'Hey, there.'

She's like, 'What abite yee?' in a friendly enough way. 'Are yee eer toxi draver?'

I'm like, 'Taxi driver?'

'Aye, we phoned for a toxi.'

'Er, no, I'm not your taxi driver.'

'Okee. Hee are yee then?'

'I'm actually just a dude. Ross or Rossi. Believe it or not, I came over here with the intention of chatting you up.'

She actually laughs. All of her mates laugh as well.

'Yee?' she goes, staring at my belly. 'Hoy old are yee?'

I'm there, 'How old do you think I am?' flirting my orse off and at the same time hoping that she guesses low. She doesn't, though.

She goes, 'Ay'd see you're un your fortays. Fortay-tee, fortay-throy.'

One of her mates – who's a focking disgrace, by the way – goes, 'Ay'd see fortay-eet.'

I feel like nearly going, 'Would you now? Look in the focking mirror, Love.'

The Georgia May one looks over my shoulder and she sees the goys all sniggering behind me. 'Och,' she goes, 'yeer deeing ut as a bat!'

I'm there, 'As a what?'

'As a bat?'

'Oh, as a bet?'

I realize I need to somehow save face here. I can't go back to the goys having just crashed and burned.

So I go, 'No, yeah, it was actually a joke. The real reason I came over was because the goys over there would love to meet you.'

'Hoy's the gay with the blond heer?'

She mean's goy, not gay.

I'm there, 'The dude with the blond hair is called Johnny Bliss,' even though it makes me sick to have to say it. 'He plays outside centre. We're a rugby team, by the way. We won our match today.'

The goys sense that the castle's defences have been broken and they all come swarming over the wall, Blissy leading the chorge.

'Johnny Bliss,' he goes, introducing himself to Georgia May, or whatever she's *actually* called. 'Do you know who you're the absolute spits of?'

That ends up being that. Their taxi eventually arrives and the goys order four or five more to take them all to a nightclub in Ballyshannon called Bualadh Bos. No one even asks me to go with them. They just thank me for putting in the spadework, then they disappear out the door, leaving me and Byrom Jones on our Tobler, drinking pints into the night.

He goes, 'Thoy absoloytloy oydolioyz yoy, Rossoy.'

I'm there, 'I don't know. Five years ago, I would have left with that bird. She thought I was forty-three.'

'Oy'm talking abaaht in terms of rugboy. Yoy royloy put your bodoy on the loyn todoy.'

'Yeah, no, I'm sore all over as a result.'

'Yoy were moy maahn of the mutch. You've got them royloy beloyving they can escoype the drop, Rossoy. I just got a tixt mussage. Bictuv lost to Sundoy's Will todoy. Knoy what thet moyns? Moyns we're aaht of the bottom toy. For the first toym thus soyson, we're aaht of the rilegoyshion zoyne.'

I'm there, 'Okay, that definitely calls for another pint.'

He goes, 'Oy woyn't, Moyte. Oy'm goying toy git beck to the Boy and Boy. Oy've got an earloy staaht tomorroy. Got toy git bick to Dublin. Ut's moy youngest son's birthday. Oy promused hum Oy'd Skoype hum.'

'Skype him? Where is he?'

I suddenly realize that I know absolutely nothing about this man who threw me, literally, a rugby lifeline.

'Un Noy Zoyland,' he goes. 'With hus mother. And his brothers and susters.'

I'm like, 'Oh?'

'Yeah, moy mirriage dudn't work aaht. Aw, long storoy, but moy woyfe mit someone ilse and, well, Oy dudn't want to watch another maahn roysing moy kuds. So Oy coym to Oyrlund. Oy've got a couple of moyts luving here. They coych schools. Everyone's koyn on Koywoy coyches so Oy thought, woy not guv ut a goy for a year or toy?'

'So, like, you were a coach in New Zealand, were you?'

He smiles mysteriously, then goes, 'Can Oy lut yoy untoy a luttle soycrut, Rossoy?'

I'm there, 'Yeah, no, what?'

'Oy've niver coyched rugboy in moy loyfe. Moy sport is cruckut.'

'Are you trying to say cricket?'

'That's ut – cruckut.'

I actually laugh. I'm there, 'So you're, like, a total spoofer?'

He goes, 'Doyn't git moy wrong, Oy'm a fen of the goym. Yoy groy up in Noy Zoyland, yoy can't avoid ut. And loyk Oy sid, Oy've got some moytes coyching schools. Thoy hilp me aaht with advoyce and that. Thoy were the ones who toyld moy Oy noydud toy foynd a ployer skulled in the daahk aahts.'

'Meaning me.'

'Moyning yoy. Do yoy beloyve in fate, Rossoy?'

'Fate? I don't know. Do you?'

'Oy niver dud. But Oy thunk Oy'm staahting toy.'

'Maybe I am, too.'

'Oy've boyn quite deprissed, Rossoy. What wuth everythung thit's heppened to moy in the laahst couple of yurrs. Look, Moyte, Oy knoy ut's oynloy koyping Seapoint in Division Toy Boy of the All Oyerland Loyg. Toy or throy months from naah, Sinnoy will join the academoy and the toym will probabloy be rilegoytud nixt soyson innywoy. But sunce yoy came in, Oy moyt as well tell yoy, Oy've staahted to foyle something that Oy hiven't filt in a long toym. And thet's heppiness. Heppiness and fuckun hoype. So, look, here's to yoy, Moyte!'

He holds up what's left of his pint. Jesus Christ, I'm suddenly on the point of tears here. It's one of the most incredible tributes that's ever been paid to me. I return the toast and he knocks back the last of his pint.

He gets up off his stool. 'And doyn't yoy fuckun deer till innyone Oy'm a fuckun cruckut coych,' he goes.

I'm there, 'Your secret's safe with me. There's a very good chance I'm going to drown tomorrow anyway.'

'Doyn't yoy fuckun deer draahn,' he goes. 'Not untul the soy-son's oyver.'

Off he goes. I feel honestly amazing about myself. I order another pint of the old Tolerance Water for the road.

The bor woman pours it for me. She smiles at me. She's about fifty-odd. Yeah, no, I'm thinking, that's about your level now, Ross.

I'm just sinking the first mouthful when my phone all of a sudden rings. It ends up being Ronan.

His opening line throws me. He goes, 'You fooken spanner, Rosser.'

I'm not expecting it, especially after all the compliments I've just been getting.

I'm like, 'What's wrong, Ro?'

He goes, 'Did you meerch into The Tipsy Wagon last night and give Scum a baiting?'

'It was more of a decking than a baiting. I would have said I decked him.'

'What the fook are you playing at?'

'Someone had to do something, Ro. It was getting out of hand.'

'We calt a fooken throoce, Rosser.'

'What?'

'About two bleaten hours before you walked in there and battored him.'

'Again, it was a decking. And if you called a truce, why did he fock a brick through Rihanna-Brogan's bedroom window?'

'That was joost kids, Rosser, fooken about.'

'Oh.'

'Now he thinks we're at war again – you fooken dope.'

'I'll talk to him and explain the situation.'

'Stay ourrof it, Rosser. You've dud enough dabbage.'

Shit, I'm thinking, those are big focking waves. I'm standing at the edge of the water and I am totally bricking it.

The goys aren't helping. They've all been in the water and they're all, like, fist-pumping and chest-bumping each other and I'm standing there in my wetsuit, trying to look invisible.

'Rossi,' Dordo goes when he spots me hanging out on, like, the *periphery* of the group? 'You haven't been in yet!'

I'm there, 'Yes, I have. You must have missed me. I was, like, standing up on, like, a surfing board, literally on top of one of those big waves out there.'

He laughs. 'What are you talking about?' he goes. 'Your suit's as dry as a bone.'

Senny and Blissy, who are easily the best surfers in the group, are slapping me on the back, going, 'Come on, Rossi. They're only little baby waves compared to what you're used to – the man who's surfed Jeffrey's Bay.'

I may have implied, with drink on me last night, that I was a slightly more experienced surfer than I actually *am*?

I'm there, 'Yeah, no, do you know what it is, though? I've got this famous rotator cuff injury that I think I may have aggravated against Rainey Old Boys. I don't want to make it any worse – especially with the match against Dungannon next weekend.'

That doesn't convince anyone. They're all like, 'Come on, Rossi! Show us how it's done!'

Me and my big focking mouth.

I'm literally shaking now. It's not from the cold. It's from actual fear. That's how terrified I am of water.

I'm there, 'Maybe I'll ring Byrom and see how he feels about me possibly risking an injury. My phone is back in the B&B.'

Except suddenly everyone is going, 'Rossi! Rossi! Rossi! Rossi!'

The last thing I want is for these goys to suddenly lose faith in me. And of course I can't pull out without looking like a complete focking tool. Senny hands me his surfboard and goes, 'Show us how they do it in Waikiki!'

Yeah, I may have also mentioned that I spent a summer surfing in Hawaii.

So what else can I do except walk into the sea with the board under my orm. I go out to my waist. I could try to stand up on the thing here, except the waves are way, way out and I don't think I'd get away with it. So I have no choice but to lie face-down on the board, like I've seen the others do, then stort paddling out to sea with my hands, towards the big waves and my almost certain death.

I'm so scared, I'm literally farting dents in my wetsuit.

The goys are all on the shore, shouting, 'Stort! Stort!' and I'm thinking, 'I have focking storted!' I must be, like, halfway out to sea at this stage.

Fock. The waves stort to become a bit choppier. I'm being tossed about a little bit now, although I think, if I'm tipped off the board, I can at least cling to it, because it definitely seems to float.

'Stort! Stort!'

Oh, fock off, I'm thinking. I'll stort when I'm *ready* to stort?

I keep paddling. I must be, like, half a kilometre off the coast at this stage and I am seriously kacking it. In my mind, I'm going, 'Please, Father Fehily, in a way, you got me into this entire mess – now you can get me the fock out of it.'

I look back over my shoulder at the goys and I notice they're all jumping up and down, screaming at the top of their voices, 'Stort! Stort!'

I notice that I'm not quite as far out to sea as I thought I was – we're talking possibly a hundred feet. I'm thinking, Will you shut the fock up with that thing. And that's when I realize that they're not shouting 'Stort!' at all. They're shouting . . .

Shork?

You've got to be shitting me. There's no way there's shorks in these . . .

And it's when I turn my head around again that I notice a triangular-shaped fin in the water, literally ten feet in front of me.

I swear to fock, I think I'm about to have a genuine hort attack. I suddenly can't catch my breath and my mouth is dry and I'm shaking so much that I manage to somehow tip the board over, so that I fall off it into the water and the board cracks me on the side of the head.

I go under, my mouth and nostrils filling up with water. Everything turns black for a few seconds, but somehow I manage to find my way to the surface again.

I'm suddenly, like, flapping around in a blind panic, with no idea where the shork actually went. I can't see it. I think it must be below, under the water, then something suddenly brushes off my foot and I manage to turn my body around in the water and that's when the fin reappears on the surface, again about ten feet away from me.

I'm suddenly screaming like a focking mad person.

The fin moves closer and closer. But then, instinctively, I lift the board and I swing it in the direction of the shork. There's, like, a dull thud as the side of it crashes down on his head and then I hear this horrible, like, gurgling noise and I don't wait around to see what happens next.

I stort thrashing and kicking in the water and about twenty seconds later I realize that something incredible is happening.

I'm actually swimming!

It turns out that being chased by a focking shork was the only incentive I ever needed.

I travel through the water like a speedboat and I certainly don't look over my shoulder. Up ahead, I can see the goys all running into the water, going, 'That's it, Rossi! Keep going, Rossi! Don't look back! That's it, keep going!'

I literally thrash the water into a salty foam. Then Maho and Gilly are suddenly in front of me and they grab me by the orms and literally just pull me out of the water.

Thirty seconds later, I'm lying on the sand, trying to get my breath back, staring out to sea at this monster of the deep, bobbing up and down on its side, blood spilling out of it, staining the sea red.

There's, like, silence among the goys. Eventually, Gilly goes, 'Rossi, you killed a shork!', like I'm somehow a hero. 'You killed! A focking! Shork!'

All the goys stort cheering and high-fiving each other, and even though I wouldn't usually be into killing animals just for the crack of it, I'm buzzing off the feeling of having just killed essentially Jaws. And I didn't need a harpoon gun. I didn't even need a boat.

'Are you hurt?' Maho goes. I can hear the excitement in his voice. 'As in, did it bite you?'

I'm there, 'It didn't get the chance. Yeah, no, I saw those big

jaws – teeth like razor blades – about to close on my orm and I acted. I was like, "It's either me or you. And guess what? It's not going to be me! Eat my board, motherfocker!"'

He laughs. He goes, 'You killed! A focking! Shork!'

I'm there, 'Hey, I'd do it again under the same circs,' becoming suddenly giddy at the thought of what this is going to do for my rep in the game. There'll be a few nervous front rows out there if this story gets out. I'd say even Cian Healy will be watching his tone around me in The Black Door after this.

'Nerves of steel,' Gilly goes, shaking his head. 'Nerves of literally steel.'

I'm like, 'Hey, to be honest, it was mostly just instinct. I noticed he was sizing up my throwing orm! I said, "Sorry, that limb is the property of Seapoint Rugby Club! And we've still got two matches left!"'

They all laugh.

And of course the other upside of this is that I don't have to go back in the water. How is surfing on top of a wave ever going to top that? How is anything going to top that? Killing a shork with a surfboard is the equivalent of throttling a tiger with your bare hands. It's a major, major deal.

And that's when I get a sudden idea.

'I want a trophy!' I go. 'I want its head! For my wall! No, no, for the front grille of the cor!'

The goys all laugh, suddenly discovering what a huge asset I am, not only in terms of what I contribute on the field but also in terms of what I bring to the porty *off* it?

'You cut that thing open and it's going to focking stink,' Maho goes.

I'm just like, 'I don't give a fock! Bring me its head!'

'He deserves it,' Dordo goes and he grabs his camping knife out of his backpack, steps into the water and storts wading out towards the thing. 'I'll get you the head, Rossi!'

There's, like, cheers from all the goys and it's incredible. It's like there's suddenly no age difference between us at all. It's like we're *all* suddenly in our early twenties?

Gilly goes, 'Dude, do you know what we should do? Nail it to the door of the Dungannon dressing room next weekend. Just to let them know that this is how *we* roll.'

'We're definitely doing that!' I go. 'We are one hundred percent definitely doing that!'

I look up to see how Dordo is getting on with the job of, I don't know, *decapitating* the thing? I notice that he's not doing anything. He's just, like, frozen to the spot, up to his waist in water, the big knife in his hand, looking back up the beach at me.

He's like, 'Focking hell,' as if he's seen a *ghost* or something?

I'm there, 'What's wrong, Dude?'

'It's not a shork,' he goes. 'Jesus Christ, Rossi, you just killed a focking dolphin!'

# 9. Head Games

It's, like, four o'clock on a Wednesday afternoon and I'm sitting in the cor pork of Mount Anville, waiting to collect Honor from drama. Her class are putting on a joint production of *The Boy Friend* with either St Andrew's or St Michael's and I've honestly never seen her so excited about a rehearsal.

While I'm sitting there, my phone all of a sudden rings. It's my old dear. I answer it. Don't ask me why. Maybe I'm feeling charitable towards her. Maybe it's because I saw a whole new side to her last week, the way she was with Ari. Maybe I've finally realized that there *is* something inside her other than Hendrick's and seal fat.

I'm like, 'What do you want?'

She goes, 'Oh, hello, Ross. I'm just phoning to let you know that she got her way in the end.'

The school doors open and the kids all stort spilling out.

I'm like, 'Who got their own way? What are you shitting on about?'

She goes, 'Ari's granddaughter. As you know, she was threatening all sorts – injunctions and all the rest of it. I spoke to Hennessy and he said, "Do you have anything to hide?" and I said, "Nothing, Hennessy! Absolutely nothing!" I told him that Ari enjoys a drink and that – as you've witnessed, Ross – we've been struggling to find a medication that suits him and that's all there is to it. Hennessy said, "Then give her what she wants. Don't let her go down the injunction road because it looks like you've got something to hide. Book him into the Mater Private. Do it now."'

I hear a bang. Something has hit the window on the front passenger side. I look up. It turns out that it was some kid's head. Honor's banging it off the side of the cor.

I sound the horn. Honor looks at me – with the kid still in a headlock – and she goes, 'What?' with a look of total disgust on her face.

And I give her a look that says, I've just had those windows cleaned.

The old dear goes, 'Who's that?'

I'm there, 'Yeah, no, it's just Honor bullying some kid. So when's the appointment?'

'It's in two weeks' time.'

'And are you not worried?'

'What is there to worry about?'

'Er, that the doctor will come down on Tiffany Blue's side and say that Ari is batshit crazy?'

'There is nothing wrong with Ari, Ross. And if I have to get medical evidence to prove that, then I will.'

'Yeah, no, whatever. Look, before you go . . .'

'Yes?'

'I just wanted to say, you know, thanks.'

'What are you thanking me for?'

'You know what for. You covered for me when Tiffany Blue tried to tell Sorcha that, you know, I *rode* her?'

It's funny, it feels awkward talking to my old dear like this.

She goes, 'I have no idea what you're talking about.'

I'm there, 'Yeah, no, I know you don't. But at the same time, thanks.'

She hangs up. I give Honor another hoot of the horn, because I'm bored shitless just sitting here. And that's when I find myself suddenly laughing out loud. Because I recognize the kid she has in a chokehold. Focking hilarious . . .

It turns out to be Caleb.

'Lick the window!' she's going. 'Focking lick it, Caleb! Otherwise, I'm never letting you go!'

I roll it down an inch or two and I go, 'There's no real need, Honor. I had it washed this morning. I got the Tri-Foam Polish and everything. Hi, Caleb.'

She tightens her grip on him and goes, 'Lick it!'

And that's what Caleb ends up having to do. Hell hath no

fury – it's that expression again. I see his little tongue poking out of his mouth and he storts licking the glass clean. After maybe a minute of this, Honor releases her grip on him and gets into the cor.

'You're a bitch!' Caleb goes, at the same time rubbing his neck – oh, he's a brave man now! 'You're a fat, ugly bitch as well.'

She opens the window all the way. 'I'll remember that next week,' she goes. 'I'm going to make you do the front windscreen then.'

I give him a wink – as if to say, You play my daughter, that's what you get – then I point the cor in the direction of home.

'So,' I go, 'you seem to be slowly getting over Caleb.'

Honor's there, 'Oh my God, you should have *seen* the way the girls were around him! As soon as he got the port of Tony Brockhurst – oh my God – *every* girl wanted to be Polly Browne. They were all like, "Me! Me! Me! Me!" Er, *pathetic*, much? Of course, the hilarious thing is, he's in love with Miss Lodge, the pianist.'

Of course he is – he's what psychiatrists call the wrong kind of horny.

'Well,' I go, 'you've just made a show of him in front of absolutely everyone. Being bullied by a girl! It's hilarious.'

She's there, 'It serves him right. He thinks he's hot shit.'

'I'm defending you, Honor. I much prefer this version of you than the other one. *The Life of Pi*. I barely recognized you. So did you get a port in the musical yourself?'

'I'm playing Miss Dubonnet.'

The bet-down headmistress. I make no comment either way. Honor sticks her nose in her phone and homeward we go.

It's just as we're coming up to the gaff that I suddenly notice a yellow DHL van pulling up on the road outside. The delivery dude is just about to press the gate buzzer when I shout out the window, 'I'll take that!'

I hop out of the cor.

Honor's so, like, engrossed in her phone that she doesn't seem to even notice.

The dude hands me this little machine – I don't know, it's *like* a credit cord machine? It has a little pen attached to it and he tells me to sign the screen, which is what I end up doing, then he hands me a big, brown envelope and I straightaway notice the name *Sotheby's* on the front.

I wait until the dude drives off, then I turn my back on Honor so she can't see what I'm doing if she happens to look up. I open the envelope. Inside are all of Sorcha's letters from Nelson Mandela, along with a covering note. I end up just skim-reading it, picking out random phrases – 'regretfully returning your items' and 'unable to authenticate them as genuine'.

It's the final line that ends up being the real killer. It's like, 'Find enclosed the report of our handwriting expert, who has concluded that the letters were not written by Nelson Mandela, but are in fact forgeries, and amateurish ones at that. Kind regards,' and blahdy-blahdy blah-blah.

I take the pages – the covering note, the report of the handwriting expert, even the letters themselves – and I stuff them into my pocket.

'Oh! My God!' Honor suddenly goes.

I end up nearly shitting myself. I spin around and I go, 'Honor, I don't know what you *think* you saw . . .'

But she's still just staring at her phone. She goes, 'There's this, like, catwalk model on YouTube who turns over on her high-heel shoe and her ankle snaps like a cracker. Hill! Air!'

So it's, like, Friday afternoon, the day before we play Dungannon. I'm going for a run through Dalkey village when I decide – real spur of the moment job – to get my hair cut. It's something I used to do before big matches back in the day – call it superstition – we're talking blade three or four at the back and sides, then short on top.

Into the borber's I go.

When it's, like, *my* turn in the chair, I end up having one of my famous rush of blood to the head moments.

The borber turns around to me and goes, 'What'll I do?'

And I'm just like, 'Give me an Ian Madigan.'

I'm doing it – I don't *give* a fock?

Except the dude turns around to me and – word for word – he goes, 'Who?'

That's what he genuinely says.

I'm there, 'Er, Ian Madigan?'

He's like, 'Sorry, I've never heard of him,' like he thinks I'm making him *up* or something?

I end up just staring him out of it in the mirror. I go, 'You're actually saying that to me? After all the things he's done for Leinster and Ireland?'

I end up having to whip out my phone and look through Google images for the best photograph I can find of him. I show the borber and he goes, 'Oh, that's a nice cut.'

And I'm there, 'Yeah, wasted on the likes of you. *Who's Ian Madigan?* You're some focking joker. Can you cut my hair like that or not?'

'Yeah, it's no problem. I'm just wondering is it a bit –'

'What?'

'Well, it's kind of a young person's style, isn't it?'

'Jesus Christ, I'm thirty-five. I'm hordly an old-age pensioner.'

'But it'd be more something that a fella in his twenties would have.'

'Ten seconds ago you'd never heard of Ian Madigan and now you're a focking expert on his hair? Make me look like that or I'll take my business elsewhere.'

'Okay, if that's what you want . . .'

'It *is* what I want. That's why I focking asked for it.'

He thankfully shuts up then and he goes to work. He grabs the razor and shaves the back and sides of my head, then he storts snipping away the top, then he combs it back and to the left, throwing a bit of wax into it to hold it in place.

I look incredible. That's my instant reaction when he's finished.

I pay the dude, although I don't tip him. He'll know who Ian Madigan is in future.

Back out onto the Main Street I go. And I don't have to wait long before I get my first compliment. As I'm running past The Country Bake, I hear a woman's voice go, 'Ross?'

I turn around and it ends up being Flidais – as in Caleb's old dear?

'I thought it was you!' she goes. 'Oh my God, you look . . . different.'

I'm there, 'I'm presuming that's a good thing.'

I can't help flirting. It's just *in* me?

She goes, 'It's like that rugby guy, isn't it?'

I'm there, 'Ian Madigan? He's, like, a protégé of mine. I got a text from him two days ago,' and I whip out my phone to show her. 'He heard I was back playing rugby and he wanted to say fair focks.'

She goes, 'Yeah, you don't need to show me. I do believe you.'

'Well, I can't find it now, but it's in there – I can promise you that. I'll probably end up saving it. So how the hell are you?'

'I'm fine. You know, I was actually going to ring you.'

'Listen, you don't have to keep apologizing for your son. It was a bit weird, that's all. I think it's fair to say it just weirded us all out. No permanent damage done.'

God, I focking love her perfectly round, cue-ball head.

'Well, actually, I wanted to talk to you about Honor,' she goes.

I'm there, 'Oh?' at the same time thinking, Fock – has she worked out what actually happened that day?

She's like, 'Caleb says she's been kind of, well, bullying him.'

I'm there, 'Bullying him? Does that not sound a bit random to you?'

'Random?'

'Think about it.'

'Well, he said Honor got him in some sort of chokehold and forced him to lick the window of your cor.'

'A girl bullying a boy, though? I'm sticking with the word random. When did this supposably happen?'

'After Drama on Wednesday. As you know, their schools are doing this musical together –'

'And I hoped things wouldn't be awkward between them. But now he's come up with this bullying story.'

'He said you were in the cor when she made him lick the window.'

'Look, I don't want to cast whatevers on your son, but he *is* a proven liar?'

'I know. It's just that, well, Thea, my daughter, told me that Honor used to bully her in the same way.'

She's the one with the underbite and the shoulders like Samson Lee.

I'm there, 'Look, I'm the one who usually collects Honor from Drama and I honestly didn't see her go near Caleb. It sounds to me like he's making shit up again. You've got a tough time ahead of you with that one – wait till puberty arrives!'

She looks suddenly sad. 'I'm sorry again,' she goes, 'about that whole business. If it's any consolation, he's seeing a really good psychiatrist at the moment.'

I'm there, 'Yeah, no, that's a definite consolation alright. Thanks for letting me know.'

She goes, 'It's been difficult for the children, you know, since I split up with their father,' and she leaves it hanging in the air for a few seconds. 'It's been difficult for me, too, being a single mum and everything!'

I'm thinking, Okay, is she actually going out of her way to remind me that she's unattached or am I imagining it?

I'm there, 'It must be shit for you alright,' just letting her know that she's got my attention.

'Anyway,' she goes, 'it was lovely to see you again.'

I'm there, 'I'll tell you what I'm going to do, Flidais, because it's you. I'm going to have a word with Honor. It's quite possible that she *is* bullying Caleb and I just haven't noticed. Some people would say she's fully entitled to after the way he tried to play her. Look, I'll say it to her and see if there's any chance she might pick on someone else.'

'If you wouldn't mind.'

'I'm not guaranteeing it'll do any good. In fact, it might make things worse for him. But I'll mention it and see if she could maybe move on to another kid.'

She goes, 'Thank you, Ross,' and she gives me the most incredible smile. I've got a horn on me like a gas cylinder. 'It was lovely to see you again.'

I'm just about to stort running in the direction of home again when my phone all of a sudden rings. I look at the screen and it ends up being Ronan.

I'm just like, 'Ro, how the hell are you?' hoping that it's not *more* bad news.

He goes, 'Rosser, you need to come and gerrus. We caddent be hee-or.'

His voice is all over the place – he sounds like a crazy person.

I'm there, 'Come and get you? What are you talking about?'

He's like, 'Just huddy the fook up, Rosser. Buckets is arthur been shot.'

Ronan calls me a faloot – a bleaten faloot. At the same time, he's looking over his shoulder through the rear windscreen of the cor every literally, like, ten *seconds*?

He goes, 'Are we being foddowed? Are you shewer we're not being foddowed?'

I'm there, 'Ro, we're not being followed.'

We're on the N11 – me and Ro in the front, Shadden and little Rihanna-Brogan in the back – on our way to The Glenview Hotel in Wicklow, where they're going to stay until things hopefully cool off.

'What about that silber Nissan Almeerda?' Ronan goes. 'It's been behoyunt us since we turdened on to the M50.'

I'm there, 'Ro, you're being paranoid.'

'Being padanoid, am I? Well, maybe I've a reason to be padanoid. You're arthur making things ten toyums woorse.'

'Yeah, no, I said I was sorry.'

'Buckets of Blood in the hospital, Nudger gone to Spayun and me hiding like a skeered . . . rat. You're a bleaten faloot, Rosser. What the fook have you done to your heer, by the way?'

I don't answer. He's only lashing out.

Buckets is fine, by the way. It was only, like, a *flesh* wound? The bullet missed all the bones and major orteries, which means it was probably only a warning.

Rihanna-Brogan goes, 'What about me reci'al? Am I going to, like, miss it?'

'You wha?' Ronan goes.

Rihanna-Brogan's there, 'Me reci'al. Ine apposed to be singing a song from, like, *Farrozen*?'

'Ine afrayud you won't be. Ine gonna have to keep me head dowun for a while now because of your grantfadder there.'

His tracksuit top is zipped right up and he's tugging at the neck like it's choking him.

Rihanna-Brogan goes, 'But Ine arthur practising *so* hord!'

Ronan just, like, roars at her then. He goes, 'I said you're not bleaten doing it. Lerrit go!'

There's suddenly, like, silence in the cor. He's there, 'Doatunt eeben think abourrit, Rosser.'

I'm there, 'What?'

'You were about to sing the next loyun of the song, you fooken faloot.'

Most people would have done it in the same position.

I'm there, 'Yeah, if you remember, Ro, I was the one who said switch it to a *Fair City* tour – and now I'm the one being blamed.'

Shadden goes, 'And there's no need to bleaten shourrat her, Ro!'

Seriously, it's like there's an actual episode of *Love/Hate* going on in my cor.

I'm there, 'Maybe we should possibly *all* calm down? It's not going to help if we all stort losing the rag.'

Ronan's like, 'What the fook are you doing, Rosser?'

'I'm taking the turn.'

'The turden for wha?'

'For The Glenview Hotel.'

'This idn't the turden.'

'It *is* the turn. You go off here, then you follow the road back over the dualler and it's in there on your right. They've got a pretty good gym, to be fair. I know the Irish rugby team used to stay here quite a bit.'

'You're bleaten setting me up.'

'Ro, I'm not setting you up.'

'You're throiving me into an ambush.'

'Why would I drive you into an ambush? Ro, you need to calm the fock down. Look, see? There's the hotel over there. I might even come in with you and check out the facilities.'

'No,' he goes, 'you've dud enough, Rosser,' and he doesn't mean that in a good way. 'Joost throp us off and then fook off.'

It hurts. It genuinely hurts.

Up the driveway we go. This is probably Shadden's first time outside of Dublin. From the look on her face, she doesn't think much of it.

'How long are we gonna be hee-or?' she goes.

Ronan's there, 'Long as we have to. Let's all think of it as a hoddiday.'

Rihanna-Brogan goes, 'When are we going home? I miss Finglas.'

The last person to miss Finglas was Hitler, when he bombed the North Strand by accident.

'Doatunt be like that,' Ronan goes. 'Be a nice little barreak for dus all.'

She's like, 'Er, I've got, like, *skewill*?'

'Forget skewill, will you? Tell you wha, foorst thing we do when we check in is we ring up roowim serbice – you can have athin you want!'

Rihanna-Brogan nods her head sadly.

'Mon,' Ronan goes, 'be an adventure for dus.'

I feel like shit. I caused this. I know it.

I pull up outside the hotel and everyone gets out of the cor. I look at Shadden, standing there in her tight leather trousers and her high heels and her big, hoopy earrings, then Ronan with his shaved head and his tracksuit top zipped up to his chin, and all I can think about is Nidge and Trish.

'What's that smell?' Rihanna-Brogan goes.

I'm there, 'Honor always asks the same thing. It's called Not Dublin.'

'Mon, Rosser,' Ronan goes, 'help me with the bleaten bags, will ye?'

I pop the boot and I help him lift them out – five matching pieces of luggage, all in leopardskin. They're like the focking Trotters going on holidays.

I help them carry them to the door of the hotel, then a dude appears with a trolley and goes, 'Are you checking in, Sir?'

And I'm there, 'Yeah, no, my son is,' and the dude grabs the luggage and storts piling it on the trolley.

I'm there, 'Look, I'm sorry again, Ro. You've every right to be pissed off with me, even though I was only trying to protect you.'

Ronan looks at Shadden and Rihanna-Brogan. 'Yous go on inside,' he goes. 'I'll foddow you in.'

Which is what they end up doing.

I'm there, 'I suppose if there's an upside to all of this, it'll give you a bit of time and space to study for the Leaving. Every cloud – blah, blah, blah.'

He goes, 'You're arthur putting eer loyuvs at risk, Rosser. Moyun, me thaughter's and me peertner's. Stay the fook away from us altogetter.'

Sorcha screams when she sees me. She's goes, 'Oh my God, what have you done?'

I'm there, 'It's only a haircut, Sorcha. Ian Madigan has the exact same haircut and everyone thinks it's cool.'

'Ian Madigan is twenty-four, Ross.'

'He's actually twenty-six. His birthday was the day Ireland won the Six Nations.'

'My point is, he's *young*.'

'And what am I?'

'You're too old to have a haircut like that.'

'Well, I genuinely disagree. And little Leo does, as well.'

He's, like, mesmerized by it. He keeps touching it to see if it's real.

I'm there, 'Hey, I've got an idea.'

She goes, 'No, Ross.'

'You don't even know what I was going to say.'

'You were going to say, let's get Ian Madigan haircuts for all the boys.'

'I think they'd look very smort with them.'

Leo suddenly grabs a handful of my hair and goes, 'Focking bollocks!'

It's another new word.

I'm like, 'Aaahhh!'

Sorcha goes, 'Ross, don't react.'

'I'm kind of reacting to him pulling my hair rather than the swearing, Sorcha.'

'Yes, but *he* doesn't know that.'

He twists it in his little hand. Fock, it's like he's trying to pull it out at the root.

'Don't respond,' Sorcha goes. 'That's it, Ross. Just ignore him. Now, give him to me.'

She loosens his grip on my hair and lifts him out of my orms.

'Shitting focking bollocks!' he goes. 'Shitting bollocksing fock!'

Sorcha puts him in his high chair next to the others. It's feeding time at the zoo.

'By the way,' she goes, 'there's still no word from Sotheby's. They were supposed to send a valuation by courier this week.'

Shit.

I'm there, 'Maybe it was all the spelling mistakes, like Honor said. Maybe they just focked them in the bin. Either way, I think it's time we forgot they ever existed.'

She's like, 'I'm not going to forget they ever existed. That money is going to hopefully pay for more than one hundred Mount Anville students to go to Botswana to have their awareness raised of the challenges that African people face there on a daily basis. I think I'll ring them now.'

Quick as a flash, I go, 'Oh, hang on, I've just remembered something. They rang.'

She's like, 'Rang? When did they ring?'

'Yesterday. Yeah, no, you were out at the time. They rang and they said they needed a few more weeks to make up their minds if they're worth anything.'

'Weeks?'

'They said weeks, but I think they meant months.'

'Months?'

'We just have to accept it, Babes. They said that that's how long these things take.'

'Where are you going?'

I've backed away from her and am moving towards the stairs as quickly as I can without looking suspicious.

I'm there, 'We're playing Dungannon tomorrow afternoon, Babes. If we win, we stay in Division 2B of the All Ireland League.'

She goes, 'But where are you going now?'

'I'm going to lie down with my eyes closed and go through my visualization exercises.'

'What, and leave me to look after our children?'

I always say that women will understand men the day that women understand rugby. And that day will be probably never.

There's, like, silence in the dressing room. Byrom is being all Mister Bright Side, but no one else is *having* any of it?

'Trust moy,' he's trying to go, 'a draw is not a baahd rissolt. You'll all foyl differentloy abaaht thus tomorrow.'

I've got my head down. I'm just, like, staring at the floor, waiting for the room to stop spinning.

'Focking Dungannon!' Bucky goes, then he kicks his locker once, twice, then three times, in the hope that it'll make him feel better.

Except it *doesn't*?

Maho's there, 'Bucky has a point. They came here with fock-all to play for. I mean, they're going to finish mid-table no matter what happens. We're the team who had something at stake and we end up throwing away, what, a seventeen-point lead in the last twenty minutes?'

Dordo goes, 'We don't deserve to stay up on the basis of that second-half performance, we don't deserve it.'

There's, like, something wrong with my vision. As in, I can't properly *focus*? I close one eye, then I open it again and I close the other. The problem is the left one. Everything is, like, blurry through it. I give my head a shake.

Senny goes, 'Are you alright, Rossi?'

I look up. I'm like, 'Yeah, no, I'm good,' even though I can only make out the outline of the dude. 'Just disappointed. Like everyone else.'

It happened just before half-time.

We were coasting. Like the goys said, Dungannon weren't that up for it – win, lose or draw, it was all the same to them. They were mostly ripping the piss out of my haircut and planning their night out in Dublin.

The end of another nothing season. Too good to go down, not good enough to challenge. They were playing for the sheer enjoyment.

A seventeen-point lead, did Maho say? I thought it might have been more.

Then just before half-time . . .

I threw myself headlong into a ruck just as their loosehead was standing up and . . .

Crack!

Our two heads came together. It was weird because I could actually hear everyone go, 'Jesus Christ!' as they winced, then turned away. And then nothing.

I have no idea how long I was unconscious for. It was probably only a few seconds, although it felt like I'd just woken up from a fourteen-hour sleep.

I remember lying there, looking up at the clouds and feeling the blood dribble down the back of my neck. I remember Eddie Rowan, our medical dude, asking me basic questions, like the colour of the Dungannon jerseys and my old dear's maiden name – the focking scrote. I remember leaving the field, my orms draped around Bucky and Maho's shoulders, like a drunken sailor. I remember Christian on the sideline going, 'Ross, are you okay? Holy shit, Charles, look at him – he doesn't know what day of the focking week it is!' and then my old man going, 'Nonsense, Christian! A little bang on the head, that's all! He'll be out again for the second half, right as rain – you see if he's not!'

I remember puking my ring up in the dressing room, then feeling suddenly better again, as the players arrived in at half-time, excited because they knew the match was won and three points was going to be enough to keep us in the division.

I felt better. I know I felt better because while Byrom was telling the goys not to be complacent, I was standing at the sink, washing the blood off my head. It was a small enough cut – we're talking an inch, maybe two, but not very deep.

Byrom went, 'Oy'm gonna toyk yoy off, Rossoy. Oy thunk yoy moyt noyd a stutch or toy.'

And I went, 'There's no focking way I'm coming off. It's just a bad cut, that's all.'

I wandered over to Eddie Rowan's medical bag and I pulled out a roll of bandaging. I wrapped it around and around my head until the entire thing was covered, then I secured it with a bit of, like, sticking plaster.

I could see Byrom looking at me, still Scoobious. 'Rossoy,' he went, 'Oy'm not sure abaaht thus.'

I'm there, 'Dude, I'll swing into the Beacon on the way home and get a few stitches put in. I feel honestly fine.'

He nodded, then went, 'Oy'm going to boy looking at yoy. First foyve munnets, Oy soy inny soyns that you're not oykoy, you're coming off – noy aahguments, understood?'

I was like, 'Loud and clear.'

And now he's standing in front of us going, 'Ut's not the ind of the world. Woy just noyd to goy toy Groystoyns in toy woyks and moyk sure woy wun – oykoy?'

Ollie Lysaght, our full-back, goes, 'You say it like it's easy. They need to beat us to win the league.'

'Well, that's a double incentuv for us to boyt them, usn't ut?'

Seapoint and Greystones are, like, sworn enemies.

'Focking Braystones,' Andy Warpole, our openside flanker, goes – that'll give you an idea of the hatred we have for them.

'Rossi,' Gilly goes, 'are you sure you're okay?'

I'm there, 'Yeah, no, I'm fine,' because the room has suddenly stopped spinning and my vision is storting to clear. 'Byrom's right, though. We need to pick ourselves up and go again.'

There's, like, cheers from one or two corners of the dressing room, but then suddenly, Frankie Hugo, our left wing, goes, 'Okay, can I ask the question that's on everyone's lips? Rossi, what the fock were you thinking attempting a pass like that in the final minute?'

I don't get a chance to answer because Senny suddenly rips into him.

He goes, 'I don't think we should be scapegoating anyone.'

Frankie's there, 'I was screaming at you, Rossi: "Don't do it! The intercept! The intercept!" I could *see* it happening!'

But, again, Senny goes, 'No one individual is to blame. We take collective responsibility. We win, lose and draw as a team.'

Bucky goes, 'Senny's right. We'd have been relegated a long time ago if it wasn't for that man there. Put it behind you, Rossi. Forget what happened.'

It's already forgotten.

You see, the truth is, I can't remember playing the pass that was apparently intercepted – as a matter of fact, I can't remember a single thing that happened in the second half.


Flidais is surprised to open the door and find *me* standing on her doorstep – although *happily* surprised, I think I would have to add?

She goes, 'Ross?' struggling hord to keep the smile from her face. 'It's nine o'clock at night.'

And I'm there, 'Yeah, no, I was just passing and I thought I'd swing in and tell you that I had a word with Honor.'

I didn't, of course – what would be the point?

She's like, 'And?'

'And,' I go, 'I think it's safe to say that I don't think you'll be having any more problems. She's going to hopefully move on to someone else.'

'Oh, thank you so much, Ross.'

'Hey, Honor is a complete bitch – but she's also a bit of a daddy's girl underneath it all.'

I'm feeling better, by the way, except for this blinding focking headache that just won't lift – although I know a good cure for it!

'Are you not going to invite me in?' I go.

She's like, 'Sorry,' opening the door wider, 'I'm forgetting my manners. We'll have to keep our voices down, though, because Caleb and Thea are in bed.'

I could be wrong, but she seems a little bit pissed.

She leads me into the gaff, then down to the kitchen – me walking a few steps behind her so I can check out her orse. It's like two bear cubs wrestling.

I notice the wine glass on the island with a bottle of red beside it – half full, half empty, whatever you want to call it. I say half full because I'm nothing if not an optimist.

'Yeah,' I go, 'like I said, that'll hopefully be the end of Honor bullying Caleb. I was actually thinking about what you were saying the other day – you know, how hord it's been on the kids since you and your husband got divorced?'

'We're actually separated,' she goes.

'Yeah, whatever. I was thinking I possibly should make the same allowances for Honor – as in, it's been pretty hord for her, you know, since me and Sorcha broke up.'

Her mouth drops open.

'You and Sorcha?' she goes. 'You've broken up?'

I'm there, 'You seem pleased.'

'Pleased? Why would I be pleased? That's awful. I mean, you've got three young babies. When did it happen?'

She takes an empty wine glass and looks at me with her eyebrow raised. I nod and she pours me a glass and also another one for herself.

'Yeah, no,' I go, 'it was actually around the time that Brian, Johnny and Leo were born. Sorcha woke up one morning and decided she didn't love me anymore – might have been some kind of post-natal whatever, but that's what she said. We just decided to stay living together for the sake of the kids. Both free agents – that's what I'm trying to emphasize here.'

She goes, 'Oh my God, I wouldn't have been able to tell from the two of you. I have to say, you put on a really good act.'

You have no focking idea, I think.

'So,' I go, 'are you, em, back on the dating scene at all?'

She laughs – she's definitely two or three glasses down the road. She's there, 'Dating scene? There *is* no dating scene for people of our age, is there?'

I'm there, 'You'd be surprised,' knocking back a mouthful.

'Well, I let one or two of my friends set me up. But, you know, all that's really available for people our age is other divorced and separated people. In other words, people with baggage. There's so many assholes.'

'They're out there – there's no doubt about that.'

'Some real creeps.'

'That's not a reason to give up, though. That's a reason for you to become better at spotting the good ones – especially when they're standing in front of you.'

She stares at me for a long time. I think it's only just dawned on her the direction this evening is about to take.

'Oh my God,' she goes, 'what am I doing here?'

I'm there, 'I don't know – what *are* you doing here?'

'I can't do this. This is mad. I've got two children asleep upstairs.'

At the same time, she's running her eyes over my body, trying to imagine what I look like underneath my clothes.

I'm there, 'We don't have to do anything. But I feel it only fair to warn you that I *am* going to kiss you.'

I move over to her. I take the wine glass out of her hand and I put it on the island.

She's like, 'Oh my God, this is such an irresponsible thing to do.'

I'm there, 'Hey, it's only a kiss,' and I lean in and throw the lips on her.

She smells of *Decadence by Marc Jacobs* and Lean Cuisine Crustless Chicken Pot Pie, the box for which I noticed on the draining board.

When I've kissed her, I go to pull away, except she's still caught in the moment. She has her two hands on the back of my neck, the fingers entwined, and she pulls my head within range again, then storts kissing me like she's searching my lips for whatever nourishment was missing from her microwavable dinner.

I manage to remove my jacket, shoes, shirt and chinos, while her hands are all over my abs and pecs like she's trying to feel her way out of a cave. She grabs me by the hand, leading me out into the hallway and up the stairs, the baldy-headed ride.

'And don't forget,' she whispers, 'there's children in the house.'

'Don't worry,' I go, 'I'll be quick.'

'I'm not asking you to be quick. I'm asking you to be quiet.'

Of course, there's nothing to say I can't be both.

Into her bedroom we go and she closes the door behind us. And that's where I'm going to close the door on the rest of you. I've been called a lot of names in my time, but one thing that pretty much everyone accepts is that I am a man of honour.

All I'm going to tell you is that the next ten to fifteen minutes end up being just what we both needed. It's a definite load off for the two of us. I'm throwing her around like I'm shearing a sheep and she's making generally encouraging noises about what I'm doing to her. She's got her two eyes shut tight in concentration and she's blaspheming like a nun who's just won the Lotto.

It's not all me, me, me either. She has one or two arrows in her quiver. She pulls a couple of real surprises on me in the dork of the room, before the whole sticky business comes to an end, with her sitting on top of me with her hand clamped over my mouth to drown out the noise. She's going, 'Don't you stop! Don't you dare stop!' while rocking backwards and forwards, with her head thrown back, like she's trying to get a donkey to run like *Barbaro*.

Anyway, like I said, let's just fast-forward to the moment *after* the deed is done? We're both just lying there, getting our breath back, when I make a sudden grab for my boxer shorts and Flidais goes, 'Where are you going?'

She sounds a bit focking sulky about it as well.

I'm like, 'Yeah, no, I don't think it'd be a good thing for me to still be here when your *kids* wake up in the morning?'

She goes, 'I'm not suggesting you stay until the morning. I was just thinking, you know, we could wait a little while and do it again.'

Sex, I always say, is like laying concrete. Do it right the first time and you shouldn't need to do it again.

'Look,' I go, 'I'd love a second crack at it, but on a different day. How does that sound?'

She's there, 'Unbelievable.'

'You sound pissed off with me.'

'I'm not. It's fine.'

Jesus, she's high maintenance. Her poor focking ex – I'd say he has some stories to tell.

I throw the old jockeys on and she goes, 'So are you going to give me your number or what?'

This is just when I'm reaching for the handle of the bedroom door. These are the morgins between success and failure when you're playing at this level.

'It's just my phone is actually downstairs in my jacket pocket,' I go.

And she's like, 'You don't have to actually *have* your phone to give me your number.'

What's that movie? *Fatal Attraction*?

I'm like, 'Yeah, no, good point. It's, er, zero eight seven,' and then I stort throwing just random numbers at her – we're talking six, we're talking four, we're talking one, we're talking blah, blah, blah.'

'Whoa,' she goes, 'stop saying numbers. This is too many digits.'

'How many have I given you?'

'One, two, three, fourrr . . . Twelve. You've given me twelve.'

'Okay, knock the last two off. Actually, knock off the last three. That should be enough.'

I leave her there with a look of, like, total confusion on her face, then I tip downstairs to the kitchen to collect my clothes and get the fock out of the gaff before she decides to try the number.

I throw on my chinos and I step into my Dubes. As I'm buttoning up my shirt, I notice that I must have lost a couple of buttons in the course of tearing it off. I'll get Sorcha to sew them back on tomorrow – if I can find them, that is.

I'm actually down on my hands and knees, searching the floor for them, when I suddenly become aware of someone staring at me somewhere in the dork. I look up and I end up getting the fright of my focking life.

Caleb is standing right in front of me, in his little dressing-gown.

'Jesus Christ,' I go, with my hand over my hort. 'You nearly gave me a focking hort attack.'

He goes, 'What are you doing here?'

I actually laugh. You could wait around a lifetime for the chance to deliver a line like this. I'm there, 'What do you think I'm doing here? I was riding your mother.'

He stares at me for a good, like, twenty seconds. I'm just grinning at him.

I go, 'See, this is what's known in the business as a taste of your own medicine.'

He's there, 'I'm going to tell Sorcha.'

Again, I *laugh*?

'She's not going to believe you,' I go. 'Sorcha thinks you're just some love-sick kid who has a creepy obsession with her. I've said it before and I'll say it again – you're the wrong kind of horny, Kid.'

He's there, 'I know it was Honor who put those things in my bag.'

'Maybe she did and maybe she didn't. But I think she was well within her rights. You used the girl to get to her mother.'

He laughs in what I would have said was a *cruel* way?

'Yeah,' he goes, 'as if I'd be interested in Honor. She's painful-looking. She's got horrible skin, horrible hair, horrible teeth – and nobody even likes her.'

'That's where you're wrong – because I like her.'

'That's because you're both sociopaths.'

'Sociopaths. Anyone can use big words, Caleb.'

He's there, 'Four syllables – is that what you regard as big?'

'Syllables,' I go. 'Oh, they're all coming out now, aren't they? Hey, you better stort being nice to me, Caleb. Because if things work out between me and your old dear, I might end up being your stepdad!'

I leave him just standing there in the kitchen, not knowing what to say.

I grab my jacket and I go, 'I'll see you round, Bieber.'

It's what you would have to call a dream exit. I'm actually feeling fantastic about myself until about, like, thirty seconds later, when I sit into my cor and my phone suddenly rings.

It's Ronan.

He goes, 'Rosser, where are you?'

What happened to *stay the fook away from us altogetter*?

I'm there, 'I'm just in Dalkey at the moment, Ro.'

He goes, 'Rosser, shut the fook up and listen. Ine arthur spoying an associate of Scum's downsteers in the loppy.'

'An associate? What do you mean by an associate?'

'What the fook do you think I mee-un by an associate? A fedda who associates with the sham – do you get me?'

'Okay, I get you.'

'Ine arthur been rumbled.'

'You're definitely sure it's not just you being paranoid. I remember Nidge got very bad, didn't he? And John Boy was the same before him.'

'Ine not being padanoid. Have you been thrinking?'

'A mouthful of wine – that's all.'

'Reet,' he goes, 'I need you to come and gerrus.'

'*Get* you?'

'From the bleaten hothel – we're not safe hee-or, Rosser.'

'Okay – and where am I bringing you?'

'I've no ithea. Someweer that's safe.'

'Hey, I know! Matter of fact, I don't know why I didn't think of it before.'


It's just after midnight when I drive around the back of the hotel as instructed.

I text Ronan. It's like, 'Outside,' then I think about adding a smiley face, then I think no, I better not, but then I think, Fock it, yeah, why not?

Five seconds later, the door of the kitchen flies open and three figures emerge from it. They're all, like, bent over. Their heads are covered with white sheets and they're sort of, like, running from the knees down.

They make it to the cor and they all pile in.

'Throvuy!' Ronan goes. 'Throyuv, throyuv, throyuv!'

So I drive.

Out of the hotel and back onto the N11, heading north at, like, a hundred and twenty Ks.

'Where we heddun?' Ronan goes.

I'm there, 'You'll see.'

Shadden's like, 'Hee-or, Ro, we left wirrout paying eer biddle.'

'Dudn't mathor,' Ronan goes. 'I gev them Rosser's credit keerd number when we checked in.'

Sometimes I think all I am to my son is an ATM. I don't mind, I'll get the money off my old man later.

'Where are we going?' Rihanna-Brogan goes. 'I was, like, half-way through watching a fillum.'

'You can watch your fillum anutter toyum,' Ronan goes. 'We had to bail – that's alls Ine tedding you.'

Fifteen minutes later, we're driving through the gates of Honalee.

'You don't mean hee-or?' Ronan goes.

I'm like, 'Why not? You'll be safe here. We've got, like, security gates, CCTV – blah, blah, blah.'

'Is Sorcha alreet wirrit, but?'

'Ro, she loves when you come to stay.'

Of course, he's never been here with a death sentence hanging over his head, but I'll get around her somehow.

As I pull out my front door key, Ronan goes, 'Smiley face. You're some fooken spanner, Rosser.'

I'm like, 'Yeah, whatever. Now act natural, okay?'

'What do you mee-un, naturiddle?'

'Around Sorcha, I mean. Until I explain the situation to her. Don't let her see that you're scared of something or that you're being chased, okay?'

'Doatunt woddy, Rosser.'

'Ronan, I mean it.'

'Game ball.'

Sorcha's standing in the hall when we walk through the door.

I'm there, 'Look who's come to stay with us for a little while!'

Ronan goes, 'Howiya, Sorcha? Where does the feed from the CCTV come in? I need to be looking at it at all toyums. Need to sleep wit one eye on it.'

I'm there, 'A nice surprise, Sorcha, isn't it?'

But Sorcha looks at me and goes, 'Ross, there's someone here to see you?'

My blood turns instantly cold.

'Shit,' I go. 'He's not wearing tracksuit bottoms and a Christmas jumper, is he?'

And straightaway I get the answer to my question. The kitchen door swings open and he steps into the hallway.

'Well, this is a fine how-do-you-do!' he goes.

No, it's not Scum. It's my old man.

And behind him, in his chauffeur's uniform, is K . . . K . . . K . . . K . . . Kennet.

I'm like, 'What the fock are you two doing here?'

And the old man goes, 'I think it's time we had a little talk, don't you, Ronan?'

'Poor Kennet here has been going out of his bloody well mind,' the old man goes.

We're sitting around the kitchen table, just the adults, we're talking me, the old man, Sorcha, Ronan, Shadden and – like I said – Kennet.

The old man goes, 'The house has been empty for days. Then when Kennet here heard about Buckets of Blood, well, obviously he feared the worst.'

Kennet goes, 'Sh . . . Sh . . . Sh . . . Shadden, if you were being threatened, could you not have c . . . c . . . c . . . come to me. I know p . . . p . . . people.'

Shadden's there, 'I ditn't wanth you getting involfed. You're oately out on temper doddy release. I don't want you going back to chail.'

Jesus Christ, it's bright in this kitchen.

I'm there, 'Why is it so focking bright in this room? Do we need the lights on?'

Sorcha's like, 'Ross, it's one o'clock in the morning.'

I switch them off. It ends up being pitch dork. So I switch them on again.

Why do they seem so bright, all of a sudden? I'm focking blinded here.

The old man brings the meeting to order again. 'Now, Ronan,' he goes, rubbing his hand through his hair, 'Kennet here has been telling me about the weeks of reprisals and counter-reprisals that have been going on between you and this chap, Scum.'

'Well, arthur this,' Ronan goes, 'there's gonna be mower – and that's not a threat, Grandda, it's a probbis.'

'But where's it going to end, Ronan? It started off with a few broken windows, the odd slashed tyre. Now it's guns!'

'Pooer Buckets – a fedda who nebber hoort addyone in he's loyf.'

Buckets has one hundred and thirty-seven previous convictions, by the way, including at least ten for grievous bodily horm. I think Ro's being *overly* charitable to him there?

Kennet goes, 'He's gonna be f . . . f . . . f . . . f . . . foyun, but. That's why this has to be the end of it.'

Ronan's there, 'Scum will be got. Ine putting the wheedles in motion.'

Shadden goes, 'It's only a bus toower, Rohnin. It's not woort dying for, so it's not.'

I'm there, 'What Shadden's talking there, Ro, is a thing called sense. You've got a daughter and a girlfriend. You've also got your Leaving Cert coming up, even though I'm hordly the one to stort lecturing you about knuckling down to the books. The point I'm trying to make is that more violence isn't the answer. Do you even, like, *remember* what happened to Nidge at the end of that show?'

'I have to hit him befower he hits me. It's kiddle or be kilt.'

'Or, if you're lucky, you get arrested and you go to jail for twenty or thirty years. Is that how you want to see your daughter grow up? Through three or four inches of bulletproof glass? No offence, Kennet.'

'N . . . N . . . N . . . None taken,' Kennet goes.

The old man's like, 'Why don't I talk to this chap and see if we can't come to an arrangement?'

Ronan goes, 'We altready had a throoce, but now the throost has gone.'

I'm there, 'I can't keep apologizing, Ro.'

'Even so,' the old man goes, 'I expect the chap wants a resolution just like all the other interested stakeholders. He's a businessman, isn't he?'

'He's a dealer,' Ronan goes. 'And a pimp.'

'Well, that's still a businessman – of a sort. You see, that's the thing I love about the free market. There's always a deal to be done. As I'm often wont to remark to my esteemed friend Mr Hennessy Coghlan-O'Hara, business always finds a way. Why don't you just leave it in my hands?'

Senny's girlfriend – we're talking Torah – is well worth a stare and I'm saying that as a connoisseur of beautiful women. She's, like, tall – almost as tall as me, in fact – not too fat, but not too thin, with a fantastic smile and a fabulous pair of gimme-gimmes.

She can dance as well.

We're in – okay, this is a blast from the past – Club 92. In other words, the famous Club of Love, where I did so much damage back in the day.

It's, like, a Saturday night. We have no actual game this weekend and Byrom thought it'd be a good idea for us all to maybe let our hair down before turning our minds to Greystones.

The Club D'Amour isn't the Club D'Amour I remember. Me and Christian are the oldest in the place by a good decade and the music is the kind of shit I hear coming out of Honor's room about three hours after she's been told to go to bed – a lot of David Guetta and blah, blah, blah.

I look over at Christian. He's in the middle of the dancefloor, having the crack with Bucky, Senny, Maho and Gilly. He's having a great time, even though he's only drinking Coke. I'm proud of the dude.

The DJ suddenly goes, 'Okay, now we're gonna take you back in time . . . with a little bit . . . of this.'

It's 'Murder on the Dancefloor'.

Jesus Christ, when Sophie Ellis-Bextor is being passed off as nostalgia, you know you're getting old.

I say that to Torah as well. She leans in to try to hear me better. She smells of *Maison Martin Margiela*.

'When Sophie Ellis-Bextor is being passed off as nostalgia,' I go, 'you know you're getting old.'

Torah laughs, even though I'm pretty sure she has no idea what I just said.

That's when someone suddenly pushes me in the back. It's, like, a hord push as well and it sends me flying across the dancefloor.

I turn around and there's some random dude just staring at me, like, *threateningly*? I'm there, 'What the fock is your problem?'

He goes, 'You're my problem – you focking pervert.'

I'm like, 'Dude, I'm just dancing with the girl . . .'

I'm wondering can he see my boner in these chinos?

He looks over his shoulder and goes, 'Senny, come over here!'

Senny arrives over. And I think to myself, Oh holy fock. Oh, focking holy fock. Because I suddenly recognize the dude.

'This is him,' he goes. 'The focking peeping Tom I found looking in your window.'

I'm there, 'Excuse me?'

I try to look as bewildered as I possibly can. Which isn't hord for me. Honor always says that clueless is my resting face.

Senny goes, 'Gav, chill out, that's Rossi – our hooker.'

But this Gav dude is like, '*This* is the focker who was looking in your window. The focker who kicked me in the balls.'

He makes a run at me and it takes the combined strength of Bucky, Dilly *and* Gilly to hold him back.

I must have left him with a couple of fine achers alright.

Senny is suddenly looking at me dubiously – as is Torah, by the way?

The music stops and the DJ calls the bouncers to the dancefloor. Everyone in the entire of Club 92 is staring.

Senny goes, 'Rossi, what's he talking about?'

I'm there, 'I've no idea,' straightening my Hollister T-shirt. 'It must be a case of mistaken identity.'

The dude goes, 'It *was* you! I was standing this close to you! You were even wearing that top!'

Blissy is standing next to Senny. He goes, 'Rossi, you need to stort talking here.'

I think to myself, okay, I can't keep point-blank denying it. It's not like lying to Sorcha, where she's coming from the position of actually wanting to believe the shit that comes out of my mouth.

I've got, like, seven or eight of my teammates staring at me and they want the truth.

So the truth is what I end up giving them.

'Okay,' I go, 'I admit it. It was me who was looking in your window that night and, yes, who gave this dope here a kick in the knackers. But it wasn't to be a filth-bag.'

The bouncers suddenly arrive, but they hang back because they can see that it's just two rugby players sorting shit out and they're obviously respectful of that.

If we were soccer players, there'd be sixty Gords with riot shields and batons in here already.

'So explain to me,' Senny goes, 'why were you looking in my window?'

I'm there, 'I thought you invited me over.'

'What? Why would I invite you over? I was having a night in with Torah.'

'I asked you if you wanted to do something together and you said you fancied a night of Netflix and Chill.'

'Netflix and Chill – exactly.'

'Dude, I'm thirty-five. I thought you were inviting me around to watch a box set and just kick back.'

He stares at me for a long time, as do Torah and the rest of the team. In fact, the entire of Club 92 is staring at me with their mouths open, including the dude whose mebs I dropkicked.

Senny is the first one to break the silence. He smiles, then the smile turns into a laugh. Then Torah laughs, then the rest of the goys, then the bouncers, then everyone in the entire club.

It's suddenly the most hilarious thing that anyone has ever heard.

I hear people repeating what I said. They're all going, 'He thought Netflix and Chill meant watching a box set and kicking back.'

I'm looking around and I'm going, 'For fock's sake – I *still* say it means that! Netflix and Chill! Have you all lost your minds?'

I know I sound like my old man.

All the goys, including Senny, are suddenly slapping my back and hugging me and telling me I'm a legend. The bouncers head off, knowing that I represent no threat to anyone.

The DJ puts on 'Murder on the Dancefloor' from the stort and dedicates it to 'The old guy in the T-shirt that's too small for him with the haircut that's too young for him who thinks Netflix and Chill means watching *Battlestar Galactica* and relaxing!'

And I think, Yeah, no, fock you, too, Dude.

'Fock Saint Mary's!'
    'Fock Saint Gerard's!'
    'Fock Saint Andrew's!'
    'Fock Saint Michael's!'
    'Fock! Fock! Fock! Fock! Fock! Fock! Fock! Fock!'
    'Fock! Fock! Fock! Fock! Fock! Fock! Fock! Fock!'
So it's, like, Monday night and me and Christian are on the way to Strength and Conditioning. We've decided to run rather than drive, from the Vico Road to – no one's fooling anyone – Ballybrack. And it's just like old times, because we're playing a game we used to play back in the day, where you take it in turns to say the names of people or places or teams or even just shit that you hate, while you're pounding the road.

'Fock Chris Ashton!'
    'Fock Dan Cole!'
    'Fock Chris Robshaw!'
    'Fock Courtney Laws!'
    'Fock Owen Farrell!'
    'Fock Josh Beaumont!'
    'Fock George Ford!'
    'Fock Ben Youngs!'
    'Fock! Fock! Fock! Fock! Fock! Fock! Fock! Fock!'
    'Fock! Fock! Fock! Fock! Fock! Fock! Fock! Fock!'
Christian goes, 'It's just like the old days, huh?'

I'm there, 'I was thinking the exact same thing.'

We're passing by St John's School and I'm like, 'This next bit is all downhill – come on, let's step up the pace!'

He's like, 'Are you sure?'

'Fock BJ Botha!'

'Fock Keith Earls!'

'Fock Conor Murray!'

'Fock Simon Zebo!'

'Fock! Fock! Fock! Fock! Fock! Fock! Fock! Fock!'

'Fock! Fock! Fock! Fock! Fock! *Fooocccckkk!!!*'

Because that's when it happens. My legs disappear from under me – and it happens in, like, an *instant*? One minute I'm eating up the path, the next I'm *literally* eating it? I get suddenly dizzy and then I can't feel my legs and the next thing I know, my face is hitting the concrete beneath me.

'Ross!' Christian goes.

I'm lying there on the ground and I'm going, 'It's okay, it's okay – I slipped.'

Except Christian's there, 'That was no slip. Your legs went.'

I go to stand up, except it's like I suddenly have no bones. Down I go again.

Christian goes, 'Don't try to stand up. Come on, Dude, take a breath. You just fainted.'

I'm there, 'I didn't faint. And I don't want that word being bandied about. Fainting is what ladies do.'

'Well, something happened.'

I think I feel strong enough to finally stand up again, so very slowly, very deliberately, I get back on my feet.

I'm like, 'Come on, we'll just walk the rest of the way to the club.'

He goes, 'Dude, there's no way you're doing Strength and Conditioning training tonight.'

'Christian, we've only got hopefully one match left. We beat Greystones, we stay up – end of.'

I stort walking.

He's there, 'Ross, I don't like this.'

I go, 'You don't have to like it. Come on, let's just get there. We'll speed-walk. And we'll change the subject. I don't know if I mentioned how proud I am of you for getting your shit together.'

He storts walking alongside me, except he still looks concerned. He's there, 'Yeah, no, thanks.'

'Lauren's going to be seriously impressed,' I go. 'I can't wait to see her face next time she's home. It's like the old Christian is back. The one she fell in love with.'

Five minutes later, we arrive at the club.

Dudser storts bawling us out of it before we're even properly in the door. I don't even have time to say hi to the rest of the goys because he's going, 'You're late, you useless fockers! Kettlebells! Pick them up! I want to see a hundred goblet squats and I don't want to see you pause for breath!'

We do as we're told – there's no negotiating with Dudser.

Anyway, I'm about fifty squats into my hundred when I notice Senny on the other side of the room, doing orm curls with the borbells, but at the same time just, like, *staring* at me?

I'm there, 'Alright, Senny? I always dedicate mine to women I want to ride. I've done twenty for Mila Kunis and twenty for Natalie Portman. These twenty are for Emily Ratajkowski.'

He suddenly drops the borbells and makes a run at me across the floor of the gym.

I'm thinking, What the fock? because the last time I saw him he was accepting my explanation for the Netflix and Chill incident and joking that my name should be placed on the Sexual Offenders Register for the next thirty years.

I have no idea what's happened to change his mind as he launches himself at me while I'm literally mid goblet squat? He actually slams his head into my midriff, sending the two of us spilling backwards onto the floor.

I'm in, like, shock, which is how he ends up managing to pin me down, with one hand gripping the front of my Leinster training top and the other hand cocked and ready to fire.

I swear to fock, he's about to drill his fist into my actual face, when I notice a rugby boot on the ground beside me. I don't even know what it's doing there. But I quickly grab it and in one smooth movement – bang! – I manage to crack him across the side of the head with it. It leaves him, like, stunned for a few seconds, enough time for Bucky and Maho and one or two others to rush over and drag the dude off me.

At the same time, they're all going, 'Senny, he's not focking worth it,' and I'm thinking, What the fock are they talking about? Where's all this hostility suddenly coming from? What have I supposably done now?

That's what I end up saying to them – straight out. I'm like, 'What have I supposably done now?'

Senny is touching his face. There's, like, blood on his fingers. I hit him some crack, in fairness to me.

'You know what you focking did,' he goes.

I'm there, 'Dude, genuinely, I've no idea what this is even about. The last time I saw you was in the cor pork of Club 92. You were high-fiving me and telling me that in other countries they chemically castrate sexual deviants like me.'

He goes, 'That was before I found out what you did.'

I'm like, 'What did I do?'

'You tried to get off with Torah?'

'What?'

'Don't even try to deny it. She told me. She said she was at the bor and you walked up to her and said, "What are you doing wasting your time with someone like Senny?" and then you put your hand on her orse.'

'Yeah, no, that sounds like my MO, but it didn't happen. Has it crossed your mind that she's possibly making it up? Girls do that shit constantly to fock with men's heads.'

He makes another run for me, except Bucky and Maho have a good, firm hold of him this time.

'You're a focking wanker,' Bucky goes. 'You'd do that to a teammate?'

I've done a hell of a lot worse than that. Ask Christian there. I rode his mother.

I don't mention that, though. I don't get the chance, because Dudser lets a roar out of him.

He's like, 'Alright, you!' meaning me. 'Ballybrack Shopping Centre and back! Do it now!'

I look at Senny and I go, 'Dude, I'm sorry. I was shitfaced. And if it's any consolation, she was probably flirting with me.'

He goes, 'Do you know something? You were actually becoming a bit of a hero to me.'

I'm there, 'I'd like to think I still am.'

'You're not! You're nothing to me!'

I step outside with his words just echoing in my ears.

It's pissing rain. I'm just about to stort running when I hear Christian call my name. He's followed me out of the clubhouse.

He goes, 'What was that?'

I'm there, 'Yeah, no, me up to my old tricks obviously. I'm a complete filth-bag. I'll probably never change.'

'It's just you seemed pretty surprised – when he told you what happened?'

'Like I said, I was hammered that night.'

'No, you weren't. You only had eight or nine pints. Why can't you remember what happened, Ross?'

I suddenly turn my back on him and I go to stort running, except he grabs the back of my Leinster training top, pulls me back and spins me around.

He's like, 'You collapsed on the way here tonight. Your legs went.'

I'm there, 'You don't know what the fock you're talking about, Christian.'

'It was that clash of heads against Dungannon. Jesus Christ, Ross, you've got concussion.'


My burger arrives not on a plate, or even on a table-tennis bat with the rubber pulled off it – it's on a roof slate, with a side of rocket with Parmesan shavings.

'Long time since I've seen one of those,' the old man goes, as if reading my mind. His steak sandwich, by the way, is served on a bathroom tile with a side of melon-studded couscous. 'And to think they said this country was finished.'

It's nice to see The Merrion Inn open again.

Kennet looks at me, a smile playing on his lips, which means a joke is coming. Eventually.

'B . . . B . . . B . . . Boy the way,' he goes, 'I like your h . . . h . . .

h . . . h . . . heercut, Rosser. When are you g . . . going back to gerrit f . . . f . . . f . . . f . . . fiddished?'

And I go, 'Yeah, no, it's called f . . . f . . . f . . . f . . . fashion, Kennet. You wouldn't know the first focking thing about it.'

He's having the Umbrian fish soup, by the way, which is served in a stainless-steel bedpan with a side of olive and Manchego bread.

'So,' the old man goes, 'I expect you're wondering why I've asked you here today. Well, I've been speaking with our friend – the famous Scum – about arranging this, inverted commas, *sit-down*. And, as I told Ronan this morning, Scum seems rather amenable to the idea, as I suspected he would be.'

'So where is it actually happening?'

'Well, naturally enough, I put forward the Members' Club in the RDS, but the chap vetoed the idea out of hand. Too far out of his comfort zone, I expect. He suggested The Fu King Chinky – it's apparently above The Tipsy Wagon in the town of Coo Lock.'

Kennet goes, 'I think he was saying he'd m . . . meet you in the fooking chinky, Cheerlie, rather than The F . . . F . . . F . . . Fu King Chinky. I think that place is called Mister Wu's.'

'But it's still focking Coolock,' I go. 'Why can't we meet somewhere neutral? Does Westmoreland Street have a Nando's?'

The old man goes, 'I've been in business for more than forty years, Ross. Where you take your meeting is irrelevant. It's how you prepare for it that matters.'

'Eeder way,' Kennet goes, 'Ine gonna b . . . b . . . b . . . be theer, Cheerlie.'

'No, you're not.'

'Ch . . . Ch . . . Cheerlie, Ine not letting you go in theer on your owen.'

'I shan't *be* on my own. I shall have Ronan with me – and Kicker, of course.'

I'm like, 'Me? Why the fock do I have to be there?'

'Scum said it was a precondition. He's absolutely adamant that you be there.'

Kennet goes, 'Ch . . . Ch . . . Ch . . .'

The old man's like, 'Kennet, we've talked about this. The terms of your – what's this you call it? – temper doddy release are that you refrain from associating with, quote-unquote, known criminals. I think our good friends, the Garda Síochána, would be only too happy to return you to Mountjoy Prison.'

'I don't gib a b . . . b . . . b . . . boddicks, Cheerlie. Ine not letting you go in theer wirrout me. Enta stordee.'

The old man looks up and suddenly spots some tosser he used to play golf with in Elm Pork. He tips over there, going, 'I don't believe it!'

I turn to Kennet and I go, 'Why are you so keen to put yourself in the firing line?'

He's there, 'Your oul fedda's been v . . . v . . . veddy good to me since I gorr ourra p . . . p . . . p . . . p . . . priddon. He's arthur gibbon me a job, muddy in me pocket, respect.'

'You don't have respect. I know I'm biased, but you genuinely *don't*?'

'Look, I wontherstand why you hate me, R . . . Rosser. I ditn't threet young Ronan veddy weddle at the st . . . st . . . s t . . . st . . . steert.'

'No, you didn't. You had him removing clamps from cors for a focking pittance – slave labour. But what I'll never forgive you for is that black eye you gave him.'

'Alls I can say is soddy.'

'I'm not interested in your apologies.'

'He's arthur been a garreat fedda to Shadden. And he's a garreat fadder to Rihatta-Barrogan, so he is.'

'Ronan's great, full-stop.'

'And that's why I w . . . w . . . wanth to be involvt in this sss . . . sss . . . sss . . . ssit-down. I wanna meck it up torrum. I owe him big-toyum . . .'

He continues yabbering away, except I'm suddenly no longer even *listening* to him. Instead, I'm suddenly staring at the old man's *Irish Times*, which he's left on the seat beside me, open and folded over on the rugby page. It's actually the headline that *first* grabs my attention? I reach for the paper in slow motion, almost not wanting to read the story, but at the same time knowing that I *have* to?

It's a story by Gerry Thornley. He gets all the focking good ones, typically.

And this one is an actual belter.

It's like, 'The IRFU has promised to investigate claims that an All Ireland League player killed a dolphin while on a morale-building team holiday in Bundoran . . .'

I'm lying on the sofa with my head hopping again and an ice pack on my forehead. At the same time, I'm texting Senny going: 'Dude wotever i said/did to your girlf it was no reason for u to report me to the irfu for killing that dolphin.'

He's straight back with: 'I didnt report u for killing anythng – get ur facts right.'

I'm there: 'Then how does GT have the exclusiv in today's times?'

He's like: 'May b cos the photos hav been up on instagrm for d lst fking week.'

Shit.

See, that's the problem with hanging out with young people these days, with their Facebook and their Snapchat and their whatever-the-fock else, everyone's a potential paparazzo. And when you've got as much to hide as I generally do, that's a massive focking problem.

I text him back, going: 'Dude we ned to posbly clear the air b4 sats match.'

He's straight back with: 'Eat fking shit.' And then – this is the real killer – about two minutes later: 'Btw you look like a sad bastrd with that haircut.'

I feel low enough to tie the laces of my Dubes without even bending down.

That's when the living-room door suddenly opens and in steps Christian. Sorcha must have let him in, even though I told her that I didn't want to see anyone.

I'm there, 'Dude, this is not a good time.'

He's like, 'Sorcha said you've got a migraine.'

'I'd describe it as a headache more than a migraine.'

'You've got the curtains drawn and you're holding an ice pack to your head and Sorcha said you were vomiting an hour ago.'

'Jesus Christ, that girl can't hold her piss.'

'Dude, you need to say something.'

'To Sorcha?'

'To the club. There's, like, protocols when it comes to this kind of shit.'

'Yeah, no, that's what I'm afraid of. If I go telling them that I'm, like, falling down in the street and forgetting conversations that I supposedly had, they're not going to let me play against Greystones.'

'But you shouldn't play against Greystones – you've got concussion.'

'We don't know for a fact that I do.'

'Ross, do you want to be around to teach Johnny, Brian and Leo the correct way to throw a ball?'

'Stop!'

'It's a genuine question. Do you want to be around to watch them play Junior Cup? Senior Cup? Ireland Schools? Ireland under-twenty?'

'Dude, don't say it!'

'You could be watching them from the focking wheelchair section!'

I let a sudden roar out of me. I'm there, 'I said focking stop!'

Except *he* shouts even *louder*? 'No, I won't stop! This is focking serious, Ross! We're only finding out about the long-term effects of concussion.'

I'm there, 'Well, if we're still only finding out about it, maybe we shouldn't rush to judgment.'

'Ross, you saved my life. I'm not exaggerating when I say that. If you hadn't got a hold of me, I'd have been dead within the year. And now I'm going to return the favour.'

'By doing what?'

'By telling Byrom Jones that you're suffering from concussion.'

He turns to leave. I'm there, 'Dude, no.'

He's like, 'Ross, you're risking everything. There's ex-players walking around out there who don't even know their own names. It's called brain damage, Ross – let's not even sugar-coat it.'

'Wait,' I go. 'Dude, please, just wait. Close the door there and hear me out – that's all I'm asking, that you hear me out.'

He does what I ask him – reluctantly, though.

I'm there, 'You know, I didn't realize until three or four months ago that I've been walking around all these years with a humungous hole in my chest.'

He goes, 'What are you talking about?'

'I'm saying that's what it felt like – like I've had a hole in the middle of my chest all these years. And do you know what shape that hole was?'

'No, I don't know what shape the hole was.'

'It was the shape of rugby.'

'Okay, what does that even mean?'

'Do you know what it's like to be shit at everything, Christian?'

'You're not shit at everything.'

'I'm shit at everything. There's no point in pretending otherwise. My daughter was more advanced than me by the time she was five. I've no exams, no qualifications. I'm a shit husband, a shit son – you know, there are days when I wonder am I even a good father?'

I can feel my eyes filling up with tears, then suddenly they're spilling down my face.

I'm there, 'It caught up on me, Christian.'

He goes, 'What did? Ross, why are you crying?'

'The focking realization. That I could have really been someone and instead I pissed it all up against the wall. It's a lonely focking feeling, Christian, to be staring down the barrel of middle age, knowing that there was only one thing you were ever any good at – and you failed at even that.'

'There were factors.'

'There weren't factors, Christian. I like to say there were factors so I don't have to take responsibility for throwing it all away. Dude, I know people look at me and they look at Drico and they say, if you'd looked at those two players in their Senior Cup years, there's only one of them you could picture going on to win Grand Slams and Heineken Cups and captaining the Lions – and that was me. But there was one basic difference between me and him. He was a winner.'

'*You're* a winner.'

'I'm a loser.'

'This is definitely some kind of midlife thing – I mean, the hair, the T-shirt . . .'

'I threw it away, Christian. All that opportunity. Jesus, all that talent. But can I tell you something else? In the last few weeks, I feel like I got some of it back. Can you understand that? That hole I was telling you about – it doesn't feel as big now.'

Christian turns his head. I realize that even *he's* crying now?

'Dude,' I go, 'I didn't end up in the cor pork of Seapoint Rugby Club by accident. I mean, I don't make a habit of driving through – let's call a spade a spade – Ballybrack.'

'Stop. I know what you're going to say and don't say it.'

'*He* led me there, Christian. Father Fehily led me there.'

'Dude, you could end up doing yourself a serious injury. A lasting one.'

'He won't let that happen. I know that for a fact. He said that to me in the hospital. He said when he died, I'd have an open channel to the man Himself. And you better believe he's talking to Him about me, Christian. Oh, he'll be in His ear: "Ross this" and "Ross that". Can you hear him?'

Christian wipes away tears with his open palm and at the same time he nods.

I'm there, 'He won't let anything bad happen to me, Dude. See, he's directing this whole focking show. Because he doesn't want me to grow old wondering. Yes, I threw it all away, Christian. But this is my chance to get it back again. This is my last shot. The dream kick and the jackpot focking question, all rolled into one. I've got eighty minutes to keep Seapoint in Division 2B of the All Ireland League. Now, you can walk out of here and go and tell Byrom the truth. But I'm begging you, Christian – please, please, please, don't take this opportunity away from me.'

'Fock,' he goes, mad at himself, because he knows that if this was any other sport, he'd do the right thing without any hesitation.

But this isn't any other sport.

He sits down on the orm of the sofa, totally defeated. And I know in that moment that he's not going to say shit.

Suddenly, Sorcha knocks and puts her head around the living-room door. She's like, 'Ross . . .'

I'm there, 'Seriously, Sorcha, you can't hold your piss.'

She steps into the room and that's when I notice that she's crying as well. At first, I'm wondering was she outside the door, listening to my little speech. But then she tells me, through her tears, that my old dear just rang to say that Ari is dead.

# 10. *Indicktus*

The old dear has a face like a –

Do you know what? I'm not going to say it. It's not a day for that kind of thing. The woman is grieving. Her face is focking horrendous. Let's just leave it at that.

Ari, it turns out, had a hort attack while he was on – if you can believe this – the treadmill in the old dear's basement. She told him about this examination he had to go for and he got it into his head that it was some kind of physical. He decided he needed to get himself fit.

She found him on the floor of the basement, in his tracksuit, with the treadmill setting switched to max. The dude was already room temp.

I'm sitting there, blinded with another migraine, wondering how am I going to go and play a rugby match after a morning like this?

Foxrock Church is practically empty. On one side, it's just me and the old dear, who's dressed from head to toe in black, then Sorcha and Honor, the old man and Helen, then a few of the old dear's friends from The Gables, the writing world, the golf club and her various campaigns to stop certain things coming to Foxrock. On the other side, it's just Tiffany Blue, muttering to herself madly – presumably drunk or high – and shooting the old dear filthy looks.

She looks very well.

Sorcha does the reading in her best Mount Anville Debating Society voice. 'A reading from the Prophet Isaiah,' she goes. 'On this mountain, the Lord of hosts will prepare for all peoples a banquet of rich food. On this mountain, he will remove the mourning veil covering all peoples, and the shroud enwrapping all nations, he will destroy death forever . . .'

The old dear reaches for my hand and takes it in hers. She

squeezes it tightly, as if she's trying to get, I don't know, *strength* from it? I look at her sideways and our eyes meet. I don't think I've ever seen her look so sad and for once it doesn't *seem* like a performance?

She goes, 'I don't know if I'll ever get over this, Ross.'

I'm there, 'You will get over it, because you've got good people around you, including me.'

'She wouldn't let me cremate him.'

She's, like, whispering, by the way.

I'm there, 'Who wouldn't?'

She rolls her eyes sideways to indicate Tiffany Blue. She's apparently taking his body back to the States after this, then she's going to bury him next to her mother – in other words Ari's daughter – and his first wife – in other words, Tiffany Blue's *grandmother*?

She goes, 'His wish was to be cremated and his ashes scattered here.'

I'm like, 'Where? Foxrock?'

'Just in Ireland. He fell in love with the country.'

'He obviously didn't see enough of it. It's a complete shithole in places.'

'Well, that was his wish. He said that way he'd always be near me. He said I'd hear his voice every time the wind blew down Torquay Road.'

She sort of, like, laughs to herself – I suppose the word would be *fondly*?

'Silly Ari,' she goes. 'Silly heart.'

Sorcha's like, 'This is the word of the Lord.'

And we're all there, 'Thanks be to God.'

I'm there, 'So why don't you tell Tiffany Blue that she's not taking him?'

She goes, 'I'm tired, Ross. I'm tired of the fighting. She already thinks I'm a gold-digger. I don't want to be called a body-snatcher as well. I need peace and quiet now. To come to terms with my grief.'

'Well, like I said, you've got good people around you. I mean, *I'll* call in all the time.'

'Will you, Ross?'

'Well, not *all* the time. That was just an expression. I'll call in, though.'

'And bring those lovely babies – em . . .'

'Rock, paper, scissors.'

'Yes, I want to get to know them better. I'm their grandmother after all.'

She doesn't ask me to bring Honor, I notice.

'And now,' the priest goes, 'Ari's wife, Fionnuala, is going to say a few words.'

I'm there, 'Are you sure you want to do this?'

She goes, 'I'm dreading it, Ross. But I know I must.'

She stands up and I let go of her hand. She walks unsteadily to the – I'm going to use the word – *pulpit*?

Tiffany Blue looks like she's trying to will her dead with her eyes.

After a long pause, the old dear goes, 'Ari and I didn't have long together – although I was always far more conscious than he was of how short our time was likely to be. Ari would talk about all the things he wanted us to do together, all the places we had to see, as if time wasn't a factor in his life at all. He was oblivious to the idea that he was aging along with everyone else. Sometimes, he would talk with great fondness about old friends – people he knew from the forties and the fifties – and how sad it was that they'd fallen out of touch. And I would say to him, "Why don't you pick up the phone?" and he'd say, "Ah, we wouldn't have anything in common, Fionnuala! He'd be an old man by now!" '

We all laugh. It's a decent anecdote, in fairness to the woman.

She goes, 'While Ari was beautifully oblivious to the passage of time, it was left to me to speculate about what our lives would have been like if we'd met when we were younger – the adventures we would have had together, the places we would have visited, the children we might have had together . . .'

Her voice sort of, like, *wavers*?

'Instead, we led separate lives, separated by thousands of miles, until fate conspired one day to bring us . . . to bring us . . .'

She suddenly breaks down, her hand over her mouth, her eyes

shut tight and her head bobbing up and down as the tears stort to flow.

I don't wait to be told. I'm up off the seat and I'm straight up to the pulpit to help her down. I put my orm around her shoulder and I'm like, 'You don't need to say anything else. We get the general idea,' and I stort walking her down from the altar and back to her seat.

And that's when Tiffany Blue decides that she can't take anymore.

'Okay,' she goes, jumping to her feet, 'this is total fucking bullshit!'

The priest goes, 'I understand that on sad occasions such as this, emotions run a little high. However, I *would* ask you to please temper your language while you are in the House of the Lord.'

The Foxrock branch, as well.

'Fuck you!' Tiffany Blue goes. 'And fuck you, Fionnuala, with this bullshit grieving widow act!'

There's, like, gasps in the church.

I can hear Honor go, 'Oh! My God! Plot twist!'

I'm there, 'Yeah, no, you heard the priest. I don't know how you do things in the States, but when we're in church, we tend *not* to swear like we're in a hip hop video?'

'And fuck you,' she goes, 'with your little dick like a packet of Lifesavers.'

Honor's like, 'Okay, I should be filming this!' and she storts pointing her phone at us.

'You're drunk,' the old dear goes – to Tiffany Blue, not Honor. It's a sad state of affairs that I have to point that out.

'You think I can't see through this?' Tiffany Blue goes. 'Standing up there, pretending to be all, like, sad because Grandpa's gone. You're not sad. Because you killed him!'

Everyone's like, 'Whoa!'

It's a definite first for the Church of Our Lady of Perpetual Premenstrual Tension, as we used to call it.

The old man is instantly on *his* feet then?

'I know you've lost someone who was very dear to you,' he goes, 'and I understand that you're very sad, but I can't allow that

calumny to go unchallenged – church or no church. How dare you suggest such a thing?'

Tiffany Blue's there, 'Well, is it not a bit convenient that he dies two days before he's due to go to hospital to have his mental state assessed?'

'You need to get yourself clean again,' the old dear goes.

'So now I can't prove that he wasn't of sound mind when he married you. Or at least that's what you think, you dried-up skank.'

'You're being irrational.'

'Why was he on the treadmill? He was ninety-two years of age!'

'Because he wanted to be fit and ready for those demeaning tests that you – his own flesh and blood – insisted he be subjected to. That's on *your* conscience, not mine!'

I'm still standing between them, bear in mind, with my orm around the old dear's shoulder. I can feel her body literally trembling.

'Why would he take a bath before he got on the treadmill?' Tiffany Blue goes then.

The old dear's like, 'I beg your pardon?'

'He took a bath, according to you, then he got on the treadmill. Why would he do it in that order?'

'Because we never got his medication right.'

'Bullshit. He'd never stepped on a treadmill before. He never took exercise in his life.'

The old man goes, 'The poor chap died of a heart attack and that's all there is to it.'

'Induced,' Tiffany Blue goes, 'by her.'

The old man's there, 'Fionnuala, don't say another word! This is bloody well slander of the worst kind and I know just the chap to get it remedied through this country's courts of law!'

'He had burn marks on his legs,' Tiffany Blue goes. 'Where did they come from?'

'From a borbecue,' the old dear tries to go. 'While we were on honeymoon. I explained it. Some coals slipped from the fire and then . . .'

I'm there, 'Hang on, what exactly are you allegating here?'

'She dropped something in the bath,' Tiffany Blue goes, 'while Grandpa was in it – something electrical – to give him a heart attack. Then she dried him off, dressed him in a T-shirt, shorts and sneakers, dragged him downstairs and left him beside the treadmill. Then she tried to have him cremated before I could get a post mortem performed on the body.'

The old man points at the old dear and goes, 'Look at her! Look at that woman grieving there! Does anyone in this church honestly believe that Fionnuala O'Carroll-Kelly would be capable of such a thing?'

There's, like, silence for a good five or six seconds – these are her so-called mates, bear in mind.

The old man's like, 'Well?'

It's only then that people stort to shake their heads and go, 'No, of course not. That's ridiculous.'

The priest looks at Tiffany Blue and goes, 'I'm going to ask you to leave this church right now.'

Tiffany Blue just stares the old dear out of it for about thirty seconds. Then she steps out of the pew, into the aisle, and clip-clops her way down the aisle and out of the church.

A few seconds later, she steps back inside just to shout, 'This ain't over, bitch!'

You can say what you want about Greystones – it's Newtownmountkennedy with nicer views; even the tide is afraid to come in; its name translated into Irish is *Na Clocha Liatha*, which literally means, 'Check your shoes – I think one of us has stepped in something!' – but this much is also true: it's a tough place to go and win a rugby match.

Seapoint versus Greystones is one of *the* bitterest rivalries in Irish rugby. It's not for no reason that it's called the El Classico of second-tier rugby in Ireland.

The two teams hate each other for, like, a whole host of reasons. A lot of our goys played schools rugby with *their* goys? We're talking Pres Bray, we're talking Gerard's, we're talking CBC Monkstown, we're talking Blackrock, we're talking Clongowes. A lot of them are still friends – *best* friends, in some cases? Plus, a lot of our goys ended up playing for The Point because – let's be honest here – they weren't good enough to make the firsts in Greystones. So they've obviously got shit to prove.

It's a fixture with more individual needles than the Liffey Boardwalk.

Byrom has obviously heard about what happened at Strength and Conditioning on Monday night because he addresses it head-on in his pre-match team talk. He goes, 'You could cut the tinsion in here wuth a knoyf. Look, Oy doyn't knoy what wint on, why you've all fallen aaht – something to doy with the loydoys, noy daaht. Oy doyn't want to fuckun knoy. What I can tell yoy from experience is that in a year's toym, moyboy toy, yoy woyn't remimber what it was all abaaht. Ut won't boy important toy yoy. But yoy *will* remimber what hippens aaht on that putch todoy. Ut'll defoyne the rist of your loyves.

'Toy months agoy, I would niver have drimt that woy'd foynd aahsulves un thus pusition. We were a laahfing stock. Do yoy remimber what Groystoynes dud when they came to Kulbogget Paahk? They scored eight troys. They were toyking the puss. But todoy we're a dufferunt toym. That's because we staahted to beloyve in aahrsulves. Lit's fuckun shoy them what koynd of a toym we are naah by stopping thum wunning the loyg. Whativer shut is goying on between yoy, lit's put it aaht of our hids for the nixt eightoy munnets. Lit's koyp The Point in Duvusion Toy Boy of the All Ireland Loyg!'

It's pretty stirring stuff, it has to be said. Everyone claps. As we're walking out of the dressing room, I tip over to Senny and I offer him my hand. I'm like, 'Dude, I'm sorry. Like I said, I was hammered. The other point I'd love to make is that making a move on each other's birds was an accepted port of the game when I played.'

He looks me in the eye. He goes, 'I'm not shaking your hand, Rossi. But I am prepared to play with you today, because I'm a professional,' which is a definite dig at me. 'And that's how professionals behave.'

The first ten minutes end up being the ten most intense minutes of rugby that I've ever experienced. Greystones – focking

Braystones – are really fired up for this one. They're determined to build an early lead and make the second half just, like, a *victory* lap for themselves? The hits are unbelievable – on both sides. The hordest tackles of all are best friend on best friend.

I'm tempted to say, that's rugby.

Worse than the tackling is the sledging. I'm throwing the ball into the lineout and one of their goys is going, 'Send us a postcord from Tullamore next year!' and 'I hope you enjoy Navan!'

There's one or two comments about my hair as well – 'Who's the old dick who thinks he's Ian Madigan?' and that type of thing.

On the sideline, Byrom is going, 'Doyn't lit thum into your hids – ut's all paaht and paahcul.'

And I'm there, 'He's right – let's not get suckered into personal battles against this pack of Wicklow focking Sandpeople.'

But it gets even worse as the half wears on, with Greystones leading 12–3.

Some dude who was in Clongowes with Senny – they're supposedly, like, *cousins*? – keeps asking him why he didn't come to play for a real team when he got focked out of Lansdowne. 'Is it because you're a focking bottler?' he goes.

Possibly as a result, Senny is having a mare with the boot.

On the sideline, Byrom is going, 'Sinny, you're litting thum unto your hid, Moyte! Doyn't lit thum unto your hid!' and I can hear my old man, a short distance away, go, 'Respect for the opposition number ten is the *sine qua non* of the game! Without it, let's just make the ball round and call it soccer!'

I'm actually doing okay – and feeling okay – until about twenty-five minutes in, which is when I stort to get a bit, I don't know, light-headed?

Bucky asks me if I'm okay. I'm there, 'Yeah, no, I'm just a bit, I don't know, dizzy.'

'Dizzy?' he goes. 'Might be dehydration.'

Someone throws a bottle of water on and I take three or four mouthfuls from it. But that's when the pains in my head stort up again. They're, like, the worst *yet*? It feels like I'm being repeatedly stabbed in the head.

'You okay?' Maho goes, as he watches me grimace.

I'm there, 'Yeah, no, the water seems to have definitely done the trick.'

A few minutes later, after seven or eight phases, Greystones win a scrum ten metres from our line.

We do the whole binding thing, then the referee does the usual, 'Okay, crouch . . .' which is what we end up doing.

And that's when the Greystones hooker, who's built like the focking robot out of *Big Hero 6*, looks me dead in the eye and sort of, like, smiles. Of course, I'm too distracted by the pains in my head to realize that he's got, like, a trick up his *sleeve* here?

The referee's like, 'Touch!'

And that's when this dude goes, 'Here, Ross, is it? What's the difference between you and an Eddie Rocket's tuna melt?'

The referee goes, 'Pause!'

'I don't know, what?' I make the mistake of going.

And the dude goes, 'An Eddie Rocket's tuna melt is dolphin-friendly!'

'Engage!'

What the fock?

Badoom!

Bucky and Maho are suddenly shouting, either side of me. They're going, 'Push, Rossi! Fock's sake, Rossi! Push!'

But I'm so thrown by the comment that I can't. My legs are suddenly like jelly.

I'm thinking, Do people know it was actually me who killed that dolphin?

'Push, Rossi!' they're going. 'Focking push! If you don't, it's going to be a –'

Pushover try. They score a pushover try. The ultimate indignity.

'Referee!' I hear the old man go. 'Watch the Greystones scrum! There's clearly all sorts going on in there!'

But the goys know whose fault it was.

They're all going, 'What the fock, Ross? It's like we're playing with a seven-man scrum.'

I go, 'How the fock do they know it was me who killed the dolphin?'

Wynney, our blindside flanker, goes, 'He's probably just guessing. Keep your focking head in the game, Rossi.'

I try, except the headaches get worse as the half wears on and now I'm feeling something close to paranoia.

Yes, it was all over Instagram and Facebook and whatever-the-fock else these dudes are into – but I never saw my name anywhere near the story. So how the fock do the Greystones players know?

A minute or two later, I'm getting ready to throw the ball into a lineout.

Bucky goes, 'Cat Germany Four!' which I instantly know means middle.

That's when the Greystones jumpers, all at the same time, stort going, 'Duh-dun!' doing the cello bit from the theme tune to *Jaws*. 'Duh-dun!'

I pull the ball back over my head.

They're like, 'Dundun, dundun, dundun, dundun . . .'

Then, just as I'm about to throw it, their number eight goes, 'Eee-eee-eee-eee-eee-eee-eee-eee!' making the sound of a dolphin. 'Eee-eee-eee-eee-eee-eee-eee-eee!'

Oh, fock!

I end up throwing the ball so long that it totally clears the lineout. Their inside centre gets his hands on it and he's a flier – he evades two tackles and puts the ball under the posts.

It's over and it's not even half-time.

The goys all *turn* on me, then, because they know we're about to be relegated and this time there's going to be no escape act.

Byrom's shouting, 'You're not ploying as a toym!'

And Blissy goes, 'Yeah – and some of us aren't playing at all!' meaning obviously *me*?

My focking head, though. It feels like it's about to explode and I've never been so relieved to hear a whistle blow. As we're walking off the pitch at half-time, I turn around to Byrom and I go, 'I want you to take me off.'

He's like, 'Toyk yoy off? Hoy am Oy putting on?'

'I don't know. Throw on one of the Thirsty Thirds. I'm done. I've fock-all left to give.'

He stares at me, then he looks over his shoulder at Bucky, who just nods.

I sit through Byrom's team talk.

He goes, 'We're oynloy twintoy-throy points daahn – woy can stull wun this mitch,' except no one actually believes him.

He doesn't even sound like he believes it himself.

The Greystones players are already in celebratory mood next door. You can hear the excitement in their voices. They're going to be playing their rugby in Division 2A next season – that's as sure as we're going to be playing ours in Division 2C.

Byrom tells one of the thirds that he's going on. No one says shit to me. That's the way it goes. You don't go crying over fallen comrades while the battle is still raging.

They run back out onto the field. I stay where I am. There's, like, silence in the dressing room. I listen out for the old man. Ten seconds later – reliable as a clock – I hear him go, 'Where the hell is Ross O'Carroll-Kelly? Seapoint's talisman, for heaven's sake!'

I run into the jacks, into trap two, and I make an oral sacrifice to Armitage Shanks, God of Porcelain.

In other words, I spew my ring. Everywhere.


'I wish you'd tell me what happened,' the old man goes.

I'm there, 'I told you, I don't want to talk about it.'

This is, like, the day after the match.

He goes, 'Well, there must be an explanation, Ross. A great player doesn't become a bad player overnight.'

I'm there, 'Well, I've just proven that sometimes they do.'

'Stuff and nonsense! I know what happened. I could tell from the way you were holding your forehead and blinking your eyes.'

'Really?'

'Well, it's obvious, isn't it?'

'Is it?'

'You were poisoned!'

'Poisoned?'

'Happened to the great All Blacks team of 1995, of course – or so it was rumoured. Someone in Greystones obviously slipped something into your water. Although given the quality of what comes out of the taps in County Wicklow, they wouldn't have had to touch it.'

We're sitting in the back of the old man's cor on the way to Coolock. Ronan and K . . . K . . . K . . . K . . . Kennet are sitting in the front.

I'm there, 'Look, I wasn't poisoned alright? If you must know, well, I think I'm suffering from concussion.'

'Concussion?' the old man goes, like it's his first time ever hearing the word. 'Where the hell would you have picked up something like that?'

I'm there, 'Where do you think? Playing rugby.'

'Concussion in rugby? I've never heard of anything so ridiculous!'

'It actually exists.'

'Exists, my foot! No, that was all dreamt up by personal injuries solicitors, a great many of whom are GAA supporters, I shouldn't wonder! No, you were poisoned, Ross! Nothing surer!'

We pull into the cor pork of The Tipsy Wagon, then we climb the iron staircase on the side of the pub to the restaurant upstairs.

On the door, it says 'Mister Wu' and then underneath it's like, 'Beijing – Kowloon – Coolock'.

Ronan tries to take chorge of the situation. He's pretending he's not shitting himself. He's doing a better job of it than I am.

He's there, 'Foorst thing we do when you walk into the restor doddent – what have I alwees toalt you, Rosser? – we look for an alternative route by which to leave.'

'Check yisser exits,' I go.

He's like, 'Check yisser exits – veddy good.'

The old man runs his hand through his hair – I'm just going to call it hair – and goes, 'Let's all just calm down. We are going to sit down and reason this out like business people do.'

Which is easy for him to say. He's not the one who punched Scum in the face and broke his glasses.

With a green, Manila folder tucked under his orm, he pushes the door of the restaurant and in we stroll, the four of us.

It's not difficult to spot Scum. The restaurant is empty, except for him, and then, sitting next to him, his three skanger lieutenants slash capos slash whatever-the-fock you want to call them.

I'm presuming everyone else split when they saw these four fockers arrive.

'Hello there!' the old man goes, at the top of his voice. It's like he's having a business meeting in the Westbury or some shit. The old man offers him his hand and Scum shakes it without standing up.

He's there, 'Chardles, reet?'

'That's right,' the old man goes. 'And you're Scum – nice to put a name to the face! This is my driver, Kennet, my grandson Ronan, whom you know, and my son, Ross, whom, I gather, you've also met.'

Scum stares at me. For about thirty horrible seconds, I'm convinced that he's going to pull either a gun or a knife on me. Eventually, he just goes, 'That day downsteers. It was a looky punch. That's why I ast for you to be hee-or. To say that to you. You caught me unaweers, you sloy bastoord.'

I didn't catch him unawares. It was a genuine decking. I resist the temptation to point that out, though.

He goes, 'Sit thowin – the ford of you,' which we do, on the opposite side of the table. 'This place does be altwees full of Choy Knees. That's how you know it's a good one – doatunt know if you ebber heerd that befower.'

He's clearly a man of culture.

Some Chinese dude – possibly Mister Wu himself – comes over then and hands us all menus – focking comically lorge ones as well.

'Now,' the old man goes, 'if I might suggest an order of business for this meeting . . .'

'You've some fooken balls,' Scum goes, 'meerchin in hee-or and throying to dicthate what . . .'

The old man runs his hand through his hair and Scum stops. It's like he's suddenly lost his train of thought.

The old man goes, 'Yes?'

'Soddy,' Scum goes, 'I caddent . . . I caddent remember what I was apposed to say. Go on, Chardles – what?'

'I was just going to suggest a running order. First item of business, we agree a unilateral truce, then we discuss any grievances that either party may have in a calm and reasoned fashion, then we agree on a way forward that benefits both parties. How does that sound to you chaps?'

He touches his hair again. I swear to God, it's like Scum is hypnotized by it.

'Er, yeah,' he goes. 'That sounts, er, feert enough, Chardles.'

Mister Wu is suddenly back, standing over the table, waiting to take our order. Ronan closes his menu. 'Chicken balls and cuddy sauce,' he goes. Kennet says he'll have the same – so do Scum and the three grunts sitting beside him.

The old man goes, 'I have no idea what that is, but when in Rome, etcetera, etcetera,' and he hands Mister Wu the menu back.

'Okay,' I go, 'just to be different, I'm going to go for the roast duck Cantonese style with egg fried rice, the butterfly king prawns with sweet and sour sauce – and do you have any crabmeat and sweetcorn soup? It's just I don't see it here on the list.'

Mister Wu just stares at me. Everyone at the table stares at me, in fact.

'You'll have chicken balls and cuddy sauce,' Scum goes. 'Thinking you're bettor than ebbyone else.'

I shrug and I go, 'Fine. Fock it, I'll have chicken balls and *cuddy* sauce as well.'

It's probably the only thing that's actually on the menu – the rest is just for show.

Ronan goes, 'So are we agreeing to anutter throose?'

Scum just stares at him for a few seconds, then he offers him his hand across the table. 'Throose, ceasefoyer,' he goes, 'whatebber you wanna call it.'

Ronan shakes it.

'That has to mean that all hostilities are at an end,' the old man goes. 'It means the war is over.'

Scum nods. 'It's ober – feerd as Ine concerdened in addyhow.'

'Next item on the agenda,' the old man goes. 'I think there may be some healing to be done and the best way to start that process is for all parties around the table to talk about the ways in which they've suffered – without recrimination, I might add.'

Scum goes, 'Cad I intedupt you theer, Chardles. I joost wanthed to say at the veddy steert, Ine soddy for shooting Buckets of Blood. Ine veddy fonth of Buckets. Ine an admoyrer. Throyed to recruith him for me own crew a few yee-or ago. That's why I says to the feddas, doatunt hoort him too bad – a flesh woowunt is alls.'

Ro's there, 'Well, if you're apodogizing for that, Ine apodogizing for slashing yisser toyers and breaking yisser windthows. And burdening yisser bus out.'

'And Ine soddy for doing the sayum to you. And for throying to moorder you with machettes.'

The old man goes, 'You see, this is wonderful progress!'

There ends up being silence then for a good, I don't know, sixty seconds or something. I'm actually staring at the blackboard with the dessert specials on it, wondering is there anything that people on this side of the city *won't* deep-fry? Then I realize that they're waiting for me to talk.

'Are you gonna say sumtin,' Scum goes, 'Or are you just gonna sit theer steerdin at the spesh hiddles?'

I'm like, 'What?'

'Seeing as we're all apodogizing to each utter, you can say soddy to me for catching me unaweers wit that punch.'

I end up having to give in to the pressure, of course.

I'm like, 'Yeah, no, I'm sorry for decking you.'

The food arrives and the atmosphere definitely lightens.

The old man is staring at his dinner like me looking at Sudoku – no idea what the fock is going on.

'When they say chicken balls,' he goes, jabbing at it with his fork, 'surely, they don't mean . . .'

Everyone at the table cracks up laughing. The funniest thing of all is that the old man isn't even joking.

Scum points at him. 'I like you,' he goes – and he says it like it's a threat. 'Ine fooken saying that now, Chardles. I like your stoyle – do you get me?'

One crook always appreciates another – that's what I'm tempted to say.

Soon, the compliments are flying back and forth across the table.

'Ronan, that was a lubbly touch of yooers,' Scum goes, 'adding the thrug mixing factoddy to your itiner doddy, where Tommy and the boys got lifted in Seerdies Two.'

And Ronan goes, 'Well, I coult say the sayum ting about you getting that Tom Vodden-Lawdor lookalike to gerron to the bus at the end of yooer toower and tell ebbyone to say theer prayers. I have to say, feer fooks to you for that.'

It goes on like this for a good, I don't know, fifteen minutes while they all tuck into their so-called food and me and the old man chase ours around the plate with our forks.

When the plates are eventually clear, the old man goes, 'Now, shall we get down to business?' and he pushes his plate aside, lays his Manila folder down on the table and opens it up. He pulls out eight little, I don't know, booklets, six or seven pages long, which are stapled together. He hands one to everyone at the table.

'The fook is this?' Scum goes.

He's obviously not a reader. My reaction is pretty much the same.

The old man's there, 'It's a business plan. I thought it might form the basis of a discussion as to how we can move forward in a way that suits everybody.'

Scum looks through it. 'Veddy detailed,' he goes, looking at the old man over the top of his glasses. 'Veddy fooken detailed.'

He's Sellotaped the earpiece of his glasses back on, I notice, instead of shelling out for a new pair.

The old man smiles. He's there, 'You see, Scum, I'm a firm believer in the market. Ross here will tell you that, as a child, I used to take him to Musgrave's, the cash-and-carry in Sallynoggin, just to listen to the tills ringing. The sound would quite literally bring tears to my eyes.'

Scum and his goons all laugh. They think he's focking joking.

Ronan suddenly goes. 'What are these figures, Grandda? On the back payuch?'

The old man's there, 'Those are the projected earnings for the two businesses over the next five years. That's how much I estimate these tours could be pulling in – provided you don't keep putting each other out of business. As you can see from the map on page 6, Scum, I'm suggesting that Ronan, Nudger and Buckets of Blood's tour operates from College Green and that yours operates from O'Connell Street. And you divide up the territory between you. Ronan, your tour will focus on Series One, Two and Three of the show. Scum, yours will focus on Series Four and Five and any future Six. I'm thinking that, far from being in competition with each other, The *Love/Hate* Tour of Dublin and *Love/Hate*: The Tour could complement each other. You could encourage your customers to do both!'

Scum sneaks a quick look at Ronan to try to get his reaction.

'Are these numbers reet?' Ro goes.

The old man's there, 'They're actually conservative, Ronan. I took the liberty of asking a chap I play golf with – he's in market research – to look at the figures for me. He's convinced that you're only scratching the bloody well surface.'

Ronan and Scum are both just nodding.

The old man goes, 'And that's where I come in. Like I said, I see this as a business with enormous potential. As an entrepreneur, I wish to invest in both The *Love/Hate* Tour of Dublin and *Love/Hate*: The Tour. I want to capitalize both businesses to help you advertise and market yourselves properly – national newspapers, etcetera, etcetera – and also provide you with vehicles.'

'We boat alretty hab a bus,' Scum goes.

'I'm not talking about one bus each, Scum. I'm talking about six buses each – and that's only the beginning. Can any of your chaps here drive a bus, Scum?'

Scum looks at them. Two of them shrug. They'll give it a go.

The old man's there, 'I want to invest €250,000 in the two tours, which, under my proposal, would become franchise operations of the same business. In return, I'm asking for 50% equity in the company.'

Scum and Ronan's eyes meet across the table and they smile at each other.

'What do *you* think?' Scum goes.

Ronan's like, 'What's there to loowuz? That's a lot of bread.'

He's un-focking-believable, my old man. You'd have to give it to him. We walk into a situation where I think there's a decent chance that we're going to be murdered, chopped up and dumped in the sea. And he comes away with a 50% share of two soon-to-be-thriving businesses.

An hour later, as we're getting up from the table, Scum shakes my old man's hand and goes, 'Can I say sumtin to you, Chardles?'

The old man goes, 'Yes, of course, do.'

'You've got a way about you – addyone ever telt you that?'

'Well,' the old man goes, 'modesty precludes and so forth!'

Scum's there, 'Well, *Ine* fooken saying it to you – you do. I doatunt know if it's the heer or what, but you have a way with people. You shoult be in poditics or something,' and I watch this register on my old man's face.

He's just like, 'That's interesting.'

I'm the first one out the door – as you can imagine. I tip down the metal staircase and that's when my phone all of a sudden rings. I check the screen. It's Byrom. For ten seconds, I consider not actually *answering* it?

I don't even know why I do in the end.

I'm like, 'Hey.'

He goes, 'Dud yoy not git moy mussages?'

'Yeah, no, I haven't been listening to them. I just wanted to drop off the radar for a while.'

Of course what I actually mean is drop off the side of the Earth.

'Yoy didn't hear the result?' he goes.

I'm there, 'No, I presume we lost.'

'Woy droy.'

'Drew?'

'Droy.'

'How?'

'Sinnoy had a bloynder of a second haahf. He was determined to

335

stop Groystoynes wunning the loyg – Sunday's Will pupped thum at the poyst.'

'So what does a draw do for us? Are we not still relegated?'

'We funushed sicond bottom. Moyns we've got a ploy-off – nixt woykind. Against Bruff. Yoy remimber woy talked abaaht Bruff?'

'The B is silent.'

'The boy is soylunt – ixictloy. Rossoy, ut's gonna be one hill of a mitch.'

'Good luck with it. I genuinely mean that.'

'We caahn't wun ut withaaht yoy, Moyte.'

'Byrom, I'm not coming back. I've lost the respect of the goys. I've lost the dressing room.'

'Just come to troyning on Tuesdoy. You moyt hear something thut'll choynge your moynd.'


So into the clubhouse I go – why, I don't know.

But the dressing room ends up being *empty*? There's, like, no one around.

Bucky suddenly sticks his head around the door and goes, 'Rossi, we're in the bor – team meeting.'

I'm thinking, team meeting? Then I'm wondering have they copped it – that I'm suffering from, like, possibly concussion?

I'm like, 'Yeah, no, do we know what this meeting is about?' as I follow him along the corridor towards the bor.

He goes, 'Senny wants to say something to the team.'

So into the bor we go. All the goys are sitting around on the benches and Senny is standing up in front of them.

I'm like, 'What's the deal here?'

Senny goes, 'Rossi, sit down,' which I do, next to Dordo, our scrum-half.

Senny clears his throat.

'Okay,' he goes, 'last week, when we were here for Strength and Conditioning, I made certain allegations against Rossi, namely that he tried to get off with my girlfriend in Club 92. Torah was the one who actually told me that he made a move on her. Well, on Satur-day night – after the Greystones match, in fact – she told me that it

336

was bullshit. She basically made it up because I didn't seem upset enough when she told me she was thinking of going to Montauk on a Ji in the summer.'

Everyone's like, 'What?'

Women. I've loved thousands of them – never understood one.

'So,' Senny goes, 'I just wanted to say this in front of all the goys – because I actually accused you in front of all the goys – I was out of order, we're talking bang out of order. You've been an unbelievable mentor to me and a lot of others in this dressing room since you came in. I hope you can, I don't know, forgive me.'

I'm like, 'Dude, it's gone – like a fort in the wind.'

'Well,' he goes, 'I also owe you an apology for something else. Look, I told my cousin on the Greystones team that you killed that dolphin. And, yeah, I knew they'd probably use it against you. I'm sorry for that as well.'

I'm there, 'I genuinely don't know why killing a dolphin is such a big focking issue. You kill, I don't know, a salmon or a cod and no one says shit. You kill a dolphin and suddenly it's all this. It's only a fish.'

Dordo goes, 'I think a dolphin is actually a mammal, Rossi.'

I laugh at that.

I'm there, 'Yeah, I've had that argument with so many people over the years. Think of the focking shape, Dordo. And if you all remember, I killed it in self-defence. And now Gerry Thornley's getting involved. Jesus Christ, Ireland just won the Six Nations and there's a World Cup just around the corner. You'd think he'd have more important things to write about.'

Bucky steps in then, like a true captain. He goes, 'If anyone from the IRFU storts sniffing around, asking questions, we tell them the same thing – it never focking happened. It's just Greystones being Greystones.'

'Dicks,' everyone, at the same time, goes.

Byrom's there, 'Look, laahst woykind, the first haahf in Groystoynes, was the first toym in nearloy throy months that woy dudn't ploy togither as a toym. Woy forgot what it was thut moyd us strong – ut was eer togithernuss. Thut's the oynloy woy we're gonna boyt Bruff. And, Rossoy, we're not gonna doy ut wuthaaht yoy. So what doy yoy soy, Moyte?'

And I just go, 'Why are we sitting here like a bunch of knobs? Let's go back to focking work.'

I wake up feeling – yeah, no – okay.

As in, I don't have a headache, although I *can* smell cigor smoke and I'm wondering is that another symptom, or am I possibly having a stroke, until I open my eyes to see the old man standing at the end of the bed, smoking a Cohiba so big you could snap twelve inches off the thing and still have enough left to stir your porridge.

I'm like, 'What the fock are you doing here?'

He goes, 'Your good lady wife let me in.'

'What time is it? It's the middle of the night.'

'It's the middle of the day, Ross. One o'clock, to be precise. I just wondered did you have any plans for Friday afternoon?'

'That's the day before we play Bruff. No, I'll probably just take it easy. Visualization exercises and blah, blah, blah.'

'Well, I'm here with an invitation for you.'

'An invitation to what?'

'To Charles O'Carroll-Kelly's May Day Political Think-In.'

I actually *laugh*? I'm there, 'I thought you'd finished with all that bullshit. I thought you'd retired from – what was it? – public life?'

He goes, 'It's turning out to be quite the year for comebacks, isn't it?'

Charles O'Carroll-Kelly's May Day Political Think-Ins were a tradition that stretched back – fock, it must be, like, forty years?

Even when I was a kid, the first day of May was always the day of the year when the old man invited around all of his friends from politics, business and the Law Library, to drink Cognac and one-hundred-year-old port and discuss, at a very annoying volume, various ways to make Ireland a better place for all of its citizens, but especially those who work in politics, business and the Law Library.

The Think-Ins stopped about five years ago, after the old man had his hort attack in Monte Corlo, then announced his retirement from public life in a seven-page letter to *The Irish Times* which they didn't bother their holes publishing.

He promised Helen that he'd embrace a healthier lifestyle and he seemed to be definitely *serious* about it? He walked to Donnybrook village every day for the paper, gave up the cheese and the brandy and cut back to seven cigors and two Shanahan's steak dinners a week.

And, of course, he was suddenly more *zen* about shit? He could watch the politicians on *Vincent Browne Tonight* without feeling the need to shout, 'Hypocrite! Hypocrite! Hypocrite!' at the TV screen until his face turned red and the veins in his forehead stood out like motorways on Google Maps. The worst you'd hear out of him would be something along the lines of, '*Parturiunt montes, nascetur ridiculus mus!*' followed by a sort of, like, knowing chuckle.

And that, the world probably presumed, was the end of Charles O'Carroll-Kelly. Until, well, like the dude just said: 'It's turning out to be quite the year for comebacks, isn't it?'

I'm there, 'So what exactly are *you* coming back as?'

'Let me just say this first, Ross. You've proved something to me these past few months. Something about second acts. I mean, first acts are all very well, but they unfold in a largely predictable way, don't you find? But it's second acts that contain all the drama, all the surprise, all the excitement.'

'You've changed since you put that thing on your head.'

'There's no point denying it, Ross, I have changed. I feel like the man I was forty years ago.'

'God focking help us.'

'The final straw was talking to Scum the other day, when he said I should be in politics. I went home and I said to Helen, if I can persuade Scum to do what I say, then there has to be a place for me in Dáil Éireann.'

'Politics? Who are you going to run for? I thought Fianna Fáil focked you out for being too crooked even for them.'

'Aha! That information is embargoed until Friday, I'm afraid! You'll get it along with everyone else!'

He turns to leave.

I'm there, 'By the way, thanks – you know, for sorting out the Ronan situation.'

He goes, 'Business. Always. Finds. A way.'

'At the same time, I'm still saying fair focks.'

'I'd better be off. I'm having lunch with your mother.'

'How is she? Not that I care – I'm just asking.'

'Heartbroken is the word! And still rather shaken up by what happened at the funeral Mass.'

'Still, two billion squids – I'm sure that's going to help with the grieving process.'

'I think your mother would happily live as a pauper for the rest of her life if she could have Ari back for even one day.'

There's, like, silence then. It's that kind of silence where everyone in the room knows what's just been said is horseshit but no one wants to actually *acknowledge* it?

I go, 'You don't think she *did* kill him, do you?'

He laughs like it's the most ridiculous thing he's ever heard. He's like, 'Ross! Listen to what you're saying! This is your mother we're talking about!'

'Yeah, no, I'm just putting it out there.'

'Fionnuala O'Carroll-Kelly, Ross! It's not so long ago that *Irish Tatler* was giving her an award for her humanitarianism.'

'Yeah, no, there is that, I suppose.'

'I rest my case!'


On Thursday night, we train like mad men, knowing that it's the last week we're all going to be together like this. Senny won't be back next season – and I *certainly* won't? A few of the others will probably drift away, too, find birds, stort careers, go travelling, maybe even emigrate.

And Byrom is on his way, too. He pulls me to one side as I'm leaving the clubhouse and he tells me the news that he's quitting after Saturday's match.

'Thet's just betwoyn moy and yoy,' he goes. 'Oy doyn't want the goys knoying – not before the goym.'

I'm like, 'Where are you going?', thinking he's going to say Pembroke or some other cricket club.

Instead, he goes, 'Oy'm goying hoym, Rossoy. Oy'm goying hoym, to Noy Zoyland, to boy wuth moy kuds.'

'I thought you couldn't bear to see, I don't know, another man raising them.'

'Soying another min royse them is a daahn soyt bitter than not boying wuth them at all.'

'I suppose.'

'Oy've realoyzed, thoyse laahst few woyks, Oy've just boyn hoyding aaht here. Ut's toym Oy minned up and wint hoym.'

I tell him fair focks.

He goes, 'Are woy gonna wun on Sitterdoy, Rossoy?'

'We'll either win,' I go, 'or die trying.'

I love it as an exit line, so I automatically turn around and stort making my way back to the cor.

Ten seconds later, I'm looking over my left hammer, reversing out of my porking space, when I suddenly spot a familiar figure sitting behind the wheel of a red Renault Clio, porked next to mine. I end up having to switch off the engine and get out.

She obviously sees me coming because she's already storted rolling her eyes and shaking her head. She still makes me tap on the window before she rolls it down, though.

I'm there, 'Hey, Torah.'

She goes, 'Hi,' but she doesn't give me any more than that, except, 'Is Senan still inside?'

I actually laugh. I'm there, 'You've some nerve showing your face around here after what you pulled?'

She goes, 'What *I* pulled?'

'Yeah, no, telling Senny that I made a move on you.'

'You did make a move on me.'

'What?'

'You tried to kiss me. In Club 92.'

'So why did you tell Senny that you made it up?'

'Because he couldn't cope with the idea of you betraying him.'

'So you took a bullet?'

'I shouldn't have said anything in the first place. He had enough on his mind, worrying was he going to get into the academy.'

I'm there, 'I tried to explain to him that making a move on one another's girlfriends would have been considered pretty standard behaviour in the rugby world I grew up in. He didn't seem to want to listen.'

'Yeah,' she goes, 'I don't particularly *care* what you consider standard behaviour?' and she suddenly puts the Clio into reverse, then backs out of her spot, but without looking in her mirror or over her shoulder.

I hear a sudden bump and then a roar behind me. It's like, 'Aaarrrggghhh!!!'

Torah slams on the brake and throws the door open. I race around to the back of the cor to find Dordo lying on the deck in obvious agony. I look down and I notice that a bone is poking out of the side of his Cantos where I know a bone shouldn't be.

He's like, 'Aaarrrggghhh!!!'

Torah goes, 'Oh my God!' when she sees him – and she doesn't even know how vital he is to the team.

I'm there, 'Yeah, fair focks, Torah, you've just taken out our scrum-half.'

All the goys come suddenly racing out of the clubhouse to find out what the screams of agony are about.

Byrom's going, 'Daahdoy, are you alroyt, Moyte?' hoping against hope – like the rest of us.

Dordo goes, 'My focking leg! It's focking broken!'

We all look at each other and we're all thinking the exact same thing: Where are we going to get a replacement number nine at such short notice?

It's a cruel, cruel game. But I wouldn't change a single thing about it.

At least we wait until the ambulance has arrived from Loughlin-stown before we stort openly discussing options.

'Is there innyone on the sicond toym?' Byrom goes.

Bucky shakes his head and he's like, 'Frankie Fallon is their scrum-half. He's getting married on Saturday.'

The focking idiot – but that's another day's work.

'What abaht the Thirsty Thirds?' Byrom goes.

Maho goes, 'Colin Carey. But he did his cruciate on the last day of the season.'

That's when I hear a cor boot slam and I spot Christian walking towards the clubhouse with his gear bag slung over his shoulder – obviously planning to do an hour in the gym.

I'm like, 'Holy shit! What about Christian?'

Byrom goes, 'What, thet moyte of yours?'

'He played scrum-half once or twice for us back in the day.'

'Could he full un for Daahdoy?'

'He's got a rugby brain, Byrom – very similar to mine.'

Thirty seconds later, Christian is in the dressing room, taking his training gear out of his bag when suddenly, like, nine or ten of us pile into the room and we're all just, like, staring at him.

He's there, 'What?'

I'm like, 'How would you feel about playing for us against Bruff on Saturday?'

He laughs. He's there, 'Are you serious?'

I go, 'Have you ever known me to joke about rugby?'

He doesn't answer – doesn't need to.

He's like, 'What's going on?'

'Daahdoy's broyken his lig,' Byrom goes.

Christian's there, 'So, what, you want me to play scrum-half?' and what's incredible is that I don't see even a flicker of self-doubt in his eyes. 'Not a problem,' he just goes.

The Jesuits raised us well.


I arrive home and *they're* in the house? As in Sorcha's old pair.

'Ah, for fock's sake!' I go, when I see *him* sitting in the living room – in my chair, by the way.

'Ross,' Sorcha goes, 'don't be rude. I told you my mom and dad were coming over for Dad's birthday.'

'I still stand by what I said,' I go – refusing to even acknowledge him or his ridiculous birthday.

They don't even have the focking TV on. They're sitting around talking – that's what kind of a family you're dealing with – about fock knows what, probably Africa and its problems because, as I pushed the door, I heard Sorcha mention 'dengue fever and other vectorborne diseases' and that's an exact quote.

I'm like, 'Where's Honor?'

'She's upstairs,' Sorcha goes, 'reading the boys a night-night story.'

It makes me automatically smile.

She goes, 'Tell her to hurry up, Ross – we're going to have birth-day cake.'

I tip quietly up the stairs and I stand on the landing. I can hear Honor's voice and then Johnny, Leo and Brian shouting their reactions to the various twists and turns in the story that their big sister is telling them.

Again, I smile – can't help it.

It's only when I get closer to their bedroom that I realize that Honor isn't reading them, I don't know, *The Three Little Pigs* or *The Gingerbread Man* or anything like it.

I give the door a little shove.

She's standing in front of their three cots, which are all lined up against the wall. Johnny, Leo and Brian are standing up, their orms hanging over the top bor, staring at her like monkeys waiting for nuts to be tossed.

'Okay,' Honor goes, 'who can say, motherfocking bastard?'

At the top of his lungs, Brian goes, 'Motherfocking bastard! Motherfocking bastard! Motherfocking bastard!'

Honor goes, 'Good boy, Brian!' and she tosses – I swear to fock – an M&M into his cot. Brian gets down on his hands and knees, searching for it like a pig looking for truffles.

'Okay,' Honor goes, 'Bollocksing shit fock!'

Oh! My! Focking! God!

'It was you!' I hear myself go. 'You've been teaching them how to swear!'

Honor turns around and sees me for the first time. She doesn't seem to care that she's been caught in the act.

She's like, 'So?'

I'm there, 'Honor, you're bang out of order here – and I'd usually be the first one to defend you. I'm going to have to tell Sorcha.'

'Tell her if you want,' she goes, an evil smile creeping across her face. 'But when I tell her your little secret, this is going to seem like nothing.'

I'm there, 'What little secret?'

'I told you I'd get you back, didn't I – for what happened at the wedding?'

'You're bluffing. I genuinely hope you're bluffing.'

'Someone with as many things to hide as you should really be more careful about what he leaves in his pockets.'

Oh. Sweet. Suffering. Fock.

It's like a bucket of ice-cold water has been thrown over me.

I run out of the boys' room and into our bedroom. Into the walk-in wardrobe I go. I grab my famous Henri Lloyd sailing jacket, then I put my hand in the pocket. It's empty. I check all the other pockets. They're gone. The letters from Nelson Mandela and the paperwork from Sotheby's saying that they're not letters from Nelson Mandela.

I hear Honor going down the stairs and then I hear Sorcha go, 'Hi, Honor, we're about to cut Grandad's cake!'

I peg it out of the room and down the stairs, going, 'Shit, shit, shit, shit shit!'

In response, I can hear the boys in their room going, 'Shit, shit, shit!' and then, 'Focking shitting bollocks!'

Into the living room I go to find Sorcha and her old pair staring at me sadly. It's like there's been a *death* or some shit?

Sorcha goes, 'Ross, Honor said she needs to talk to us about something serious – something that's been, like, *troubling* her?'

I'm there, 'I'll be very interested to hear what this is about, Babes.'

Honor goes, 'I've been carrying this secret around with me for, like, days now and it's really upsetting me.'

Sorcha's old man goes, 'Spit it out, girl!' because he can see that she's tearing the orse out of it and he doesn't trust her anyway.

Sorcha goes, 'Dad, stop! Can't you see she's upset? Honor, what's this thing that's upsetting you? I'm so glad you and I have the kind of relationship where you feel you can confide in me.'

Honor's like, 'It's something that you're going to be – oh my God – so upset about. It was something that Dad did.'

Sorcha's old man's ears instantly prick up. He's only dying to believe the worst about me.

Honor goes, 'I'm really sorry, Dad. I tried to keep it to myself, but I just think Mum needs to know?'

'Honor,' Sorcha goes, 'what did your father do?'

And Honor looks me in the eye and goes, 'He killed a dolphin!'

I freeze. Holy shit. *That's* her secret? Me killing a dolphin?

She goes, 'What happened was, I was looking for that photograph that he took of us all last year when we went to Tayto Pork. I wanted to delete it because I look fat in it. And I just happened to accidentally go into his text messages and he was talking about how he killed a dolphin. It was when he went to Bundoran.'

I actually laugh – it's *relief* more than anything? I'm there, 'Yeah, no, it's true. I'm going to have to hold my hands up to that one. I literally did kill a dolphin.'

I can't tell you how happy I am. But then I look at Sorcha's face. She's very definitely *not* laughing?

She goes, 'Do you think this is funny, Ross?'

I'm there, 'No, I don't think it's funny. All I'll say in my defence is that you don't know the circumstances in which it happened.'

She gives me a look of just, like, disbelief.

'The circumstances?' she goes. 'In what *circumstances* is it okay to kill a dolphin, Ross?'

I'm like, 'Sorcha, don't be so naïve. People think they're great just because they go around smiling all the time. Dolphins can be pricks, Sorcha. Wake up to that fact.'

'Pricks?'

'Yeah, I'm using that word. And this one was a real prick. He pretended to be a shork.'

She doesn't have an answer to that. But just as her old man senses that I'm getting the upper hand in the conversation, he decides to throw his thoughts into the mix.

He goes, 'Bundoran? Wait a minute, I read about this incident – in *The Irish Times*.'

I go, 'Yeah, I think it comes as a surprise to everyone in this room that you even *read* the sports pages.'

Honor is obviously worried that Sorcha has bought my mistaken identity storyline, because she goes, 'I've been really upset about it, Mom. I've been having nightmares. I think I'm disturbed.'

I'm there, 'We've all moved on from this, Honor. I can't believe you're still talking about it. I was surfing and I saw a fin in the water. I thought it was a shork and I reacted by smashing it over the head with my surfboard. There's nothing more to say about it than that.'

Sorcha is still dubious, though. She goes, 'Ross, do you know how much money I've given to dolphin conservation charities over the years?'

I'm there, 'A lot would be my guess.'

'I've got three standing orders.'

'Yeah, no, I thought it was going to be more that that.'

'And you're going around just gratuitously killing them.'

'Seriously, Sorcha, you're worse than Gerry Thornley. We kill millions of fish in this country every focking day. I don't know why everyone's so obsessed with this one focking dolphin.'

'A dolphin isn't a fish, Ross. It's a mammal.'

'Think about what you've just said there, Sorcha. Then think about the focking shape.'

Honor goes, 'I really feel I've been affected by this, Mom – I'm talking, like, *mentally*? What if I end up becoming a serial killer?'

I'm there, 'If you ended up becoming a serial killer, Honor, I honestly think I'd say, "Hey, she could have turned out a lot focking worse."'

Sorcha goes, 'Ross, can you please leave the room?'

I'm like, 'I haven't had any birthday cake.'

Then she says it again – except she *roars* it this time? 'Ross, can you please leave the room?'

I'm there, 'Fine. I probably shouldn't be eating cake anyway. I've got an important match coming up in two days – if anyone in this house knew the first thing about rugby.'

As I'm leaving the room, I hear Honor go, 'Oh! My God! Hill! Air!' even though – little does she know – the joke is actually on her.

Five minutes later, I'm lying on the bed, reflecting on another one of the Rossmeister General's famous escapes. Better to be hung for a dead dolphin than a dead South African president. That's my philosophy.

But that's when the question suddenly hits me out of nowhere. If Honor didn't steal the Mandela letters from my pocket, then who the fock did?

And the answer comes to me straightaway.

Oh! Focking! Shit!

It had to be Caleb.

Flidais looks at me in a way that I can't even put into words. It *is* eight o'clock on a Friday morning. And she's probably copped by now that the phone number I gave her was basically horseshit.

She's like, 'What the hell do *you* want?'

The more I disappoint women sexually, the more they seem to want me. What's *that* about?

'I'm not here to see you,' I go. 'I'm here to see Caleb. He stole something from me that night I was here.'

She's there, 'Oh, let me guess – your underwear?'

I go, 'No, nothing like that. It was just some letters from Nelson Mandela. It's a long story. Suffice it to say that if I don't get them back, my marriage is going to be over.'

'You told me your marriage *was* over.'

'Hey, maybe you just heard what you wanted to hear.'

'No, you *actually* said it, Ross. You said you were only staying together for the kids.'

'Jesus Christ, grow up, Flidais. Seriously, if you're thinking about going back into the dating game, you'd better develop a better bullshit detector – that's all I'm saying on the subject. Now, is Caleb home or not?'

That's when he suddenly appears in the hall behind her. He tips down the stairs, dressed for school.

I'm there, 'Caleb, I need those letters.'

He goes, 'What does this idiot want?'

'Caleb, look, I know you and me didn't exactly get off to the best of storts. A lot of that was down to me – I'm going to admit that. But you could do a lot of damage with those letters.'

'What letters?'

'Come on, don't play the innocent. The eight letters that Nelson Mandela wrote to Sorcha – which are of massive sentimental value to the girl – and then the letter from Sotheby's saying they're basically bullshit.'

He looks at his old dear, pretending to be baffled. He goes, 'I have literally no idea what he's talking about.'

I'm there, 'Look, I need them back. So, as a gesture of goodwill, I'm going to do something for you,' and now it's my turn to look at Flidais. 'Your son didn't steal Sorcha's bras,' I go. 'Or her knickers for that matter.'

She's there, 'Excuse me?'

It's a bit early in the morning for all of this and I'm saying that in her defence.

I'm there, 'Look, he was definitely perving over her and generally creeping us all out. But he didn't take her underwear. Honor planted all that shit on him. She set him up because he was only using her to get to her old dear.'

Flidais looks at me, appalled.

'You let me think it was Caleb?' she goes. 'And you knew the truth all along?'

I'm there, 'Don't twist this around to make me seem like the bad goy. It was Honor who did it. And she had her reasons. Your son made her feel like she was just a Plain Jane, which she probably is, in fairness. Okay, Caleb, I've done that for you – now give me the letters.'

He's there, 'I already told you. I don't know anything *about* any letters.'

He seems to be telling the truth.

Flidais goes, 'You heard that, did you? Now get the hell away from my door.'

She slams the door in my face. She's hurt. I'm not saying she doesn't have her reasons.

I shout through the door, 'There's bigger wankers than me out there, Flidais! You'll hopefully find that out in time.'

Then I turn on my heel and I walk back to the cor. I sit there for, like, a minute or so, just turning this thing over and over in my head. If Honor didn't take the letters and Caleb didn't take the letters, then what the fock happened to them?

It's turning out to be a genuine mystery.

I'm just about to turn the key in the ignition when there's a tap on the window on the passenger side. I look up. It ends up being Caleb. I open the electric window.

I'm like, 'I can't believe I got you off the hook for nothing.'

He smiles at me. 'Not for nothing,' he goes, then he reaches inside his school jumper and pulls out an envelope, which is, like, folded in two. He opens it out. I can see the little logo on the front saying Sotheby's.

I'm like, 'Caleb, please – I told your old dear the truth.'

He's there, 'Yes, you did,' and he hands the envelope to me through the window.

'Look,' I go, 'I'm sorry for everything, including – you know – doing the dirty deed with your mother.'

He's there, 'She has a weakness for assholes.'

I laugh. I suppose I can *afford* to?

I'm like, 'Look, either way, you don't know what it means to me to get this back. I can actually fully focus now on tomorrow's match and the job of keeping Seapoint in . . . wait a minute, this envelope's empty.'

He's there, 'Yes, I know.'

'So where are the letters from Mandingo and the bit of paper from Sotheby's saying they're a crock?'

He smiles at me, like he's waited for this moment for a long time.

'I cycled up to your house this morning at seven o'clock. I posted them through the letterbox – in an envelope addressed to Sorcha.'

Shit, I stepped over that on the way out the door half an hour ago.

I look at the clock in the cor. It's, like, ten past eight. If I really put my foot down, there's a chance I could still get back to the gaff before Sorcha finds it.

Caleb's there, 'Drive carefully, Ross!' as I do a quick wheelspin and tear off in the direction of the Vico Road.

Five minutes later, I'm walking through the front door. The first thing I do, of course, is check the floor. Shit, it's gone.

Then I'm thinking, Okay, try to think of a way to spin this. You've got out of tighter corners than this, Rossmeister.

And that's when I hear Sorcha's voice from the end of the hall-way. 'It's okay,' she goes, 'I found it, Ross.'

I can see from her face that she's been crying. I notice the Nelson Mandela letters in her hand.

Of course I still fancy my chances of bluffing my way out of it.

I'm there, 'Bad news in the post, Sorcha?'

She goes, 'This didn't come in the regular post. But funnily enough, do you know what did, Ross?'

'Er, no.'

'A letter for you. I accidentally opened it. It was from a solicitor. That woman from the Computer Laboratory in Sandyford is suing you for sexual harassment.'

'Random. I take it that's the reason you're upset?'

'Well, for most wives, that'd be enough, I suppose. But when you're married to someone like you, Ross, you never know what's coming next. So I opened the second envelope – a brown one. No stamp. Someone obviously pushed it through the letterbox.'

'Again, I'm going to say random.'

'It turns out that those letters, which I've cherished all these years, weren't written by Madiba after all.'

'Any specific idea who did write them?'

'There was also a note in the envelope, Ross. From Caleb.'

'Caleb? Why is that name familiar?'

'He said he found them in your jacket pocket. While you were upstairs with his mother.'

There's no point in me lying here. But, equally, I think, Fock it, I might as well give it a go.

I'm there, 'That kid and his lies again. I think he belongs in psy-chiatric care.'

Coolly, calmly, she goes, 'Ross, I want you out of this house.'

I'm like, 'Sorcha, can we possibly wait a day or two to do this?

I've got this match tomorrow, bear in mind, and it's important that I don't let anything affect my focus.'

'I've packed you a bag. It's upstairs on the landing. Kiss Honor and the boys goodbye.'

'Sorcha, do you not think you're possibly overreacting?'

'I've spoken to my mom and dad.'

'Yeah, I'd say *they* had a lot to say on the subject.'

'Yes, they did. And now I need some time by myself to decide what I'm going to do.'

I arrive at the old man's gaff in the early afternoon, with my bag slung over my shoulder, to find the place full of *his* old mates.

I totally forgot it was the first of May.

The gaff is so rammers, in fact, that I end up having to literally fight my way through crowds of people to even find him. It's just like old times, except there seems to be even *more* excitement for whatever reason.

I hear some barrister mate of Hennessy's go, 'He's like Charles O'Carroll-Kelly from years ago! No, no, he's the Charles O'Carroll-Kelly I knew thirty years ago!'

I finally spot him through a scrum of bodies in the living room. He's smoking a Cohiba, running his hand through his hair, and he's telling the story about the time at a charity auction when he outbid the great Michael Fingleton for the prize of dinner at The Dorchester with the great Jack Kyle.

I end up spoiling the punchline for him.

'You ended up inviting Michael Fingleton along to The Dorchester as a third guest,' I go. 'I can't believe you're still dining out on that story.'

He's not even pissed off with me. He's like, 'Kicker! What about this turn-out? Like the old days, eh?'

I'm like, 'Yeah, no, whatever. I'm going to be staying with you for a while. I hope Helen's cool with that. Sorcha's focked me out of the house.'

He's pretty shocked by the news, in fairness to him. 'She's thrown you out?' he goes. 'What, the day before Seapoint take on Bruff with their All Ireland League Division 2B survival at stake?'

'There was no talking to her?'

'Did you mention that you needed to remain focused what with the match tomorrow?'

'Tried to. But you know what women are like.'

'*Amare et sapere vix deo conceditur*, Ross.'

'I don't know what that means.'

'Does anyone, I'm inclined to wonder?'

'I'm probably going to need some money, by the way. I may need to pay off an Indian I supposedly sexually harrassed. That's got nothing to do with why Sorcha focked me out, by the way, before you try to make that connection.'

'Well, it's not a problem, Ross. I'll talk to Hennessy about making some kind of settlement.'

'Do you not want to know what it's even about?'

'It'll be something or other, I'm sure. Anyway, before I make the big announcement, Hennessy and I have a tradition that we must observe!'

Off he goes.

I'm about to head upstairs and get settled into my room when all of a sudden Christian arrives. I'm pretty surprised to see him here, but not half as surprised as he is to see me.

I'm like, 'What's wrong? You're still playing for us tomorrow, aren't you?'

He's there, 'Yeah, of course. But I just called out to Honalee. Sorcha said you two were having problems and you were going to be living here for the time being.'

'Yeah, no, the day before we play Bruff,' I go, 'and she decides to spring that one on me. She knows how to pick her moments, I'll say that for the girl.'

'So what happened?'

'I might as well tell you. She found out that those Nelson Mandela letters were forgeries – even though I should have told her about Oisinn's port in the whole thing. Then there was me killing that dolphin. And riding a woman with a skinhead. And another thing where I sexually harrassed an Indian.'

'Jesus Christ, Ross.'

'I know. I need to possibly simplify my life. And seeing as it's all coming out now, I should possibly also mention that I lied to you.'

'To me?'

'About Lauren saying that she'd come back to you if you got your shit together. I only said that so you *would* get your shit together. It was the carrot-and-stick approach. Lauren was the carrot.'

'Ross, me and Lauren are over.'

'I know that now. She's no interest in you. I should have told you that from the beginning. Some dick called Loic. A cinema photographer, by all accounts. He sounds like a real piece of work.'

'What I mean, Ross, is that I'm cool with it.'

'How could you be?'

'Ross, I've met someone myself.'

'Who? You're a dork focking horse!'

'Look, I might as well tell you, it's Sorcha's friend, Muirgheal?'

'Muirgheal? From that focking Africa thing?'

'Yeah, we've been seeing a bit of each other.'

'Here, settle an argument for me, will you? Does she still make that funny slurping noise when she kisses?'

'What?'

'Forget I said anything. Fair focks is what I actually mean.'

Suddenly, I notice the old man take his place on the sofa. Then Hennessy sits down beside him. There's a lot of excited chatter in the room. It's, like, an air of *anticipation* or something?

I turn around to Christian and I go, 'You know Hennessy there is going to destroy you in the divorce courts?'

Christian laughs. 'Yeah, I know,' he goes, 'I've got all that to look forward to as well!'

I notice Kennet appear from nowhere. He goes, 'L . . . L . . . L . . . Layties and genteddle men, can we p . . . p . . . p . . . please have sidence ford a moment.'

I'm suddenly thinking, They're not going to do it, are they? They're not about to do the Cock of Foxrock?

There's, like, suddenly a *hush* in the room? I'm thinking, Oh my God, they *are* going to do it.

The Cock of Foxrock was an annual endurance test in which my old man attempted to eat a 200-gramme block of mature red Cheddar faster than Hennessy could drink a pint of lager with a dessert spoon. Traditionally, the winner – who was crowned the Cock of Foxrock – got to make the keynote speech that was the centrepiece of Charles O'Carroll-Kelly's May Day Political Think-In and set the tone for the twelve months ahead.

Middle-aged professionals can be terrible dicks when they get together with drink on them.

I suppose the Cock of Foxrock would have to be classed as an extreme sport now, given the medical histories of the two men about to contest it. The old man's not even supposed to be drinking (which he is) or smoking (which he is), never mind shoving a block of Cheddar into his face (which he's about to). And Hennessy's not exactly triathlon material either, with his fur-lined orteries – the only thing about the man that's even remotely cuddly.

Kennet places a block of Davidstow Reserve in front of my old man and a pint of, I'm presuming, Heineken and a spoon in front of Hennessy.

Then he's like, 'M . . . M . . . M . . . Meerks . . . S . . . S . . . S . . . Set . . . G . . . G . . . G . . . Go!'

There's, like, a lot of cheers, or rather roars of support, most of them for my old man, although Hennessy also has *his* supporters, too, to be fair to the focker.

The old man tears off a mouthful of cheese, then tries to work up enough saliva to persuade it down his Jeff Beck, sweating himself two collar sizes thinner, while at the same time stealing sly looks at Hennessy, to see what kind of progress he's making with the spoon. There's, like, chanting and roaring and it would have to be described as boisterous – these are all, like, Horseshoe Bor regulars, remember – with support about seventy/thirty in favour of my old man.

Ten minutes in, Hennessy is only, like, halfway through his pint, while a good, like, three-quarters of the cheese is gone, although some economist dude, who the old man knows from Doheny & Nesbitt's, points out that the old man has 'gone with the front-loading option' and, while he appears to be making quicker progress, most of the cheese is still in his mouth, hordening into a big dry ball – like one of those golf-ball soaps I buy him every year for Christmas. And for his birthday.

The good news is that Hennessy is slower than usual. He supposedly injured his wrist playing nine holes in Elm Pork yesterday and has had to switch to southpaw, placing the old man at a serious advantage.

'Come on, Charles!' the roar goes up.

'Go on, Hennessy!' comes the reply.

The old man forces the last piece of Cheddar into his face. Now, all eyes are on his Adam's apple – the question being, can he persuade that giant boulder of hord sludge down his throat. He, like, coughs and splutters once or twice and a senior counsel friend of his offers him a glass of Seppelt, but he ends up getting shouted down by fans on both sides.

'Just the focking cheese!' they all go. 'Nothing to wash it down!'

They're sticklers for the rules, these people – well, today, anyway.

Hennessy suddenly storts to speed up – or maybe it's just the way the pint glass, like, *narrows*? – but he's suddenly getting closer to the end. And that's when the old man storts working his jaw like a literally lunatic, trying to get his spit glands into production to help him break up what's still in his Von Trapp.

It ends up being pretty much a photo-finish at the end. The old man swallows the last piece, then opens his mouth to show the room that it's empty, just as Hennessy is picking up the pint glass to pour the last bit of liquid onto his spoon.

There's, like, a humungous round of applause, with literally everyone joining in – even Hennessy. The old man struggles to get his breath back, then he stands up.

He goes, 'Let me begin by extending my commiserations to Mr Hennessy Coghlan-O'Hara, who, as ever, fought a good and noble fight – although I must remind him that the score now stands at nineteen victories to eighteen! And so, m'learned colleague, it falls to me to say something to set the tenor, as it were, for the year ahead, 2015 – hopefully our final year under the rule of Enda Kenny,

Cabinet Secretary of the German-controlled Vichy Republic of Ireland.'

That gets a massive cheer.

'And, as fate woud have it,' he goes, 'I have an announcement to make of some considerable import. Ladies and gentleman, after five years in the, inverted commas, political wilderness, Charles O'Carroll-Kelly has decided . . . to return to politics!'

The roars are loud enough to upset the foundations of the house.

'I was born in this country,' he goes. 'And I love this country – oh, yes – for all its faults and for all its problems, which *are* many. So independence didn't work out quite the way we hoped it would. But that is no reason to go surrendering our future to Berlin and Brussels and their battalions of unelected, faceless bureaucrats who think they should tell us how to live. I, for one, am frankly tired of watching Enda Kenny and Eamon Gilmore and all the other secondary-school geography teachers, whom we have somehow elected to represent this country, having their backs slapped by unelected Gerhards and Jean-Claudes and being told, "Good boys!" for visiting austerity on this country's citizens in line with the demands of international financiers and global bond speculators – no offence to some of you present.

'There currently exists, I think it's generally agreed, a political vacuum in this country. Voters are looking for an alternative to the parties who have governed this state for nigh on a century. That is why, here, today, I am announcing the arrival of a seventh force in Irish politics – or eighth if you count Renua, which, I think I'm correct in saying, nobody here does.'

No one says shit.

'People are tired of the old same old faces and the same old political marriages of convenience,' he goes. 'Fianna Fáil and Labour! Fine Gael and Labour! Fianna Fáil and the Progressive Who-Even-Remembers-Anymore? Who knows, one day it might be Fianna Fáil and Fine Gael!'

Everyone laughs.

He goes, 'The good news is that, next time out, there will be a new name on the ballot paper – a political party that represents a new way of doing politics. Which is why, today, bloated though he is with cheese, Charles O'Carroll-Kelly is announcing the formation of . . . New Republic!'

There's, like, suddenly mayhem. People are cheering and chanting, 'CO'CK for Taoiseach! CO'CK for Taoiseach! CO'CK for Taoiseach!'

I turn around to Christian and I go, 'I might go and lie down.'

He's there, 'Are you okay?'

He's genuinely concerned about me.

I'm like, 'Yeah, no, I am. The headaches have stopped by the way. And the blurred vision and the memory loss. It turns out we were possibly worrying about nothing.'

'Ross,' he goes, 'that doesn't mean you don't have concussion. The symptoms can come and go. That's why it's such an insidious thing.'

'Whatever that even means. Yeah, no, I'm just going to go and lie down and clear my head of all this other shit that's going on.'

'Do your visualization exercises.'

'You took the words out of my mouth. Tomorrow is probably going to be the last rugby match I ever play, Christian. And I'll tell you something, Dude, by five o'clock tomorrow, all of the questions are going to be finally answered about the player I could so easily have been. And I won't have to grow old wondering.'

# *Epilogue*

It's finally here. The day, the hour, the moment. It's incredible, given what's been going on, but at the same time it's a fact – I'm in the zone.

'Ut's boyn a long, haahd royd,' Byrom goes. 'But nah ut comes daahn to thus – oytoy munnets of rugboy thut'll determine whither Seapoint ploy their rugboy in Duvusion Toy Boy or Toy Soy nixt soysun. Whativer hippens aaht on that putch todoy, moyke sure yoy loyve nathing behoynd. Because beloyve moy, the rist of your loyves is a long fuckun toyme for regrits.'

All the goys are, like, clapping and cheering and kicking the fock out of the lockers.

I turn around to Bucky and I go, 'Look, I know I'm not the captain, but do you mind if I say something here?'

He's like, 'Go ahead, Rossi – you've earned the right.'

I stand up and I go, 'The coach is right. And I'm saying that as someone who's got enough regrets for five focking lifetimes. I spent the last fifteen years of my life telling myself that next week, next month, next year would be my time. I'd get my shit together and finally become the player that the likes of Tony Ward predicted I would one day be. But the years just fell away and suddenly I found myself at thirty-four, thirty-five years old, remembering something that Father Fehily, my old mentor, used to say: "One of these days is none of these days."

'By that he meant, don't put shit off until tomorrow – because there might not be a tomorrow. So do it today. Recognize the moment. The moment is now. Four months ago, I was one seriously depressed man. I was staring down the barrel of middle age, thinking about all the things I could have done and a lot of people would say should have done in my life. Winning Heineken Cups and Grand Slams. Obviously captaining the Lions. It never happened. Any of it.

'And then one day, something led me to this very field in the middle of – you know it as well as I do – Ballybrack, where I met a bunch of great young goys, who decided to give a fat, washed-up has-been like me a break. And after a difficult stort, I think I helped you realize that we didn't have to accept the inevitability of relegation. It was in our hands to do something about it. And you helped me realize something. And it wasn't just that I could still carry off a muscle top or a young person's haircut at the age of thirty-five.'

Everyone laughs.

I'm there, 'It was that saving Seapoint from relegation was my Grand Slam, my Heineken Cup final, my Lions call-up, all rolled into one. One of these days is today. One of these days is right now. So let's go out there and beat these bog-hopping cabbage fetishists!'

Out we walk, onto the pitch, our heads up, our shoulders back – the black, blue and green of Seapoint.

I turn around to Christian and I go, 'Still sure you can do a job for us at scrum-half?'

He's like, 'After that speech, I feel like I could walk into machine-gun fire.'

It's an amazing thing for me to hear.

I'm there, 'Dude, whatever happens today, I want you to know, I am so proud of you.'

He goes, 'I hope you're still saying that at five o'clock.'

I look over my shoulder for Senny. Something tells me he's going to be our key man today and I possibly should have a word in his ear, as someone who's been there and done it. But when I look around, there's no actual *sign* of him?

I ask Blissy and Ollie Lysaght where he is and they say he must be still back in the dressing room.

So back I go.

He *is* still in the dressing room? He's sitting down, tying, then retying the laces of his boots.

I'm there, 'Dude, what the fock?'

He goes, 'I can't get these focking things right. They're either too tight or they're too loose.'

And I'm suddenly worried, because as I always say to Mads – just as I said it to Johnny Sexton before him – when you're in the zone, you shouldn't notice shit like that. When you're in the zone, you could put the ball between the posts in your granny's slippers.

I'm there, 'Dude, come on, this is the moment.'

He goes, 'I'm well aware that this is the focking moment, Rossi. But these laces have to be right. There's a lot riding on today.'

'Yeah, I know – the future of Seapoint in Division 2B of the All Ireland League.'

'More than that. The goys from the academy are here again – to watch me.'

'I don't see how that's bigger than Seapoint Rugby Club staying up.'

'Maybe that's why you never actually made it in the game. Because when it came to it, you never had that ruthless streak.'

'Dude,' I go, 'I'm going forget you said that and just put it down to pre-match nerves. Tie your laces and I'll see you out on the pitch.'

Out I go.

I spot the old man on the sideline. The leader of New Republic or whatever the fock they're called. I catch his eye and he goes, *'Carthago delenda est*, Ross! *Carthago delenda est!'*

And then, standing next to him – I end up having to do a double-take – it's Oisinn! He's back, looking tanned and happy – and beside him is JP, here to support us.

'Eat nerves,' Oisinn shouts, 'shit results.'

I smile at him and then – oh shit, oh shit, oh shit – I suddenly get this, like, stabbing pain in my head, just behind my eyes. Not now, I think. Give me twice this pain tomorrow – just don't do this to me now.

Senny finally joins us on the pitch. Bucky asks him if he's okay and he goes, 'Just focking concentrate on your own game, will you?'

The Bruff players stort with the mind games straightaway. Their loosehead walks up to me while I'm doing a few stretches and goes, 'Tis a cure for sore eyes to see you – and you only a scrap of shop-bread! I pledge my immortal soul, I'm grateful to God, His son and the entire communion of saints for putting yee fellas in our path this day! And may all be safe wherever the tale is told!'

Word of my heroics has obviously reached Limerick because they've clearly decided to target *me*? Their hooker decides to add his two yoyos to what his mate said.

'It comes best from you,' he tells him. Then he looks directly at me and goes, 'Let me tell you, upon my word, you've got the full of your hands of thrubble this day, for I'm only waiting for the wind of the word to knock the steam out of your pipe!'

I'm just thinking, Let's see if you're still saying that in five minutes' time.

Christian shouts, 'Come on, Seapoint, let's focking do this!'

My head is throbbing like it's never throbbed before. Senny gets the ball in his hands, the referee blows the whistle and the match is suddenly underway.

After three minutes, we win our first scrum. As the two front rows are getting ready to come together, their hooker looks at me and goes, 'Look at you! You're only the turf of the rick and you living in mortal dread of me! There'll be a long day before you – and tis the barren hope for yee!'

I slip my right orm out of the bind on the way in and I punch the focker so hord in the face that I feel his cheekbone actually move. Down their scrum goes.

I go, 'They're deliberately collapsing, Ref.'

He awards us the penalty.

And if the Bruff players didn't know it before, they certainly know it now – they're in a match.

I'm out on my feet.

I can't even walk in a straight line and I mean that quite literally. I feel like I've been in a plane crash. My body is beaten up, but my head is even worse.

The pain – I can't even begin to explain it to you. There are moments when the only thing that helps is to close my eyes. But I can't close my eyes – not for more than a second or two, because we're still in a match.

We're still in a match, but we're losing. It's, like, 12–6 to Bruff, even though we've dominated in terms of possession. We'd be ahead if it wasn't for Senny, who's chosen today to have a mare. He's missed four of his six kicks – none of them particularly *hord*? – and he also knocked on when we had a chance to score early in the second half, with the Bruff defence finally broken and three of our players screaming for the ball out wide.

Plus he's making wrong decisions – we're talking left, right and centre.

Bucky goes, 'Senny, you need to relax. We've got time here.'

And Senny lets a roar at him – his captain, bear in mind. He's like, 'You focking relax!'

Our man of the match – no question – ends up being Christian. I can hear people on the sideline going, 'Who's the Seapoint scrum-half?' and then the old man going, 'Christian Forde! Won a Leinster Schools Senior Cup medal for Castlerock College back in 1999, along with the Seapoint number two! I was one of the fortunate ones who was there to witness it!'

But the minutes are ticking by.

The Bruff players are getting inside Senny's head, going, 'I'd take my oath that you'll not kick nine points this day!' and he's letting it get to him.

His game is, like, full of mistakes.

They're going, 'Will you look at him! He's as tormented as an ass tethered in a storm – and he without half the sense!'

We know we're getting relegated unless something dramatic happens. But there's only, like, thirty seconds left.

We have possession of the ball right on their twenty-two, but we know that, as soon as we surrender it up, the game is going to be over.

We win a scrum.

Christian pulls me to one side. He goes, 'Are you okay?'

I'm there, 'No – I feel like I'm going to focking vom.'

'You really should go off.'

'I'm not going off – end of conversation. Dude, we need something special here.'

'Okay,' he goes, 'do you remember when we were at school, we played Mungret in a friendly? It was the first time I ever stood in at scrum-half?'

I'm there, 'You're not talking about –'

He goes, 'I am.'

'Okay, let's do it.'

I turn around to Bucky and I go, 'Tell Senny to get in the pocket.'

Bucky's like, 'What are you talking about? Three points is fock-all use to us.'

I'm there, 'Bucky, trust me, okay?'

He just thinks, Fock it, what the hell, then goes, 'Senny, get in the pocket!'

You can see the confusion on the faces of the Bruff players. Mind you, they're from Limerick – a lot of them look like that all the time.

We crouch, we touch, we pause, we engage. A rip of pain goes through my head again.

Christian puts the ball in. We give it one last, humungous push. The Bruff scrum moves back a foot or two and Christian wheels around the back of us to pick up the ball.

Senny is in the pocket. Christian makes a movement like he's about to offload it to him and the Bruff players chorge forward to try to slap down the kick. But Christian doesn't release the ball. He tucks it under his right pec, sneaks around the back of the scrum and, with his head down, makes a break for the line.

The Bruff players see what's happening, but they cop it a split-second too *late*?

We're screaming at him, 'Go on, Christian! You're in, Christian! You're in!'

He crashes over the line, grounding the ball in the corner.

And all hell breaks loose. He's suddenly, like, swamped by bodies. It was a Father Fehily move – me, Christian, JP, Oisinn and the old man are the only people here who know it.

When he gets to his feet, I chest-bump him. I just decide the moment calls for it.

But of course the work isn't done yet. Senny still has to put the conversion over and the angle is horrible. It's from, like, right on the sideline and, as usual, there's a wind blowing across Kilbogget Pork like you wouldn't focking believe.

'Just take your time,' Bucky tells Senny, throwing him the ball.

Senny grabs a cup and spots it. He takes however many steps backwards, then he looks from the ball to the posts, then back to the ball, then back to the posts, then back to the ball.

He takes a deep breath. We all take a deep breath. And then . . .

He stops.

We're all, like, looking at each other.

He looks at Bucky and he goes, 'I can't do it.'

Bucky's like, 'What?'

He's there, 'I just . . . can't.'

The pressure has got to him. That much is obvious.

On the sideline, I can hear the old man going, 'What in the name of Hades is going on?'

My head is hopping at this stage. I feel like if I lay down on the pitch now, I would be asleep within seconds.

The referee tells Bucky we need to hurry up or we won't get to take the kick at all. Bucky goes, 'Just give us a second,' and he tries to persuade Senny to take the kick. He picks up the ball and hands it to him. 'Just feel it in your hands,' he goes. 'Then visualize it going over.'

Senny's like, 'I can't. I just . . . can't.'

And I go, 'Gimme the ball.'

Bucky looks at me. He's like, 'What?'

So I say it again. 'Gimme the focking ball.'

Which is exactly what he ends up doing – or, in actual fact, I pull it out of his hands.

I can hear the old man going, 'Good Lord! Ross O'Carroll-Kelly is going to take the kick!'

There's, like, literally gasps all around the ground.

I place the ball in the cup, then I stand up and I look at the posts. Christian tips over to me. He's there, 'Are you okay?'

I laugh. I'm there, 'Fine – only one problem.'

'What's that?' he goes.

I'm like, 'I can see three posts.'

'That's okay,' he goes. 'Aim for the one in the middle.'

Silence descends on the ground. I take a deep breath. I measure out my steps – four backward, then three to the left. Then I run my

hand through my hair. I look at the middle post and I let myself become aware of the wind on my face, trying to work out how strong it is and how it's going to affect the flight of the ball. I take another breath – a deeper one this time. Then I run at the ball and I send it into the air with my boot.

I know it instantly. I know it from the second I strike the ball. That's experience.

I blink my eyes once, twice, three times, to try to focus on the ball, to see where it's going. But then I don't *need* to see it? Like I said, I already know.

And then I hear the roars of the crowd, my old man's loudest of all, going, 'He's done it! He's only bloody well gone and done it!'

I fall flat on my face, through tiredness, pain, emotion, whatever.

Suddenly, I'm pulled to my feet again by Byrom, who has run onto the field because it's all over, and he's going, 'Yoy luttle beautoy! Yoy luttle fuckun beautoy! Oy knoy yoy'd doy ut! Oy knoy yoy'd fuckun doy ut!'

The other players lift me up onto their shoulders and they carry me around the pitch. I've got, like, tears rolling down my face and I'm so happy it feels like I might never stop crying.

The old man is blubbering like I don't know what. At the top of his voice, he's also going, 'Let this be a lesson to everyone who witnessed it! Age is not an impediment to anything! Today might well be the oldest you've ever been, but it's also the youngest you will ever be again!'

I'm going, 'Shut the fock up, will you?' but at the same time I'm hugging him. 'You're making an actual show of me.'

He laughs, then he holds me at orm's length and goes, 'I'm so bloody proud of you. Are you okay, by the way?'

I'm like, 'Yeah, no, I'm fine – just wrecked.'

'One of your eyes looks a little, well, droopy.'

'I just need to sleep, that's all. But first I'm going to celebrate.'

His face suddenly lights up then and I realize that he's looking over my shoulder.

He goes, 'It looks like someone is here to share in your moment of triumph, Ross!'

I turn around and I see Sorcha, pushing the stroller towards me. I'm like, 'You came!'

The boys are all in full voice, especially Brian, who's going, 'Fock you, you focking fock!'

I'm there, 'Sorcha, tell me they saw it – the moment the ball went over the bor?'

Except she doesn't respond. She seems upset about something and I notice that she's, like, deathly pale.

She goes, 'Chorles, your phone is switched off.'

He's like, 'Well, of course it's switched off! I'm at a rugby match!'

Leo shouts, 'You bastarding prick!'

I'm there, 'Sorcha, why are you upset? What the fock's going on?'

And she goes, 'Your mum just rang, Ross. From Blackrock Gorda Station. She's been arrested and chorged with Ari's murder.'

# Acknowledgements

My thanks as ever to Rachel Pierce, my superb editor. Thank you to my wonderful agent, Faith O'Grady. Thanks to Alan Clarke for your extraordinary artwork. Enormous thanks to Michael McLoughlin, Patricia Deevy, Cliona Lewis, Patricia McVeigh, Brian Walker and everyone at Penguin Ireland. Special thanks to George Hook, Johnny Walsh, Stephen Walsh, Paul McCarthy and Alex McCarthy for allowing me to pick your brains. Thanks to my father, David, and my brothers, Mark, Vincent and Richard. But most of all, thanks to Mary, my wife, with all my love.

# *He just wanted a decent book to read ...*

Not too much to ask, is it? It was in 1935 when Allen Lane, Managing Director of Bodley Head Publishers, stood on a platform at Exeter railway station looking for something good to read on his journey back to London. His choice was limited to popular magazines and poor-quality paperbacks – the same choice faced every day by the vast majority of readers, few of whom could afford hardbacks. Lane's disappointment and subsequent anger at the range of books generally available led him to found a company – and change the world.

*'We believed in the existence in this country of a vast reading public for intelligent books at a low price, and staked everything on it'*
**Sir Allen Lane, 1902–1970, founder of Penguin Books**

The quality paperback had arrived – and not just in bookshops. Lane was adamant that his Penguins should appear in chain stores and tobacconists, and should cost no more than a packet of cigarettes.

Reading habits (and cigarette prices) have changed since 1935, but Penguin still believes in publishing the best books for everybody to enjoy. We still believe that good design costs no more than bad design, and we still believe that quality books published passionately and responsibly make the world a better place.

So wherever you see the little bird – whether it's on a piece of prize-winning literary fiction or a celebrity autobiography, political tour de force or historical masterpiece, a serial-killer thriller, reference book, world classic or a piece of pure escapism – you can bet that it represents the very best that the genre has to offer.

## Whatever you like to read – trust Penguin.